BLOOD

1990 - 2005

15

YEARS OF
EXCELLENCE

GLB
Publishers

BLOOD WARM

novel by

Robert Burdette Sweet

GLB Publishers®   San Francisco

Second Edition
Copyright © 2005 Robert Burdette Sweet
All rights reserved. Printed in the U.S.A.

Published in the United States by
GLB Publishers
P.O. Box 78212, San Francisco, CA 94107
www.GLBpubs.com

Cover art by the author
Cover Design by the author and
GLB Publishers

This is a work of fiction. Names, characters, places, and incidents are either the products of the author's imagination or are used fictitiously, and any resemblance to actual persons, living or dead, events, or locales is entirely coincidental

Library of Congress Cataloguing Control Number

2005924904

1-879194-56-2

First printing June 2005
10 9 8 7 6 5 4 3 2 1

DEDICATION

In Gratitude to
Susan Eastwood, Will Patterson, and
members of Arts Anonymous:
Paul Christensen
Tess Crescini
David George
Mike Newman
Pat Perrone
Sheila Rowan
D. Lester

Robert Burdette Sweet

is the author of many works, both fiction and non-fiction (see list below). His short stories have appeared in over sixty magazines and been listed and on the Roll Of Honor in Best American Short Stories. He is also a painter, sculptor, and composer. Oh yes, he is also a retired Professor of English from the University of California at San Jose and still lives near-by.

The plaudits of his contemporaries are numerous and expansive. Anais Ninn: *Sweet has a real gift for creating atmosphere and ambiguity.* Gordon Lish: *...a remarkable talent.* John Gardner: *Your writing is terrific.* Gary Elder: *You go for the most dangerous game of all: Truth Absolute. I can't forget your work because it gives me the human honor of thinking and rethinking.*

Other books by Robert Burdette Sweet

WRITING TOWARDS WISDOM:

THE WRITER AS SHAMAN

THE MAMBO

AKBAR THE GREAT

DAME AMERICA

JOURNAL FROM THE APOCAPLAGUES

JIMMY AND THE DREAM THAT FLEW

MEMORIES OF FIRE

MOUTH OF THE JAGUAR

WHITE SAMBO* (See last page)

Author can be reached by e-mail: r.b.sweet@worldnet.att.net

Part 1

THE TOWN: ST. GEORGE'S

1

Blood Warm

I tried shoving my suitcase and typewriter through the torn mosquito net draping the bed, but couldn't figure out where the netting attached. Growing up in Chicago had not prepared me for my first skirmish with the tropics. It was already late afternoon and the sweltering heat made the simplest undertaking arduous. Yet I was in a hurry. Better to end my life today than draw out the inevitable.

At twenty-five I had traveled to the island with the goal of plunging myself into the sea to drown. Death as in a Joan Crawford movie—where she flails away in a flapping white nightgown striking out toward the center of the Atlantic—struck me as a clean and vigorous exit. Cold water, however, seemed unnecessary. Suicide in the Caribbean might be less noble than Joan's immersion in the frigid Atlantic, but it would be more womb-like, soothing. I unbuckled my bag to feel around for a notebook and pencil. I had no intention of dying without taking notes.

Managing to wrap the mosquito net over the rectangle of wire suspended from the bedposts, I leaned back against the two hard oblongs I took to be pillows. "**October 10, 1955**," I scribbled. And then underneath, "**Grenada, British West Indies**." I gnawed the eraser. It tasted as vapid and sullen as I had felt for a long time.

Extremely agoraphobic, I've never traveled beyond my front door expecting to return alive. So in a private sense I had already passed beyond. Checking into the St. James Hotel and beginning my suicide note were mere formalities. "**Dear Mom and Dad, colleagues, friends, acquaintances and all lovers I will never meet.**" I smiled at my expansiveness. "**Should you be informed that my (corpse) (body) (remains)...**" Well, which would it be when finally I washed ashore? It depended on how long I had been submerged. And that would depend on how far out I paddled before I sank from exhaustion. My parents would wonder why I hadn't just jumped into Lake Michigan. Not to mention the expense of flying to a tiny island in order to finalize my existence, which might necessitate the return of my (corpse) (body) (remains). This would be an additional fiscal burden for them, who already had postponed paying off the house loan due to their sacrifices for my college education.

Behind me, outside the open window, I heard the waves smacking over rocks and the yawp of gulls before the next crash. I had never smelled sea salt before. It smelled sharp as the scent of blood. Bluntly, I decided upon 'corpse', crossed out the less accurate possibilities and proceeded: **"Should you be informed that my corpse has washed ashore, please accept that my drowning was no accident. Not a murder,"** I dramatically added hoping to salvage the reputation of any islander who might come under suspicion. **"Nor is it anyone's fault,"** thinking as I wrote that it sure was. **"I have simply decided that my life is untenable."** I yawned, stretched my arms and inadvertently snagged dangling portions of the net which abruptly unraveled with a muffled thud, shrouding me like a winding sheet. I felt stunned, as though with the descent of this curtain I had already finalized my plan. **"Chin to the wind!"** With a flourish I signed my first, middle and last name.

Feeling much better, I fell asleep.

* * *

"Is there a piano on the island?" I inquired a week later of the woman behind the reception counter at the hotel. She was attractive, big black eyes staring out of mocha skin. Other than the governor, myself and a few others, I discovered that on the island there existed two other colors: mocha and black, neither of which had much to say to the other. The mocha, much to my chagrin, called me 'Boob.'

The West Indian dialect, sounding more Scottish than anything else, had accents tending to fall on surprising syllables.

"Why for a piano? But, of course, Mr. Boob, you must seek to play one yourself?"

"It's Bob with one O," I corrected.

She went on, "I might know of where one is. Tomorrow, Mr. Boob. Tomorrow I will fetch one out." Her lips trembled so flirtatiously, I guessed wrongly that she had something in mind for me for herself. Well, I was lonely. I kept my suicide note tucked in my back pocket for security.

Grenada was off the beaten track then. Tourist boats were yet to dock. I would learn that drums throbbed the forest while tasseled, voodoo nuns groaned in tongues and fell in cataleptic seizures upon the earth floors of bamboo huts. The blacks called me "Sir," and no plea, no matter how desperate on my part, would stop them. So to them I had no name. I was simply a perpetually sunburned, sweating "Sir."

The following morning the receptionist hailed me with a note—tiny blue forget-me-nots twining the margins—announcing that a Mrs. Jessamine Hempstead would expect me for tea that afternoon at four.

"She's the piano," the receptionist confided, grinning and slapping at the metallic bell for no apparent reason other than to appear busy. "You follow Green Street up, up and up. You'll know the house. It looks like a steamship."

Stumbling along the cobblestone street that wound steeply away from the harbor—the afternoon heat made progress difficult—I hummed a tune while licking sweat off my lips. Being invited somewhere, anywhere, improved my disposition. Though I seemed to have put off my suicide, as I did most things, I still couldn't accept who I was, much less where I was.

Identity is a slippery concept. The gorgeousness and ease of island life, the unfamiliarity of every sound, odor and sight had quickly eroded whatever sense of self I'd originally sought to annihilate. Chicago, with its rows of gray apartment buildings, gray streets and sidewalks, the bare black branches of ice-locked elms scraping the brooding sky, seemed a distant memory.

My suicide plan now appeared to be unnecessary, not merely due to Mrs. Hempstead's invitation, which gave me an immediate purpose, but because the first day I had strolled across the street from the hotel through a heavy, warm rain smack into paradise.

Beyond an iron fence on a hill rose the twin spires of an Episcopal Church. Surrounding the Gothic facade and its high, stained-glass windows, frangipani trees glowed in cascades of white and yellow flowers, their leaves shining from the shower that by then had ceased. Inside the church a choir rehearsed, the sound of the voices rising into a rainbow, neon and brilliant, arcing across the steamy island. In front, upraised, white boxes appeared to drift down the hill in a scrim of haze. An occasional high cross flashed gold in the fitful sun. The air, thick with the heady pungency of flowers, was the temperature of blood. I wanted to fall to my knees.

I seemed to be challenged by beauty itself—swallowed by it like Jonah inside the whale. To celebrate my survival, that day I had decided on the spot to play at being Gauguin and paint in order to implant the tombstones in my memory. But nowhere on the island was anything but house paint to be obtained. So I opted for toothpaste. On a cardboard sheet, with a toothbrush and paste—fortunately for my purpose streaked with red—I quickly approximated marble: sarcophagi, crosses and all, and tacked the finished product to my hotel room wall. A maid and the janitor to whom I eagerly showed my painting found it tolerable, even interesting. Their kindly condescension, however, changed to intrigue and even awed alarm when I called them in to view the painting hours later after the heat of midday had melted each toothpaste tomb, cross and conch into gradual shifts and slides so that the graves appeared to erupt into frothy spirits, a kind of otherworldly emanation that thrilled what I guessed to be their basic Voodoo orientation.

That had been only yesterday, and as I pushed on toward Mrs. Hempstead's I congratulated myself again and again on my artistic attempt. Walking alone makes my mind spin and twist, repeating itself over and over. The street to Mrs. Hempstead's, still spiraling upward, was deserted. Long shadows cast by broad-leafed breadfruit trees offered some relief from the heat. I stopped to breathe and mop my forehead. I looked back down at the town of St. George's, its white, blue and ochre-colored buildings clambering up the hill to terminate in green clouds of gum trees. The distant ocean, streaked by long waving lines of improbably ponderous pelicans, flashed yellow and silver.

Stucco houses had given way to shacks. Since there were no house numbers I had to assume I was on course. Too much effort had already been expended to turn back. I plodded upward. Two bends in the road further I recognized my hostess' house. It did resemble a steamship. Despite its peeling white paint, the house was the largest I'd seen on the island, girded as it was by square pillared porches rounding both the first and second floors. Huge dogs hurled themselves at me from behind a fence. The animals' fury bent the fence dangerously in my direction.

Not only do I become witless when any dog takes notice of me, but particularly I had already learned to fear the tropic dog, a scurvy beast incapable of affection. I am willing to speculate that, for a thousand miles on each side of the equator, dogs increase in viciousness just as their numbers become startling. They stand in the streets, lie on the doorsteps, poke their heads from open windows, even recline upon the low flat roofs with their tongues lolling and their eyes running like sores. "Hi there, Cerberus," I attempted to calm myself and the monsters with my deepest voice whose quavering timbre eased neither of us. Dogs indigenous to the area are not easy to distinguish from each other. They're large, always tan or clay-colored, with several inch-long black whiskers circling their stubby muzzles. As they strutted toward me with a wily, audacious carriage, I shouted, "Mrs. Hempstead? Mrs.

Hempstead?"

Expecting a matron of sorts to appear on the porch ineffectually brandishing a cane as a gesture of welcome amid the cacophonous snarls, yips and barks that surrounded me, I was not prepared for the sudden emergence of a lovely girl, her mocha skin and flashing black eyes set off by the whirl of a short lace dress as she bounded down the steps to intercept the dogs and swing wide the gate. "You must be Boob." She extended her ringed fingers.

I naturally assumed this diaphanous charmer to be a daughter or a surprisingly friendly servant on her way to a christening. "Mrs. Hempstead should be expecting me."

"If you're Boob, I greet you. Call me just Jessamine." She turned to rush ahead of me, shooing the dogs under the house with a stick. "Come. Come. It's safe now. Oh, I apologize for the mess this garden is."

Actually, I was stunned by the bananas, palms, hibiscus and especially by a tall flamboyant tree tonguing red flames over the tiled roof. No one consciously gardens in the tropics. Her apology was a reference to what she assumed I was used to in the States. On the island gardens simply are, an unappreciated given. There's something very mundane about the rules of gardening I'd been accustomed to, because she proceeded to lop off the yellow head of a hibiscus with her stick.

"Since Janet, everything has been crazy." She kicked the flower under a bush.

A year before my arrival, the island had been devastated and subsequently demoralized by the hurricane called Janet. Most boats had been destroyed and no one thought to build more, so the fishermen no longer fished. Children were sprouting bloated bellies from a diet of plantains, dasheen and bananas. Gnawing too much sugarcane rotted their teeth. Yet no one did anything about it except talk and even obsess about Janet.

So Jessamine and I drank our initial tea with cookies among a flurry of her stories about the horrors of the hurricane. The wind did this and then it did that. This blew here. That blew there. They hid. They trembled. Nothing would ever be the same. The British sent care packages of sweaters. Even I laughed, dabbing, as I continually did, my dripping forehead with the back of my hand.

To my wonder, Jessamine seemed sophisticated and naive in equal proportions. And she was vivacious and broody by fits and starts. After tea, she took both my hands and held them. Caressed them with her long fingers while staring into my eyes. Why are women's eyes usually so much wider than men's, so much rounder, as though they can see right through you?

Like Lara's eyes, I thought while forcing a smile and glancing out the window. Lara in Chicago.

"What are you thinking?" Jessamine placed my hand on her knee, arranging the fingers wide so that they cupped the knobby bone.

"What?"

She stroked the hair on my arm. "Thinking of the States? Lonely for home, are you?"

She *could* see through me. Though not accurately. *Free* from home would be more like it. Free from the mess I'd already made of my life. And Lara's. "Can I trouble you for a glass of water, please? I'm thirsty. The hike up here in the heat..."

She brushed aside my hand and rose. "And I'll bring a wet towel for your drippy forehead. I should have invited you later, toward evening. I've heard Americans have trouble adjusting to the tropics." Jessamine stood over me smiling. "I hate it here, too," I thought she muttered, padding on her bare feet toward the kitchen. Lara, also, had preferred to scuff off her shoes at the least provocation. Though Lara was educated and white and Jessamine uneducated and black, I wondered if I wasn't going to use and be used by them similarly. I stretched out my legs and tried to get comfortable in the stiff cane chair. We take our needs with us wherever we go. Jessamine made me feel welcome. Just as Lara had.

Initially, Lara had seemed wonderful. Hysterical, but in her way divine. I ignorantly assumed she might be the agent to straighten my bent and make me acceptable to my parents, the high school that employed me as teacher, and the world in general. I had pled in my heart, if not my groin, for reprieve from Chicago's fairy-faggot underground with its commingling of lust and fear, the *Liebestod* of strangers. Lara, a potential divorcee with two children, was as genuine as I would like to be. Curly-haired and frisky, Lara was not only pretty but proved to be sexually aggressive as an unspayed mouser.

Gay guys screw women in more ways than one. I'd never have junked all of that and escaped to the island had I not still been, in the evenings I did not spend with Lara, a lurker in the bushes for trade. Winter, fall, or summer, it made no difference. The happier I was with Lara, the more I felt free to unleash the forbidden me. To my credit, I imparted not all, but many, of my peccadilloes to her. She replied, "But that's not how you act with me!"

I responded, "The love you think you feel is not what you're getting." Males tend to stick it anywhere it can be stuck. At nature's command. They are under the aegis of that great god, the Future-Forever. Youth is that god's slave, his gonadal hireling.

"I'm pregnant," she whispered.

I heard my father, the school principal, and the head of the English department all laughing, but their laughter was cold, derisive, ironic. Blinking rapidly, her lashes beating hard, like a spasm or tick, Lara insisted, "Of course, I'll have an abortion. My divorce isn't final. I'll lose my children if I enter that courtroom with a distended belly. And you, look at you, what a waste!"

Chicago's seamy underpinnings being familiar to me, I ferreted out that most dedicated teacher of human despair: the illicit, usually incompetent abortionist, who for an exorbitant price would kill nearly anything you had enough money to requisition. In a room under the roar of the elevated train, there Lara screamed and screamed and bled and bled. My, our, child wrapped in rags and tossed into a slop bucket had never had the honor or horror of one breath.

If memory is who one is, I shuddered at my recollections. I was relieved when Jessamine returned, bearing a glass of water cubed with ice. Ice! A house on the island with a refrigerator! I sighed as she wrapped a cool towel around my forehead. "You're a saint." I drank greedily. The previous tea had done nothing to quench my thirst.

"I'm a woman."

I wondered what that was supposed to mean.

"There's the piano," she invited. "Play. Play for me, Boob."

Near the far wall of the ample living room away from the windows stood a baby grand, the ivory missing from many keys. I feared for its tune. My fear proved justified. But I tried some Schubert, some Chopin and Bach. Keys stuck, I kept forgetting where I was in most pieces, the wires twanged and clinked. The towel slipped from my head and got tangled about my feet. It was a rout, but Jessamine seemed to love it all. "More, more," she giggled, at me or with me, I was not sure.

Though I've never performed on the piano with finesse or even with particular concern, from the age of six playing the instrument has been a satisfying habit, like brushing one's teeth. Hence my desire to find a piano on the island. Most of what I've ever learned about anything came from attempting to come to terms with playing music. But what you know and can maneuver yourself through one week, without constant renewal and continual effort you won't be able to manage the next week. All performance artists are Buddhists whether they acknowledge it or not. They must accept impermanence.

Which is a wisdom I've never been able to accommodate. Knowing is not believing. I still want permanence. Which is another way of admitting that too much of what is real has always gotten in the way of my presumptions.

Just as I pretended to misconstrue what was to become of my relationship with Jessamine. I at first assumed that this island beauty wanted me for me. And for a time the affair did appear to be how I thought it was. We became lovers the evening of our first meeting, after the tea, the ice water, after my pianistic fiasco, on her upper porch, as night rolled in on the thousand, thousand flashes of fireflies igniting the arching flamboyant tree above our heads.

Possibly it's a gay thing, but I've always suspected that if strangers don't have sex right away, later familiarity will bore them into not wanting it. With acquaintance arises, all subliminally, a kind of incest taboo. Besides, initial sex is rather tentative anyway, the yowling and clawing a month or so up the road. Also, a young man has no basic function other than to try out whatever is around. I hadn't had sex since the dwarf I'd encountered in New York's Everard Baths, the first stop on my way to the island. I enjoyed other guys, too, while at the baths, but specifically I recall the dwarf, cute and hairy as a furball, cuddled on my lap, lapping my cod like a starved kitten. His dong was longer than his chest, his tiny legs twitching upward toward an air vent that dripped with steam. I had deplaned in Trinidad dripping with clap, a green scum leaking unremittingly like snot from a runny nose. I searched out a doctor to stab penicillin into my behind, concluding that if it was hell I wanted and hell I deserved, I had arrived at its approximation.

But Jessamine's eagerness annulled my sense of desperation and, as had Lara's, made me question my natural proclivity. The affair, what was to become my constant welcome in her house, her friends, the gossip I became privy to, all put my fatal fear of rejection and estrangement momentarily to rest.

Jessamine was very open and told me most of what I wanted to know about her, sometimes by intention, sometimes by accident. People follow patterns. We grow to become programmed as any machine. Her program, I eventually realized, was to screw white. It wasn't my penis she desired, but my pinkness.

During our inaugural tea, I had presumed her to be naive. Projection, I was to discover, colored my insight. "My life before you was as nothing," she liked to pretend.

But how then had she become, by twenty-nine, one of the wealthier inhabitants of the island? Even though what wealth she had was more appearance than actuality—she worked at the telegraph office most mornings and some afternoons—appearance is much of what wealth is. Her maids—especially the nosy Lemba who kept, rather pointedly it seemed to me, interrupting our trysts—all made Jessamine appear to American eyes as anything but needy. Especially since it was the luxury of servants who kept her two children, both preteen girls, as much out of our way as they were.

We would attend dances called jump-ups at the shack bar on Grande Anse beach. The wild rhythms and melodic trilling of the steel band made everyone frenetic. So did the rum. The islanders seemed to believe that perpetual sex and alcohol are the best ways to endure paradise. Because paradise, as Dante and Milton have assured us, is boring to the point of ennui. "Tiresome," Jessamine would admit.

Which is where I came in. I had, however invisible to myself, the words 'exit' and 'escape' pulsing like a neon sign on my blistered forehead. I was to be someone's savior—the girl at the hotel desk had decided after learning I intended to remain on the island for a year—and it might as well be her appealing friend Jessamine. Everyone wanted out of where I had escaped into. The United States and Canada had stringent immigration policies. Marriage was...

But let me reveal Jessamine in as many of her own words as I can recall: "I come from the back country. Poor. All hated me, because my skin was lighter. I don't know why. I don't know how..."

It was All Saint's Night when Jessamine told me this. She had persuaded me to accompany her to the cemetery that sprawled down the hill around the Episcopalian Church, where each grave glowed from encircling candles. I agreed because the place was already meaningful to me, and the night when dead spirits might walk encouraged my need for romance as much as did her body. We strolled arm in arm into the flickering light. Hunched crowds cowered around the upraised sarcophagi that caught at the fire, making the graves appear to erupt and move as in my toothpaste painting. She searched out her husband's plot, one of the few with a cross reaching up into the stars. She'd continually referred to him as Mr. Hempstead, but a glance at the stone indicated his first name was Julian and he had died three years before my arrival on the island. We sat closely together on his sarcophagus while sounds of mourning and bursts of song wavered through the gutting light.

She clutched my bare leg where it jutted from my short pants, the finger with the simple gold wedding band toying with the hairs on my thigh. I leaned against her husband's cross, scraping an itch on my back, aware that I had inadvertently chosen the embossed year of his death, 1952, for a scratching post. Can adultery be committed against the dead? And in their own bedroom, as it were?

"Do you miss him?" I wondered.

"Who?"

"The man we're sitting on."

"Oh, Mr. Hempstead. I think of him sometimes. Look, there's Marilee." Her hand swept from my thigh and vigorously waved. "Everyone will be here tonight." I recognized the receptionist from my hotel, who had arranged our introduction, as she waved back.

"I didn't know that was her name," I said.

"Who?"

"The woman you're waving at. From the St. James. Marilee is her name, you say. She's lighting candles." I watched as Marilee bent to touch a wand of fire to the candles she'd already staked out around a modest mound of piled dirt garnished with sea shells.

Jessamine commented, "That's the place a child of hers lies. I hopes I never has to bury more than this Mr. Hempstead here." She rapped on the sarcophagus as though for luck. "Nights like this that are special and ceremonious make me marvelously to wonder."

"About what?"

Jessamine tipped her chin up and closed her eyes. "They make things happen. By doing what's always been done, things happen. Like when the goat was bled dead so that Mr. Hempstead could come to know me."

Clearly, this was no ordinary date.

"When I was thirteen and a feast day occurred, and the drums were beating and a goat was to be sacrificed...for me. For me! And they'd strung the goat upside down, hanging from the thick bough of the bo tree, and Lemba, my guardian, Lemba..."

"Why the goat?" I wanted to know. "And why then?"

"So the goat would take away with him my blood. To heaven. To hell. I never understood where or why. But there Mr. Hempstead was. It had all been arranged. But I didn't know, I couldn't realize . . . He was old, bearded and pale. He had chosen me by noticing where I drew water from the river. Only Lemba understood. It was she who held the knife, at first close to her stomach and then raising it, bright in the moon, before slashing the throat of the shaking goat, and the drums, pounding and pounding."

Jessamine lay her head on my shoulder, her long, nearly straight hair coating my arm in a glistening fall of darkness. The churchly choir, robed and with candles, meandered by, singing among the graves "While shepherds watched their flocks," until Jessamine, who had begun choking out tight sobs, collapsed, her head on my lap. She said nothing for a long time.

I watched the candles mirror in the luminescent conch shells near our feet. I heard the choir grow distant as, still singing, it slowly wandered off toward town. A wind, rife with rain, its temperature warm as blood, whipped the candles until one by one they flickered out.

Head still couched in my lap, she whispered, "After our meeting he took me to the house I still live in. We had the two girls. He was nice. Very nice to me, Mr. Hempstead, he was."

Lightning flickered over the ocean. We could see it repeatedly dive into the dark water. The crowd had dispersed. We were alone, with only the death of her Julian to provoke whatever we might do. She raised her head, kissed me and held me close. "And then he died." After a pause, she hugged herself and shivered slightly. "So here we are, Boob. Just us and the night."

2

Goat with Two Legs

Dining in the St. James Hotel was a bland affair. But since there were no restaurants or bars on the entire island, you ate and drank where you slept. The hotel's monthly rate was five dollars a day, including food. I took the monthly rate. The dining area was pleasant, white table cloths, white-jacketed black waiters, but, for weeks, no diners except me and a sandy-haired, lanky Britisher who, characteristic of the breed, never spoke or glanced in my direction. While eating, he read thick books on agriculture.

After days of this, I began seating myself at a table that faced him. He read on. I stared, marveling at his insouciance while spooning soup through his mustache, nary a dribble marring hair, book or table cloth. Having been raised never to ignore someone within speaking vicinity, but also guessing that he must have been taught the opposite, I appeared one evening armed with *Crime and Punishment*, heavy enough to be impressive.

I had consumed several rum punches in my room, so I felt steeled to confront this wall of a human who was near my age and coloring. There ought to be some distant genetic connection, I reasoned. I look very British, my ancestry being predominately Welsh, though like most Americans at that time I really didn't know much about my heritage and have never managed to care since. You are, socially anyway, however you were raised. The hereditary past is for the desperate to seek out, as is a heavenly afterlife for the poor.

I eased my Dostoevski between the shiny glasses for wine neither of us ever ordered, tried propping it against the tin sugar bowl, only to have the book slip toward my plate while shoving the bowl to balance precariously on the table's edge. The waiter, observing the near catastrophe, rushed toward it. "Sir!" he mumbled decorously, trying not to laugh. Black pants hugged his protrusive buns. I was already smitten. "Sorry," I muttered.

When he brought the soup, I was beside myself. I could not fathom how to hold the novel open, focus on the words and spoon liquid into my mouth at the same time. The Britisher, other than with a slight raise of a tawny eyebrow detectable above his reading material, remained impassive.

The inevitable waited for the main course of mutton, which was imported in cans the cook just pried open and plopped on a plate. Anglican cat food, I dubbed it. I dove my fork into a section that might have passed near fire when, beyond my control, Dostoevski collapsed flat down into the mire. In basic American I exploded, "Aw, shit!"

The waiter giggled so hard he had to hide himself behind a partition, where, from the sound alone, I gathered he flailed himself helplessly. I glanced over at the Britisher who had stirred to peek around his pages to eye me with curious disdain. "I wasn't aware Americans read." His voice came at me clipped and dry.

"Some of us even go to college," I defended. When caught off guard, I've always tried to explain and excuse myself simultaneously. The ploy never works, though I keep thinking it should.

He chuckled, gasped, finally glaring at me in stupefied silence. The ceiling fan went womp, womp. Then he snickered again. "Oxford," he sobered himself to announce.

"Cornell College in Iowa," I shot back.

The waiter, with a smirk trembling his full lips, waved his cute butt in my face as he carefully resurrected the soiled pages from the stew. A squished canned pea already dried in a green streak across that odd name of Dostoevski's antihero 'Raskolnikov.'

"What happened to New York?" my antagonist challenged.

"Brothers, I think. The Brothers Cornell founded both the university and the college. Methodist ministers, the two of them. Besides," I rattled on, "if you've ever heard of an educational institution, don't go there. That's my motto. I've been to Northwestern University, too. A terrible place. All professors do in famous institutions is show off. They tell, don't show. And teaching should be an art, don't you think?"

"*Au contraire*," he countered while sipping his tea. A gold wedding band flashed its warning.

There's nothing more intimidating to a midwestern American than a language other than what he speaks. I nervously rose to my feet, extended my hand into the air between our tables. "How do you do. My name's Boo...I mean Bob."

He looked stunned. His mouth flew open exposing a coated tongue. "Henry," he eventually grunted. "Henry Collingsford." His face disappeared again behind his book. He continued sipping his tea. I remained hovering a moment, confused and irritating to him, I guessed, as a fly.

I realized that my insistence upon extending this confrontation exposed my fatal flaw. But I couldn't help it. Like the ancient Greeks, I believe it's possible for a pervasive and tragic flaw to seize us while we're young and shake us until we exhaust or come to recognize and thereby moderate the patterns responsible for our discomfort. Little can be done for the flaw except to weather it, blunt it through knowing. Not comprehending one's flaw can make young men, especially, dangerous to themselves and so to others. I was dangerous when I arrived on the island.

The cankerous core of my constant and near-fatal flaw was and is and will be a terror of isolation, loneliness and insignificance—for which I claim no originality. Although the intensity and obsessiveness of my anxiety marks me as perhaps more irritating, grasping and wracked than most—as well as more forgiving, helpful and even tail-wagging in compensation—I suggest that the degree to which we are afflicted is what first reveals us to others and finally, dare we face it, to ourselves.

Despite my grating manner while introducing myself to Henry Collingsford (all flaw and little sense), we became friends. Sent by the Crown as an agricultural advisor to the unenlightened—to him an evident fact because they were black—he jaunted each day into the hills and farms in a jeep that permitted him to bounce across fields of sugarcane and through banana groves destructively on his mission to redeem ignorance. He invited me to join him on several occasions. One day as we lurched over a rutted road through arching banana leaves that slapped our faces with vicious whacks, I convivially shouted, "How many kids do you have?"

Henry was reading a map as he raced the jeep. A leaf had just torn free and snagged itself under the windshield wiper on his side. "Two, I think," he said gritting his teeth in the wind while standing to lean over the windshield and pull on the leaf with his right hand, his left still clutching the map, his eyes fixed on me. I sang tremulously, "And He walks with me and He talks with me," fearing as I always do with exuberant drivers that the end is near and that celestial points might be earned should decapitation be accompanied by a hymn. I grabbed for the emergency brake.

He slumped into his seat, flicking my arm aside with the back of his hand. "I know what I'm doing. You Americans," he sniffed, "with your religious clap trap. It will be the end of you one day."

I decided to ignore the obvious truth of his observation. "How come you only 'think' you have two children?"

"I'm not home much."

"And never intend to be?"

"Not if I can help it."

The jeep burst out of the banana grove and ground down the corner of a sugarcane field before Henry righted us to wheel into the parallel troughs that might serve as a passage through the stalks. Blacks in short pants and straw hats stared as we kicked sand in our wake. Several of them shouted, in protest I believe. "Damned natives," Henry grinned happily, fluttering his map at them in salutation, "probably never seen a real jeep."

Abruptly, the tracks we followed ended in a broad stretch of sand walloped by waves. We were on the other side of the island, near the town of Grenville, or so Henry surmised as he cut the motor. The hiss of breaking water made sea shells of my ears. When we got out of his vehicle I looked for the town but nothing could be seen of it, just miles of beach, misty and wind blown.

I sat on a mound of sand, my fingers discovering shells underneath, all broken and aged, and then I came upon shards of broken pottery crisscrossed with dark lines. Then the heads of odd creatures appeared in my hand. I recall the discovery well and remark upon the extraordinary artifacts now because to this day I have no idea what artistically accomplished peoples created them.

The natives called them Carib stones. The Carib Indians, for whom the sea is named, are virtually extinct, having leapt en masse like lemmings from a cliff, preferring suicide to domination by the first white visitors with muskets. But then the Caribs had pushed out the Arawak Indians who first inhabited the island, so the antagonism is tribe versus tribe, color becoming merely a more convenient marker as the world got more homogenized. 'I belong, you don't' is the cry that marks our species. The fault is inherent, probably genetic.

Did the Arawaks create the figures? Other than that they were formed of clay and embellished with heads, all were parts of bowls, some with handles still intact, the artwork itself resembling nothing I've seen in books or the anthropological exhibits in museums. What primarily characterized the figures were the eyes. Though carefully and skillfully formed, there was no attempt to make them human. All eyes were perfectly round, protrusive and centered with a deep hole. The noses, too, were not human but rather more pig-like, or long and slightly curved like a tapir's. The lips, typically twin ovals, jutted outward yet were thin. Though human in no particular detail, the shape of the head caused me to read the figures as human. In no way did these ceramic shards resemble Aztec, Maya or Olmec art, the oldest cultures near the island.

Henry came down with malaria. Though anyone sleeping near the ocean had their beds draped with mosquito netting, I had yet to see a mosquito. Yet there Henry lay, sweating, shivering and hallucinating. "Martha, Martha," he moaned. A reference, I assumed, to his wife since wedding bands are a form of bondage not even the unconscious is supposed to veer from. A corpulent black with an even blacker bag came and went. Henry thought he might be a real doctor and I decided not to disabuse him of that hope. I fed Henry aspirin and when the fever still remained too high, swathed his forehead and shoulders with ice-packed blankets.

I liked doing this. It made me feel necessary, no longer a vagabond. Should altruism be the power play I've always thought, I mastered the part with joy. When Henry finally recuperated sufficiently for soup, I ladled the broth through his mustache almost faultlessly as he could. He whispered between slurps, "You've saved my life, Boober." Calling me Boober was to him affectionate, West Indian and funny.

Years later, while traveling in London and staying at a gay hotel, I phoned him. He enthusiastically greeted me as the man who had once saved his life, but when he discovered where I was staying refused to see or speak to me, "ever in the future" is how he put it.

My teaching salary at one of the most prestigious high schools at the time was three thousand a year. I had saved only a few hundred in order to survive on the island. So when I returned one evening from a day with Jessamine to pick up a note from the manager of the St. James Hotel stating a refusal to continue the monthly rate he originally had agreed to, I exploded. Precisely why, I demanded, would he dare such a thing? His response was that he suggested I move, because all his rates were about to be doubled. But why? I insisted. His swarthy face, though glistening with sweat, remained implacable. There are reasons, is all he would mumble.

Had this happened to Henry, I wondered banging on his door. No, but then he was going back to England within the week, his agricultural stint on the island drawing to a close. I'll sue, I confided to Jessamine. "You'll lose," she wagged a finger at me. By which she meant, but was too polite to say, that didn't I realize the judge was black, the hotel owner might be black, and I had no connection with the governor whatsoever.

Idealistic as youth used to be, believing that the planet, despite all evidence to the contrary, was a rational place, I insisted on my day in court. The judge and barristers all wore flattened, yellowing, once-white wigs that looked like road-kill sheep. Their black hair broodingly margined the creased wool. Sweat slid gracelessly down their furrowed brows. The judge was not at all nice. "Has the manager of the St. James signed a document assuring your monthly rate unto futurity," he wanted to know. "And could you produce said document?" In his left, cloaked arm, the gavel was already raised.

"The agreement was verbal," I squeaked out.

The gavel descended with a whack. "Case dismissed!" His smile was not apologetic. I wondered if I had learned what it was to be a minority. My Caucasian features might remind him of the slave traders who shackled his ancestors, at the rate of ten thousand a year, and brought them to be beaten on island plantations where their life expectancy was less than ten years due to the grueling labor. I exited the courtroom, my fists clenched. It was the kings of Dahomey and Nigeria, your own kind, who captured and sold your forebears. The Brits I resemble merely bought the already tortured goods.

I was in a state when I joined Jessamine that evening. For the first time I recognized that her smile might be more amused, even haughty, rather than kind and accepting regarding my presence. "I warned you," she grinned. Nevertheless, she consoled me with what she insisted was a present. She'd bought a Christmas tree. Would I go get it? The *Isle de France*, the only luxury boat to dock during my year on the island, was to arrive that night—Jessamine's employment at the telegraph office offered her extraordinary information—in whose hold were some authentic northern pines the islanders prized. She'd already reserved one. Besides, Ernest Hemingway was aboard.

The next day found me wandering about the *Isle de France*

improbably in search of a Christmas tree and Ernest Hemingway. I hovered around every deck chair that contained a body. What would I say to the icon, I could not imagine. But maybe: When you were my age you wrote some wonderful stories, so what happened? Or, since with a fist you knocked your fellow writer Sinclair Lewis out for implying you were gay, does that mean you're repressed?

Fortunately, the Papa remained in his room gracing neither a deck or the island with his presence, but I did claim Jessamine's tree which we decorated with popcorn that night, aided by Lemba and Jessamine's two girls. The salubrious weather on the island made the passage of time impossible to note. There seemed to be no particular beginning or end to anything. The approach of Christmas surprised me no more or less than the green flame that spurted out from the sun as it sunk over the watery horizon each evening.

To further assuage my anger at losing my suit in court, Jessamine invited me to inaugurate the holidays by accompanying her while she visited many of her friends. I very much enjoyed drifting among the finer houses, then on to tin-roofed shack to palm-roofed shack to drink and chat with their occupants, all who welcomed me with what I took to be wondrous grace. We drank rum, usually straight, and it was not long before I was bobbing my head to the music of steel bands which seemed to emerge from every banana grove and alley. When I was initially blessed with cloth scarves of various startling colors that were wrapped around my neck, I accepted them with gratitude and joy. I even got to laughing and prancing to the drum beats and the lively pinging of the beaten oil drums, letting the scarves wave in the air to the accompaniment of appreciative laughter from our hosts. "The best Christmas parties I've ever been at!" I hugged Jessamine.

As I did, I came to the realization that Jessamine had not been presented with any scarves. Her throat was quite bare except for a necklace of seashells, pale blue and soft white, a striking contrast against her skin. "Your friends don't like you as much as they do me?" I shouted over the din. She cupped hands around her ears indicating she couldn't hear over the noise.

But she took hold of my hand and led me to the back of a peculiarly squat shack composed of rotten wood balanced uncertainly on slanting supports. Behind the shack, around a pond fringed by reeds, women in turbaned kerchiefs and men in either khaki shorts or dirty white pants swayed to the drumming and the raucous steel band whose harsh notes fell like stones into the murky water.

Two more women presented me with scarves, one blue, one white. I'm rather tall so they had to leap in order to drape the banners around my neck and over my shoulders. I began to feel burdened by their gifts, especially since I saw that not only Jessamine but that no one else had been so honored. I spotted Jessamine's maid Lemba doing a bent-kneed jig on the far side of the pond. I waved at her in recognition when she wiggled her way to the water's edge on squat, bowed legs and heel-digging bare feet.

The drumming quickened, the music intensified, the steel band players thrashed their cloth-bound sticks across the colored triangles that marked the notes. They played a furious glissando which sounded like lightning and then rumbled thunder. I sat on the big, flat stone where Jessamine had suggested I situate myself, my bannered gifts lifting in the breeze around my ears. This is all marvelous, I thought. Like a free trip to Dahomey or Nigeria. Were it not for the steel band, of course. Though I would always rather be involved than a spectator, in this instance I was both relieved and amused to act as spectator. And, after all, I was white, clearly the respected guest of Jessamine who, apparently better to view the activities around the pond, had crawled onto the lower, wide limb of an enormous bo tree that wreathed one side of the yard. She lay on her side, one leg hanging down, mouth moving as though singing.

Actually, the whole crowd began swaying, rhythmically digging their heels into the sand and humming as they inched closer to the pond.

Somebody offered me more rum, this time in a gourd exquisitely bound in fish netting. I sipped cautiously. No sense passing out on Jessamine, I promised myself. I crossed my legs under me and leaned eagerly forward, blinking into a world I had heard of but which I never thought I would see.

A boy in a T-shirt that proclaimed 'Hold me!' pushed a small drum onto the rock near my knees. He rapped on the animal-skin covering with his knuckles. "You beat, sir. Sir, you beat." Because the drumming was now repetitive, even monotonous, I thought of the syncopation typical of African recordings I'd heard, and so decided to offer them a Nigerian authenticity their genes could only guess at. Thump da, da thump. I lurched into my act, slapping the hide with a vigor that caught even me off guard. As I wildly pounded my way toward what I assumed might well make Grenadian musical history, an old woman, toothless, hairy breasts drooping out of her skimpy dress, tapped me on the shoulder. I turned, instantly enveloped by the horror of her breath, but immediately engaged by her forced smile. "You ain't doing it so good now." She slunk back into the crowd.

I obeyed by imitating what I was hearing, constant, relentless, unvarying beats that in my inebriated state were difficult to maintain. The banners around my neck rustled as the evening breeze stirred them. I felt my eyes going glassy.

A large man, black neck straining, a white cloak draped over his huge shoulders, strutted forward from the crowd. With bare feet he waded into the scummy pond. "Damballah. Damballah-wedo!" his deep voice roared over the drumming. The steel bands fell silent, their players staring at this impressive fellow who balanced a large wooden bowl in each hand. On either side of him women, also in white, dipped fingers into the bowls and flung lumpy masses of food into the water. The crowd hummed and crooned. "Damballah, Damballah, wedo, wedo," cried the cloaked man. He then graced us all with a broad, beneficent smile as he archly inquired, "You ask for a pig. I will give you one. You ask for a goat with two feet. Where could I get it to give to you?" His black eyes searched among the people. The drums abruptly began to hurry their rhythms. I could not keep up, so I rested back on my haunches, arms at my sides, the various cloths around my neck tickling my ear lobes. As the imperious man backed out of the water with a splash and much kicking of his grimy feet, several women fell to the ground, writhing. The drumming continued, as did the humming.

I glanced over at Jessamine, still nestled in the tree, arms charmingly cradled under her head. As I try to recollect this now, forty-three years later, I believe that she, too, was wearing white. Which would not have surprised me, since she often wore white, the perfect contrast for people of color. But am I right or wrong in remembering that her dress on that occasion was unusually long and artfully embroidered? I seem to recall that information with a start.

The giant man, whom I was soon to acknowledge as a mambo, circled the pond calling out over the rolling drums, "Where is this goat with two legs? Where, where is he?" And he stopped, his arms raised, directly below Jessamine as though she would know. "He is a bold fellow, this goat with two legs," the mambo continued while gesturing at Jessamine. "His bit of sweet potato is bold. His banana is bold."

Silence fell. Even the drums ceased. No one laughed. Not even I. Particularly since Jessamine had languidly raised herself on one elbow and pointed, smiling, at me. "Damballah-wedo," everyone shouted, shuffling in my direction. The drums cracked noisily but, again, monotonously, continuing their thumping as Jessamine's eyes rolled back and she began trembling, at first like a leaf, then violently, until utterly and terribly possessed. Though quivering, she nevertheless unmistakably began to imitate me. First came a series of my barking laughs. Then her fingers twisted through the air mimicking my playing the piano. She squeezed a mock toothpaste tube and pretended to smear it over empty space. She shouted in tongues a word that sounded like "Ezili. Ezili!"

Members of the party who had not given into trance or possession approached me where I remained stunned on my rock. They reached their hands out toward me, fingering my skin and twisting the gift scarves so tightly around my neck I feared strangulation. But while doing this they laughed. Their laughter did not seem derisive, so it calmed me. As did my drunken condition.

"Boob. Boob!" I heard Jessamine's voice directly behind me. Without my noticing, she'd clambered down her tree and now showed no signs of possession, her eyes normally fixed on me, her lips inviting. "Let's go home now, my Boob."

"Party's over?" I practiced breathing in and out to steady myself.

I've since learned that Elizi is the patron goddess of lovers in the Voodoo pantheon and has strong matrimonial associations. I suspect I got married to Jessamine. Certainly, I was the goat with two legs and the bold banana, and she did appear to be taking on my persona.

When I finally broached the subject of our Voodoo nuptials to Jessamine, she expressed surprise. "You got drunk and I took you home with me," was her entire explanation.

3

Daisy, Mr. Edmonds, and the Governor

Despite my Voodoo marriage to Jessamine—or perhaps because of it—renting a room in her house was out of the question. Actually, she never offered. Maybe the possibility never occurred to her. But then, as I was further to witness, it's typical of the tranced and possessed to recall nothing. Or at least never to admit recalling anything.

The Christian/Voodoo dichotomy on the island can best be visualized as an orange, the skin that encapsulates the fruit being Christianity, while the pulp, the essence, is Voodoo. Christianity was the conscious, Voodoo the unconscious. That Jessamine knew how obvious our relationship was to anyone who cared cannot be disputed. Yet along the coast, in the towns such as St. George's where consciousness reigned, Christian rules, thanks to British colonialism, held sway.

Forced by the court to vacate my lodgings at the St. James Hotel, under duress and with considerable irritation, I moved to a guest house called the Green Gables. The Gable's proprietress, Daisy Renick, was as mysterious, vicious, resentful, kind, distant and lovable as any harlequin of mixed characteristics and heritage could be expected to encompass. A mulatto, with feisty pride, Daisy sported the negative characteristics of the disparate races that comprised her. Her nose was long, hooked and pointed, the nostril openings mere slits from which poked twin black hairs. Her lower lip hung fat and pendulous half way down her tiny chin. Her glistening black eyes glared between puckered lids. To fortify the impression of Daisy as a harlequin, her skin was patchy and mottled, grading itself from gray to lemon to plum, depending on what any disastrous slant of light might encourage.

The Green Gables itself swayed in the wind on impossibly long, thin stilts that attempted to support the porch. Though a small door

smeared with blistered green paint led directly onto the street, most
of its structure yawned out over a steep hill, a half mile from the
sea. Though cramped, the porch had views of the town and the
harbor which was always rife with sailless rigging listlessly rolling
amid the dinging of bells against the evening's parade of clouds.
It was on that porch each evening that Daisy, Mr. Edmonds, and
I shared rum punches before dining at our separate tables in the
Gable's dour and dank refectory. While eating, the only
sound—except for Daisy's occasional scathing indictment of anyone
who "Doesn't know their wines. Disgusting!"—tended to be the
clink and scrape of forks and spoons against plates and the
mesmerizing womp, womp of the ceiling fan.

Mr. Edmonds was Daisy's only other guest. He had resided
at the Gables, I gathered, for years. He was thoroughly sweet,
incomprehensible and unnerving. Mr. Edmonds bore skin so pale
as to resemble the translucence of a cave worm. His lips were thin,
tight and red as a bloody gash. The tan suit he always wore fell
upon him like the skin of one who has strenuously dieted. Since
he never appeared in any other garb, his suit had taken on a hide-
like permanence. His smile was wan but frequent and exposed one
eyetooth of pure gold.

"Oh, Bob," he addressed me where I lay couched in the porch
hammock, my usual perch, "just look you at that sunset." I collapsed
the book I was reading over my stomach and stared with him, as
we did most evenings, at the brilliance. People, even though not
naturally conducive to each other, approached an easy kind of
muted intimacy when there weren't TVs, VCRs, compact disks
and roaring car traffic to intervene. Daisy, Mr. Edmonds, and I
asked very little of each other, our lowered expectations and quiet
tolerance warming us almost tenderly, though our main entertainment was to snipe, however subtly, at each other and with
unbounded viciousness at any one on the island whose name had
the misfortune to come up in conversation.

I agreed with Mr. Edmonds as I did each evening that the sunset could not be more spectacular, when Daisy waddled onto the porch with our rum punches and three addressed envelopes for me and one each for the two of them. Daisy's lower lip rode tight against her teeth in anticipation. "The Governor, the Governor. Look a' there," waving an embossed envelope, "his H. E. his self has..."

"That bastard," cooed Mr. Edmonds.

I companionably offered, "We're to be arrested, Mrs. Renick?" After a spate of many weeks I'd returned to *Crime and Punishment*, which I slid down over my crotch, identification with the protagonist causing me to feel guilty about nearly everything.

"All three of us has been for...tomorrow?" Daisy already had daggered her finger through the envelope, squinting at what she declared was, "An invitation to tea and cocktails, five PM sharp." She read aloud slowly and with staggering difficulty. "At the mansion," she whooped.

Mr. Edmonds had eased his unopened invitation into a side pocket of his wrinkled armor. "Thank you very much Mr. Governor, but I shall decline." He grinned unnervingly, crossed and wrapped his thin left leg around the right. "You, Bob, and you, Mrs. Renick, will comport yourselves remarkably, I am sure, at the house of His Eminence...quite without me."

I leaned out of my hammock, "But you've been to H. E.'s before, Mr. Edmonds?"

"Many times," Edmonds assured me, his gold tooth winking between the blood of his lips. "H. E.'s a reprobate. I'll have none of him."

Daisy sank into a wicker chair, her eyes shifting uneasily under the multicolored puffs of the lids. "We must all refuse," she plucked at a nose hair apparently for emphasis, as though the decision were hers in the first place. "I, too, have been to the mansion before and found it... well..." She searched for a proper and therefore British expression. "Tiresome," she seemed to recall from deep in her memory from where she also dredged up, "in the extremity." Just as Jessamine had mined similar words and phrases in an effort to impress.

"In the extreme," corrected Mr. Edmonds, blinking steadily at her.

"There it goes!" I shouted, jabbing my punch glass toward the green ray that proclaimed the departure of the sun.

Daisy and Mr. Edmonds sang out, "Bravo!" brandishing their glasses before them.

"Well, I'm accepting the Governor's invitation," I announced.

Daisy scuffed off to abuse the cook for some imagined offense. Mr. Edmonds slunk back into his chair, arms now protectively enfolding where his chest might be, lost in thought. I opened my other letters which arrived in the weekly mail, one from my mother, the other from Margo Athens.

I had met Margo Athens at my apartment mate's wedding two days before my departure for the island. I was best man and Margo, the bride's best friend, was maid of honor. Only the four of us and the minister had huddled in the echoing chapel. Margo was even more striking and classically beautiful than the bride. Her alabaster skin, her waist-long hair shimmering a vinaceous amber, and her green eyes made to glisten beneath dark mascara—all assured her of being astounding. Which was her intent. To astound was her business. She was very devotedly a high-class prostitute who, in the letter I then read, to my astonishment and with little warning, promised to intrude upon the chaos I was creating for myself on the island.

Margo had written me once a week since I'd given her my island address. She had proved herself to be witty, thoughtful, and knowledgeable about nearly everything. She had just completed *War and Peace* for instance, and complained regarding what she noted as the disappointing brevity of the book, and so at my suggestion, had plunged expectantly into *Anna Karenina*. She previously had hinted she wished to vacation from her vaginal labors with me in Grenada, and in this particular letter she projected her arrival to be within two or three weeks. As I recall, I was more appalled than jubilant. But having always considered myself fate's plaything, I simply swigged more punch, congratulating myself for being kicked out of the St. James Hotel, for not being in the least encouraged to stay at Jessamine's, and for by default ensconcing myself at Daisy Renick's three-dollars-a-day-with-food Green Gables.

A lodging Margo clearly would consider intolerable. Her milieu, I already knew, was nightclubs, one of her recent clients being the comedian Shelly Berman who "could only get it on dressed in drag," she had written to complacently inform me of the oddities of her trade. Clearly, she needed a rest. I would arrange for her to stay at the swanker and newer Santa Maria Hotel.

Having decided this in my mind, I turned to my mother's letter. "Dear Sun," she wrote, which was a typical dyslexic error of mine that had begun in college with letters and remained lodged in her more rational but brutal mind, "You've hinted that this lady 'friend' of yours just might visit where you've run off to. Can't accept you'll take a whore on as companion…"

How the hell did she know Margo was what she was? All I had done was to describe Margo briefly. I didn't recall suggesting that Margo would visit. Clearly, my mother was a witch with supernatural powers and should simmer in her own cauldron. Feigning innocence, I penned a swift reply. "Best you not write me if you can only heap disparagement upon my acquaintances." Not until after my father died fifteen years later did my mother write me again, and then all letters until her death were weather reports.

It's the specifically personal, the subjective, the eccentric in our lives that either fans or snuffs out the original coded stuff of fate. For the first six years of my life I was repudiated by my mother and given over to the care of nurses. After six days and nights of screaming my mother had her hips rudely broken in order to eject her forceps-wounded offspring, and so reminded me always, but particularly when I misbehaved, that I was the one responsible for almost annihilating her, so best the little cutthroat shape up.

Dinner not being ready, and while Mr. Edmonds sunk deeper into his doze, I nestled into my hammock, switched on the yellow bug light and prepared to resume the Dostoevski. It did pass through my mind however, how inconvenient but fabulous it was that a queer such as I had a mistress I seemed to have mystically wed and was about to import a prostitute I assumed I was to bed. When in fact Daisy's servant boy, Ralph, had a bicycle I often borrowed, and I was happiest in the knowledge it was the memory of his behind I sat on.

Then it happened. How I survived without snapping my back in two and being paralyzed for life is as wondrous as wondrous events tend to be. I had reached that part in *Crime and Punishment* where the desperate protagonist, with whom one is forced to identify, creeps, ax in hand, slowly, to smash the unsuspecting pawnbroker woman's head...he raises the weapon, pauses, and then plunges it into her brains—at which instant my hammock broke.

Termites I've often honored as being responsible for my most intense reading experience. And yet there I was, crumpled on the porch floor, moaning and shrieking so loud even Mr. Edmonds roused himself to uncharacteristically bellow, "Shut up!"

I struggled to my knees and was stretching each appendage tentatively into the air assuring myself that my spine had not disintegrated, when Daisy reappeared to announce dinner. Observing the demise of the hammock, she attacked. "That will cost you," she said, leaning over my crouching form.

"I didn't do it," I muttered.

"Ha," she said.

But with Mr. Edmonds' head under one armpit and Daisy's under the other, they supported me, sniveling as I was, down into the semidark of the eating area. Over viscous soup and, of course, canned mutton, as though nothing had happened (but then to them nothing had), Daisy pontificated to the ceiling, "Yes, I've decided differently. I will be attending the Governor's *soiree*. With you,

Mr. Sweet. You'll need some assistance, I suspect. I'll consider it my duty."

Mr. Edmonds commented from his corner table where he liked to hug the wall, "Surprise. Surprise."

Daisy ignored the sarcasm. "I'll order a cab, Mr. Sweet. You pay, as compensation for the hammock."

So it was settled. After eating, I painfully inched my way upstairs to my room small as a jail cell, containing a cot, a table for my typewriter, a cane-backed chair, and two windows covered by sticky once-white curtains with musty pink flowers blown inward on the sea breeze.

I have a photo of myself lying on that narrow bed. I do not recall who took it. I did not have a camera. My eyes are shut as though I'm shocked by the intrusion. I'm naked, a light cotton blanket tucked close to my body reaching just below my navel. The wrinkles of the blanket, like the silk of a robe in a Renaissance painting, are emboldened by shadows that whirl restlessly over legs and groin. A light yet steady flow of brown hair feeds down from the dark, deeply indented navel, fanning out over the well-formed chest and prominent nipples. A luminous cast of light from the window behind me glances over the sternum and ribs that appear to be strong, the flesh that covers them neither excessive nor spare.

Is destiny our bodies? In the eyes that view us, probably yes. From our own vantage, the issue becomes mixed. I've always had to stare in the mirror each morning to assure myself that how I think of myself is not true. By now expectation and fact tend woefully to be merging. Cancer-riddled as I am, with a heart prone nastily to attacks—all symptoms presently quiescent, only age itself insisting that the calm be not for long—I merely reach for the recollections that might best encapsulate who I was.

I look at this photograph of myself forty-three years ago with amazed approval. I was almost a hunk. My head on the two pillows piled behind me sustains features that are not unpleasant. The aquiline nose, the bee-stung lower lip, the puffed boyish cheeks, the curly hair, the glistening slant of light I'd swear would show in the hazel eyes were they open, combine to make me look cuddly and unalarming. As though my only intent were to appease.

All of this is hindsight, however. My aching back made it difficult to sit at the typewriter the next morning. My novel about the high school I taught at wasn't going well: too many first person points of view. For instance, it was difficult trying to be in the mind of Sherry, an earnest, blonde, accomplished pianist who had fallen for a student teacher whose homosexual tendencies she had every intention of correcting. I was including the situation in my book only because it was true—when Daisy flung open my door without knocking to remind me that the cab to the Governor's mansion I was to pay for would arrive at four-thirty and that, not unexpectedly, Mr. Edmonds had decided to join us and wouldn't that be just fine.

As the cab jounced through the potholes and dodged around palm fronds broken off in that afternoon's shower, Daisy admonished Mr. Edmonds—as though they'd been married for years—to pull up his socks, which had the unfortunate tendency to sag exposing his blotched ankles.

"Why did you ever leave England?" I directed my question at the back of Edmonds' head as he bent to fumble down around the floorboards. I had always wondered and the excitement of approaching the Governor's mansion encouraged me to broach the subject I sensed to be forbidden.

"What…" Mr. Edmonds began, straightening his back, his vermilion lips gaping wide into a swollen O.

Daisy advised him, "No need to answer. No need that I can see," while staring out the window at a flash of sea between the trees.

"My mother…" Edmonds pressed the palms of both hands against his cheeks in consternation. I do not know if he would have said more, because then Daisy interrupted, "Here we are. The Governor's!"

The cab had taken a side road through arching ferns, and no mansion but a rather large English cottage replete with roses and a picket fence came into view. Guests milled about in the garden, all gradations of black, I noticed. As we alighted from the cab and strolled through the high gate, Daisy observed, "How satisfactory that all people is welcome here."

The Governor has a choice? I mused. Also, it would be political and administrative death for him to even hint at the same inequality that was practiced among the island's inhabitants or the inequality taken for granted in my own country. The Governor, by circumstance, must be forced toward enlightenment.

He came toward us, rotund but solid, a gray mustache, gray eyes, white jacket with golden medals, his right hand stretched toward us. "Mrs. Renick," he slightly bowed as Daisy kinked her knees. "And, ah, Mr. Edmonds and..." He reached for my hand and pumped it. "Our island's guest, no doubt."

"From Chicago."

He touched my shoulder with his left hand. "I'm so sorry."

He steered us inside the modest but pleasant house, aiming us at a punch bowl steeped, I guessed rightly, with rum. Daisy and I thrived under his attention. Mr. Edmonds, of course, wilted, hugging his jacket close to him with folded arms. "Yes, I'm much enjoying my stay," I replied to the Governor's kind question.

"And how long might we have the honor..."

"Possibly a year. That's my plan."

"That long?" His eyes searched mine. He decided to be blunt, albeit indirectly: "There have been those who wash up on our island's shore for no apparent reason."

"Except escape."

He motioned me away from the crowd to the bay of a window where banana trees crowded close to the house. Their obscene blooms pushed out beyond a cornice. I noticed them, shadowed, through slats in the Venetian blind.

"Yes. And one wonders what they are escaping from. And

why." He toyed with the cord of the blind. "That Mr. Edmonds you're staying with. Do you know much about him?"

"He seems to be a harmless fellow. Awfully shy, though."

The Venetian blind shot up several feet. Under where it had been rolled I noticed a dead fly on its back, legs rigid. I felt it incumbent on me to change the subject. I wanted to protect Mr. Edmonds and I didn't know how else to do it. "I've been surprised by the presence of Voodoo."

"On Grenada?" His eyebrows arched in amazement, whether mock or real I wasn't sure.

Since I didn't wish to confide in him regarding my possible marriage and the strange rites that attended it, I merely offered, "I've heard the word mentioned." Which was a lie. In truth, I never heard anyone, not Lemba, not the folks back country, no one in town ever utter the word during my entire stay.

He hissed harshly, "On this island, sir, there is no voodoo. This is a Christian land."

I couldn't guess how to respond. After all, this was his house, his party, his island. So I chatted on trying to change the subject again. "I seem to have been cast out of the St. James Hotel. Under trying circumstances. I still don't know why." Since I was soon to learn that he owned the St. James, I was in, as they say, deeper than I guessed at the time.

Yet he responded to my complaint cheerfully while urging me back to the table where a servant with a red bandanna on her head and a secretive smile ladled punch for me into a glass. Other guests had arrived and Mr. Edmonds and Daisy had plunked themselves side by side in a Victorian love seat, Mr. Edmonds' socks having re-rumpled their way down over his shoes. I could see what Daisy meant. His ankles were veined, pasty horrors.

The Governor suddenly enthused, his mustache crawling over his ochre teeth, "But didn't you know? Don't you know by now? I thought the news was out."

I sipped at my punch waiting for him to proceed.

"Hollywood is about to grace our dear island, sir. Harry Belafonte, and the great, I think, Joan Fontaine, and James Mason…you've heard of them? They're your people, after all. Your preoccupation. And there weren't enough rooms for all these STARS." His voice rose near a howl. "Two hotels do not a cinematic dormitory make." He chuckled at his witticism. "And somebody's hair dresser…a Dorothy, Dorothy Dandridge, I believe, will be lodged at the Gables. That's why you were encouraged to leave the St. James. Oh, I've had a time of it, arranging, arranging. Sorry for any inconvenience to you, though. Mrs. Renick! Mrs. Renick!" He left me to hurl himself toward Daisy. Mr. Edmonds stood, grinning frailly as was his wont, permitting H. E. a seat beside the Gable's proprietress.

The crowd had intensified, wide-brimmed hats and even some suits and dotted ties and several wing-tipped white and brown shoes. The noise of laughter and general conviviality was getting on my nerves. Groups of more than eight people paralyze me into inertia. I pled with the servant who wore the red bandanna for a refill. She had that quiet grace yet studied efficiency I've always found disturbing. As the punch gurgled into my glass, the dark woman this time fixed me directly with her secretive smile. "How be that Jessamine?" she conspiratorially cracked her lips to inquire.

God, what a small island.

4

Star-struck

Shaped like a paramecium, the island held some hundred thousand folk who did their thing in twenty square miles: tropical and lush toward the south, dry with cactuses on its northern end, centered by the rain forest and volcanic lake Grande Etang. The general effect was rural, dotted with villages balanced on cliffs. The houses, of wood or stucco, often were painted in startling pastels and typically nestled between breadfruit trees whose wide, notched leaves dappled the corrugated tin roofs with shade. Above, mountains heaved their shoulders hairy with palms, while below rank valleys steamed with glistening banana leaves and the darker, squat but spreading nutmeg.

Despite the island's smallness, I seldom saw people I recognized, even in St. George's where I lived. I felt increasingly avoided. My whiteness isolated me. In a society as stratified by color as Grenada's, my being ostracized was more a mark of honor than of disdain, I decided. Yet it unsettled me that everywhere I went, every move I made was noted and possibly remarked upon. The circumstance aggravated my pervasive fear of being exiled.

So I stuck to the few friends I had and wrote incompetently on my book each morning. When it got too hot in my narrow room by afternoon, I often walked or rode the bike I borrowed from Ralph, Daisy's handyman, toward Grande Anse beach to splash about in the tepid water. In truth, I was suffering after four months from serious culture shock. Every flower, every tree and smell and each startlingly vacuous person refused to resonate in my mind and thus fortify my sense of self. I decided that each of us is made up of three quite distinct personas. The first is genetic predilection—the fated hard-wiring—that we spend our entire lives struggling to acknowledge. The second is the social milieu within which we were raised, whose dictates nine times out of ten attempt to deconstruct our initial programming. The third is the archetypal unconscious, the deeper source of purpose and meaning we share with all peoples and animals and plants, with the sky and rocks and stars, with the infinite but ever-expanding universe itself, black holes and all.

It was the second, the personal memories and constructs, I grieved for—the mirror that would reflect back to me who I was supposed to be—made up of oak trees, elms, snow and sleet, choked highways, symphonies, conversation whose pointlessness I could follow. I began to drink too much rum. In order to sleep, first there had to be the rum. I swigged it straight out of the bottle. It was cheap.

I had decided to walk to the beach one afternoon rather than borrow Ralph's bike. I remember bouncing a knapsack containing towel and swimsuit and a book across my back and tapping a long stick—meant for chasing off feral dogs—at the pitted, tar road. I heard a rare car approach from behind me. I turned, mopping at my forehead with the T-shirt I'd taken off, stepped politely into a ditch waiting for what I could now recognize as a taxi to pass. But the vehicle slowed while the car's passenger leaned a tousled head of sandy hair out the window to shout, did I need a ride? His smile was wide and friendly. I was awed as a native by his comparative whiteness. It was like confronting an albino.

I adjusted myself in the seat next to him. He appeared to be tall, gangly, with blue eyes and a face that can only be described as tremendous. Tremendously gorgeous. Not classically perfect, but craggy, strong, overblown—as though stamped on a coin like a Roman Emperor's. But then he hadn't starred in *Ben Hur* yet. He said his name was Stephen Boyd.

The name meant nothing to me. He said he couldn't wait to see what he'd heard was the world's greatest beach—to which I retorted that, well, there was a lot of sea and sand out there, when the taxi stopped at the barracks-like changing rooms. The Caribbean coruscated beyond some palms behind it. Chatting gracefully on about the island's beauty, he gestured me into the same tiny changing room with him so that, he insisted, our conversation wouldn't be interrupted. Irrationally, I prayed that was not his intent at all. Besides, why had he bothered to pick me up? My chest hairs prickled.

Slowly unbuttoning his shirt, Stephen Boyd politely wanted to know what I was doing on this windward spit of land. Mesmerized by his bare chest, I nevertheless managed at least a partial excuse for my existence by explaining that I was a writer while pretending to tug at the belt around my short pants. I wasn't wearing underwear, as I tend not to when it's warm, and decided this entire experience was proceeding at too rapid a pace, particularly since my banana already headed down toward my right knee.

"As for me," Stephen Boyd responded to my query, "I'm sometimes an actor." He bent to stuff his shirt into a leather satchel he'd brought with him. As he stood, I noticed that his chest, between the nipples, appeared to be caved in. Though I assumed it to be a birth defect, his chest looked to have been struck a blow from a large hammer. Subsequently, I have observed in his various films—usually with historic backgrounds —whether in the Roman equivalent of a steam room or driving a chariot, his chest is strategically draped with a towel or coated with armor.

I had greater and greater reason to forestall dropping my pants. After all, it had been months since I'd dallied with a male, and the ecstasy of the clap-ridden dwarf in New York's Everard Baths could not still my genetic predilection forever. Besides, Stephen Boyd's physical imperfection made his heroic face less threatening—and him, I hoped, more accessible. I suddenly remembered I still had tennis shoes on and eagerly busied myself with the laces as Stephen Boyd undid his belt and stepped out of his pants in one seamless gesture while explaining, "I'm here with some others to make a movie. *Island in the Sun*, it's going to be called. From a book by, I think, Alec Waugh."

Inspecting my shoe for the whereabouts of a stone I'd felt lodged near my toes, I responded imperiously, "I only read Evelyn."

Fortunately, he did not register my snobbery and continued, "I arrived this morning. Couldn't wait to take a swim. Staying at a hotel. The Santa Maria." He talked on and on, his voice subdued yet energetic. "Joan Collins…ever heard of her? She's already had a row with the manager. Something about a ceiling fan. Couldn't stand the ruckus so I headed toward the beach. Couldn't wait." It dawned on me that Stephen Boyd had no intention of ceasing his chatter. He was revealed to have underwear on. Jockeys. The bulge respectable but not over much.

Tennis shoes off, I dropped my shorts. Stephen Boyd kicked his way playfully out of his shorts.

Staring at my swollen privates, Stephen Boyd coughed in what I at first took to be an appreciative spasm. But, "We'll be needing stand-ins, you know," he went right on. "The lights, the lights need to reflect off white and you're…"

"Pink?" I offered.

"Pink is fine," he said slipping into his shapeless, boxer trunks.

I noted his organ remained somnolent. Clearly, I had misconstrued friendliness for lust. So I grew testy with chagrin and challenged, "How much would I get paid?"

He slung a towel retrieved from his satchel around his shoulders and proceeded to bump his way backwards out the door. "I think it's five dollars a day."

Wow, I thought, wriggling into my form-fitting suit, that's a dollar a day more than I spend, including rum. "So what do I do?" I shouted after him.

Stephen Boyd was already flinging sand with his running feet as he raced toward the sea. "Whatever they tell you." He tossed his towel aside and plunged into the water with a smack.

We bobbed together in the limpid waves, the salt making it easy to stay afloat, his extraordinary head against a background of marching, orange clouds. "What's it like to be an actor?" I wanted to know.

"What's it like to be a writer?"

"I'm not sure I can answer that." We both stared back at the empty beach, heavenly palms and glittering sand miles in both directions.

"Me either," grinned Stephen Boyd.

He had his taxi drop me off at the Green Gables before returning to the Santa Maria and, apparently, the disgruntled Joan Collins, whoever that was. Sounded to me like a summer drink.

My one-sided confrontation with Stephen Boyd was not the only time desperation and loneliness had led me to desire the unobtainable. It was, in fact, my unrequited love for one of my students that was the real reason I junked my life in the States and proceeded with my disappearing act on the little-known island.

Most students I encountered at that very special school were extraordinary, but then I primarily taught the exceptional, overachieving juniors, seldom encountering one whose testable IQ was under 150. Except for Phillip Weight whom I uncovered in one of the occasional spit-and-drool classes I was assigned 'to keep my feet on the ground', where he dourly doodled, I suspect waiting for someone like me to rescue him. Due to the incessant whining, coughing, paper airplanes and guffaws, I dreaded spit-and-drool hour every day. To shut my charges up, and after some explaining but not much, I threatened them with expulsion (which I had not the power to grant) unless they wrote seven to fourteen poems a week for one month. To my amazement, each poem handed in was better than the one before. Philip's were cynical, mournful, precise and publishable.

I transferred him from spit-and-drool to the cashmere-sweatered set whose sharp eyes glinted with gem-like flames, whose only untoward gesture was an occasional arched and mysterious smile. Quietly he outshone, out-maneuvered, and out-tested them all. One day as the class was leaving while I stared through the blinds out the window, he came to stand very near me intoning, "We know.

Don't we. Yes. We, you and I, know."

I had no idea what he thought he meant. And yet my entire body felt suddenly immersed in some thrilling essence. I tried not to notice his tight ass, his already hairy arms, the sparks from his buck-dark eyes. "So, drop down into my basement apartment some afternoon."

He did. Over and over. Winter slid into spring. We talked about his poetry, mine. Everybody's. We ice-skated on the DesPlaines River, observed the wild flowers by May, and ran, falling exhausted upon each other after running miles through hills and forest paths. I came to tremble for even one touch of him.

I entered class late from a meeting one day and Phillip stood in front guiding the group in a pointed satire of my teaching style, the exaggerated nuances of satire writhing the cashmere sweaters into convulsions. Had he not been him he could have been me. His parody was not mean, but was overblown enough to be hilarious. And dangerous. Dangerous as transference is.

And yet nothing is worse than a dry, unadmitted love. It never gets to move through desire's usual stages. It overreaches itself like some terrible fungus, clogging all pores and the lungs until you cannot breathe. Students may be neither struck nor fucked. I've usually stuck with that.

So, when Stephen Boyd dropped me off at the Gables, I climbed the stairs to the porch, congratulating myself that nothing worse had happened than what had. And that Stephen Boyd had been as casual and accepting as is possible for an apparently straight male to be.

Daisy hooted soon as I had made my way to the porch in time for cocktails and sunset, "I wants you to meet the star Dorothy Dandridge's star hair dresser."

She pointed at my accustomed place in the hammock, repaired since my unfortunate mishap, at a person of undetectable sex lounging enormously within the confines of the netting. "Surely, you have a name of your own," I peered through the uncertain rays

of the yellow bug light. I meant my greeting to sound poised with
a sprinkle of wit.

"Good God," wheezed the personage, shifting its body so that
the hammock swung dangerously out toward the last spurt of the
dying sun. "That horrible plane ride, this wretched accommodation
and now... Who are you?" the creature demanded.

"He's the writer who also reads," Mr. Edmonds answered for
me, his voice fairly lilting with sarcasm. My peculiarities were
fodder for his insecurities. I felt as though I'd been 'outed.' "And
your hotel mate," he added.

The inhabitant of the hammock tried heaving itself upwards
by the elbows which, since this feat is virtually impossible to
manage while wrapped in netting, fell instantly back with a grunt.

"Mrs. Lotti, meet Mr. Sweet," Daisy attempted to rescue the
situation.

I plunged my hand through the bug light into the squirming
morass, but withdrew it when no welcoming hand was offered me.
Nevertheless, Mrs. Lotti—and I'll just have to take her word for
it as her appearance and behavior seemed quite to the contrary—muttered sullenly, "You're hired."

"For what?" Mr. Edmonds wanted to know, his lips pulsing
blood red.

Daisy waved a rum punch over the hammock. It was accepted
by Mrs. Lotti who explained in a very throaty voice from her
darkness that I would—as though any choice on my part were out
of the question—aid her client, an actress famed for her role as
Carmen in *Carmen Jones*, to learn her lines. "At the Santa Maria,
a hotel with some elegance and decency to it." Daisy looked
shocked, even hurt, her nose hairs twitching. "Tomorrow morning
at ten, room 304. I'll be there to introduce you."

Which she was. In fact, Mrs. Lotti opened the door to 304 in
response to my knock. I was about to inquire what remuneration
I could expect, but a glance at Dandridge, seated in a chair with
her perfect features and skin aglow in the morning light, caused

my lips to snap shut. The presence of beauty can be its own reward.

Dorothy Dandridge offered me a chair opposite while she tucked her feet under her buttocks. A typed script lay open across her knees that were encased in flowery slacks of a silky material. "I'm so glad you can help me...I hope...with these lines. They keep flying right out of my mind." One hand fluttered its fingers illustratively around her ear.

There I was two feet from the first black actress to seemingly defeat the color barrier, the first to grace the cover of *LIFE*, who had just returned after creating a sensation at the Cannes Film Festival—and all I could think about was how closely she resembled my mother!

At least pictures of my mother taken when she was Dandridge's age. The same high forehead, slanting brows, wide dark eyes, high cheekbones, finely sculpted nose, luscious and expressive lips, twin melon breasts borrowed from the vine of life itself. My mother's icy beauty had revealed itself often to me, naked in the bath or whispering a terse good night, her swan neck sheathed in pearls, hurrying to whatever it was flappers did by night.

Although Dandridge's skin appeared to be burnished by the sun to a coppery sheen, my mother's, like mine, tended to fry pink then peel when the sun cursed rather than kissed it. But I'll have to applaud my mother's beauty over Dandridge's, giving her credit for being graced with real hair, wavy and thick. Dandridge wore a wig. Always, I came to realize. When I rose at her bidding to accept the bound script, I noticed the cross-hatch of netting transverse the upper portion of her forehead. Because I was to watch her perform a scene three hours later, her face in close up, I've always wondered why the black threading never showed up on movie-house screens. Possibly, Mrs. Lotti was capable of more wizardry than immediately met the eye, as her own wig in daylight proved to be unfortunate in all respects.

At Mrs. Lotti's departure, Dorothy and I got down to work. I read the part to be acted by John Justin, the white district commander whose torrid affair with the lustful, dark Margo played by Dandridge, causes him to urge her to flee with him to England. "Have you read my novel?" I announced the line with enthusiasm, it being one of the many occasions when I've discovered life and fiction to be so inextricably mixed that one could not be distinguished from the other.

"Just read the lines, Robert," Dorothy Dandridge smiled, amused. "No need to try acting, dear friend."

"But *I'm* writing a novel." I stared across at her, my mouth, I'm sure, wide open.

"So Mrs. Lotti has told me. But the point is…just to let me…learn my part. Proceed, please."

"My novel?" I tried again in a flattened voice. I waited for her to pick up the cue.

Dorothy Dandridge meshed her glued eyelashes, ran a pink tongue over her glossy lips. Finally, "Oh…and yes," she reiterated dully, with the precise shade of indifference my friends always exhibited when coerced into reacting to one of my own manuscripts. For me, this experience held all the discomfort of a *deja vu*.

"Well, and what did you think?" I read on, my voice rising in anticipation. I couldn't help throwing something of myself into the script. After all, it was a writer I was performing, and I could only hope John Justin would do as well—who probably hadn't written two sentences strung together in his life

"I'm not deaf," said Dorothy Dandridge, her eyes flashing wide. "Just speak the lines. Now, what do I say back? I've forgotten."

I cleared my throat trying to swallow the lump that developed as I prompted her: "You say, 'It's fine, really.'"

"That's all?"

"That's what's typed in your script."

Her ringed fingers kneaded the chair cushion, apparently in consternation. "Little wonder I can't recall these lines. They're so, so bland, blah, meaningless."

"It appears not to be a very inspired script," I agreed.

She churched her long, sensitive fingers under her divine nose. "What would *you* have me say?" she seemed to wonder aloud.

I thoughtfully pulled on my ear. "Does this Margo woman, whom you're supposed to be, really want to go with him" (I almost said 'with me') "to England?" She nodded. "Why then, she'd have to show extraordinary appreciation, hyperbolic enthusiasm, such as what's declared on the dust jacket of books."

"Which is?"

"'Stunning,' 'brilliant,' 'awesome,' 'never before realized,' come to mind."

Dorothy Dandridge stared at me. A cloud seemed to veil her face. "Is it all mockery?"

She scooted out of her chair, strolled across the room to flick on a switch for the ceiling fan which obediently commenced its womp, womp. Between the opened slats of the blinds, I noticed the Caribbean spraying white sheets of breaking waves against distant rocks. The Santa Maria was balanced on a slim branch of volcanic slag capping the horseshoe levy that shaped the harbor. Over the fan, I managed to hear the occasional screech of gulls flying by.

"Mockery?" I stalled. If she felt that similar words and phrases had been used to describe her were as bloated, as false as any book jacket, she might well be correct. "In some instances they might be taken as true honors. It all depends." My attempt was to be vague.

"You'll never know. Few do." She stood over me, lovely face pushed into a contortion that betrayed anguish. Possibly, Dorothy Dandridge was, in modern psychiatric parlance, bipolar. In other words, for me at least, someone to cherish. I've always sensed that depressives are the only authentic people, equipped as they are to comprehend the tragic nature of what it means to be human. When, earlier, she referred to me as 'dear friend', I took that to mean that we understood one another instantly, no passage of time or words required.

"Now let's get on with it." She curled back into her chair. "I think your novel is...beyond reproach. Brilliant. Insightful."

She was doing better than could be imagined, but then it was Dorothy Dandridge who was the walking novel, and I only the novice re-creator of the already tired genre. "Shall we, freely, just alter the dialogue as we see fit?"

"Oh, yes, yes." She clapped her hands. "So feed me my lines, you keeper of the verbal zoo."

"You're funny," I said.

"So are you."

* * *

And so it was that one scene of the script for *Island in the Sun* got altered and neither the director Robert Rossen, nor the producer Darryl Zanuck, to my disappointment, noted the difference.

Three hours later, we all gathered at a bamboo hut the film crew had just constructed in some brush not far from the hotel. I had already strutted in front of the camera where John Justin was to walk. As a stand-in, you just pace back and forth until all lights and camera angles can be adjusted to your movements. Dorothy Dandridge had already taken her position, lounging on a couch, a bowl of fruit by her side.

By this time I was standing outside the hut, between what appeared to me to be an old man and a younger look alike who might well be his son. "What the bloody H—," I whined, "are grapes doing in that bowl? Where in the holy J— did they come from? Grapes don't grow in the tropics." Though my voice was audible, I complained mostly to myself.

"They came by boat. From refrigerators in the boat," the ancient on my right, who later declared himself to be Darryl Zanuck, decided to explain.

"But why? Why grapes?" I wanted to know.

The fellow on my left, about my age who did turn out to be

Zanuck's son, took it upon himself to inform me that audiences expect to see grapes in bowls beside pretty, Cleopatra-types. Dandridge was a pretty, Cleopatra-type, hence the authentic grapes.

While we conversed, numerous native boys climbed over the roof with buckets of water apparently poised to rain down on whoever entered the hut. "But this is the dry season," I rasped on, "and this scene, which I've come to know intimately by coaching Miss Dandridge, has nothing to do with rain."

"Dear God," exploded John Justin who had just arrived on the set, "nobody told me there was going to be a monsoon." The boys had already doused many of us with experimental releases from their buckets, shrieking with delight at each miniature deluge. "I'll need a raincoat," John Justin announced, seating himself, legs crossed, on a palm stump.

I wanted to inform him that nowhere in the tropics could a raincoat be found, because they were too hot—when I recalled with a start that I and I alone possessed a raincoat. It was a gift from my Aunt Alice who had urged it upon me hoping, no doubt, I'd get smothered in it and never return from what she referred to as my "Reckless sojourn into nowhere."

I confessed my ownership and Dorothy Dandridge, who had nervously munched far too many of Zanuck's precious grapes, assured everyone that I would solve the problem by fetching my raincoat. Which, star-struck and bludgeoned as I was, I did, racing to the Gables on Ralph's bike, then back to the set again. During my absence, the native boys had managed to spill most of the water but, buckets replenished, had just regained the roof. The cameras were set to roll, or whatever it is cameras actually do. Generators roared, powering the lights. I tossed my Aunt Alice's raincoat at John Justin, who sprang to his feet, grabbed the coat, adjusted it over his shoulders and dashed just as breathlessly through the deluge as he was supposed to, flung my raincoat at a chair and bellowed, "Have you read my novel?"

Dorothy Dandridge, in mid slurp of a grape, looked

startled—just as she was supposed to. "Well, yes," she said, swallowing hard and fast.

"And what did you think of it?" shot John Justin leering at Dandridge's bursting globes.

Her reply, trust me, was better than any dust jacket. The words bounced into and through the hyperbowl. As for the rest of the scene, she recalled her lines pretty much as I had invented them, which were less cumbersome than what some Hollywood hack had concocted.

Or so I thought at the time.

5

Frames

My thinking that Dorothy Dandridge's beauty resembled my mother's has not only oedipal implications but also brings up the curious question of what beauty is: cultural indoctrination? Since my mother was white and Dandridge is famous for being black (which she wasn't, copper-toned is more accurate), what is this shady difference in skin color that threatens the very stability of modern nations?

The conflict rivals Byzantium's preoccupation with the Trinity. Was Christ a man *and* a god or all God? Centuries of mayhem ensued over this theological question, just as contemporary politics remains paralyzed over the issue of race. It's a cliché by now to admit it, but I have to join with the ranks of those who claim our species to be terminally absurd.

So it's absurd for me to view Dandridge as black and my mother as white since their appearance was so similar. If race is class and not color at all, Dandridge had a far more elevated background than my mother. Dandridge was raised to be the star she became by her thespian mother who, not so coincidentally, was a lesbian. My mother was born in a sod hut on a homestead claim in South Dakota and was raised fending off obstreperous Indians. When the family finally built a wood house, a vast improvement over the original sod walls and dirt floor, my mother dedicated herself to cleaning, which became her life-long obsession.

Dandridge's Caucasian father was an architect who deserted his family. My maternal grandfather became a grain speculator who, when the price of grain fell, locked himself in his office and, with a Colt revolver, blew his brains out. His suicide cursed my mother with a terror of desertion, which she transferred to me. My fatal flaw began with my grandfather's splintered skull.

We all have our unchosen reasons for being as we are. And we are as fated to be discontented with ourselves as we are to admire or worship or attempt to emulate those we perceive to be superior. The two weeks the movie people spent on the island convinced me that I was no more free of the enticements of charismatic fame, hence star-bludgeoned, than anyone else, despite my attempts to remain blasé.

I looked forward to encouraging Dandridge to alter her lines in the morning and to pacing in front of the lights for John Justin or Stephen Boyd in the afternoon and evening. It made me feel involved, occupied, busy: the values I was raised to extol. And yet, in my small way, I only cooperated in demeaning the integrity of literature itself. Because, though Alec Waugh's *Island in the Sun* is not a great novel, it is still a good and earnest one, and Hollywood's decision to expunge the entire climactic scene—where the natives fall like rabid mongooses to dismember a pale politician they've been taught by their black leaders to hate—took all the teeth out of the racial intrigue the film purported to explore.

I had just left my session with Dorothy and had several hours to dispose of before aiding in the preparation of a scene with Stephen Boyd and the still mysterious Joan Collins, so decided to have an early punch at the Santa Maria bar where Mrs. Lotti was the bar's only occupant. I guessed it would be wise to avoid that unusual person's raspy and perpetual complaints about the island, so I ducked around a corner where I'd never been and noticed a piano, a spinet, its wood blistered blond from the sun and salt. Casually, I pressed down on a few keys, noting to my dissatisfaction that it was more out of tune than even Jessamine's piano, but what the hell, I settled myself on the bench deciding that the only Bach prelude I might be capable of recalling would best accommodate itself to the distraught strings. With the roar of the sea against the rocks outside as an orchestral aside, I launched. Mrs. Lotti and the bartender be damned.

Though the first few tries exposed a bewildered memory on

my part, more notes resurfaced with each attempt and eventually I was rattling on nearly to the end. I felt certain that persistence itself would cause the master of Weimar to eke his way out through my brain, when I sensed someone drawing up a chair behind me. I heard the drag of the legs over the stone floor and became spookily aware that the someone had actually begun to listen.

It is as rare for a musician to be earnestly heard as it is for writer to be seriously read. But as if music were indeed the food of love, accompanied by the crashing waves and the piercing rebound of notes off the plaster walls, I played on. The extraordinary moment inspired in me a faint nausea.

Determined to seem oblivious of the listener's presence, so that I might come off as quaintly practicing rather than performing, I paused just long enough to poise my fingers for yet a fresh foray into the prelude—my seventh, I believe—when I heard the clap of hands. Breathless, I turned around. And nearly fell face forward onto the lap of Harry Belafonte.

I recognized him from his album cover of folk songs that my dry student love, Phillip Weight, and I had listened to in my basement apartment near Chicago. Harry Belafonte's face was fiercely pretty. He lilted at me with his strained, tenor voice—of a similar timbre to Mrs. Lotti's— "Wonderful. Wonderful."

Which, of course, my rendition of Bach obviously hadn't been, so I questioned him with my eyes and gasped out, "Oh?"

When, to my chagrin, he amended, "I mean here, on this island, what a surprise. What a pleasure...to hear Mozart."

I stared at him, flabbergasted by the sheer *gravitas* of his presence. "But you didn't." I was more horrified than amused.

"What?"

"That was supposed to be Bach," I snickered nervously. After all, this was not a movie star rendition of my mother, this was a movie star rendition of my most salubrious of wet dreams. Belafonte also had about him an aura of anger. Despite his facade of gentleness, underneath he seethed. So attractive is this negative quality to my neuroses that I wanted to yelp excitedly from the sting of it. Abuse me, abuse me, my unconscious moaned.

So, agreeably, he did, although rather backhandedly. "Perhaps it's the atrocious piano but the melodic line seemed so…fluid."

"Like a sewing machine," I by accident quoted one of my sillier professors, an authority on Eliot, so what could she know about Bach and why was I compelled to ape her silliness? "But Mr. Belafonte," I tried pulling myself together, "music is, after all, music." I pressed my lips tight in prayer that whatever words repeat and alliterate just have to be taken as meaningful.

An adage with which Belafonte apparently was acquainted for he laughed lightly, "And I sing just because I sing."

We both roared, tipping our heads back, eye teeth pointing toward the ceiling. His knees were aggressively wide apart, hands grasping the chair rung: haughty, animal, gracile. I knew our audience was to conclude even before he rose, without a further word, slinging the chair over his shoulder and stalking out of the alcove.

What was it about being in the presence of these movie people that made one feel like a cow confronted by a wolf? I've since concluded that it's because they have a frame around them—in fact while they are performing, in essence when they are not. I remember attending a New Year's Eve party where the guest of honor, around whom everyone salaamed, was Betty Furness. What she did for a living was to open refrigerator doors for a Westinghouse ad on early TV. She never said a word. And scarcely smiled. But she had a frame around her. And frame means fame.

The Greeks with their sun rays and the Byzantines with their haloes originated the concept of the frame. The 16th century let haloes slip to become a ruff to reflect their Protestantism, and Easter hats and bowlers of even our own secular century only hint at the halo's—and hence the frame's—former glory. But that was before the over-powering framing instituted by the movies and TV whose inspiration, I suggest, we harness to serve all humanity once again.

Because most of us suffer from impaired self-esteem and a gross sense of anonymity, a clothing designer might design dresses, suit coats and jackets of all sorts with thin aluminum wires protruding from shoulders to encase the head in the all important frame. The mind boggles to imagine how fancifully these aluminum frames might be decorated. With lights, possibly, that flash for the perpetually depressed, or shrouded in a subtle felt for the manic. Think of it—walking, vibrant TV images, all of us! Frame is fame and equals worthiness.

I meditated on this possibility that afternoon as I aided the cameras to adjust for Stephen Boyd and marveled at the stunning arrival of the then unknown Joan Collins. We all surrounded a rock that jutted precariously over the ocean watching Joan gracelessly ascend the rock on the skinniest, shortest legs I'd ever witnessed, notwithstanding the dwarf in New York. But once she arranged herself on the smooth summit, and the sinking sun dragged the usual diaphanous russets and yellows toward the violet sea, the light on her face and the face itself was so exquisite we all gaped.

She shook her black hair, her features cameoed in the orange sun, haloed by the ephemeral glow. Despite the heat of the day which hadn't yet waned, she appeared to be carved in ice. Perpetually and immortally the siren, her skin a sheath of ivory, it was she who seemed to illuminate the sun.

I felt fingers poking into my ribs. I struggled out of my trance. It was Stephen Boyd, sandy-haired Helios himself. "Excuse, please. You're in my way."

As cameras whirred, or whatever it is that cameras do, he strolled toward Joan Collins' rock. She leaned down. He scrambled part way up. They kissed and separated, then kissed and separated again. A love scene. Or at least what I like to call stage two love, where one becomes hesitant, wondering what the heck he is getting in to. Through Stephen Boyd's maneuvering, I'd got thrust back among the curious natives so I couldn't hear a word of dialogue. I began watching, through the waning light, glittering fleas bounce from shoulder to black shoulder, like exploding sparks from the dying sun, each tiny one of them.

* * *

Jessamine wanted to go to the Mourne Rouge that night, the shack of a bar on Grande Anse beach, where she'd heard James Mason intended to pass some time. She had a fascination for James Mason. His particular frame seized her with awesome fervor. Her usually velvety voice wobbled when she spoke his name.

But the instant she entered the taxi I'd employed for the occasion, I knew something was wrong. She slammed the door. Usually graceful and cuddly, she stuck her pert nose out the open window. "You're late," she announced tersely.

"A long day on the set," I tried excusing myself. Her nose seemed to poke out even further into the warm night, the smell of crushed nutmeg and ginger wafting between us as the car slowly eased past dark palms and the glow of kerosene lamps flickering from huts.

"Those are not our people," she said, obviously referring to the silhouettes crouched around tables inside the huts. I didn't know how to respond. Because, of course, those were her people, those who had given her life and raised her. I guessed what she meant: that by dating me, having married her prosperous Mr. Hempstead, and sashaying off to view her movie hero in person, she felt and properly so, that she'd slept her way out of one class and into another.

I glanced at her sideways and discovered she was staring at me, her white dress shimmering along her body. "You've got a hole in your shirt, Boob. A real tear."

"Sorry." I felt around the shoulder discovering where the hem had indeed separated. "So how was your day at the telegraph office?"

She shuddered.

"Is that how you found out James Mason was going to be at

the Rouge?"

"Besides, you don't look good in yellow." For some unaccountable reason she continued to vilify me via my shirt. Her nose stuck its way again out of the window. The breeze lifted her black hair around a gardenia she'd affixed near her ear. "I learn much from working at the telegraph office."

"I like the gardenia," I offered. My unconscious reveals itself quite willy-nilly, for I heard myself maliciously add, "The effect is for James Mason, no doubt."

A short, spurty giggle bubbled from Jessamine's lips. Her hand flew to her hair as though to protect the gardenia. The car tires ground through sand as we approached the Rouge. Torrents of steel band arpeggios assailed us while red lights rimmed the stars as we left the car to ascend the rickety wood steps, hand in hand, as would any apparently perfect couple doomed to destruct.

The band played even more ferociously than usual, the singers spitting their guts out, vibrant with charm, as the drummers throbbed and smacked their towering array of instruments. The raised stage for the band and bar hovered over the oblong dance floor that was surrounded by wood benches upon which Hollywood seemed to have arranged itself in a tense row, like gawking gulls on a wharf. James Mason, to whom I'd not spoken but instantly disliked because of Jessamine's infatuation, seemed to be more amused than his coworkers. You could tell he'd just discovered the delights of the island's rum punch and kept a glass pressed against his puffy chin. Joan Fontaine, who appeared older, more rigid and bloated than she might have wished, looked stunned, the noise having so afflicted her ears that she covered them with ringed fingers and winced.

Spotting James Mason, Jessamine squealed, "Oh my Gawd," grabbed at my shoulder further exasperating the rip in my shirt and began shaking like a divining rod over a hidden spring. "There...over there...."

I snatched her pointing finger from the air. "When under stress, act calm," I shouted over the music. Besides, other than the stars themselves, and a few islanders, the Rouge was nearly empty this early in the evening and Jessamine's eagerness struck me as unwarranted and embarrassing. James Mason looked old—he might have been in his mid forties—and smarmy, like he was trying to scrape dog shit off his shoes without anyone noticing.

I went to get our punches. Returning with the drinks, I observed to my horror that Jessamine was on the dance floor breaking into a shuffling, side-step of a dance, butt grinding, wagging her way into James Mason's proximity. Miffed, I seated myself, a drink in each hand, on the far side of the dance floor, next to, as it turned out, Joan Collins. I ground my teeth, sullenly taking in Jessamine's display of all the native wiles she'd distanced herself from not twenty minutes earlier. "Those are not our people, my ass," I grumbled.

"Thanks for the drink," Joan Collins said relieving me of Jessamine's punch while staring straight ahead, her profile frigid and exquisite. We hadn't met on the set and I didn't know what to say to yet another star. So I said that kind of wrong thing I've always been prone to, "I'm not a waiter, Miss Collins."

She turned her head slightly toward me while sipping Jessamine's punch, her eyes seeming to glaze over. "Now how was I supposed to know?" She pursed her red lips.

It was difficult for me to concentrate on who was going to become one of the world's more famous women while my island mistress gyrated her tush in James Mason's face. Jealousy, I've concluded, is essentially the prerogative of males, my genes chattering loudly about how I wasn't to let any scamp of a movie hero seed my chromosome pool, when Joan Collins proclaimed, "I was perfect on the set today. Just...perfect."

"You knew I was there?"

"I know where everyone is. Always. But how could I miss a face pink as yours in this charcoal pit of an island? In the film I'm supposed to have a Negro grandmother. Me? Me? Can you imagine.

That's why I'm afraid to marry Stephen Boyd. A tar drop for a child would dent his peerage. But I won't talk shop. I just won't. Yellow is not your color," she fixed me with her terrible blue eyes veiled in reams of intermeshing lashes. "And your shirt is torn. See, up by your shoulder." She sniffed in distaste.

"Little wonder you took me for a native waiter."

"What are you doing here? I'm in the films, of course."

"Writing a book."

"My sister writes books. And so shall I one day. What's yours about, the island?"

"No. Actually…" I was aware I was going to sound irrational, "my book is about a high school in the U.S. I'm not at all sure why I'm writing it on a tropical island."

Joan Collins yawned, her ivory chin tilted upwards, her nose that would launch a thousand TV episodes surrounded by her artfully bewildered hair. Then the music stopped. The patrons, who had by now swollen to a crowd, milled about boisterously. I stood. Where was Jessamine? Between the jostling shoulders, I saw that she had seated herself, her white dress a wilted flag of distress, between Joan Fontaine and the dreaded Mason. Even from across the dance floor her eyes glowed like black onyx. Her hair around the gardenia brushed along James Mason's jowl. Too much, too much. I gnashed my teeth.

I began elbowing my way through the crowd, nearly colliding with Harry Belafonte who danced by himself after the music had stopped. His feet sprang wildly about in all directions to rhythms of his own invention, when, just like that, the band started up again and everyone shouted, "Come, come calypso like me!"

And the jump-up commenced with asinine enthusiasm, everyone doing just that: jumping up and up. The two dull light bulbs dangling from the palm-roofed ceiling which were covered by cute wicker baskets—the work of the island's only incarcerated criminal and the only resident artist—jiggled with jovial abandon. From everywhere came the smell of sweat, and the fleas went bounce

bounce from shoulder to shoulder timing their leaps to the joyous drums.

I continued my lurch toward Jessamine just as she executed a stately whirl and a graceful return, tight into the arms of Mason. Though he seemed to have no idea how really to jump-up West Indian style, he clutched Jessamine closely, ballroom romantic, and so I screamed vengefully at them, "There's a lot of mesmerizing frames around here."

"What?" Jessamine pretended interest as she pirouetted under one of the star's armpits. Mason stared at me aghast. Jessamine waved me away with a distracted arm.

I searched about for Dorothy Dandridge who would of course, and with pleasure, dance with me. But she was nowhere. Nor was her Mrs. Lotti. Clearly, I was desperate.

Dancing with Mrs. Lotti, who must certainly be a transvestite, would cause an island sensation I could never live down. I spun about distractedly. Joan Collins was bending over Joan Fontaine not two feet from where I distractedly spun, empty punch glass clutched in my hand.

I tapped Joan Collins on her bare back—I sensed her skin crawl—and bellowed, "May I have this dance?"

To my surprise, she snugged into my arms murmuring, "To England. I want to go home. To England." Which I had guessed from her attitude and accent, but had no idea I was to become the burgeoning star's confidant. I thrust my punch glass at Joan Fontaine, who eyed it distastefully letting it slip through her fingers to crash on the floor, and Collins and I were off, I sweeping her arms this way and that, proper for a Grenadian jump-up. What James Mason had no idea how to do, I did. I just hoped that he and Jessamine would appreciate the performance I was about to give. I clutched Joan Collins in a rather harsh embrace in preparation. Not realizing how truly miniature she was, I experienced dismay by her voice intoning throatily from the vicinity of my navel where her lips seem to have gotten embedded in my yellow shirt, "I hate this damned hell hole."

Referring, I assumed, to the island, not my inny. Was Jessamine watching? Ah, she was. I sprang back from Joan Collins, my arms reaching, ecstatic as only youth can be, toward the light fixtures while grinning down at the diminutive future dominatrix of *Dynasty*, "Now leap like me!"

And up I rose, higher than any islander, floating around the dried palm fronds long enough to glimpse Jessamine, her mouth open, one hand aiming toward it as though to stifle a groan, her creaking consort grasping her protectively close. My arc exhausted, I plummeted downward like some Icarus reborn to the sound of beaten steel...onto Joan Collin's foot.

"You fucking goddamned fucker pimp," she gestured with the hand that wasn't wound around her foot, middle finger raised threateningly. She hobbled around the dance floor, the English primrose swearing like a stevedore. Mayhem ensued. Beware of tiny people. They're easily injured and congenitally angry. Both band and crowd fell silent. The ocean outside could be heard licking the sand. Joan Collins whimpered and by now managed to seek out Harry Belafonte, into whose arms she strategically collapsed. "Get that fucking fucker of a spastic jumping frog out... Out!"

"Yeah. Exit her pond," growled Harry unable so soon to grasp what might have occurred, yet his eyes rolled menacingly.

So this is what happens, I thought, when males act out how nature primed them to be. Jessamine came over to me. She squeezed both my hands in hers, glared straight up into my eyes. "Oh, my dear, dear Boob."

6

Sea-change

Jessamine and I walked down the back steps of the Mourne Rouge and out onto the wharf, her high heels clomp-clomping on the rotten wood, bare arms folded over her chest. Neither of us had spoken since leaving the dance. The silence between us became a weight. Even the sea moved sluggishly, like coffee being stirred by an invalid: dark, warm, and fretful as that.

I felt relief at the renewal of the bar's steel band music, whose sharp yet somehow mellow pings flew up into the icy spray of multifarious stars. When we reached the end of the wharf, we turned to face the music and a dirty hubcap of a moon rolling through cloud wisps behind black palms.

"Is Mason a nice guy?" I finally asked, the friendly tone of my voice meant to assure Jessamine that her bout with the Hollywood frame was understandable, if not thoroughly forgivable.

"Oh, he's wonderful," she assured me.

I tried to let that ride. After all, the extent of my own hypocrisy, particularly regarding our relationship, went beyond comprehension. She was for me a dalliance, an amusement and, yes, a receptacle. She had no idea who I was. And I couldn't tell her. She would have no way of comprehending.

Unlike my own country where derogatory words regarding my sexual predilection came constantly from newspapers, papal missives, presidents, ministers, parents, neighbors and friends, my months on the island had produced no reference to that sexual possibility, positively or negatively. What an American child would habitually scream at you was, to Grenadians, apparently an unknown. And how can you be what there is no word for? How can you explain to your mistress, and under the mysterious auspices of voodoo your wife, that what she sees and feels is not what she's actually getting?

"So how was that tomato," Jessamine loved all images peculiarly American, "that Joan something-or-other?"

I tried to laugh. "She'll never be the same."

"A Grenadian knows where to land," she said.

"I'm sorry about everything. Let's walk the beach."

Stowing our shoes among the washed up coconut shells under the wharf, we began our stroll. At night the tropics seethe into the unconscious and percolate. Unlike the day, the night warmth soothes rather than intimidates. The stars, free of smog, gush like frozen fireworks across the sky. And everywhere there are fireflies, winking high up in the palms, down through the acacias, glittering over seashells in the sand. And to wade through the warm water whose sluggish waves barely hissed across the sand is to splash through phosphorescent plankton and become enraptured in wet fire. This was not the world of now, but the world of then—back when we swung arboreally, blessed and blessing all unaware.

Jessamine's words startled me from my reverie. "Yes. I learn much from working at the telegraph office." With her toe she kicked a little fireball of froth onto the beach.

"Meaning?"

She hitched her dress into the elastic of her panties and waded deeper into the water. We were far from the Rouge whose music floated a bare scrim of sound across the distance. "Meaning quite a bit," she addressed the dark horizon.

It was about this far down the beach that we frequently had committed our most successful intercourse. I took off my pants and jockeys with every intention of repeating the exercise. When you're on a roll, roll on.

I followed Jessamine into the sea, naked and joyous, whooshing handfuls of glowing water toward the sky as she turned to me, the whiteness of her dress shimmering around her shoulders, her face, in the moonlight, contorted when, like Niobe all tears, she flung at me, "Who is Margo Athens?"

At first I didn't know. Her accusatory tone made my mind go blank. The Christian name of the character that Dorothy Dandridge played in the movie came to mind, which seemed irrelevant. "Got me," I said, watching the water lick her hips.

She paced past me, heading toward the beach, pushing the water into shining whirls with her knees. "You're a very strange man."

"I've heard that before," trying to be funny.

"Then everyone seems to know except me?" Clearly, she thought her question rhetorical. It took me moments to recollect my equilibrium. I watched Jessamine arrange herself on the sand, dress splayed out around her like the petals of some enormous nocturnal flower. It all looked like paradise. But the ominous tone of her voice was beginning to make it feel like hell.

I jiggled my exposed privates back to the shore. I stood over her dripping, shiny, I hoped, from the moon glancing off my skin. Well, the stance had worked before.

"Better sit down," she commanded from between clenched teeth.

I adjusted myself uncomfortably in the clammy sand. Nakedness increased my sense of vulnerability because by then I had recalled that Margo Athens was the Chicago prostitute who was going to visit me in what Margo assumed to be my island seclusion.

"A tel—a telegram?" I stuttered out suddenly comprehending the portentous underpinnings that had threatened the entire evening. I tucked my yellow shirt around my groin, which made me feel even sillier. "Oh, she's just a friend, an acquaintance actually, who said she just might drop by the island for a few days. She's just a friend of friends. Studying to be a nun," I unaccountably decided to add. I glanced at Jessamine with a lopsided grin. I already knew that one of Margo's clients was an archbishop so my lie was not entire, were one merely to construe the work place for the work.

And yet Jessamine could have no way of divining Margo's profession from a telegram. But my mother had surmised by merely gleaning the information through the blank spaces in my misspelled letters.

I heard Jessamine rambling on: "Because I know better than anyone when telegrams are delivered, expect to receive, between the hours of twelve and five tomorrow, a cable from the States. Wherever you will be. The telegraph office will find you out." She smacked her lips in satisfaction, as though a fencing match had taken place and her sword had pierced my liver.

Yet how could I realize that Margo, whom I barely knew, would actually arrive on this tiny hunk of land off the shores of British Guinea? Or that Jessamine, spurred by Margo's imminent intrusion upon our world, would feel forced to reveal what she'd apparently intended to keep wholly secret?

Jessamine leaned toward me from out of her petals, a pistil struggling through stamens, her black eyes big as a starving child's: "I'm pregnant."

The horizon line looked inky. At this inevitable juncture with the women I've known and, yes, sort of loved, my response has never been what they hoped for, nor what I might have hoped for. I became paralyzed, as though all the darkness of all the world's nights were inhaled into my lungs and festered there. I had obeyed the world's dictates, denied my own being, and by so doing must pay. As would they.

"Of course, I'll take care of it," Jessamine was saying. "I know now my dreams with you will come only to dust."

"Take care of it?" I wondered, whispering. I imagined a stalwart youth with my perfect nose but with olive skin, painting, writing beneath a spreading nutmeg. Not like Gauguin's idiot half-caste son. Nor a girl whirling in a pinafore, pining for a guy like me she'd never get. But a clone. A cute, hairy one whose eyes have the glint of pomegranate seeds.

"I'll kill it." Jessamine's words blasted my fantasy.

"Just like that?"

She patted her skirt close around her thighs. The tide was coming in, its little eddies sucking between her painted toenails. "What would you have me do?"

I was supposed to say, 'Marry me in a Christian ceremony and return with me to Chicago.' What I was supposed to say hovered an invisible dirigible over my head. 'Be decent, be decent,' the waves hissed along the sand where long pincered crabs burrowed in the ooze. My mother's voice hurled straight down from the dirty, pitted, hubcap of a moon: 'You did it, now pay with your life. Your life is owed to others. Did you think it was yours to live?' It was the same curt voice she had used after discovering me masturbating when a child, warning that a sign would be hung on my back because I was a monster, except that everyone knew anyway by just looking into my eyes.

I stared at the sand between my legs, speechless. I couldn't even take Jessamine to a restaurant in the United States without being kicked out for dining with a Negro. And I didn't have enough money to take her to a restaurant even were it to accept us. And where could we live? Not only did I know full well that I was queer, but I could only financially afford to be queer. On the island, I had merely performed as would a long-imprisoned straight male, except with more dire consequences.

Did I fit the profile of a murderer? I cannot believe that flushing a child down the toilet is not infanticide, or so I'd thought when Lara in Chicago conceived by me. But then I have never understood of what murder consists—swatting a fly, nibbling a carrot, the pig grease I consumed for breakfast, the cow for dinner? When does murder stop and survival begin? And yet Jessamine's threat reminded me of how we take ourselves everywhere with us, conniving to act similarly and for the same reasons. Life is a series of circles—the only relief is when we've forgotten what we've done, before entering the next identical circle. In my case that's due to my pervasive dread of rejection, which is so strong that I'm perpetually catapulted into betraying myself and so those closest to me in my thankless endeavor to 'fit,' to 'please,' to be 'accepted.'

Being called 'fag,' 'pansy,' 'sissy' throughout my life by most persons of consequence took its toll. My father referred to homosexuals as a particularly low form of planetary life. 'Like apes,' he had slapped hirsute fists on the table. 'Or sailors,' he added strangely, concluding that were I to grow up slimy as that he'd kill me. My parents slept in separate beds and never touched. Sex, as I understood it in my adolescence, occurred only between a man and a woman who apparently seldom did it, so I had smiled blissfully during my father's interrogation assuring him I had no intentions of becoming a sailor.

To Jesssamine's query as to what would I have her do, I finally responded, "Whatever pleases you. If having an abortion is what you want, I'll cut sugar cane to pay for it."

To which she snickered, "You? With the back country people? Bundles of cane over your shoulders? Ridiculous, mun." She touched her lips with her index finger. "Be quiet. Someone's coming down the beach. Look, there's two of them."

I snugged my shirt tighter around my organs. It wasn't entirely wrong to be naked on a beach at night, it's just that it wasn't really acceptable. So engrossed was the hand-holding couple in whatever it was they imparted to each other that they passed in front of us without noting our presence. It was Harry Belafonte and Joan Fontaine, her beehive, ash blonde hair plunging through the fireflies like a schooner in full sail. In the film they were lovers, but Harry rejects her because she's white. In whatever may pass for real life, it appeared that Belafonte was the aggressor, occasionally nuzzling her neck the up-swept hair exposed, Fontaine's response being a shrieking, defensive giggle.

They hadn't walked far beyond us when Jessamine, noticeably quivering, billowed up into the dark, her dress cascading sand, her lower lip pulling away from her teeth in a stricture of awe. "Oh, my Gawd!" rumbled up from deep in her throat. Then, "Golly, by golly, gee…." For minutes the iconic passage of the stars obsessed her, robbing her of breath, dignity and selfhood.

Which, under the circumstance, proved fortuitous. We got some relief from facing ourselves. I chatted nervously, "That's the kind of phenomenon democracies bring into being. When the ordinary rule, the extraordinary ideal has to emerge from somewhere." Jessamine paid me not the slightest attention, so I went on: "To thrust one's self onto seemingly superior others is to be momentarily free of our own inconsequence. That's what love is, too. A giving of yourself away because you don't like who you are."

"Love?" Slowly she turned toward me, her lips now pursed and shaking. "You are going to dare tell me what love is?"

I understood that she must think me awful. I, too, had been taught, especially from the movies, that love is what made the world go round, despite all evidence to the contrary. I wanted to shout at her that convenience is what makes the world go round and that she was proving herself to be inconvenient. Instead, I merely inquired, "Do you really love—whatever that means—me?"

She bent over to yank a conch shell from the sand, pressed it against her ear. "I hear the shell murmuring," she said.

"Does it speak to you?"

"It speaks to me." By the way her eyes squeezed shut I guessed I didn't want to know, but she told me anyway: "I hear it whisper that it's you who has no love for me nor anything."

I assumed she was in the process of dismissing me from her life…over Margo who was barely an acquaintance? Or because she had neglected sexual precautions (none of which existed on the island anyway, to my knowledge) so that, consciously or unconsciously, she would conceive by a white man and her way off the island might become a possibility? Or had she sensed, and bitterly, that for me she was but a lark: a marvelous conduit to the exotic wonders of an island my very soul embraced and that she couldn't wait to get out of.

"That's what my mother always said, that I felt no love."

"What?" She stared down at me incredulously.

"That I have no love for her nor, for that matter, anyone or anything else."

"Mothers know," she said. "Everything." Suddenly she collapsed onto her knees and then rolled on her side, forehead pushed against my thigh. "I'm afraid." Her hands clawed toward my face. I pulled her against me, nestling her glossy, tickling hair under my chin. "I'm afraid of…all of it," she mumbled.

"The abortion?" I hated the word, much less my easy acquiescence to yet another sacrifice of one of my own children. "Where will you go? Trinidad?" I hoped she wouldn't have need to encounter that scary doctor who had administered the penicillin for my clap, whose office smelled of formaldehyde—not disinfectant but formaldehyde.

But then, I reasoned irrationally yet with all the hope I dared muster, voodoo must have a solution, some herb, a lizard's tongue soufflé, a tincture of jellyfish slime. Something! I was realizing that all this could well mean Jessamine's death, as it might have meant Lara's. We were all caught in compulsions. Not only our own but by the conveyors of Christian malignity who would insist that Jessamine's life in St. George's will be intolerable if she didn't appear innocent or commit herself to a marriage with me that the known world would condemn as racial heresy were it sanctified. All this because she'd not only aspired to, but actually entered, the social class she had decided on for herself.

In the back country, I was to discover, in the forests and smallest villages, all a woman had to say was that a spirit had voodooed her, preferably under a bo tree by moonlight, and no more questions were asked. I was never certain whether sex and childbearing were viewed by the natives as being in the least connected. Sex was entertainment and children were raised by the village, so all could proceed much as nature had intended. Which explained why Jessamine never referred to her parents. She seemed to have a very distant sense of either one. But now she was propertied and longed to further enrich her investment in the middle class whose values experience had taught me to detest.

"Shall we go back?" I tried to sound compassionate, the truth being I was exhausted. Besides, I thought it best we retrace our tracks before the movie stars retraced theirs. I definitely did not want to be recognized by Belafonte, the dangerous roll of his eyes still sharp in my memory. Any chance of a re-meeting with Joan Collins too awful to contemplate.

Jessamine strode ahead of me, headstrong and angry. I admired her for that. Sand flew in all directions, her tiny body thrust forward as though combating a ferocious wind.

*   *   *

Dawn broke around Daisy Renick's Green Gables with steel bands rippling streams of music down every street. I had forgotten that today, at the movie director's contrivance, the entire island would convulse itself into a mock carnival. Heavy drum thuds resounded even from under the Gable's porch. Groggy from last night's misery, I peeked over the railing to see Ralph and his cohorts wildly flailing at goatskin percussions of all sizes in preparation for being immortalized in celluloid. The instant I realized the stakes, I apologized by applauding the potential revelers below. What the islanders truly cared about was fun. And fun was whatever relieved the monotonous, hum-drum pleasantness of their paradise.

Mrs. Lotti, wig askew, in a bathrobe of oriental design, flung an arm flap of embroidered bamboo over the balustrade. "Just stop it," she whirled the bamboo sleeve over the drummers who, unable to hear her, assumed she cheered them on and so walloped their instruments with increasing vigor.

"Hey there, mun," they called upward, "we's practicin' for carnival." Bang, wallop, bang.

Mr. Edmonds joined us garbed in green silk pajamas stained at the crotch.

"We're in for it," I commented companionably.

"We're in for it," he sighed. "Out of sync, out of season. The movies have wrought havoc upon this land."

Daisy, fully dressed in a black knapsack of a skirt and blouse,

shouted, quite beside herself, "We'll have tea. That's what we'll do."
So we did, though the towel I'd wrapped around my waist
proved to be an uncertain drape as I endeavored to defend my
modesty while slumped casually on the balustrade, teacup in hand.
Mrs. Lotti said, "Los Angeles is a human place to be," sucking
the tea up through her puckered lips, "not like this barbarous
outback." She flipped shut the wings of her kimono so we couldn't
see what she did or didn't have underneath. Mornings invariably
drove her voice deeper.

"But it's Los Angeles that's inspired all of this buffoonery," Mr.
Edmonds grinned.

"Nevertheless," Mrs. Lotti assured us, "there are on this globe
better places."

"Than paradise?" I wanted to know.

"Paradise," Mrs. Lotti stated, full throated and finally
thoroughly at her ease, "is a matter of definition. *N'est-ce pas?*" And
she predictably curled and quivered her pinkie over her cup.

Mrs. Lotti, I thought, is how all gay guys are perceived to be
by average persons: drag queens framed in kimonos chortling
dastardly critiques with quivering pinkies.

That afternoon, when the carnival was in full swing, I managed
to fit into my own frame of significance—all by accident and
through no particular talent, which is how I suspect most frames
get affixed. I had scrambled up onto a wooden podium erected for
the occasion that oversaw the cacophonous parade below. My intent
was to demand payment from Darryl Zanuck for my labors with
Dandridge and my stand-in duties. I hesitated, wondering how
to approach the seated mogul whose lips appeared to have got
permanently sucked into an orange bull horn, when a tiny black
lady clad in a khaki uniform spat up into my face, "Is youse Robert
Burdette Sweet of the Gable's Green?"

"The Green Gables?" is all I could think of saying, the sweeping
crowd of dancing, drumming, thrumming, shouting paraders
blocking all egress to auditory awareness. She stuffed a telegram

into my hand. I opened it there, with Grenada itself as my witness, and read, "Will arrive. Grenada. Four-fifteen. Wednesday next. Love. Margo Athens." So many of the island citizens observed my receipt of the telegram on the haphazard stage that I was mistaken for months thereafter for, as they phrased it, 'a moving star.'

Well, this 'star' moved all right. I jumped off the platform into the parade, became instantly shaken to the core by the calypso that pulsed my heart and flooded arteries. I dimly recalled what I'd originally been about—Zanuck could write me a check later—and I hurled myself along with hundreds of others into exuberant leaps, wild gyrations and general misapplications of various body parts. My feet barely touched the cobblestone street, my arms reached for the clouds that lowered darkly foreboding rain. Was this escape? Had I escaped into the rhythmic frenzy of an obsessed crowd? So be it. I began leaping, hysterically, higher than in my escapade with Joan Collins. Over and over, up and up.

And should you ever see *Island in the Sun,* there I am, a blurred spasm of Caucasian desperation, careening from stage left to right, higher than any native, darting, actually, like a jism-squirt across the screen, my framed second of glorious denial.

7

Cursed

A day after the faux carnival, Hollywood departed secretly, under the cover of darkness. Mrs. Lotti evaporated, owing, Daisy claimed, the price of numerous rum punches. Zanuck never paid me the twenty-five dollars I had been promised. Nothing was left of 20th Century Fox but the wooden platform in the middle of town and the hut where Dorothy Dandridge had munched the grapes. Though still stricken with star fever, the island soon relapsed back into its usual torpor.

I had neither seen nor heard from Jessamine since our confrontation on the beach. Not knowing what to say to Jessamine, I put off contacting her. Only a few days had passed, but it was already time to meet Margo's plane.

I rode Ralph's bike toward the airport, which was inland between two mountains. Struggling up the pitted road fringed with tree ferns, I wheeled off onto a dirt path that the heat made me fantasize as a short cut. Traveling across a ridge, a rock wall on my left, a craggy incline on my right, my shoulder brushed against what I took to be a small green boa constrictor nestled in a sugar apple tree. The snake lay furled, like an intestine, its gold eyes flaring. Margo will really love it here, I thought.

My brush with the boa did help me decide I was pedaling in the wrong direction, so I hopped off the bike, turned it around on the narrow trail, and proceeded to retrace my tracks. But a small animal blocked my progress. The size of a large cat, it refused to let me by, its eyes seething, head lowered, saliva dangling from its jaws. I assumed it was a mongoose and a rabid one at that. Mongooses were beginning to take over the island. Originally imported to eat the rats, they now dined on anything available, even sugarcane. I didn't know if they could be rabid but realized the creature's misery might well become mine were I not very patient. Its head swung slowly back and forth, breathing heavily, eyes sniping at me. I got off the bike, leaned it against the rocky wall, and swayed there, breathing heavily myself. And sweating. How was I going to credibly explain to Margo that the reason I hadn't met her plane was because I'd been waylaid by a rabid mongoose?

But then I reasoned, a mongoose was nothing compared to the fer-de-lance snakes, poisonous as anything living, that had been imported into the neighboring island of St. Lucia to convince the slaves not to escape. At least that was the islander's explanation for their lethal presence. How clever of me, Margo, to pick Grenada over St. Lucia where the snakes still slithered long after their existence had no human purpose.

I often despair of being on forested trails by myself because of the infernal babbling my mind insists upon. "Hey there, mongy babe," I cooingly addressed the animal, "you go your way so I can go mine. OK?" After a pathetic, weak lunge at me, the mongoose finally struggled off the path. But I still saw its quivering tail trembling between boulders. I got on the bike and furiously pedaled past the shaking animal back to the road. "Airport or bust," I muttered scraping the fern leaves in my effort to avoid the occasional taxi presumably heading to intercept the same flight.

My plan had been to rent a taxi after greeting Margo, shove the bike in the trunk, and thus save some money. By the time I turned into the airport a light rain had begun. I stood by the bike under a banana tree hoping for the rain to stop.

The original Grenadian airport, before the huge Cuban project that would eventually pressure President Reagan to attack, had one short runway between mountains so steep that were one perchance to land safely one would hesitate to dare press one's luck by attempting to depart. I sat cross-legged under dripping banana leaves observing the one small outbuilding topped by a limp and soggy weather sock. Though not accompanied by wind, the rain beat harshly against the palms—and then stopped suddenly as it had begun. A streak of sun flashed through the clouds and white butterflies resumed their dashing sprints from orange to yellow to red lantana bushes.

I watched as several people strolled from the building, suitcases in hand, toward the runway. One was a woman whose walk seemed familiar but whose wide straw hat obscured her face. Then she turned in my direction, yet she couldn't have seen me hidden as I was by a drape of banana leaves. The sun glanced for a moment across the mocha face. It was Jessamine.

I was about to run toward her, when I stopped cold. I felt as though all breath had been knocked out of me. Why was she here? Why now? Then I understood: of course, her intent was dramatically to board the plane Margo would debark from and thus proceed to Trinidad, I guessed to dispose of the child we'd agreed to abort.

I cowered under the trees staring at her. She looked to her right and then her left, fingers curled about the arm of her maid, Lemba. Pulling on the arm actually, until Lemba responded to her entreaty by helping her search for whomever it was Jessamine seemed to insist they discover. Both women, one in the wide-brimmed hat of straw and the other in a blue bandanna, cast their eyes about and then turned their backs to me. I breathed again, yet began to accept that the person they wanted was me. Preferably, I assumed, before the plane bearing Margo arrived, when I could be approached unencumbered. Just the three of us while Lemba—or so my guilt caused me to imagine—made a dive at my hair, armed with clippers to help herself to some curly strands she might concoct into a voodoo soup. Were the soup consumed by her, she might assume power over my undoing beyond even what Jessamine may have wished.

The better I'd gotten to know Jessamine, the more I realized that Lemba was more than a hireling, she was the matriarch of the household. Black and wizened as a raisin, she nevertheless seemed ageless. Her tendency was to scurry rather than walk, her mottled, plumpish arms beating the air like the gills of a fish deprived of water. Whether fluffing a bed or sweeping the porch, all activities were accomplished with skill and vigor, no matter how hot the day or sultry the evening. Her deeply-socketed dark eyes with their yellowing whites always sparked with wary glances. She knew everything, attempted to control everything, and had from the very start viewed me with such suspicion that I learned to feel unnerved by her very presence. Lemba was Jessamine's jungle past which I came to understand she could no more dispense with than could I the omnipresence of my puritanical mother, whose witchiness and all-knowing rivaled Lemba's. Jessamine and I had never individually been left to encounter one another. We were accompanied always by our shadows.

And with the arrival of Margo imminent, I could not emotionally afford to counter Lemba, or for that matter, Jessamine in any way. I remained under my banana clump, so motionless that flies sucked on my sweat.

But not for long. Accompanied by the full glow of the evening sun, Margo's plane appeared over the mountains and banked to make a landing. I wondered if I would recognize her, my whore-friend from Chicago I'd only met once at my best friend's wedding. Jessamine and Lemba backed away from the blasts of air the small plane stirred about itself. Like Adam, I emerged from leaves, wondrous as to what fresh female encroachment would further galvanize my fate.

Jessamine spotted me instantly. Her arm went up as though to wave but fell back to clutch her thigh as though vaguely confused, vaguely terrified.

A small ramp was being pushed toward the plane whose propellers continued to whirl. Jessamine, Lemba, and I along with several other travelers circled about the ramp, our hair blowing, Jessamine's hand crushing her hat tight to her head. When the plane's door opened the propeller noise continued to be terrific. A black man and two black women, all unaccountably carrying cages of chickens, minced their way down the unsteady ramp. Then Margo appeared, radiant, even splendiferous.

She paused uncertainly the moment her feet touched the ramp. Whether she paused for dramatic effect or because she did indeed feel uncertain—as well she may have—I could not ascertain. Whatever, the sight of her with head tilted slightly back to permit her waist-length auburn hair to drift like seaweed around the mermaid sveltness of her body, sheathed as it was in a black knit dress, presented an image of mythical proportions. Was this Diana, Athena, Aphrodite herself? Total artifice, Margo pivoted gently and slowly, oh so slowly, and began her descent, hips revolving, hair dappled by the sun, eyes squinting in a terrible effort to seek me out. She was, I discovered, quite near-sighted.

In short pants and T-shirt, I wheeled the bicycle to face the ramp. Eager flies still stuck to my sticky face as I shouted up trying to smile, "Welcome to paradise."

I noticed Margo's lips moving, trying to say, "What?"

And so I shouted again, "I'm here. Over here."

"Oh, Robert," her face with its high cheekbones and glossy lips broke into a strained yet tinkling laugh. "Where am I? The other passengers with their chickens quite did me in." And she fell into my arms weeping and laughing simultaneously. I didn't know what to say, so I just held her, watching my flies tumble through the vastness of her streaming hair.

Finally she bent her head back and stared at me critically. "Oh my," she coughed delicately.

"I was in a tux when last you saw me. Remember?"

"I do. Indeed I do."

Passengers who sought to board now crowded about us aiming their suitcases at the ramp. The propellers whirred even louder preparing once again to heave the plane over the glowing mountains. Margo, still in my embrace, shook her hair, and behind her and through the auburn cascade, I saw Lemba's stern face peering at me. All I could make out were her eyes, glaring and seething as had the stricken mongoose's. Why didn't Lemba board the plane or wish her mistress farewell and head back toward town? What could she be doing standing directly behind Margo? Had she decided to clip Margo's hair instead of mine?

"Follow me," I barked at Margo. I led her toward my banana grove. I noticed that her black pumps slogged deeply into the brown mud. No Chicago nightclub, her usual habitat, could prepare her for the steamy confines of the muck and the canopy of shiny leaves.

"Where are we?" her voice quavered as from a disastrous dream. Margo was tall, her six feet matching my height now that her heels were mired in the ooze.

"Turn around." And as she did the very female heft of her posterior shifted in what she must assume to be a seductive grind while I searched the turbulent wonders of her hair for the missing strands.

"What are you doing?"

"Admiring your hair." That she could well understand. And would expect my admiration, and so submitted dumbly to my investigation, assuming that her luxuriant veils of auburn already intrigued my male desire for any physical difference there may be between us. She even slightly sighed and quivered as my fingers wandered, stroking her gleaming tresses. Unfortunately, I discovered what I dreaded: an inch wide and two inch long cut, not on the surface but underneath, devised so that the victim may never notice. I decided on the spot not to mention the voodoo incursion I now knew Lemba had managed. I nervously readjusted Margo's hair about her shoulders.

What originally alerted me to the possibility of hair theft I can only assign to an occasional rather otherworldly prescience that had marked my youthful existence. As any run-of-the-mill paranoid schizophrenic, I have heard voices. And, yes, they've always presented themselves totally disembodied from some vibrant ether above and beyond my right ear. Am I proud to share the symptoms of someone certifiable? No more proud or alarmed of that than I am of my murky brown eyes. And no more proud than I am to be mentally and emotionally androgynous, the leitmotif that drives the ironies of this, my autobiography encapsulated in one island year.

It is true that I've never felt my unusual traits to be particularly disturbing—my voices, for instance, more interesting or instructive than demanding or demeaning. Perhaps that's why, though now noticeably stoop shouldered, I strut through my sixties with enthusiasm and not a thorazine shuffle. Even modern psychiatry might find it unnecessary to medicate visions and voices as entertaining as mine.

My first auditory revelation posed as an angel who forgave me for what I'd just done, which was to let an acquaintance pull my pants down in a field causing me to come when he scraped his belt across my erection. We were both twelve. I had already learned to assume that guilt was directly proportional to the degree of pleasure experienced. So right off, before the semen had even dried, divine intervention attempted to annul my terror. The angelic voice, I must add, was rich, deep and reassuring.

The second pronouncement, during the summer of my sixteenth year when I was working as a riveter in an icebox factory, came direct from God Himself, or whoever it may be intoning from between parting clouds over the factory steps during my peanut butter and jelly lunch, insisting that I become a writer. Which might not have been bad advice, since riveting seemed not promising as a career. Except that the voice failed to warn of the future conglomeration of publishers and bookstores, the plethora of words made meaningless by the ease of Xerox machines and word processors, and the rapid growth of the moneyed unenlightened whose eyes paid more to be glued to movies and TV screens than to books, whose very pages depend upon the deforestation of an already devastated planet and whose shaky existence would be extended only by the elimination of compound, complex sentences such as this one. Yet know that for me the voice was declarative and powerful. And, yes, from somewhere in the sky above my right ear.

So, unlike Joan—not Crawford, nor Fontaine, nor Collins, but the saint—my voices were infrequent, yet before my arrival on the island they had already proved to be a facet of my personality. Therefore, when I envisioned Lemba cropping my own hair for the purpose of voodoo vengeance, I took the image seriously even though I had little knowledge of the machinations of voodoo itself. I had not, however, guessed that Margo's relative innocence might better serve Lemba's purpose, until I had observed Lemba standing close and directly behind Margo.

Though my voices, my visions, are only accurate up to a point, they contain more substance than even I wish to admit. Because within five years of her hair being snipped by Lemba, Margo will die from unusual and especially horrific circumstances—the disease which will precipitate her suicide being so lingering and finally corrupting that its inception might well coincide with our first embrace at the old Grenadian airport.

As I struggle to recall precisely as possible what did happen so long ago, I cannot remember whether Lemba got on the plane then bound for Trinidad or whether she merely entered the taxi Jessamine must have hired and traveled back to Jessamine's house which Lemba pretended to preside over in the guise of a servant. I am certain that I never mentioned any of this to Margo, thinking at the time that I had no right to foist on anyone the possibility of their being under the influence of a voodoo spell. Also, as I understood it, a curse only had power to work if the victim knew of, and believed in, the curse. Or so I thought then.

The propellers of the Cessna still roared. Attendants in short pants and nothing else positioned themselves to wheel away the ramp upon which Jessamine stood, her hand still cupping her wide-brimmed hat to her head, the plane's doorway yawning black behind her. I can still see the frozen, expressionless look on Jessamine's face as Margo and I walked with the bike between us from the banana grove to the airport's one small building where Margo hoped to retrieve her suitcase, the cosmetic paraphernalia alone I supposed she could not be without. Jessamine's dress was blue, loose and plain, her feet tucked in black sandals. What appeared to be a tiny gold locket glimmered from the velvet of her neck. Her feet were wide apart as she braced herself from the shake of the plane. Her left hand, the long fingers equally spaced, appeared to be clutching her stomach. A last strike of the sun glowed in her piercing eyes as they followed my slow progress with Margo across the field.

I turned, continued walking, feeling her stare burn my back. It was Jessamine who obsessed my day, not Margo. Her eyes, even from that distance, probed whatever essence of my being I still presumed to be intact.

I stopped, leaned the bike against my thigh, looked toward her and waved, both hands high above my head, wildly, like the semaphore signal for help, had I any idea what the semaphore signal for help might be. I only knew that I wanted to gesture like that to the familiar Jessamine and to the moribund embryo, fetus—I'd never asked how many months—whose execution Jessamine's entrance into the dark of the plane would finalize.

"Who is that…that woman?" Margo peered near-sightedly, her alabaster hand with its tapered false nails shading her eyes.

"Oh, just an island friend," I said. "An acquaintance, really."

"On a trip to Trinidad, is she?"

I watched Jessamine duck backward into the bowel of the plane as the pilot reached around her to pull shut the door.

"To shop," I said. "Upper-class natives shop there," I tried to explain. "They shop in Trinidad."

"And do you then offer them all such an enthusiastic bon voyage?"

"It's conventional," I invented, both hands now back to steadying the bicycle, "like in Hawaii. Or Italy where good-byes are important."

"You left out Japan."

"What?"

"Sayonara and all that. Does she have a name?"

The plane turned and snorted while rocking, as though to gather courage before it rumbled through the grass down the runway.

"I…I think her name is…Lemba," I lied complacently, churching fingers under my chin.

Margo said, "I think I'm going to cry."

I said, "But you're in paradise," hugging Margo close as I could across Ralph's bicycle seat.

"There the plane goes," remarked Margo as the Cessna raced toward its ascent over the mountains.

"How wonderful you're here," I resumed my usual sincerity while the plane breached the roiling, sunset clouds. "Island life can be so isolating."

8

Weeping Bullets

The evening of the fourth day of Margo's visit to Grenada, we sat at a round table on the verandah of the Santa Maria Hotel where I'd reserved a room for her. Due to the departure of the movie people, she was the large hotel's sole occupant. The night before she'd shouted, echoing down a long corridor, 'Bring out your dead', as though a plague had stolen away all the guests. After the hubbub caused by the stars, I found the silence a relief. She did not.

That the waiter, bartender and manager all assumed she was yet another movie star made the situation even less tolerable for her. As Margo liked to inform me, 'armies of men' were after her. On the island we'd all become lackadaisical regarding extraordinary beauty, and this diminished, though it did not extinguish, the impact she was used to creating. The waiter still trembled and shifted his feet nervously as he approached our table, just as Margo would have expected. And the bartender had spilled two of her punches before managing successfully to angle a third between the cleavage she rested on the counter. The manager had already asked her out on a date as though my presence meant little or nothing at all, yet Margo still seemed to feel bereft of significance.

But then that was in part due to the cold sore pushing its way out on her lower lip. On her first day we'd spent the afternoon on a small beach near the hotel. The sun seared us with its usual vibrancy. She got thoroughly burnt and four days later began to develop the sore. Prone to sun blisters on the lip myself, I was sympathetic when every two seconds she dabbed more of the rubbing alcohol I'd given her in order to assuage the irritating sensation and to attempt drying the blister up.

"I've never had one before," she winced, pressing the soaked cotton to her lip. "Please, please go away," she addressed her imperfection, sipping at the same time through a straw on the last of her punch and painfully attempting a grimace.

"The pain will be gone in hours," I tried to reassure her, though I suspected the sore would last a week or more and would grow and crust and finally bleed. Margo and I were about to live through a disaster to be made horrendous due to her obsession with her beauty which, during the remainder of her stay, I imagined would be severely compromised.

"Let's have another drink before dinner," I suggested.

"Yes, let's." She arranged herself straight and bravely in her wicker chair. I had intended to show her much of the island, but scratched the plan when I understood how even the lushness of the foliage alarmed rather than intrigued her. The sea urchins, with their long black barbs, had prevented her even wading into the water. She felt best there in the Santa Maria, ensconced in wicker, a glass of iced tea, at least, in her hand, a burning cigarette in a long silver holder circling wisps above her head.

"I'll get the drinks." After I returned with them, we continued to sit quietly, she dabbing her lip while I listened to the crash of the sea, feeling the warm air as it gently stirred folds of the table cloth. I wanted to ask why she'd come to a tropical island she wouldn't like in order to visit someone she hardly knew, but I kept hesitating. There was something thick and heavy clouding the air between us.

We'd already had sex several times and sex can make the simplest of behaviors seem awkward. Besides, her preparations for an encounter were so extended and complex—involving diaphragm, douche bag, various jellies and creams crammed between her legs—that I nearly fell asleep on both occasions before any contact was made. She'd also thoughtfully brought rubbers for me which meant I'd feel next to nothing no matter what happened. Once positioned for action however, her professionalism came into mechanical yet enthusiastic play.

"Just lie there," she'd say.

"On my back?"

"And don't move."

She'd straddle me and insert into her rubbered self my rubbered self and begin to spin and slap her behind against my thighs. I'd just about get interested and she'd stop sliding down my shaft while pulling aside her awesome tumbles of hair to peer at me with eyes flashing from the light of the bedside lamp. "That's how the archbishop likes it," she'd grin.

"So that's how I'm supposed to?"

"Men," she flung back her neck so the hair whipped, whistling through the air, "are the most passive creatures on the planet."

"Except when they're not?"

"You mean when they're pretending to be how they're supposed to be?"

She had trained her vaginal muscles to tighten and revolve about relaxing prophylactic sheaths so that, despite our virtually motionless bodies and the amusing conversation, my interest got renewed. "So it's that knowledge about men that's made you successful?" I pushed up into the jelly, encountered I assume the diaphragm and strategically retreated.

She smiled in evident satisfaction, "I'm twenty-two and well-to-do."

"Cute rhyme. But is it true?"

"Oh yes. Stocks and bonds. An account executive, saddled with a wife and five kids, teaches me how to play the game. Every Friday night he advises me more."

"And pays you more?"

"And more and more," she gracefully twirled around so all I could see of her was her hair shining down her back. I had to raise my knees and consciously shove into her or I'd have lost my grip upon the conversation. Because I realized, this is how and when Margo really communicated.

She went on, "People are my education. Schools are for those who have no clue how to know the right people. And for those who can't read."

She tipped her head back toward me in a rare spasm of enjoyment, her hair flooding across my lips. I took the opportunity to search for signs of Lemba's voodoo curse upon her. Yes, there across my chest lay an area of her hair that had been raggedly incised. I pressed the palm of my hand against it. "And that explains your interest in the Russian novelists?" I referred to information regarding her reading habits I had gleaned from her letters. "But why, really, the Russians? There are so many books out there to read."

With that same graceful twirling motion which shocked my nerves down to my toes, she again faced me while easing herself slowly up and down my personality. "In a word," she said, "they're long."

At first blush I assumed she referred to me, but quickly I corrected with, "Russian novels you like because they're long?"

"Yes," she said simply. "A good book should never end. A bad one shouldn't have been started in the first place."

"And so what's a good book?" I inquired curiously, massaging her nipples that graced not particularly ample breasts. I suspected her bra to be heavily padded.

Margo lashed her hair with a quick turn of her neck. It went whoosh and then smacked her back. "A good book is about what's real. Unabashedly, unashamedly real. Well, have you had enough?" She disengaged herself from my appurtenance which appeared to my horror shrouded in wrinkled rubber, glistening from the jelly now foaming down her thigh.

"I've had enough if you have," I acknowledged politely.

"No. You're the important one," she said collapsing onto her back by my side.

"Look at me," I said leaning over her.

"Why?" with eyes closed.

"Because you always want me to be looking at you, that's why."

She rolled over onto her side facing the wall. "There's a

difference," she sighed. "Women attract, men are attracted."

"What if I'm not? I mean, just what if?" Silence. The silence lengthened. Shadows from a moth flickered across the wall.

Finally she yawned audibly, "Impossible." The moth thudded against the light. Just as it was supposed to.

Watching her now on the hotel verandah sipping her punch, dabbing the cotton against her lip, I stared at her in wonder. Her intent had been to be thoroughly in control. Of me, of herself, of everything. With me, the island and now the canker marring the beauty of her lower lip, she must be comprehending that she was in control of nothing. The metaphor of beauty she so carefully embodied had been cracked at its seams, though not through any conscious effort on my part. It's just that metaphors are strong, staunch and forever, but any human attempt to wear one of them as a second skin is a precarious fit at best.

"You are very beautiful," I said, not only to reassure her, but because it was true. Yet as I viewed her across the table from me in the fading evening light, I concluded that what she had actually accomplished was to harmonize her imperfections into an entirety that astounded. She announced to the world that the whole can indeed be greater than its parts. Her forehead was high and wide, eyes too close together—slightly pinched from near-sightedness but green as emerald—her nose long and almost bulbous at the end, her upper lip narrow while the lower awkwardly widened toward the middle. Her cheekbones however, were a wonder of sharpness and her chin just wide enough to soften the triangular face. Her hair freshly scalloped, waved and lifted toward a thick-braided crown whose auburn made it glow like embers.

"I try," was her truthful response to my comment on her beauty. Because, as anyone must know who claims to be a walking example of art, artifice redefines the natural incoherence of nature. The cosmetics with which she accentuated and diminished various features were pervasive yet subtly applied. The work that led up to the creation of herself seemed nearly undetectable. Which is what art is.

Her body under close scrutiny appeared almost bovine. But she moved her large bones with a slithery yet regal grace. Her impeccable posture made her appear imperious. Her background I discovered to be lower middle class—raised in a slum near the steel mills of Gary, Indiana by a divorced mother. I had to guess that even her poise was a recent invention. A brave front actually to the bleak environment that had spawned her.

The unfortunate effect of acquired characteristics is that they usually appear to the observer as unnatural as they are. Being with Margo was like attending an endless recital whose virtuosity never ceased.

When she desisted dabbing at her lip for a moment to comment, "I'm so happy to be here with you, Robert," I didn't know how to reply.

"Are you really?" I heard myself wondering.

"You doubt me?" as though I didn't dare.

"It's just that I'm curious, Margo, as to why…" I hesitated and then pounced, "Why you've come all this way. To such a strange place. I'm honored, of course."

From a silver case she plucked out a cigarette with just the tips of her long lacquered nails, tapped the end in the same methodical, unconscious way she had inserted her various jellies, and said, "To see you, you damned fool."

Though obvious, the admission nevertheless startled me. "But that doesn't explain much." I gulped my punch.

She jabbed the cigarette into the silver holder, pushed a box of matches in my direction, and leaned forward for me to ignite the cigarette…as though training me to serve a goddess. Or merely to remind me that this is how males were meant to serve their women.

We'd already had trouble with doors. I kept forgetting to open them for her. I never could get it straight how a woman is supposed to precede her male and yet when confronted by some obstacle, the male is expected to dart in front and remove the impediment without knocking the woman aside. Although, as we already knew from our movies of the '50s, no woman could run without holding onto a man's hand and he must always be slightly ahead, pulling at her frailty with his strength.

Margo had leaned across the table for some time before I understood that she was unable to light her cigarette when a man was present. I grabbed for the island matches which I knew full well had little or no incendiary ability and began scratching one after another ineffectually against the box.

"It shouldn't be happening like this," Margo languorously smiled despite the fever blister.

"It's the matches," I said. "'The match that ignites must needs be wasting,'" I quoted Melville, innocent at the time of the line's implications for our particular circumstance.

"Waste not," she said irritably, without her usual verbal freshness.

Finally I maneuvered one of the splinters to burst into a tiny explosion I then thrust under her missile. We both settled back, relieved that our mutual missions had been accomplished. Smoke lazed about her lambent crown. She flicked ashes into an abalone whose pearlescent shell had the misfortune in death to function as a tray.

"Robert, I hope you don't object. But I've come here to love you. All this way. To love. You."

I think very slowly when surprised. And I'm surprised often. "Love you too," I mumbled thickly, stalling for time.

"Naturally," she said agreeing to my insight with an exquisite toss of her head.

I listened to the waves hurling against rocks beyond the verandah. I glanced over her head into the mystery of the clouds scudding piles of soaring violet. I heard the ding of bells from rigging in the harbor. Was I to take seriously her dramatic announcement?

"I'm a bad catch," I managed to whisper. Little could she guess how bad.

"Not as I perceive it," she said.

"I'm a high school teacher with no predictable future," I tried excusing myself.

"You'll be a great writer," she said. "Some day you'll prove to be for me the perfect consort."

My ears pricked up. I'd pulled my chair closer to her without realizing it. My palm quite helplessly grazed her thigh. Her dress was Grecian in design, casually elegant and blue, which she knew to be my favorite color. In truth, since I share red-green color-blindness with a high percentage of the male population, blue is one of the few colors I can specifically identify. I'm a color-blind painter and a writer who can't spell.

"What causes you to think I'll be a great writer?" I was painfully aware of my lower lip hanging down in awe at her perception. That she'd read no literary effort of mine seemed to make no difference.

"I've read your letters," she nodded reassuringly. "Brilliant in concept and execution." Margo blew a ball of smoke into my face. I breathed in the gray furls like the incense inspiring the Delphic Sibyl.

"I just typed the letters out hurriedly." I hung my head shyly.

"And with a little help from a dictionary they will be priceless." She rested her cigarette on the abalone shell and clapped her hands at her witticism. In those mid-century days, many of us wrote letters for a posterity we believed would care. Our correspondence was a lengthy, confessive attempt to comprehend ourselves. Staring at her across the table, it crossed my mind that personalized compliments were how Margo maintained the archbishop as a paying client—by fawning over his ability to pray mightily and thus predicting his ascent to heaven, for instance. Or the businessman with his stocks, his shrewd selection of which she must assure him would only make him richer. The mind boggles. But I only suspected what I know now for certain, that the enthusiasm of others regarding our future serves them more than it does ourselves.

How salient were Margo's hopes for me. How enslaving.

Margo's hand fumbled with her cigarette case.

"May I light your next cigarette?" I eagerly held out my match box while thinking: show me the doors I may open for you, the coats I may hold for you, the chairs I might pull out for you. Just keep reminding me that I can be who I want to be. That it's all worth while.

"I'll have another drink." Margo inspected her empty glass. Clearly, she could not fetch her own and so I leapt to get her another punch.

The bartender, listening to calypso on the radio and half asleep, mentioned, "You sure, sir, you wants more?" arousing himself to observe me carefully.

"Make it two." I tossed him some crumpled BWI dollars.

Shuffling back with a drink in each hand, I reminded myself that we should eat soon. My wicker chair had difficulty shifting itself properly to accommodate my behind. "I'm gay," I blurted. One foot got unaccountably tangled about the chair leg. While struggling to extricate my foot, I managed, "And that puts a crimp in your expectations. For me. And us."

I slid her drink over toward her, waiting for some response to what I hadn't in the least meant to confess. Silence and obscurity are a gay person's primal defenses. I had been steeled to purport myself as slightly aloof and mysteriously incomprehensible. Despite this former training, I had now unintentionally exposed myself as being criminal and perverted. I waited anxiously for her reaction.

"But Robert," she sighed at last, "you are in fact quite morbid. And that's precisely what attracts me to you."

Her misunderstanding was excusable. The word had only recently been coined and only a few felons such as myself were aware of it. Even now I hate the word. 'Makes us all sound like bliss ninnies,' Christopher Isherwood had remarked upon hearing the unfortunate coinage.

"No, no," I attempted to amend, "I'm a..." I couldn't say it. In fact, I hesitated even to think it. It's extremely difficult, daily, trying to live knowing you are assumed to be scum.

"Dear," Margo purred, "what is it you're trying to tell me?"

"That I'm a homosexual," not even believing it as the word plunked out.

She rapidly blinked her emerald eyes. Ground the cigarette relieved of its holder into the abalone. "What makes you think so?" curiously watching me now as though I were something growing in a petri dish.

"Because..."

"Keep your voice down. The bartender might be listening."

"Experience, dreams, and expectations," I tried whispering obediently.

"You're serious. I believe you're being serious," her eyes spread wide in amazement. "Oh my God!" she shrieked awakening the bartender who peered groggily over at us. I gestured, assuring him we didn't need anything.

"Let's order some dinner," I suggested meekly. "It's time we ate something."

"This whole trip for nothing?" She furiously dabbed at her swelling lip with the soaked cotton. The pink skin was beginning to percolate and crack over tiny spirals of feverish flesh. She was a mess, and knew it. Everything was a mess now, and I knew it.

"You hurt me. You sting me," she cleverly projected her sore onto me. Her eyes squeezed shut, the almost bulbous end of her nose trembled. I watched mesmerized as Margo squirted out tears, mascara gradually streaking her cheeks until she looked bewitched and besotted.

"Let's eat," I tried again by picking up a menu.

"Eat?" she whimpered dangerously. "Impossible!" She stood abruptly, kicking the chair loudly back. "Take me to my room."

What was I supposed to do, carry her? "I'll follow you," I offered humbly. Which I proceeded to do as she stalked off uncertainly, her shadow wavering beside her down the hall. She paused before her door, shaking and copiously weeping bullet after bullet.

I opened the door for her, then flattened my back against the outside wall, arms flung wide like a crucified fly.

She swept by me, her blue dress long and rustling. "My intent was to love you." She slammed the door.

Beyond the door I could hear her muffled sobs and the ceiling fan whirling womp, womp.

9

Bait

Before my fateful revelation, it had been decided that Margo would dine with me the next evening where, as she put it, "You live on the island. I want to know all about your life here."

It was now almost five, the hour planned for her arrival in a prearranged taxi. I paced the floor of my tiny room in the Green Gables assuming that, since she already knew more about me than she could have desired, she probably would not appear. Daisy and Mr. Edmonds had been warned, of course, and at breakfast showed signs of irritated anticipation.

Daisy fussed about which wine would be appropriate, though I had yet to see a drop of that divinity ever fill a glass at dinner, and she had generously decided on chicken rather than canned lamb to honor the occasion. I could attest to the chicken's freshness; from outside my room reverberated the throttled screaming of a hen's last moments, followed by a whack and an awful thud. Then came Ralph's protestations: "Damnee bloody messy," followed by the headless scurry of jerking feet. I've always resented being a carnivorous mammal. I shudder at the deaths required to sustain us.

But then I shudder at most reality. Even at Margo's decision about whether to attend or not to attend our planned meeting. Telephoning her was out of the question. The Gables did not have a phone and I couldn't risk the quarter of a mile walk to the phone at the St. James Hotel, fearing Margo might arrive during my absence. Besides, Jessamine's friend at the St. James' desk would hear every word I said. She undoubtedly knew why Jessamine had flown to Trinidad, and I would have difficulty facing her. I had all day to think this out. I assumed that somehow I must be responsible for the discomfort I foisted upon others as well as myself. Yet I thought then and still think that it's not the tangled web we weave so much as the tangled web that is woven for us. Upbringing, genes, accident, take your pick.

I sat tensely on the edge of my cot, absently brushing aside cookie crumbs. Every day I consumed nearly a box of imported British tea cookies whose staleness collapsed them into crumbs before tongue and teeth could wrap around and snare them. My culinary desperation attested not so much to the fitness of my surname as it did to the meagerness of Daisy's servings. So despite the dread, I cocked my ears, anticipating and even yearning for the chicken holocaust to proceed.

"Damnee bloody messy," Ralph bellowed as another whack rent fresh screams, followed by the scamper of feet that didn't know they were dead yet. I shuddered and salivated simultaneously. Which are pretty much the nervous responses that define life, I decided while peering at my watch.

Almost five o'clock. Surely Margo would have the sense not to keep this date. She had every reason. And yet what else would she do? She could not leave the island until the next plane which was days later. I didn't know her well enough to guess how she might react to protracted adversity. At breakfast Mr. Edmonds had offered to buy a new tie for the occasion. Was he at that moment wrapping it around his skinny, corded neck into a pinched, crooked knot? Should I wear my usual T-shirt to assure Mr. Edmonds that his judgment regarding the innate vulgarity of Americans was correct? And Margo, should she appear—how might she expect a queer to dress?

I fumbled through the cookie box and found one splintered ochre circle at the bottom. Margo's hysteria had prevented me from eating the night before and breakfast had been the usual marmalade on toast. I was starving, hung over, and miserable as the hapless chickens whose slaughter I identified with and yet from whose demise I intended to profit.

I stared at my toothpaste rendition of the churchyard tombstones tacked onto the wall over the washbasin near the foot of my bed. It was during the torrid heat of late afternoons when the marbled paste grew agitated, and the tombs shifted in melting spasms and glacial glides. Jessamine's husband's cross, which I had accidentally chosen to center the picture, had decayed and dripped by then into an unrecognizable morass of cloudy effluvium. How could I have presumed when I executed the work that within months I would have impregnated the widow of the man under the memorial? I saluted the picture with my cookie just as the church bell gonged the first of five melodious rings. I gnawed my wafer.

Having decided to awe even myself by donning my midnight blue shirt with the stitched red alligator and khaki pants and raw white sneakers, I heard distantly down the stairs the front door thud with heavy, hollow raps. Daisy called up, "Catch the door, Mr. Sweet, will you?" At least Daisy assumed Margo had arrived.

I hurled myself into the clothes, thundered down the stairs, and pulled open the door to be faced by a red-turbaned Lemba whose fist was still raised to pummel, if not the door, then me. "What's this?" I gaped at her.

"I is no a this." Lemba gradually lowered her arm whose apparent aim had been the door after all. "I is for mistress here." I never could decide what language Lemba thought she spoke.

"Here?" I echoed stupidly. "But she's not..." Carefully I eyed the street for Margo's taxi but detected only a few mongrels slurping offal out of the gutter in front of the Gables. Lemba shoved a hand at me. Her dry, cracked, earthen skin gathered tightly about her lowering, yellowish eyes. "For youse." She slapped a tiny sheet of pink note paper into my open palm. My fingers automatically closed over it.

I glanced warily up and down the street again. For Margo and Lemba actually to meet could precipitate a disaster beyond my comprehension. Except of course that they had already met in a most consequential sense days earlier.

"So, you didn't go to Trinidad with your mistress?" I tried

chatting amicably to Lemba wondering why, since she'd delivered her missive, she didn't leave.

Her words came up at me gutturally, much like a mongrel snarl, "This island here me homey." She stomped one foot for brutal emphasis. I noted she was wearing white sneakers.

Attempting to dispel the gravity of the situation, I eased my sneakered foot next to hers and kidded, "We're almost alike. The two of us."

To which she snorted in disgust, turned, jumped with surprising agility over the wide gutter, stabbed with her walking stick at two dogs yipping in frenzied copulation, and retreated toward Jessamine's house up the cobblestone street.

I unraveled the pink note paper I'd crushed in my hand: "My love, my love, I cannot and will not survive lest I press you to me. Tomorrow? Tomorrow? Oh, my love, my sun, my moon, my man of men."

I nearly fainted. I glanced up from reading as Margo's taxi glided to a stop. She shouted through its open window, "But where are the gables? And it's not even very green!" She was smiling and wriggling her long pale fingers at me, one of which flashed with a gigantic diamond I had never seen on her before. The diamond glinted in the sun that still crushed the street, and glared on the panting dog in full thrust, and the retreating figure of Lemba tapping her stick along the cobbles.

Margo opened the cab's door suspiciously, eyeing what to her must appear to be a drainage ditch burdened with unspeakables. I jumped over it to reach the car. "Just rotting mangoes mainly," I tried to reassure her regarding the truly questionable contents of the trickling runnel. As she tentatively emerged, I instantly grasped the problem: she had sheathed herself entirely in white. Virgin white? From head to mesh hose and patent slippers she rippled with the essence of sacrifice.

She reached for my hand. "I'm moved, actually, that here you are, in the street, awaiting my arrival."

"Could you have expected otherwise?" I stuffed Jessamine's pink note paper deep into my pocket.

With a heave and a push I managed the princess over the moat, and as I rushed her up the narrow steps of my castle *noire* I observed that she carefully arranged folds of cloth to shade her face in wafting billows—as though she were in purdah. Apparently she meant to present herself to Daisy and to Mr. Edmonds—whom I'd already described as my island family—as a woman pure, unknown and unknowable. Untouched and untouchable.

"Oh, Miss Athens." Daisy greeted her on the landing that led to the porch. "Well, well," Daisy seemed to be swallowing her breath as she took Margo in with a gasp. If being tongue-tied can be mistaken for poise, Daisy's verbal reticence proved her to have drawing room potential. Garbed in her usual black, Daisy had nevertheless swathed her neck with a double strand of gold balls which unfortunately leaked flakes of dust that already glittered her bosom.

"And you must be Daisy," Margo rested her ringed hand a moment on Daisy's shoulder. Daisy's eyes nearly crossed in her effort to appraise the ring. "You Daisy, me Margo." With a light laugh she almost carried off the Tarzan imitation popular in those times.

As we moved out onto the porch, I noticed Mr. Edmonds—already nestled in his green wicker chair—unwrap his legs to stand as we approached, his mouth with its bad teeth bloating into a spectacular grin. I watched his eyes gulp Margo in from snowy snood to shiny pumps. Which surprised me. I had assumed Mr. Edmonds to be either asexual or terminally repressed.

He strolled boldly up to Margo and held out his hand which she clasped. For a surprisingly long time. Both of them hanging onto each other. Though Mr. Edmonds may look to have been conceived by timid parents through a sheet in a frail diaspora of strained genes, the chromosomes demanding replication seem to have somehow scored. "Bob here has told us much...." Mr.

Edmonds' tongue darted across his vermilion lower lip.

"Yes, we're great friends." Margo announced what now might define our relationship. She circled my waist with the arm that wasn't occupied with Mr. Edmonds and pulled me to her. The hours we had spent apart must have settled her mind concerning our inappropriateness for marriage.

Mr. Edmonds guided her to his chair, fluffing the cushion with stringy fingers, pulling the chair invitingly forward. Margo sank into it with an appreciative sigh. "What a lovely view," she remarked while squinting out over the palms toward the harbor. "And what a lovely tie," she tried focusing on Mr. Edmonds, who remained bent over as though mesmerized, his new tie, a brazen power tool of the '50s, dangling a wide pointed drape toward her lap.

I eased my way along the chair so I could better view this outstanding accent to Mr. Edmonds' usual soggy tan suit. I knew that the island, encouraged by its selection as a locale for the movie, intended to prepare itself for tourists, but that Mr. Edmonds could so quickly avail himself of a tie that would appeal only to the disoriented and diarrheatic traveler astonished me. A wind-whipped palm splayed its tortured fronds over an orange-rayed sun sinking into a wave-capped azure sea. Tiny purple cloudlets spiraled toward and around the bulbous knot. Mr. Edmonds yanked on it self-consciously. "The Governor himself came to market to hawk some."

"And was the Governor his self sporting one?" Daisy wanted to know. Mr. Edmonds shook his head. "I thought not," said Daisy blinking slowly and steadily at the ghoulish Mr. Edmonds still hovering over Margo, who reached for his tie to stroke the dying sun with her diamond finger.

Mr. Edmonds was finally and rather forcefully persuaded by Daisy to disengage himself from Margo, which he managed by uncharacteristically perching himself on the porch railing, legs swinging aggressively wide apart. "And now the drinks, Mrs. Renick. Is a rum punch suitable for you, Miss Athens?"

We nodded our heads and Daisy hurried below, undoubtedly reminding herself of her duties as proprietress. I arranged myself carefully in my accustomed place within the hammock, having first pulled on the ropes holding it, in the belief that horrors replicate themselves whenever possible. "Ah, catch that sunset," I exhorted. While all dutifully craned their necks, I took the opportunity to observe Margo in her wondrous get-up. Both bare alabaster arms lay spread along the back of the chair while the amorphous icy silk trembled in the slight breeze over one cheek and half of her lip. Which, I realized with a start, explained everything. Because as the breeze further stirred the whirls of material, I saw that the sore on her lip had worsened and the crusting, leaking fester had spread into the skin. She had attempted camouflaging the unfortunate eruption with lipstick, powder and what have you. So there she reclined, her last name, Athens, properly defining her, resembling a marble caryatid supporting the Parthenon, brutally hacked at by marauding Turks.

And yet like so many fragmented sculptures, the imperfection embellished her with added significance. I swung toward her in my hammock and whispered, "Who are you really?"

"But, Robert, you already know. I'm whoever anyone I want wants me to be," her eyes wide with mock innocence.

A professional stance, I assumed, but, "Isn't it that you are never you at all?"

"Nor are you!" she shot back.

"Nor is anyone?"

I don't know where this joust toward defining personality might have gone because Daisy reappeared with our punches on a tray covered with glass overlaying blue morpho butterfly wings. As with Daisy's gold baubles, I'd never seen it before. We were usually served on a cork-bottomed beer tray.

"From B.G.?" I pointed at the tray, meaning British Guinea, the closest place where the morpho soared.

"Not only that," burbled Daisy bending down into an awkward

curtsy before Margo, "but me goldy chunks too." She twined her free hand through the flaking strands. Why she curtsied to Margo I couldn't imagine. Except that everyone seemed to present themselves to Margo precisely as her persona demanded.

All, that is, but me. Since I didn't yet know who I was, I had no reference point for accommodating others. I guessed it would take more moxie to presume as Margo presumed than I would ever be able to muster.

Margo had turned her attention once again to Mr. Edmonds, the only male she'd been properly introduced to within some thousand miles whose testosterone, however slight, seemed to fidget in her presence. "You must be from England." She lit a cigarette which sent Daisy scuttling for an abalone shell. "Your accent is a marvel." Margo wafted a wreath of smoke in his direction, cautious always to veil half her face. Had I not recognized that she was performing for Mr. Edmonds precisely as she had performed for me, I'd have been amused.

But then, hell, one has to know that however any person reacts to you, they identically react to others. No matter how intimate or scathing, dishonest or kind. Margo was simply no exception. Besides, I'd already made myself persona non grata as far as she was concerned and should have foreseen vengeance, no matter how subtly manipulated. But with Mr. Edmonds as bait?

"To smoke is bloody fine. Let me smell." Mr. Edmonds leaned forward flaring his tiny nostrils. "Ah." He tipped his head back, eyes shut, and I feared for his balance on the unsteady rail. "Were it not for my mother…."

"Yes, your mother," Margo instantly pursued, having so soon grasped his preoccupation. "Tell me, what was your mother like?" quickly moving in to target her prey. But Mr. Edmonds was obviously poor, frail and ugly. What on earth…but then I understood. Or thought I might have understood. It wasn't the money she whored for, and certainly not the sex since she had not an erotic bone in her body, but solely for the admiration, for validation of the self that she had connived into being.

Mr. Edmonds drained his drink, a tall one, in one swallow. "My mother," he muttered. His head slumped to his chest, his knees pressed together. He rocked precipitously as the sun gleamed, orange as his tie, directly behind him. Before the backdrop of raucous clouds he swayed, a scissored silhouette.

Daisy, who leaned against a post, hissed, "Quiet now Edmond." Mr. Edmonds had a first name? But Edmond Edmonds? Daisy's voice now came strong, pleading, "There's no purpose to digging the past. Please, Edmond, please." The porch boards squeaked as she moved gingerly toward the railing. "We'll go down to have our supper now. All right, everyone?" She gestured with her drink at the sky behind Mr. Edmonds' head. "Sunset's nigh. Time to eat."

Margo stubbed out her cigarette in the abalone while persevering, "She was a saint, your mother?"

Mr. Edmonds, to my relief, edged his scuffed brown wing tips toward the floor. Looked directly at Margo. "Yes. A saint. And so I killed her."

Giddy from the rum myself, the shock had the impact of a joke on my confused sensibility. I pumped my hammock into rocking heaves and guffawed into my drink.

Daisy shrieked, "Dinner time." Grateful for being told what to do we all huddled together and silently followed her down stairs.

10

Breathing the Darkness In

Dinner dragged under the strain of mundane conversation and prolonged silences. Margo and I were seated at a tiny table along one wall, Mr. Edmonds by himself as usual in the corner, and Daisy by herself in front of the partially shuttered window. Dark clouds had rushed in obscuring the sun before its accustomed green flame could signal its departure. We expected rain. Distant thunder mingled with the steady womp of the ceiling fan.

Ralph served nervously since this was not his typical task, his efficient yet always wordless sidekick having been called to his village for the funeral of a man who might have been his father. One never knew with any certainty. Soup spilled out of bowls onto the plates beneath, spoons were missing, crackers quickly became soggy in the sudden humidity. Daisy clearly was mortified. Especially because she had opened several wine bottles in a flurry of largesse. She had meant this to be a real occasion. I was proud of her and grateful.

However, the more the conversation lagged and the more the various courses appeared to have been poorly prepared, the more we drank. Your typical island chicken is so malnourished though muscle-wrapped from perpetually being chased by dogs that to touch it to a frying pan is to char it. I missed the usual canned lamb. Even the legs of Ralph's fresh kill proved to be mere bones to which a scant crust of burnt skin adhered. Margo's feverish blister made it almost impossible for her to eat. A light stab from a pointy wing bone had already grazed the sore, for it began to leak thin wisps of blood. I never know how to address lettuce strands clogging someone's incisors so I was not up to informing Margo of her problem. Nearing starvation, I crunched the fried skeleton before me and sucked the marrow with a whistling wheeze.

The sound apparently could be heard above the fan across the room, because it caused Daisy pointedly to clear her throat and launch into a tirade about the island's governor. She was certain Margo would despise and admire him precisely as she did. Margo responded by describing Chicago's mayor in such revealing personal detail I feared for his reputation, but most of all for his wife's.

Mr. Edmonds nibbled on his chicken breast while dabbing with his napkin at sweat dappling his forehead without uttering a word. The unfortunate cuisine aside, it was Mr. Edmonds' surprising announcement that he had dispatched his mother and my thoughtless guffaw in response that had shattered the evening. We were all busily avoiding the possibility that Mr.Edmond Edmonds might actually have done what he said he had done.

Apparently Daisy thought she knew. Margo acted intrigued as hell. I wondered if it could be true. And, if so, how had Margo stimulated his confession? But then I recalled that on previous occasions Mr. Edmonds had mentioned his mother with a pained pucker of his rosy lips, only to be interrupted each time by Daisy. Presumably it was not he who avoided confession but Daisy who prevented him. Now I knew why.

Ralph shook our saucered coffee cups down in front of us before clearing the dirty dishes. Daisy gestured wildly at her own plate, imaginatively wafting it off toward the kitchen, a reminder that Ralph should do the same. Ralph paused in the middle of the room staring at her in confusion. His eyes were big and glowed from the candle on Daisy's table. His flat wide nose with flaring nostrils pointed shyly at his feet. His skin, held taut by cheekbones regal as Margo's, shone stark as rain on a tree limb. He was all jungle: lianas choking ferns whose tongues lick fire into the glisten of a mahogany's trunk, where everywhere is dark and vague, heavy and muffled, rank with essences. It was Ralph's stolid, brooding grace and indifferent whimsy I wanted to embrace, not Margo's pretensions or Jessamine's social climbing. Nor, for that matter, this insufferable dinner charade of masked fears and avoidances.

With a wrenching scrape I pushed my chair back and stood. Gusts of wind whirled around the Gables, buffeting the whole guest house into unnerving creaks and swayings. I held my hand out to Margo. "Let's take our coffee on the porch." I glanced at Mr. Edmonds. "Will you join us?" I couldn't bear his awful loneliness. I profusely thanked Daisy. Thunder rolled closer now and so there must be lightning and I wanted to see it. Electric storms are rare over land masses as small as Grenada. "Blow wind, crack your cheeks,'" I recited, guiding Margo up the stairs and into Mr. Edmonds' storm, as it would turn out. He did, as I hoped, follow us, coffee cup jiggling in its saucer, a tight little grin pinching the corners of his lips.

Margo already occupied the wicker chair, so Mr. Edmonds pulled the camp chair next to her. Margo had crossed her legs and stuffed a cigarette into her silver holder while furls from her white snood fluttered across her face. With the next hurl of wind, the entire island went dark. Margo laughed, clapping her hands. "I love it!" I suspected that the sudden darkness caused Margo to feel better as a presence than actually being seen. Ghosted in flapping white, she smoked serenely, aware I felt sure, of Mr. Edmonds' closeness and his eyes upon her, while occasionally pressing a laced hankie to her infected lip. "Just like home," she announced.

"What?" I was so cognizant of the smell of salt, rotting fish, cinnamon, and crushed frangipani blossoms that to compare our present circumstance with Chicago's air pockets of burning sulfur seemed inappropriate. "Oh, you mean the lightning, the wind, the lights going out."

"Robert, we'll be such great friends whenever you leave this place. For our mutual benefits." She fumbled in the dark for the abalone ash tray. "We travel the same underground railway, you and I. We understand each other far better than you dare admit."

"If you mean that friendship is more rare and trustworthy than the racy frequency of loves that come and go, I'll buy that. And, yes Margo, we do ride that same lurching underground train. You by choice. Me by fate."

She leaned forward, cigarette waving above her head. "Only a man could so flippantly misunderstand."

I noticed Mr. Edmonds edging ever closer to Margo, one hand now resting on her chair arm. "I didn't mean to say what I said... earlier...about..." he mumbled.

Big, splating drops began to fall, thunking on the banana leaves below. Responding to Margo's accusation I inquired, "Do you mean men in general? As for me, I'm a truth-monger. Not that I know what truth is, but I suspect it's what isn't supposed to be exposed."

"Why?" Mr. Edmonds eyed me directly. "Why would you claim to care about what isn't polite...to care about?"

My initial response was to explain that I wasn't British, but fortunately I annulled the conceit and actually heard myself insist, "Because the forbidden is more interesting. Reality fascinates me. I've no other explanation, Eddy." Boy, was I getting friendly —which precipitated an unexpected result.

Edmond Edmonds, presumably upon hearing his nickname for the first time in many years, lapsed abruptly into tears. Like the rain beyond the porch, water splattered from his eyes, plunking into Margo's shiny ashtray.

Margo recoiled. Such behavior did not fit her expectations of a male who indicated interest in her. Because expressiveness is so pronounced a trait in the female that life always owes them more traumas than they can adequately emote, Mr. Edmonds' outburst upstaged Margo's very being.

But utterances not only clarify pain, they also relieve us of it. I joyed in the spectacle of Mr. Edmonds' weeping. I couldn't manage more sympathy for him—his previous reticence had already accomplished that—but I would be satisfied if maybe, just maybe he might be positioning himself for some sort of relief from his chronic state of emotional constipation.

Like a typical male I distanced myself from his collapse and clambered into my web of a woven hammock, all ears. I actually enjoy listening. That's one of the symptoms that defines my androgynous nature.

Margo, female to her painted toenails, seemed quickly to rally from her distaste for Mr. Edmonds' breakdown and flung an arm around his slumped shoulders. In the dark, Margo's skin and shrouds of silk made her appear spot-lit, as on a stage. "Hush, hush," she crooned. "Are you weeping for your mother?"

Right on target.

Mr. Edmonds shuddered, clamped tight his eyes and gradually aimed the twin holes of his tiny nose toward the roof. The roof was tin and the rain now clobbered it raucously. He keened above the clamor, "My love..." He paused. I listened to the rain, felt smacks of it occasionally strike my face, thinking that, yes, to males particularly, even the word 'mother' is primordial. Primordial as the waves I watched lit by lightning, tossing themselves to a frenzy in the harbor.

In so many languages the word for mother is similar to the word for sea: *madre* and *mare*, *Mutter* and *Meer*. It is the French who retain symbolic exactitude with their *mere* and *mer*. All are European languages, but African languages too, even those of an inland origin, mimic in sound and meaning the salty connection between the twin chalices of life.

Margo was urging him, "You loved your mother?" As if there were a choice.

"And despised...and feared," keened Mr. Edmonds. Which is much the way love goes.

"But why?" Margo insisted, her voice calm, full-throated, almost deep. Her head, veiled in wafting skeins of white, arched over him like the mother her profession forbade her to become. She was reaching out, yearning far from her professional self. And yet what else is it that prostitutes do but give, should they have perfected their art. And to be remunerated for giving is the only proof of success possible.

"Why should you have despised," Margo continued, "she who

gave you life?"

Mr. Edmonds was quick this time to respond. "Because I hate life? Have always hated it?" Rhetorical questions, for Edmonds seemed the embodiment of discomfort, reluctance, restriction.

"I too have felt that." Margo lit another cigarette. "I think everyone does at times."

I heaved myself out of the hammock and went to my room for a candle and a bottle of rum. Returning, I placed the candle in a quart jar on the floor between them where the wind was less likely to snuff it. I poured us each a glass, straight. I curled back into my hammock. Had I ever wanted to kill my mother? Yes. Had I ever thought life not worth the living? Yes. Was Mr. Edmonds a form of me? Yes. Was Margo? Yes. Why must so much that seems disparate be actually our reflection in a mirror.

Mr. Edmonds sipped his rum, leaned back, eyes still fixed on the roof. "But...I...I...resent life...always. Especially since... When it happened."

'It' happened I wondered, as though he had nothing to do with it? Yet I could almost understand, because when my mother joined my father to make scathing remarks about fairies, when she covered all the furniture with plastic because everything and everyone was dirty, when she sold my piano because my emoting on the instrument embarrassed her, when she accused me of being incapable of love, I too had felt murderous.

"Eddy, Eddy, what happened?" I was growing impatient. My identification with Mr. Edmonds unnerved me. For relief I wanted to leave Mr. Edmonds and Margo to their own devices and meet with Ralph whose body had tingled my imagination for months. The way Ralph had glanced at me during dinner, signaling through lowered lids that his need might finally match mine, made me hope our time had arrived. I wanted his skin to sweat on my skin, to rut in the muck of physical sameness. The fantasy of Ralph, the odd congress between Mr. Edmonds and Margo all flickered across the screen of my mind at once. The brain is a rapid simultaneity machine. I still heard my words, 'Eddy, Eddy, what happened' booming over the rain.

Mr. Edmonds rose to his feet, his glass of rum pressed so hard to his lower lip it indented the skin. He shuffled toward my hammock and peered down at me. "So I'll tell you," he whispered. The candle light was behind him and his face hung shadowed and masked above me. He seemed more a presence than a person. "I... bludgeoned her." Edmonds gulped more rum. "I hammered her insensible. Bleeding, finally breathless."

While he spoke, a jag of lightning split clouds over the harbor. I cupped a hand over my mouth and chuckled. I'm aware that it is surprise which usually erupts us into laughter. It is the expected—the anticipation of the inevitable—that grows finally to be horrifying.

Margo by now had come up behind Mr. Edmonds. Taller than he by more than a head, she wrapped her arms around his chest and lay her cheek against the bald circle capping his thinning hair. "There is love," she began. "Think, think of the joy...."

Only to be interrupted by Edmonds' shaking down onto his knees. I heard his next words coming up from under me through the hammock's mesh, "Love? Through love is how it happened!"

Was it incest, committed or imagined, that might have turned Mr. Edmonds from innocence to criminality? I was never to find out. Margo followed him down onto the floor where they lay stretched together, his head between her breasts, she stroking the back of his wrinkled jacket.

"Whatever we've done can be undone," Margo assured him. She seemed to be as caught up in her role of earth mother as she'd been as a femme fatal. There lay Margo, her white outfit besmirched by floor dust, blessing Mr. Edmonds' despair. From the moment I met her I had discovered Margo always to be framed—never by cameras, only by her own assumption that what we represent is always far more than who we are.

'Whatever we've done can be undone' my ass, I thought as I

flailed to disengage from the hammock. "More rum, anyone?" I tried righting myself on unsteady legs. The rain had stopped and all the darkness around us dripped. "Margo? Eddy? More rum?" I stepped over their reclining bodies as at a high school slumber party. Neither responded to my invitation.

I meandered down the two flights of steps and walked through the kitchen and out into the wild place under the porch around which banana leaves still clung with long strands of rain water. The moon leaked through scudding clouds. I sat on the palm stump where the chickens had lost their heads. I deeply breathed the mystery of the darkness in.

Ralph came up behind me. I guessed it was he. Not because Ralph and I had made any specific arrangement, but we had somehow, during that ghastly dinner, possibly as his elbow brushed against me while serving the soup, silently promised each other something. Something we had inadvertently been promising each other for a long time. I felt sure of it. Each time I rented his bike actually—though I didn't know he knew and he couldn't know I knew.

I reached back and took hold of his hand. It was a large hand, caked with calluses. His fingers wove through mine. Still holding his hand, I stood and turned toward him. "Ralph," I whispered.

"Mr. Boob," he said.

He was barefoot, no shirt, short black pants. Young Grenadian men were typically muscled, stocky rather than tall, often garnished with protrusive belly buttons. Ralph was no exception. I pressed close to him. He didn't flinch. I trundled my shirt over my head. His arms circled my waist, his hands clasping my butt. I lay my cheek against his and muttered, "You want this as much as I do." I felt the twist of his extended belly button scrape below my belt.

"You feels…" Ralph jerked his head back to stare at me. "Good, mun." He seemed surprised. "But I knows…"

I felt between his thighs.

"I knows. I knows." His eyes closed. His lips furled away from his moon-bright teeth. "Ah," he said. "Ah," and his legs began to shake, trembling against mine.

I pulled back to see his milky glimmer sliding down the black leg. I gritted my teeth. Sex is always interesting even when it's not in the least bit satisfying, my desperation caused me to conclude.

"Nasty," he said stumbling away from me. He shook the leg. "Shit, mun," Ralph grumbled.

"No...no," I said. I watched him through the darkness, appalled as he scraped his leg against a banana leaf. Without looking at me, he shrugged his huge shoulders and made a dash through the mud toward the kitchen.

Guilt is as universal as the needs that feed it. Right, Ralph? Right, Mr. Edmonds?

11

The Rabble

After my misfortune with Ralph near the porch, full of frustration I changed clothes and hurried toward the St. James Hotel to call a taxi for Margo. The island's feral dogs had been made particularly exuberant by the storm and the subsequent blackout, and slunk like big furtive rats through the puddles. The church bell bonged ten rings. It was still early—typically the dogs did not become dangerous until around eleven, when all the town's streets emptied and the canines gathered into packs, growling and howling, moon or no.

I meandered around puddles, warily glancing from right to left. When a mangy mongrel scrambled stiff-legged and sniffing out of the burbling gutter in front of me, I froze, wrapping my arms tight across my chest, tucking hands under my armpits. I'm always afraid dogs will nip and flay the tips of my fingers.

It is difficult to explain why man's best friend unleashed imbues me with such primitive terror. Or why it is that others don't share this terror with me, because to my way of thinking our frail-toothed, unclawed hairlessness and sluggish pace is no match for the pack-hunting wolves dogs are hereditarily primed to be.

Since I've never been bitten or clawed, my phobia seems to have been implanted by an incident that occurred when I was four or five. My mother had a cat, Patsy, to which she was fanatically devoted. So smitten was she with the cat, who appropriated her affections for the entire twenty years of its life—from my birth to my graduation from college—that I was raised to view the feline as "my furry sister." I accepted the moniker as a compliment to me, not the other way around. I was squishing ants in the garden with my tiny booted feet—Patsy ineffectually bashing at cabbage butterflies—when a police dog loped into our yard, toppled me over, and attacked my now screeching sibling. Because I understood

Patsy to be the unquestioned dominatrix of our matriarchal household, all worldly rationality, to my raw eyes, disintegrated instantly in a flurry of yips and flying hair. Patsy survived the onslaught by attaching herself to the creature's neck and flailing away as though the dog were a scratching post. I screamed and screamed.

And still do, deep down in my medulla oblongata, when confronted by dogs. I've even scissored out newspaper clippings which report maulings of people by their best friends. The one describing an old woman who, while preparing dinner, got her entire arm gnawed off at the shoulder by her pet Doberman especially validated my fear. All of which proves the value of research in support of a thesis, should we guess that most theses are really phobias in disguise. Otherwise, why else would one work so hard to prove them?

Though the distance from the Gables to the St. James was only a few blocks, I scuttled rapidly and each time a cur neared me I increased my pace, skulking close to storefronts, desperate to effect invisibility, behavior which even the most cataract-impaired bone-cruncher found impossible to ignore. Their ears pricked in my direction, their nostrils flared with intrigue. If I can control my phobia, I thought, and stroll boldly, they'll slink off as they do from most people. I'm one of the king of beasts, I tried calming myself, while terribly aware of their claws clicking along the cobbles close behind me.

My knees wobbled uncontrollably by the time I oozed up the hotel steps.

"What can be the matter with you...now!" Jessamine's friend Marilee glared at me from behind the lone candle that lit the counter, her voice more clipped than usual. "Why you so out of breath and shaky? Has the storm done you in?"

"Dogs," I gasped. "Everywhere." I gestured behind me out the doorway.

"They do you no harm," she attempted placating me, just as

everyone always has. "But here," she offered while rolling a stick across the counter she'd extracted from a niche behind her. "Keep this if it make you feel better. Compliments of the St. James," she grinned.

I grabbed the phone and was already dialing the taxi number. "If they're harmless, why does one need a club to clobber them with?" I spoke into the phone, "Yes, from the Green Gables to the Santa Maria." I hung up relieved that though the storm-struck lights had remained out the phone still mysteriously worked. I reached for the stick. It was weighty and knobby.

"You needs a protection if you scared. People who ain't scared needs none. Simple as that."

"Violence *is* fear then." I tested the stick by thumping it on the floor. You never know when you're going to borrow a realization so I mouthed again, "Yes, violence is fear. Always."

I caught her looking at me as though she questioned a white man's ability to grasp the obvious. "You be seeing Jessamine tomorrow?"

I squinted at her. I had guessed she knew why Jessamine had flown to Trinidad. And now I had to assume she knew about Jessamine's pink note delivered only hours before proclaiming Jessamine's love and demanding my presence. "Maybe," I blinked unsurely. "Tomorrow or the next day." I shrugged shoulders trying to remind myself that even though this woman had arranged my initial introduction to Jessamine, she had no right to insinuate that my life was transparent. I turned and began down the hotel steps, my stick like a snake's tongue probing the still cloudy night.

I snickered to myself with all the braggadocio I could muster. At least Marilee would never know about Ralph and me. In that brief brush with my own reality near Daisy's porch, I had transgressed upon taboos so entrenched that for all practical purposes the incident might just as well have not occurred. Not only had I violated sexual comprehensibility but also crossed the island's boundaries of class and color. Margo was right, I was an underground kind of guy. And I was very much beginning to appreciate my forbidden appetites that assured me of partial invisibility.

Even the dogs seemed to cower now and keep their distance, doubtlessly intimidated by the adrenaline of personal understanding that persuaded me to swagger and wield my stick as though I knew what I might be about.

Margo was already entering the taxi when I reached the Gables. Mr. Edmonds clung to the last shimmer of her dress as she tucked it around her. Margo waved confusedly at me while Edmonds slammed the door and the car took off. Mr. Edmonds staggered by me and up the stairs. "A saint, a saint," I heard him whisper. Then the lights flickered back on and I watched him heave his saggy butt toward his room, inebriation forcing him to lean heavily upon the narrow railing.

I followed him, and then up one more flight to my own room. I remained so seized by Mr. Edmonds' personality or lack thereof, so haunted by him and alarmed, that instead of collapsing onto my bed as would be expected, I fluffed the pillows, lay back, slid the spiral notebook I kept notes in onto my stomach and uncapped a pen. That I had spontaneously laughed twice at Edmonds' confession of matricide alarmed me. What we laugh at nakedly reveals us. "Here I am," I scribbled, "admitting that I've chuckled twice when a fellow occupant of this guest house confessed to the murder ...of his mother. Which certainly is no laughing matter. Am I some kind of insensitive clod, a real brute? Or is he, this Mr. Edmonds, the brute? He is a negative, repellent person...with whom I closely identify. Indeed, he is who I'm afraid I really am. Not the murderous part so much as the restricted, hopeless, desperate part. But why should I, less than half his age, be forced to identify to the point of terror with this wretch? Easily!"

Then I began a fictional revitalizing of Mr. Edmonds' dilemma. As I scribbled, Mr. Edmonds' character instantly began to merge with mine. He is revealed to be as obsessed and fearful of dogs as I am. In truth, the real Mr. Edmonds had no interest in dogs,

positively or negatively. But his character quickly absorbed my
phobic preoccupation. I absorbed him into myself, much as a dry
sponge does a spill. I wrote:

> He did not know why he hated dogs. Perhaps it
> was merely the commonness of the species, for a
> man like Mr. Edmonds would have to choose
> something inevitable to despise.
>
> His life had been unfortunate, not due to any
> cruelty of fate—that might have challenged him to
> an act of deliverance—but because he had experi-
> enced an extraordinary absence of good luck. Within
> that very year financial indiscretions had forced him
> to flee his London flat and try an existence in the
> tropics. On the West Indian island where he chose
> to settle, no one would know of him or, for that
> matter, care if they did. He could submerge himself
> among comparable expatriates, all who would cling
> unquestioningly to each other in the face of the
> island's vegetative morass, the abrupt fall of night,
> and the heat that fogged sight.
>
> Edmonds faced his exile as one of many inconve-
> niences he had been taught to expect. Each lash of
> life prolonged an inner numbness rather than
> elicited rage or even the quick narrowing of the eyes
> in acknowledgment of an adversary.
>
> But had he realized that in his new home he
> would find himself plagued by an intensified version
> of the ever-present dog, he would have feared for his
> sanity. Because to Edmonds the dog was the
> miscreant, the absolute miscreant he was wont to
> maintain, of all creation.

Hawthorne, the first serious writer I read as a child—because
his book of short stories happened to be on my aunt's library shelf
which held ten books in all (my parents had even fewer
books)—still dominated my mind. That word 'wont' is a dead give-

away, as is the nineteenth century heft of each sentence. Well, you have to start somewhere and from somebody, a progenitor who plants his foot square into your unsuspecting gray matter.

Mr. Edmonds and his mother had shared the flat in London in which they kept birds, mostly parakeets, and one large cat whose presence in the aviary had been as amusing to Edmonds as it was alarming. There is something about wanting to decimate one's immediate environment that attracted and held his attention. Upon his mother's death, he gave the wildlife away and forged several checks attempting to cover her medical and final expenses. His lack of criminal talent ensnared him before her funeral and he ran, leaving his mother unembalmed and above ground to cope with her spiritual effects as best she might.

The island's torpid, ancient town to which he came was small, faced the sea, and was backed by a promontory upon whose crest resided the dead. They were in exposed marble boxes topped by crosses, sprawled haphazardly beneath palms and the fanatic sun. All the town's major streets, cobblestoned and tortuous, began at the ocean and literally petered out at this place.

Mr. Edmonds took residence in a guest house as near the sea as the threat of malaria permitted. There he began a life of seclusion, waiting for the time when he might rejoin his mother in some less earthy, more permanent aviary—in the stars perhaps, for his thinking grew increasingly fantastical as his nostalgia for London grew.

But if he was to feel antagonism toward dogs, the particular island he had chosen because it was still part of the British Commonwealth turned out not to be the place for him. The tropic dog, he discovered, was a scurvy beast not capable of affection. What most people think of as the dog's loving nature disappeared the further south that beast was to be observed. Mr. Edmonds came to that conclusion with alarm but hardly with surprise. A thousand miles each side of the equator, just the area of his safety from the law, dogs increased in both viciousness and number. Fortunately, he had spent most of his life in a temperate zone where seasonal changes seem to confound the dog's potential for evil, reducing them to inane obsequiousness or mere trial flashes of temper.

Why had I ducked Mr. Edmonds' killing his mother, if that is what sent me to record the piece in the first place? Because, I suppose, the dogs as metaphor took over. Had they taken over because of the walk I'd just taken to the St. James? Something deeper than that? Stories write themselves, and like a poem are best grounded in one pervasive image. The story had already defined itself, given itself perimeters on its way to drawing blood. My blood.

During his residency on the island, Mr. Edmonds came to sense what lay beyond the tearing mongrel's eyes, the irritating snarling. They were the proletariat, not so much in the sense of class as in attitudes or poses of being. The intolerable heat of the tropics excited the brutes while it caused men like Edmonds to languish in an ease that usurped his vitality.

The sun always blinded him; the collar from which his gray neck poked soon turned yellowish as antique ivory. He was aware that the canine population looked askance upon his timorous tread and his habit of carrying a large stick with which he tapped the cobblestone streets. As Edmonds rose early and walked to his small office where he pretended to work, he caught the dogs yawning in the new sun, playfully nibbling fleas or urinating with an abandon curious to one as restricted as himself.

The man's humming and the gastronomic rumblings of his hasty breakfast apparently aroused the dogs, for many of them would bark teasingly or nip his heels until he was forced to raise his stick and cry, "Get out of here, go away." Though more and more often, as he fancied a new depth in his understanding, he found himself cajoling them, murmuring, "Hello there, fellow. What a pretty dog," until his natural terror proved too much and he hurried down the street with the now curious animals scampering in his wake.

On one of these occasions a black native stopped him and said, "They just full of fun, sir." The native cocked his huge head. "They noble and fine. And brave. They brave, sir."

"They ought to be done away with, they ought to be shot," muttered Edmonds.

And then he had turned to face his adversaries. Their numbers were startling. They lounged on the cobblestones, lay on the door steps, poked their heads from open windows, even reclined upon the low flat roofs with tongues lolling and eyes running like sores.

I could only assume that the real Mr. Edmonds feared people-power as intensely as I do. Paranoia is a legitimate response to what I've come to call our Age of the Proletariat, 'not in the sense of class or color but in attitudes or poses of being.' And yet is it moral to deny people access to whatever they need or want, even if what they want is bad for them?

Evenings, it was Mr. Edmonds' habit to sip a rum punch on the porch of the guest house. To the left of the porch towered a royal palm swaying in the twilight breeze. The sun, straight before him, began to sink into the sea, dragging clouds with it. By six o'clock, claiming he had recently returned from tea at Lord and Lady –'s, he would enter the porch with feigned breathlessness, seat himself in the high-backed wicker chair, fold his left over his right leg, and await with great patience the opportunity of greeting the occasional guest. His suit hung loosely like the skin of a man who has strenuously dieted. And since the suit was seldom cleaned, it had begun to take on a skin-like permanence. His face had the porcelain whiteness of a doll, the features just that delicate, the lips extraordinarily red, as though constantly bitten. His smile was wan and frequent and exposed one eye-tooth of pure gold.

"It's lovely," he would say in his bland voice to the guests, who on this evening were a couple from the States excitedly admiring the sunset.

"Oh," fluttered the woman, "it is fantastic. The colors. The drama."

Mr. Edmonds lay his head back, languidly blinking his eyelids. It was sometimes a quarter of an hour, sometimes more, that he could almost wordlessly hint at his social position on the island, the unique and mysterious circumstances that caused him to live in such exotic environs. Edmonds' sense of isolation encouraged him to affect a sickly, aggressive manner when confronting anyone. There was something about the very whiteness of his skin, the delicacy of his nervous hands, that appalled.

Though he nodded his head and gestured with pale fingers, Mr. Edmonds' washed-gray eyes fixed the unwary Americans with the look of a starveling. They don't see, he thought with wonder, they don't know. What he meant was his desperation, his need, which had long since ceased to have an object. But the Americans did sense it and sat increasingly stiff and cautious before him. They continued asking him questions about the island and laughed sharply when he dribbled his drink upon his tie.

"Oh, that tie," he smiled. "It is nothing."

Then the tropic night descended upon a single waft of wind. Instantly, the dogs began their night-long howl. The southern dog is actually nocturnal. Night is their time to sing, to court, and to possess the streets which they roam in shadowy packs.

"Hear them!" Edmonds whispered, "hear them howl. No sleep tonight. None." And he sat upright, tensed in his chair, his hands gripping the wicker arms.

"Why, whatever do you mean?" wondered the American woman, her fingernails clicking in sudden impatience upon her straw handbag. "We own two retrievers that we adore as much as we do our children."

"More," offered the husband.

Mr. Edmonds turned in his chair. His eyes quietly surveyed the guests, the twist of his neck like that of an invalid child. His eyes held immense vacuity. "The dogs, they are everywhere."

A yipping and howling and a tireless dry bark spread in waves through the darkness from one end of the town to the other. Now the barking came from the furthest hill, then it traveled down the curving streets until the center of the marketplace raged. Arias, threats, pleadings and peals of their incessant dissatisfaction resounded and, to Mr. Edmonds, reverberated with the force of an explosion.

"They are infidels," he burst out curling his fingers into fists. "You know," he confided intensely, "they won't leave you alone. At night they rule this town. They march in bands. They intercept the late traveler."

Both Americans laughed quickly with alarm. That which had placed its sullen paw within Edmonds' being seemed to touch them with an intimidating, rough dryness.

"Now, Mr. Edmonds," placated the woman, rising to lead her husband to dinner, believing it actually was her hunger that drove her from the presence of one so seemingly innocuous. "Perhaps you think about them too much." She shook her head, reprimanding him. "They're only dogs, after all." The couple moved across the porch. They had just entered the dining room when the woman began chiding her husband about his not having opened the door. Her eyes seemed to snap at him. Her head swung loosely and her jowls hung pendant and oddly decorative from her tiny chin. She had had to open the door herself! Edmonds heard her tensely whisper before they disappeared.

"Oh, I've tried to love them," Mr. Edmonds attempted to explain, though the porch was now deserted. Stepping to the railing, he peered down into the street at the mongrel shadows that drifted just outside the radius of lamp light.

How we feel about ourselves often does not jibe with reality. I still often *feel* that I'm a Mr. Edmonds. I suspect that Mr. Edmonds and I share the same pervasive and fatal flaw: a fear of abandonment so great that we bring it about.

Mr. Edmonds had again signed the register at the governor's mansion. This was a technique resorted to by guests of the island so they might be invited to the state's receptions. That a resident of the community should employ this method for social purposes was unthinkable. Each time Mr. Edmonds signed his name, he was aware of his singular lack of pride. As he confided to himself: Humility is the final defense of both the desperate and the wise.

The reception concluded at six with the governor standing at the door, grumbling farewells he hoped his guests might misconstrue as deeply gracious, since he hadn't the real regard nor energy to simulate respect. Mr. Edmonds had lingered tastelessly behind to realize more exactly the grandeur of the mansion and so was the last to grasp his worship's hand. The governor, upon placing his casually bored flesh against the soft, corrupted essence of Edmonds, felt himself strain impulsively away—even turn his eyes from the parchmented, wizened face that smiled so wanly, flashing its gold tooth. It was as though the little man before him were inquiring into the governor's nature, an interrogation from which the governor could not emerge unscathed. The governor muttered ferociously, "It is late. Good night," remaining motionless, his autocratic hand still thrust in the air behind him, paralyzed in the act of repulsion.

When Edmonds found himself on the street, the cars and cabs had already departed. The cobblestones were scraped by drying leaves and the sky was rapidly filling with pink-gray tubers. So there is going to be a storm, he mused. The wind, craving and restless, clacked the palm fronds. Putting his head down, Mr. Edmonds hurried toward his room. He was aware of the dogs, restless as animals are before a storm, whining past houses, slinking stiff-legged through gutters.

With the first drops of rain he turned the corner toward the guest house. Through the rustling sounds of the fronds which everywhere tongued toward the sea, he detected the clicking pat of feet. Whirling, his vision blurred by the thickening rain, his eyes seized upon a dog-shape, then others like shades, following closely. One might expect dogs to leap promiscuously upon each other, he thought, sniff excrement and otherwise carry on with idle dog pleasures. But the nocturnal, tropic dog, he knew, was a beast whose military bearing should cause consternation. Their pacing of the streets with noses purposefully learning the ground boded ill. Where armies are, war is, and travail and slaughter. Oh, why did no one else see the danger? Mr. Edmonds paused and, unable to go forward, reminded himself to be calm. He would approach his room from another direction.

So he turned left, followed a narrow alleyway that was steep and led directly upwards. He had not gone far when other dogs marched toward him, howling at his intrusion upon their domain. Edmonds' skin flushed bright with alarm. They went so far as to leap out of the shadows at him, and he wondered to his horror if they were not the same dogs he had been trying to elude. If they were, a kind of malicious intent would have to be ascribed to them.

He had observed that dogs indigenous to the area were not easy to distinguish from their fellows. They were large, always tan or clay-colored, with several inch-long black whiskers circling their stubby muzzles, and they strutted with a wily, audacious carriage.

Mr. Edmonds shouted at them to go away, waving his stick through the air. Rain began falling with greater intensity and, lips quivering, Mr. Edmonds peered through the veil of water, shielding his eyes with his forearm. Attracted by his strange figure and the barking of those already gathered, new dogs every moment arrived, because the lurking shapes just beyond his limited vision multiplied, their movements agitated.

"Now wait a minute," began Mr. Edmonds. His small body, wrapped about by sagging cloth, seemed to dangle at the end of the stick he kept raised in the air. On tiptoe, he appeared to be attempting to dance his way beyond the present. The dogs waited, backing from him. Their ribs showed and their skulls looked slick and cruel. Edmonds' awareness of their aversion to him was acute, but he did not, perhaps dared not, directly cope with it. He would cling to that little stick which was neither club nor baton, yet was all that might protect him.

Reluctantly he continued his struggle upward, his stick now dragging behind him like a useless appendage. Several times he slipped on the uneven, wet cobblestones. Then finding the road suddenly more even, Edmonds tried to run, his thin legs propelling him awkwardly. The dogs burst into enthusiasm, pressing him on, until he stumbled over a cement block and fell. White tombs angled in all directions. Pale crosses jutted through the rain. Because he did not get up, the dogs moved in, sniffing and whining, and one dog breathed its rancid breath into his face. Leaning on one arm, Edmonds frailly raised himself and murmured, "You want me..." His eyes grew large, burning with a strange fire. He wondered if he were not crazy to speak to animals. But his mother had, confiding more to the cat than to him, whispering to her cat with her lips pressed deep within its fur.

He got to his knees. A younger, less comprehending dog darted its head and snagged Mr. Edmonds' ear with its fangs. Blood hung like a jewel matching the red of Mr. Edmonds' lips.

He clambered over the graves. The size and angular shapes of the tombs seemed to confuse the dogs, kindling their rage. The rain had slowed to a drizzle. The night steamed and shone. Mr. Edmonds stopped, exhausted. He climbed upon a tomb, warily watching the dogs circle around him. Their jaws gaped from running, their tongues lolled like separate creatures dangling from their mouths. His own breath so choked him he wanted to be sick. But instead he held out his hands toward the animals below him. Perhaps startled by the sudden gesture, those in front held back while those behind pushed forward with strained growling. He said to the snarling mob below who seemed awed by his voice, "When you're down, nobody, nobody helps you—and you know that, don't you?" His voice had an edge on it. His doll-like face poked out of the darkness toward them.

The dogs sniffed as they advanced toward him, their eyes modestly viewing the ground. "Stop!" he stretched his lips exposing the gold tooth. They stopped, but glowered.

Edmonds' arms fell powerless at his sides. The fingers of his left hand were obscured by the disarrangement of his coat upon his shoulders, but the fingers were laid bare. The thin hairs on his head flung themselves across his ears in blowing wisps.

A particularly large dog rose on its hind feet to rest its paws upon the tomb, with a snarl it wickedly snapped at Mr. Edmonds' shin. The pain did not cause him to move or scream. The dog sniffed the blood seeping across his ankle and looked up at him with great, tearing eyes. But still Edmonds did not stir, except for a trembling about his lips.

Finally he murmured, "I am overwhelmed by—"

The word 'disgust' was barely audible in the man's voice, garbled as it was by rain and wind and the renewed and awesome clamoring of the dogs.

12

Clawed and Nipped

Dawn had already cast a blush over the curtains and roosters cracked their throats as I titled my story "The Rabble," tossed the notebook with its squiggley writing on the floor, and fell asleep restlessly dreaming of how my mother and I killed my father by tossing him out the second floor window.

My mother grasped his head, I his feet, and with a one-two-three hurled him down into the garden where he landed with a thud. He didn't struggle. Neither mother nor I spoke as we concentrated on balancing and heaving his considerable mass through the dark.

The dream didn't end there. It lurked for what seemed hours, twisting and sparking across untrammeled synapses, while I fearfully wondered what to do with the body. Since all three of us had wordlessly agreed to his dispatch, I had only to concern myself with the disposal of his splattered remains. In the garage? The back seat of his car? The trunk?

Mother and I were guiltless. My father's famed affability would have it no other way. His spectacular, long-standing indifference to both of us had simply culminated in his righteous dismissal from this earth.

I tried wresting my head from the sweaty pillows. Snuggled back. Tried again. Finally I maneuvered my still stockinged feet over the edge of the bed, grateful for the feel of the splintery boards. I felt through the stubble on my jaw, beginning to realize why I had in my "Rabble" story side-stepped Mr. Edmonds' alleged murder of his mother. Having appropriated the character of Mr. Edmonds for my own fictional purposes, my unconscious demanded not matricide but patricide and so apparently I'd blocked the whole issue. We are remarkably exposed by what we don't say, aren't even aware of thinking.

Finally managing to extract myself from the crumpled bed, I padded to the cold water sink whose peeling zinc jutted from the wall under my toothpaste painting, brimmed the bowl with water, plunged my head gargling bubbles around my ears. Gasping for breath, I recalled Jessamine's romantic imperative delivered by Lemba minutes before Margo's visit to the Gables. Yesterday's complications had prevented my answering it. Hastily mopping myself dry, I tore a page out of my notebook and penned, "How about my seeing you next Saturday? This afternoon the governor has invited my acquaintance from the States for tea and it's only polite that I accompany her since she'll be leaving in a few days." A partial lie of course, but so unobtrusive and protective for all concerned that I determined it the best course to take.

Still clothed from the evening before, I rushed down to the kitchen intending to pay Ralph a BWI dollar to deliver my deception to Jessamine while I ran to the St. James to call Margo about plans for the day. I was happy to see Ralph, his muscled arms sunk in a tub of dirty dish water, butt shoved tight and high in the same shorts he'd worn for our assignation the night before. I greeted him cheerfully, an emotion he evidently found impossible to reciprocate. Big hands remaining plunged in the murky water, he pivoted on his sandaled feet, his crotch, I noticed, attractively stained. "Whats youse wants...sir?" He seemed to pay my Caucasoid status reluctant homage.

So I said, "Please, Ralph, no sir-ing me. OK?" I smiled pleasantly, blowing drying hair out of my eyes. After all, we'd almost mingled semen not many hours before and sex should make democrats of us all. "My name, as you know, is Bob."

"Whats you wants...Mr. Boob?" He whirled his arms among the dishes, his behind shifting warily as he scrubbed.

I longed to hear Margo's warm use of the more dignified yet intimate 'Robert.' "Can you take time off... I hesitated because the sinews down his corded, bare back seemed to shiver. "and deliver this note to Mrs. Hempstead up the hill? For two bills?" That meant fifty cents to me, a day's wages for him.

Ralph was already shaking dry his enormous arms. Of course he would. With that much money he could buy two whores down at the wharf to assuage his guilt from his accident with me. Ah, lust!

Or bust: the male disposition. As Ralph ambled off, illegally shirtless according to town rules, striding the cobblestones toward Jessamine's, I loped to the St. James galloping the hotel steps two at a time.

"Winded a bit are we?" smiled that same damned friend of Jessamine's, Marilee, who seemed to do all her eating, relaxing and conniving right there behind her desk. Prankster merry Marilee, panderess of the Windwards. "Did we make it home safe last night?"

Infuriated by her sudden inclusion of the royal 'we', particularly since I didn't know what degree of sarcasm she intended, if any, I pushed sweat off my forehead with a sweep of my forearm and demanded, "The phone, please," shoving the equivalent of a dollar in torn, crumpled bills toward her. Which she stuffed as usual under the flounces of her blouse.

The Santa Maria answered immediately, but it was a while before Margo's voice, husky from sleep, managed to sexily whisper, "I'm packing. I've decided it's polite of me, Robert, to leave a day early. I've discovered to my surprise that there's a flight this evening. I've made reservations which they've telegraphed through Trinidad. All is arranged. Also, we've been invited to a late lunch at a friend of yours. A Mrs. Hempstead, she said she was, who phoned last night. Won't that be fun? Mrs. Hempstead described her house as having pillars, so I'm going to dress quasi-antebellum. After the lunch we'll proceed to the airport. Oh, I miss you already. I'll come around in a cab at two. Ta-ta." And she hung up.

Just like that. Open mouthed, I stared at prankster Marilee who yawned back, a guarded gesture I took to imply duplicity. Yet, "I'm lunching at Jessamine's this afternoon," I still confided, needing to share and thus come to terms with the trepidation Margo's information stirred in my gut.

"I know," she said.

"Is there anything about me you don't know?" I faced her square. "Just curious."

"I is but a friend of Jessamine's." Lips fluffed into a quivering pout, I feared she might force a sob. If you stand up to them they weep, if you're weak they stomp all over you. I hurried down the steps and jostled through the basket-carrying street crowd back to the Gables.

To be greeted by a return note from Jessamine that Ralph must have slid under my door: "For lunch today, my darling. Two-ish." That's all. She didn't even sign her name. But then she didn't need to. Having arranged it all, Jessamine's attempt at reconciliation or vengeance would now simply have to play itself out. She probably had been at the telegraph switchboard when Margo changed her reservation. Because the telegraph office was only open during the day, Margo must have altered her plans before dining with me, Mr. Edmonds and Daisy the night before. Hum-tra-la, I tried to boost my spirits with song. Humm-tra-laaa, but the notes fell flat around my feet. I shoved their uselessness back into my vocal chords. The disaster of Margo meeting Jesssamine I had desperately, and I thought shrewdly, tried to prevent was about to strike anyway. There was nothing I could do about it. Or so my penchant for accepting the inevitable led me to believe. Not one of the three of us could possibly exit Jessamine's house unscathed.

* * *

Margo sat luxuriantly between her two suitcases in the back of the taxi. In the moment before I slid into the front next to the driver, I noted that she had managed a Scarlet-like appearance, her dress long, impertinently red with white strips that angled her

breasts like a T-square, her shoulders bare, a necklace of jade
dangling into her cleavage. "I'm disappointed you're leaving," I said
slamming the door. "To Mrs. Hempstead's," I instructed the driver.

"Hurry then back to Chicago and home. Do you even know
why you're on this island?"

Actually I didn't, so I said, "Because it's meaningful for me."

"How?" she pressed as the cab bumped over the cobbles.

"Because I don't really live here. I only pretend I do. So I'm freer
to live more?"

My question hung precarious as a November leaf as the car eased
to a stop in front of Jessamine's gate and her dogs rushed wickedly
to claw at the pickets. "Is Mrs. Hempstead elderly?" Margo asked.
"I assumed so by the hesitant, breathless tone of her voice on the
phone. Whatever," she pushed open the cab door and planted white
pumps on the narrow wood planks that bridged the drainage ditch,
"the house is lovely and I do much appreciate matronly women.
It's so like you, Robert, to befriend a mother figure during your
stay here."

I didn't know how to respond because there Jessamine stood
on the porch, crinkled in white ruffles from hem to bodice. At that
distance she could easily have been mistaken for a teen.

Which Margo's nearsightedness caused her to do. Shading her
eyes from the sun that sparkled through the flamboyant tree
bowering the porch in vibrant blooms, Margo ogled, "And there's
one of Mrs. Hempstead's daughters. She said she had two. What
a pretty, gracious creature."

Closely following Margo as she struck out toward the gate, I
suggested she keep her voice down when she whipped her head
around and hissed, "If you can get so hung up on your own sex,
so can I."

"Oh Boob, Boob," Jessamine called, wandering toward us
through the orange hibiscus blossoms, her voice screechy as she
struggled to be heard over her dogs who by now had bared their
dripping teeth and yipped inanely. For once I was grateful that

propriety insisted females proceed males. Let Margo deal with the hellish mongrels. Force her at least to share my terror, because no matter how often I'd entered Jessamine's yard my legs always wobbled and it's difficult trying to present yourself as a swashbuckling suitor while awash on watery knees.

But the instant Jessamine unlatched the gate, Margo was bending over, an ivory hand lifting both dog's muzzles where they sniffed along her pumps. "I love dogs," she burbled to my horror. "What soulful eyes. Look, Robert," she fondled the muzzle of the shaggy, mangy one and aimed the drooping eyes right at me.

"They're not soulful," I grinned wanly, doing my best Mr. Edmonds imitation while leaning back against a picket for support, "they're eyes of fired coals." Which sounded harsh, and so I added, "Or beer bottle glass," trying to make light of my anxiety.

Jessamine was rapping at their haunches with a stick that she always had nearby and the dogs scurried to whine under the porch. Trying to compose myself, I explained to Margo, "Dogs aren't pets here, they just prevail." Since Jessamine waited, twirling the end of her stick into the sandy soil, I finally managed, "Jessamine, I'd like you to meet Margo Athens, my acquaintance...."

"Come into the house," Jessamine interrupted. "It's hot and I gots punches poured." Her abruptness seemed ominous, yet I was certain Margo could not detect the least strain as we followed Jessamine's jouncing ruffles up the steps. Margo addressed the stairs with that hip-grinding stride that was both lascivious and dignified, her long hair swinging loose, alluring yet demurely straight. I was aware that Jessamine had not hugged me, her usual mode of greeting, nor had she taken my offered hand. Apparently as awed by Margo's beauty as anyone, she had decided to humble herself and treat Margo and me as a couple. Which in no way tallied with the loving demands implicit in her recent messages to me. I was confused. And relieved.

But not for long. Upon entering the bare-floored, sparsely furnished living room I noticed a guy nearly my age half-sitting and half-sprawling in one of the cane-backed chairs. He stood at our approach, tall, gangly, cut-off pants ragged around his thighs exposing hairy, sunburned legs of indeterminate musculature. "Name's Peter," his voice boomed. "Peter Petrocelli, from Poughkeepsie."

I advanced. "Bob from Chicago." I let him squeeze my hand, a dynamic he prolonged with increasing vigor. "Sorry I don't alliterate," I cleverly apologized while working my hand free. "This is Margo Athens, also from Chicago, who doesn't alliterate either." I snickered at my nervous attempt to be socially adept. Who was this American doppelganger of mine—hairier, true, and with a nose like an anteater's, but physically my double all the same? How had he secretly washed up on the island's shores presumably to be welcomed by Jessamine, 'O brave new world that has such creatures on't'?

I raised eyebrows at Jessamine where she'd tucked her bare feet under her on her flowered cushions, Dorothy Dandridge-style. Her sorrowful black eyes had also come to remind me of Dandridge. Margo seated herself, long legs crossed, next to Jessamine, lifting her abundant auburn to tumble down the furniture's wicker back. Jessamine murmured, "Yesterday. On the beach. At the Grande Anse. I met Peter while swimming. He wanted a drink. So I showed him where. At the Mourne Rouge."

Our beach! Our bar! "Unbelievable," I flared, thinking that nothing could be more believable. Jessamine, I suspected, was able to spot an aquiline nose protruding from the water a mile out and would be drawn to it much as must a winter-hatched fly to a light bulb. And Peter's nose, his distinguishing feature, was Italian as a chandelier, pendulous and shiny. If male facial nozzles do indeed predict their possessor's privates' enhance-ability, I had to consider myself liberated from Jessamine's pining for me as of, presumably, yesterday. Last night, possibly, while I cavorted briefly with Ralph counterfeiting the tumultuous leap of stags.

"And where are you staying?" I questioned Peter as I handed

a drink to Margo from the windowsill where I'd observed the punches all lined up pink as pig snouts.

"A hotel called the St. James," he roared. His voice was very loud. "Great place."

"Convenient." I stared hard at Jessamine. "At least it's convenient to here." I took a long draw on my drink. "You've met that woman behind the desk?" I squinted now at Peter. "Marilee, I think her name is."

"Oh, her," said Peter.

"Jessamine and you met by accident? On the beach?" I arrowed in again on Jessamine, guessing that the panderess of the Windwards had worked her magic again by substituting my doppelganger in order to revive Jessamine's hopes and affections. On the island where nothing seemed to happen, one had best not blink.

"Peter and I are only...acquaintances," Jessamine responded derisively. "That's your word isn't it, Boob, for such... arrangements?"

Smiling and amusing herself by flirting ostentatiously with Peter, Margo had no idea what was going on and suddenly wondered aloud, "But where is the Mrs. Hempstead whose house this is and who so kindly invited me to lunch with her? Perhaps she's napping." Margo sincerely tried excusing the absence of who she assumed to be the missing hostess.

"Ise aint nappin'!" Jessamine snapped, succumbing to island lingo as she often did when under duress.

Margo pushed out her lower lip, her cold sore so artfully concealed with lipstick and God only knew what other cosmetic concoctions that her affliction could well go unnoticed. She seemed to hold her breath for half a minute before summoning up an unmistakable graciousness to remark, "But only to think, my dear, that you might as well be your own daughter. By appearance, at least. You can't imagine how much I admire that." Seemingly nonchalant, Margo flung an arm over Jessamine's naked foot and wove her pallid fingers through the mocha toes. "And yet none of this is what I might have expected." She jerked back her arm and blinked steadily at me. Then Margo appealed to me directly, "Is Jessamine the woman you waved at when you picked me up at the airport? The one who was on her way to Trinidad? Oh Robert, admit the truth, just for once!"

It was already evident that I was the one to emerge from that luncheon gathering clawed and nipped at by my two paramours. My doppelganger rival, Peter, lurched back into his chair, splayed wide his hairy thighs and barked, "I've been through Trinidad. What a noisy, squalid mess of a town." He eagerly plucked at a hair in his gigantic nose. "Full of thieves and cheats." Abruptly he turned to Jessamine. "And why did you go there, my island girl?"

Jessamine pinched her chin between thumb and index finger. The next seconds passed like an hour of silent accusation. Her eyes closed. Then her black lashes began to mesh intermittently like grinding gears from which pearls of water seeped down her cheeks, runneling into the corners of her mouth. She shook her head, her lips mouthing, 'No, no' over and over. All watched, amazed and unprepared for this display, except of course for me, the only one who could guess at the recent memory of the abortion and its subsequent pains that incited Jessamine's grief. Finally her eyes fluttered open, the ducts still oozing tears, and like a stricken, uncomprehending beast shrieked, "It was awful. All of it. Awful!" Her entire body began quivering, as though possessed in a Voodoo trance. Her shoulders shook like the wings of a stunned bird. Her hands looked to be shackled behind her back. Bare legs clamped together, her heels ground into the floor, the muscles in her calves accomplished lightning leaps.

Peter ran to her, clutching at her shoulders while Margo leaned over clasping Jesssamine's forehead with her fingers before her auburn veil of trembling hair mercifully shielded Jessamine's terror from my sight.

I was about to rush into the kitchen for some ice, for water, rum, anything, when Lemba materialized blocking my way, her rough hands akimbo her broad hips, a kerchief of red and white stripes strangling the puckered lines creasing her dark forehead. The color and configuration of her kerchief precisely mirrored Margo's dress. By accident? By design? "Youse all has you lunch there," she pointed out the door, "on that a-there porch. Now, mun. Now!"

"But your mistress, Jessamine..." I protested. "Something is quite wrong here."

"There's that's been wrong for considerable, mister. Glad youse finally knows what Ise knows. And youse is part'n parcel of much, much a it...sir, sir, sir!" she began screaming and waving me off out the door and onto the porch as though I were a wasp whose sting must be deadly.

13

Exiled

Looking back on my expulsion to the porch by the irate Lemba, I still wonder why I perceived that all present at Jessamine's lunch thought me reprehensible. I recall sitting on the balustrade, leaning against a pillar, staring into the wide window at Margo and Peter as they hovered over the trembling and moaning Jessamine. I felt culpable, but couldn't grasp why.

Like Adam I was being assailed by knowledge. Not the knowledge of good and evil, but by awareness of self under the tutelage of others' reactions to me. The experience was a kind of photographic portrait I'd prefer had not been captured. But then most, though not all, real photos snapped of me throughout my life seem to portray images of someone else. I am forced to conclude that the lopsided, sly grin carried by the puffy lower lip, and the heavy-lidded, sardonic, narrow eyes bear no resemblance to the man I've ever believed myself to be. Also the perpetual, if faint, aura of idiocy suggested by the thrust-forward, thin neck and the small, round head approximating a golf ball on a tee...no, that is not me. Not a chance.

With similar disavowal I peered through Jessamine's window, convinced that her collapse, Margo's premature departure from the island, the presence of Peter, and the possibility that I had set in motion Lemba's penchant for vengeance, could not represent the fruits of my actions. I impatiently thudded the heels of my sneakers against the flaking, crisscrossed slats under the railing. Where the flamboyant tree and a gold hibiscus shaded the verandah's far end, a table had been set for four with glasses, napkins and shiny yellow plates. Apparently Jessamine's daughters were eating, as they often did, in the kitchen. Above their mother's ululation I heard their piercing giggles.

Through the glass I watched Lemba, head lowered, dash past the piano over to the couch and forcefully push Peter and Margo aside from their continued ministrations to Jessamine. The back of the couch was low so I had a partial view of Jessamine's heaving chest and shunting eyes. Lemba bent over her, stubby hands held behind her back, and as Jessamine's chest rose in a spasm Lemba affixed her ragged lips to Jessamine's smooth, lush ones and looked to be exhaling hard into her mistress' lungs. Though muffled through the glass, the sounds of Lemba's steady breaths were audible to me as they entered the gradually calming Jessamine. Her breasts gently rising and falling like anemones in a tide pool rhythmically soughed by waves, Jessamine finally seemed to sleep.

I strained forward attempting to deal with what was happening. On my terms, of course. All the world may be a stage but the role we've carefully rehearsed for emergencies can only be ourselves playing ourselves. I reluctantly admitted that some of my actions may have spawned the discomforting circumstances I was forced to observe. Yet I had not put the make on either Jessamine or Margo. Nor Lara back in Chicago for that matter. The loves and deaths resulting from my passivity were only circumstantially my fault. Yet how could women know I was not fodder for their enterprising and romantic notions? Contrary to Ralph Ellison's claim, it's not blacks but gays who are the invisible men.

My culture's customs had created an off-rhyme with my innate character, and up to then I had permitted culture to override character. Not only because I was a coward, but because screwing women, with all the implications of that word, was forced upon me by my community's expectations. And my fatal fear of being exiled assured that, despite little to no initial desire, I would plow them dutifully.

Struggling to see through the window's glare, I noted how Margo reached for Jessamine's hand and enfolded it in her own. Peter spotted me and formed with his lips the words 'go away'. Suddenly I found myself accepting that exile from all I had known would be inevitable. To be blunt, it was going to be difficult figuring out even how to feed myself when I returned home. The head of my department in the high school where I taught insisted, before I left for the island, that I had to marry and soon, or be let go. And yet if he suspected what I knew about myself, he wouldn't have hired me in the first place, even though I had signed the loyalty oath demanded by the ship of state helmed by the zealous Senator McCarthy.

Lemba stomped out onto the porch, the inky irises of her protruding eyes riding high under her brows. "Eats," she announced, her callused hands with the yellow palms reaching to tuck her red and white kerchief into a mound centering her crinkled forehead. "Ise means youse, mun." Lemba scanned me with distrust.

Following her sauntered Margo, willowy and regal in her dress with its white stripe and hectic-colored silk rustling a brash statement that Lemba's turban could only hint at. "You hungry, Robert?" Margo's tongue darted to check her camouflaged sore. She was clasping Jessamine's hand, the seemingly recovered Jessamine, who appeared docile, secretively smiling, composed and possessed again of her own spirit.

"Oh, Boob, it's so nice that you're still here with us," Jessamine commented off-handedly, rumpled ruffles lurching about her throat. Jessamine then turned to Peter, who had just bolted out the door slapping his sandals along the creaking porch boards like a dog desperate to poop. "Seat yourself, Poughkeepsie friend, there at the table. Anywhere you like." As though nothing of consequence had occurred in the living room. "Watch for ants that drop from flame tree blossoms. Prettiness is never what it seems," she tittered coyly.

All had been resolved through the ministrations of Lemba apparently. Can spiritual breaths huffed into gasping lungs revive as do real breaths a victim of drowning? And if so, who really was Lemba, just a life-long servant and guide of Jessamine's, or could she be in fact the Mambo, the supreme priestess of Voodoo I had heard comments about from various townspeople? "By theys acts youse knows them," is all I remember the people saying.

I detached myself from the balustrade and skulked toward the table. I wished I could leave, my usual ploy for avoiding discomforting circumstances, but I felt responsible for getting Margo to the plane as I had promised. Margo and Jessamine had arranged themselves side by side, fingers now loosely wound through each others' on top of the white table cloth. The table cloth was so starched its corners crisped out like a ballerina's tutu. I stared at Margo's alabaster twined through Jessamine's brown agate. If males publicly touched each other like that they'd be jailed or shot.

I glanced down at the already-seated Peter, who renewed his attack on his evidently stubborn nose hair. I had no choice but to sit beside him and tried my hardest not to gaze at his curly-haired thigh that brushed my pant leg before he jerked his leg away as though I were barbed wire. Yet I felt relieved that someone there was normal, that is to say socially predictable. Since Margo stared wordlessly and voluptuously into Jessamine's eyes while tightening her hold around Jessamine's fingers, I concluded it best to chatter: "The yellow of the hibiscus touching the red of the flamboyant blossoms is a marvelous sight. Indeed," I hurried on, "this island's a garden. Haven't you found it so, Peter?"

One of my habitual tactics to cover for my social trepidations is to talk. Preferably about something, but not necessarily. The point, I've decided, is to connect and you've got two sure ways to accomplish that, sound and touch. Because extroverts such as myself fear desertion each instant, we are always babbling and clawing. An introvert might never perceive estrangement to be at the center of things. Or care if they did.

Peter slapped his nose with a loud whack. "Mosquitoes," he growled. "Nasty suckers."

I saw no mosquitoes about. Though on the island catching malaria was a possibility, the carriers were seldom evident. I could only guess that my mere mention of flowers, to say nothing of Margo's absorption in Jessamine, caused him to invent an irritation external to the real situation.

So I jumped onto a fresh topic, "Fishing," I pounced. "You like to hook things."

"Naturally," Peter Petrocelli from Poughkeepsie yelped. "The bigger the catch the better. In Korea we did more than..." He stopped. Stared feistily at Margo. "Margo, you've known my island girl for long?"

"Have you?" Margo arched her plucked-thin eyebrows. However she did release Jessamine's hand much to Jessamine's obvious relief. Since I had never guessed Margo to have any interest in women other than as competition, I could only assume that the show was for my benefit. A form of behavioral sarcasm. But with poor Jessamine as dupe? "Robert knows Jessamine well. For many months now," she viciously informed Peter.

Peter eyed me sideways. "You're familiar with Jessamine's house then..." He hesitated.

I leaned toward Jessamine. "I play here often." Jessamine's eyes widened in alarm. "The piano mostly," I politely amended.

"What are you doing on this island?" he challenged me.

"I was going to ask you the same."

Our sparring was abruptly halted by the reappearance of Lemba, ostentatiously balancing on her head a big tray laden with soup bowls. Head-balancing was a mode of transportation for anything from banana clumps to car doors in the back country, but it seemed giddy and outlandish on the verandah.

Lemba slammed the tray down in the middle of the table and then backed her way toward the kitchen in a mock charade of servility. To my horror I recognized the bowl's contents to be cold fishhead soup, a favorite again back country, but good God, not presentable on a Victorian porch.

We all dutifully slid a bowl onto our yellow plates. "How interesting," Margo said, soup spoon raised curiously in the air. "Fresh, I suppose," she squinted weakly into the bowl, unable to trust her poor vision.

What I saw in mine was a severed head sunk in broth whose scummed eyes wept strands of filigreed parsley. The jaw was speckled with chaotic red and black spots and gaped as though the amber broth had embalmed it in the act of screaming.

All focused on Jessamine in hopes of explanation and instructions as how best to proceed. "It's the rip tide," she commented dryly.

"Oh?" we all wondered.

"Off Point Saline. Tosses the fish into eddies. Easy to catch. And they're…" She paused searching for the right word, "irresistible." To our mutual alarm we watched her skewer an eye with her fork and snap the orb with a pop between her tiny but precise incisors. Cuddling her throat with curved fingers, she swallowed luxuriantly.

I could not help adoring her. Jessamine's airs, her simplicity, calm beauty, and yes, her seething, manipulative, primitive core fascinates me even in memory. She has appeared to me in dreams, warm, protective, ensconced in sea shells, tree ferns wreathing her wind-blown hair.

I lanced my own fish eye in courageous imitation, beginning to wrest its tenacious nerve from the socket. "I'm sorry," I said to the fish and to Jessamine, for somehow the two were one at that moment, and punched the extracted eye down my throat in a quick gulp, feeling it slide cool and slick as honeydew.

"Sorry? Sorry for what?" Peter must have sensed that I was apologizing to Jessamine but decided to believe I only meant to address the detached head. "It's only a damn fish." He speared his entire lunch, held it dripping in front of his mouth, then nipped into the head above where the lips stretched taut and freckled.

How dared it be that though I adored Jessamine and Margo, I was physically attracted to Peter whom I disliked intensely? He represented all I found to be reprehensible. I fantasized holding him tight in the muck of a foxhole in Korea, easing my hand under his belt, encountering hair and the warmth of musky maleness. The only reason I wasn't in Korea is because during my medical exam the ophthalmologist asked me what I would do if I weren't drafted, and I mumbled I'd get a masters degree while continuing teaching, and he scribbled a big 4F on my chart, and I've never heard from the military since. Luck is a whimsical lady.

Because I wanted to encourage Peter and Jessamine to proceed with their affair, even though I knew he'd leave her stranded as had I, I tried to further deflect him from seriously considering the obvious connection between Jessamine and myself. And so I inquired, "Peter, what are you driving in Poughkeepsie these days?" I had already learned to my amazement that when student eyes went droopy all you had to do was drop the word 'automobile' and their faces swarmed with excitement. Peter, as expected, proved to be no exception. After nibbling the brows off his fish and then tentatively licking an eye, he held forth for seemingly endless uninterrupted minutes on not only the Olds he cherished at present but all the cars he had owned and intended to own. And polish, and race, and covet, referring to each one as a sweetheart this and a sweetheart that.

Jessamine was all ears. In abstract rapture she tore at the flesh of the rip tide catch, initially using the fork and finally lurching into the feast with sharp teeth, dangling the head over the bowl, finger thrust through the mouth for support. When Peter at long last paused for breath, she quizzed, "And there are long roads in the state where you live, and autos in little sheds next to houses…"

"Garages," I interrupted.

"And moving actors and buildings tall as mountains and…" She couldn't contain herself. "And things to do always, night and day, gliding everywhere always in automobiles."

"It's great," Peter sighed.

"Well, twenty-three skidoo," whooped Margo. "And tomorrow I'll be home. In Chicago. And then you know what?" She managed to slurp some broth around her sore. She had evidently decided to ignore the fish head. Her hair cascaded gracefully over her ears.

Her sculpted cheek bones shone. "I'm thinking I'll go on to New York."

"The Big Pear." Jessamine looked dazzled.

"Apple," I corrected. "Why New York?" I queried Margo.

"To have an affair."

I narrowed my eyes. "Any guy in particular?" thinking that she's got a rich one stashed somewhere who will keep her in 5th Avenue splendor.

"Why must it be a guy?" Margo stared at me. "Why should only the expected confine anyone...to anything?"

Jessamine gasped while Peter snorted.

"After all, Robert, you've never confined yourself to the expected." Margo shook her hair until it hung lushly over the back of her chair. An interminable, and for me, terrible silence ensued.

Jessamine slid her bowl with its glinting skull to the center of the table, indicating she was sated. "Boob has never what?"

Peter shoved his bowl next to Jessamine's having never pried out either fish eye, I noticed. "You *are* a scuzzy creep," he whispered loudly out the corner of his mouth.

Jessamine looked about confusedly. "What is being said here?" I saw a dash of yellow from the hibiscus behind me reflect in her wide eyes.

"Why go all the way to New York for an affair with...anyone," I tried to ignore the snarls of warning I heard advancing in my direction.

Margo tossed off, "So no one where I live will know. So I won't have to be responsible."

I never quite understood how Lemba managed to soundlessly and suddenly take shape, to abruptly appear with no indication as to how she'd gotten anywhere, but there Lemba was bending over Margo, hand retrieving the soup bowl, inspecting its contents with a sniff. "Lady ain't bein' hungry," Lemba crooned at Margo. The stripes and colors of her kerchief so precisely echoed Margo's dress that one would assume she'd copped a swathe of the material to adorn herself for this occasion. Possibly some island cohort of hers, while cleaning Margo's room at the Santa Maria, had helped herself to some material at the biding of the Mambo, should that be who Lemba was. But then it is the educated Westerner's curse to ascribe rational intent and methods to events, as though existence were meaningful, when happenstance is likely the truer explanation.

"The soup was very nice," Margo carried off the moment with panache. "The broth delicious." She winked at me as though the party were concluding satisfactorily for her. "Jessamine must be pleased to maintain you as cook." She glanced to the side where Lemba had been, ignorant of the fact that Lemba now stood directly behind her, the exactness of the colors that adorned both of them visually merging the one into the other. "What's the time, Robert? Don't want to miss my plane."

"Getting toward evening," Jessamine said. "The late afternoon flight for Trinidad. *That* flight." She glanced at me, just for a second, but in panic. The panic had passed by the time she demanded of Lemba, "Finish clearing the bowls."

Lemba jerked herself free from her contemplation behind Margo and blithely resumed her task as maid, chucking our bowls one into the other with loud clacks.

"Glad to have met you," Peter muttered unconvincingly while rising to shake my hand as I stared up into his averted eyes. "Have a good one."

"But I'm not leaving," I smiled. "Only Margo is. I'm just accompanying her to the airport."

"You'll return to the Gables then, won't you." Jessamine made it a statement of fact. What a difference a Peter makes in lives, I thought, especially the eager Peter Petrocelli from Poughkeepsie with the big nose. It became clear to me then that Jessamine had arranged the lunch before meeting Peter and that Margo and I had proved to be inconveniences at best. Whatever Jessamine's original intent had been, her purpose for entertaining us had altered.

After scraping back our chairs, we all stood. I went over to

Jessamine and embraced her closely. I even snuggled my nose against her neck under the ear where she liked it. I felt her fingers tremble as she sunk them into my shoulders. "Oh, Boob," she said pulling away, "play the piano once again for me. So I'll remember...what I'll want to remember."

At that moment I realized how rejected I actually was, not only from her body but from her house as well. Like Mr. Edmonds, I could hear the beasts howling for my arraignment, subtly of course for this was polite intercourse, but howling nevertheless. And I comprehended then that what had driven Edmonds mad were the social mores which the dogs signified, nipping and drawing blood from all who could not participate in the horde's sanguine expectations.

"How about the Schubert?" I suggested, deciding only a gay composer could help me express my disquietude. Besides, the Impromptu was about all I thought I could recall under the exigencies of the moment. I needed to hide behind melody, richly poised with its question and answer but particularly in Schubert's resonant yearning.

The impaired grand stood against the far wall of the living room near the doorway leading to the kitchen. I was grateful everyone remained on the porch. I'm one of those who likes to pretend they are being heard rather than really listened to. The spotlight I've always sought would only blind me. Yet if depression is a sense of powerlessness, it can also supply the ink for the pen, the paint for the brush, the impetus to song and, when not totally debilitating, sow the seeds of empathy and thereby compassion.

I played very well.

Returning to the porch amid a smattering of hand claps, I urgently ushered Margo down the steps to the waiting taxi. I noticed with a catch in my throat that Margo's hair showed a freshly scissored gap, and if I really believed in the power of Voodoo and in Lemba's strength as the Mambo, I would have pointed out to Margo that her life was in jeopardy.

But at the time I continued to view Lemba as merely irritating and meddlesome. If she were the Mambo, which I continued to doubt, I decided to consider her no more threatening than the archbishop who paid Margo for her services and had the gall to request spiritual counsel on the best way to enter heaven.

14

Stone Gardenia

Before entering the taxi, Margo bent to pluck a gardenia from a bush near Jessamine's fence. She twirled the glossy bloom in her hand.

"Put it in your hair," I said. "Pretend you're in Hawaii."

"But I'm not, now, am I." Nevertheless she found a pin in her purse and stood grinning as I finally managed to arrange the flower near her ear.

As the taxi chugged slowly up the winding road toward the airport I observed, "You were cruel. To me. At Jessamine's."

"The only real difference between us, dear one, is that my cruelty is conscious. Yours is cloaked in an insufferable innocence."

The road ran through ferns and nutmeg, gum trees and palms clustered around waterfalls that tumbled down cliffs. I wanted to wander in the forest, not to hide but just in order to be. I needed to confront head-on the loneliness I dreaded and try to learn how to embrace it.

Margo stroked my hand where it clutched my knee. Her monstrous diamond glowed where the sun struck. I wondered if it was the bishop or the business executive who had tried to own her through the gift.

"Despite what I've just said, we'll be friends." She squeezed my hand. "And you'll write about me some day. I know this because I mean more to you, and will mean more to you...I am, Robert, who you need. And so it will be." She began fumbling through her purse. "I feel..." The purse snapped shut. "...so tired. Exhausted, really. Almost trembly."

"You can sleep on the plane. It's a night flight to Chicago from Trinidad. You'll be in Chi Town this dawn."

"And you will come to me when you finish your strange

business on the island? I will be waiting."

"In your fashion?"

She laughed weakly. "If I appraise your sarcasm rightly, know that 'in my fashion' is what will protect you in the long run. Just as your peculiarities protect me from you. It's normalcy that's the pits. An optional existence gets rid of the needing, the clinging, the unwholesome concept that love is a burden." Again Margo reached into her purse, this time retrieving lipstick with which she expertly and quickly refreshed her pout. "I feel so sorry for normal people. Their cage is so tight and narrow."

As became, within five years, her grave. I do not know for certain if the physical weakness she experienced on our way to Grenada's tiny landing field presaged the disease that would force her to suicide, or if Lemba had anything to do with what ultimately happened. When I finally did leave the island, Margo and I continued our friendship, and even the sex, pleasing each other more with each tentative experiment. Her other lovers and mine at first spurred our interest in each other just as she predicted. But as our caring for each other grew so did the element of threat. Her increasing exhaustion made Margo less and less resilient. She began to cling. I became frightened, less available, more critical. She retired from her profession as courtesan, languished for a while as a legal secretary, then wed a black lawyer who had divorced his wife for her. Margo's 'Negro' we called him, 'black' was then still an epithet. Though he forbade her seeing other men, and brutally, I thought, confined her to their apartment, she still managed to sneak out and spend occasional afternoons with me. We often met at a sexually ambiguous and elegant bar in the Palmer House Hotel.

And yes, I have tried to write about her. After Margo's gutting her brains out with the gun, I realized it had to be a ghost story. Besides, only the dead are truly alive, because I often see my dead when I least expect them, sitting in their favorite chairs, coming upon them in a crowd. The closer through age I am to joining them, the more frequently they appear in my dreams. I wrote "Stone

Gardenia" as a story after her death, when Margo had already made herself at home in the pantheon of my being. As Margo kept scrambling through her purse for accouterments to enhance her loveliness, so have I creatively scraped through my memory for shards my life has been built upon.

I narrowed my eyes. Blinked rapidly. Could that be Margo? The auburn hair and alabaster skin, the long neck and haughty, almost imperious posture of the woman seated behind a small marble table in the far corner of the lounge seemed unmistakably familiar. But Margo was dead! Had been dead for—how many?—five years at least.

But I kept squinting at her over the amorphous heads of ad executives, legal secretaries, classy prostitutes, closeted homosexuals, all cruising over their cocktails. It was an elegant lounge—inlaid mirrors, mahogany counter, diffused lights, no music—on the lower level of the Palmer House Hotel, Chicago. The management must pay off the Mafia who paid off the police because the place had the unusual reputation of not being raided. Ties for guys and heels for gals were mandatory. The ambiance restrained yet intense: no music, only subdued chatter.

I had first became aware of this replica of Margo from my position at the bar where I had been eyeing and was being eyed by other men. She sat near the corner at a tiny marble table with a gentleman in a dark pinstripe suit. Seeing her, I was more confused than terrified. It is not unusual, I tried to assure myself, to mistake the living for the dead. Happens all the time, especially when walking down a street and someone you miss, but know has died, appears for sometimes minutes at a time until you realize that longing has caused you merely to mistake an identity.

I turned back to my gin and tonic, letting the ice rest against my lower lip. Margo and I had often met at that bar, before and after her marriage to the black lawyer, before and after my affair with her.

Pressing the cool lip of the glass against my chin, curiosity and even dread forced me to twist my head over my shoulder in another effort to contend with—my visual error, or this apparition— whatever the woman might represent. Her profile was clearly outlined despite the dim light. Were she a specter, her figure would not reflect in the mirror directly behind her head, but from my angle I could not test the legend that ghosts do not reflect. Though the shoulders of the pinstriped man shifted as he talked, the woman's head was cocked to the side in considered concentration on the man—precisely as Margo would have charmed anyone, by attentively listening.

The woman lifted a tumbler of clear liquid, a yellow wedge of lemon impaled on its rim, toward her red, smooth lips. Her skin was luminous, gardenia satin stretched over taut high cheekbones. I stared, fixated, at the glowing auburn hair cascading over bare shoulders.

If that were in fact Margo, the drink was water, and her hips, hidden now by the table, would be too broad but disguised by the careful cut of her shimmering dress. And her eyes would be too wide apart, the imperfection obscured by eyeliner and subtle mascara, the skin between them slightly pinched from nearsightedness. Her hair would be dyed. Yet she astounded now as much as always. Or at least the woman seated near that dim corner astounded.

"I want armies of men to follow me."

"So you can deny them?"

"But not you, Robert."

"Hey, can I buy you a drink? You look so sad. Like you need a friend. Anyway, at least a fresh drink." An older man in a blue suit, pearl cufflinks winking at his wrist, eased himself between me and the bar. Black hairs, which caught my attention, curled around his silver watchband encouraging me to nod 'yes' before musing that a drink could commit me for an evening, or even a night. Or if the fellow were married, which his attire hinted, a quickie in the bus depot john, or the very raidable steam bath on Clark Street...after a phone call to the wife, of course. It must be my own, male, 'I'm-hungry-so-who-cares-what-or-where-I-eat' attitude that made me wonder if I, too, didn't want armies of men to follow me.

While Cufflinks gestured, trying to get the bartender's attention, I spun my stool around to once again view the woman with auburn hair. Did she have green eyes, like Margo?

I drained the drink I'd bought myself and started on the bribe the older man had now shoved into my hand. "Gee, thanks," avoiding the man's glance, moving my leg away from where the blue thigh had begun to press casually. Let the guy believe he'd made a mistake. You can't tell the players without a program, friend, especially not here. There are advantages to being a chameleon.

I mumbled to myself while fixating on what appeared to be Margo, "But I can't believe..."

Cufflinks glanced at his watch nestled in the black hairs. "A lovely creature," quick to observe my preoccupation with the woman in the far corner. "I'll just make the train for home. Enjoy your drink." His blue suit was already edging through the crowd toward the door.

Oh, back to the suburbs, the dog and kids, and the wife who can't quite grasp your kindly indifference to her; embarrassed and threatened, because if I were hetero, maybe dangerously religious, I could turn belligerent, even to blackmail. But, fella, you didn't make a mistake, I wanted to apologize to the retreating back. I'm just remembering, caught between some disparity in time when my friend blew her lovely brains and face out over her bedroom walls with not one but two bullets from the handgun, the first shot misaimed, barely grazing her flawless cheekbone and embedding itself in the molding near the ceiling.

What nerves were there left to pull the trigger twice? What determined panic kept synapses firing after the first miss? She must have tentatively raised the gun again to probe the muzzle through the fall of hair over her temple, struggled to reactivate her swollen finger tight against the trigger, fumbled—finally managing to slide the barrel along the ridge of her high cheekbone and shot again, the second bullet tearing her.

I eased myself off the bar stool and, drink in hand, stepped into the crowd, drifting toward the small wrought iron and marble table, staring at the woman as her cascade of auburn hair caught the muted light. I wondered who the man in the pinstripe suit was, remembering that on many occasions I had hunched forward in that very chair telling Margo all that I dreamed for my future and receiving her gentle warnings but often enthusiastic approval. It may have been the way Margo expressed herself, or the studied poise evidenced by the sensual crossing of her legs, the receptive state of her pale green eyes, that often made me surmise that much of her encouragement was not authentic. Just as

her appearance was more a pose than a reality.
"I care about your paintings."
"Why?" Careful. I needed the praise too much.
"Their colors. The artificiality..." pausing to dab
with a Kleenex at the lipstick veneering her sensual
lips. "Later, tonight, you'll show me more of your
canvases. I feel close to you through them."

I stopped within a foot of the round marble table,
swaying in confusion directly behind the shifting
shoulders of the pinstripe suit, assuming that,
viewed closely, the woman would prove not be
Margo, that Margo still rested, rotted in her
grave...that at least something in my involuntary
sub rosa existence might be taken for granted.
Though I had begun to stare right at her, she seemed
unaware of my lanky presence, the obsessive
blinking of my eyes. I sipped my drink. Pinstripe
would soon become aware of my reflection in the
wall mirror opposite him, merging with what could
be Margo's in the distorting beveled edges of the
squared segments. My brown, cow eyes and lightly
freckled skin danced in the refracted light and the
moving shadow just beyond what appeared to be,
but could not be, Margo's head.

More on impulse than after a considered decision,
I found myself leaning over, about to address the
apparition, to make my move before Pinstripe could
prevent it—at the same time realizing that if the
woman were Margo in fact, and not some discomforting trick of time and memory, she'd be wearing
the enormous, gross diamond on her fourth finger
right hand, a gift from one of the richer johns
entertained the same year as my affair with her. But
only on Friday nights had she intrigued this one.
"Tell me about them. Your hordes of men."
"Besides you, there's only one now. Never come

to see me on Friday nights."

"You're phasing out of the business?"

She sat up in her bed, tucking long legs under the black silk sheets, her neck bent. Exquisitely. Like the imitation Ming horse I had given her: defiant. "I'll tell you about him," dragging quickly on her cigarette, then just as abruptly stabbing it out in an ash tray.

"I don't think I want to hear about this one."

"I want to tell it, and that should be enough. He has a wife and children and I'm like another child to him. It's simple as that. He never touches me. I merely sit for him...naked. He's a very dear man. We exchange...confidences, I guess you'd call them. And interests. We talk about Chekov sometimes...his plays, you know. And Dostoevsky. And he tells me I'm beautiful. Over and over he tells me that."

"He pays you for what you want?"

"It's no loss to him. He's old, but I love him. Once he touched my thigh and then...we couldn't talk anymore that night. I invest the money he gives me. In bonds mostly. Do you think I'm a fool? God, Robert, you exhaust me sometimes. Your pigheadedness exhausts me." Reaching into a large pink jar on her night stand she began smoothing Queen Bee Jelly with her pinkie finger very gently under her eyes. "And you lie. About yourself. About everything. Don't you think an underground lady would know about an underground man?"

I began pulling on my pants. Buttoning my shirt. "Our sex is normal enough."

"For whom, my dear?" Margo shrieked with laughter. The enormous diamond glowed where her fingers fluttered over the black sheet. "The words sex and normal should never be used in the same sentence. No one would know that better than you."

The idea of the diamond absorbed me. If the woman wore an icy blue stone, then I would have to accept that the dead return— that no reminiscence of them could be dislodged and that they might appear at whim. I edged closer, looking now over Pinstripe's shoulder. The man still hadn't become aware of my reflection as he continued leaning toward the woman, talking, talking, shoulders shifting. His head remained bowed so that I couldn't make out his features in the mirror. But his hair shone black and straight, as though ironed. Like the lawyer that Margo eventually married.

I hesitated before actually addressing the woman. Besides, anxiety dried my tongue. First I would have to discover if she did or did not display the diamond ring and then decide if I should have the temerity to interrupt their conversation. It was then that the woman, maybe Margo, stared haughtily down the long row of tables, head cocked, hair cascading over one ear, lips moving as she talked, her perfect teeth for a moment glistening. I strained to hear. I caught not a word but managed to observe her right hand, the fingers curled around her drink glass garnished with its wedge of lemon. No diamond flashed at me, but the long lacquered nails, precise and false, were familiar and startling.

Yet perhaps this woman purchased them in the same store as had Margo, the color, crimson, being common enough. Her other hand, the left, remained hidden from me on her lap under the table. Then I recalled that Margo wore the ring on either hand, depending on whether she wanted to appear available or not, even after her marriage. Again, the woman's mouth moved, talking. But not for long, just like Margo, whose words had always been concise, stark, dramatic.

*"It's downhill from now on, Robert." This after
the Kennedy assassination. And when the assassin
of the assassin died suddenly and mysteriously in
the asylum before he could testify, she pronounced,
"It is finished!"*

"Another drink?" The cocktail waitress in a long
glittery gown, red tray balanced even with the
sequined strap overlaying her shoulders, glared at
me from behind catty eyelashes. My drink was
almost full. Maybe she felt suspicious, possibly
alarmed that I hovered for no apparent purpose over
that marble table and its oblivious occupants.

I placed my glass on her tray. "Sure. Freshen this.
It's gin and tonic," grinning companionably to
assure the waitress that I wasn't drunk or malicious.
"Tanqueray," I added, as though a select brand name
would cover for my apparent lack of purpose. I had
learned long ago to deflect unwanted curiosity with
a brusque, self-assured manner. I had managed to
hold on to my teaching job even though, years
before, I had been informed by the department chair
that if I didn't marry, and soon, I could kiss the job
farewell. "This institution can afford only responsible
faculty," not as apology, but as frank opinion. And
threat. So when Margo brought up the idea of
matrimony:

*"Despite your predilection," she suggested, "we
could protect ourselves. With each other."*

"And from each other?"

"That too, dear one."

I had thought about it. Hard. Invited Margo home
for dinner with my parents. My father was fascinated by her, even a bit walleyed and slobbery from
the intrigue she emanated. But my mother: "Marriage, yes. But with a whore, for Pete's sake?"

"I don't mean to say goodbye." I leaned against

the white wall of Margo's apartment, between two slick aluminum chairs with white cushions, near the Ming horse on a glass table under a tall lamp. "It's just that I can't approve of all of you."

"Then you approve of nothing in me. You're cruel, Robert. I've had to make do with what I've got."

"It's not that I object to your profession. My life is no Hallmark Card." Then I said it. "I'm embarrassed by what you look like."

Margo shivered in a kind of nervous terror. Her hand, as was a habit, caressed her hip. She stood in the doorway of her bathroom, body and head toweled in white, clasping a douche bag, its nozzle trailing on the tiled floor. "There's something ludicrous about two people arguing about who they are. It's a sad kind of funny, Robert. Really." She whipped the hose, snapping it around her neck where it clung like a featherless boa. "I'm going to flush you clean from me. Wash you out of my cunt, honey. Want to hear me talk like a whore? Go fuck your queer self, babe. Get jabbed real good." She bent over, hands grasping her knees, but whether laughing or sobbing, I couldn't tell. Then she straightened, her eyes green and glassy. "For little things I cry. For big things I stand like this, staring." Slowly she unwound the douche bag nozzle from her stately neck, let the bag fall with a squish to the floor. "At last I'll have an evening to read the Dostoevsky. Russian authors, at least, have no sense of ever wanting to end anything they had sufficient wit to begin. As for you, the only vital painting you do is on toilet paper. Now get out!"

The waitress was waving her red tray displaying my refreshed drink under my nose. "Excuse me," she said with a young girl's high-pitched lisp, "but

don't crowd the folks behind you. Bar rules." So I
was being observed. My curiosity had been evident.
I had to do something. "That'll be a dollar please,"
she squeaked as I reached for the glass. I tried
fishing two dollars out of my wallet—a tip that
generous should shut her up—but I couldn't open
the wallet with the drink in my hand. Didn't dare
return the drink to the tray because the diminutive
lisper seemed now to be an adversary. Without
thinking, I turned sideways and observed with
surprise, and even shock, my hand that held the
drink clatter the glass down on the same marble
table that I and Margo had shared so long ago. I
stuttered out, "I'm sorry, really. May—may I rest
my glass there a minute?" The woman who would
be Margo, yet couldn't be—I'd been to the grave, her
name there in the granite—tilted her regal chin,
cheekbones casting long shadows across her face,
and grimaced, presumably at the clank of the glass.
Then she smiled vaguely, almost invitingly, just how
Margo would have taunted any man.

Pinstripe turned his head, sharp black eyes
glinting from dark skin, a wiry walrus mustache
twitching with irritation, to announce dryly in a
startlingly deep voice, "Sure, take your time about
it, buddy."

I tried to remember what Margo's black lawyer
husband looked like. I had only met him once, at
an outdoor art fair, and recalled vaguely that he was
tall, surly, and gripped my hand with evident
distaste. Pinstripe's present sarcasm caused my
heart to trip while I managed the two dollars onto
the waitress' tray. She bobbed contentedly, knees
pushing at the sequined dress, then darted off
through the crowd.

I returned to my confrontation with what must

represent my past. Though it was difficult to catch my breath, I explained, "Just didn't know what to do with my drink for a minute."

"Join us. Please do." The woman removed her purse from the empty chair, arranged it on her lap. A ring? The same hand that had held her garnished glass reached for the purse, so I couldn't be certain yet. "We were talking about... Yes, what were you talking about?" smiling at Pinstripe. Preparing to light a cigarette, with evident disdain she slid a silver lighter toward Pinstripe who indicated he was accustomed to the honor. Naturally, in order to have armies of men you've got to at least challenge as you proceed down the line. That had been Margo's flaw and charm.

I slid into the empty chair. The wire back dug into the skin under my brown suede jacket, so I leaned forward, my face inches from the apparition that might be Margo.

Pinstripe chuckled without mirth or charm, "Have it your way, then. You always do." He straightened, crossed arms over his suit jacket which was carefully tailored and pressed, the shirt underneath white as his teeth, a pristine handkerchief peering out of a lapel pocket. An offprint of the white oppressor.

"Darren, here, who is a lawyer, was telling me about a case of his wherein this dizzy 'working woman', or so he calls her, comes down with this awful, incurable disease, obtains a gun from a Mafia connection she's met while 'on duty', shall we say, blows her head to smithereens...all quite justifiable and of course understandable, her disease, something strange, turning her to stone, all her organs solidifying...."

"Scleroderma," Pinstripe interrupted. "A disorder of coal miners and young women."

My back stiffened with apprehension. Margo's disease, her mode of death, precise, exact. My tongue thickened. I tried moving it dryly along my teeth. "Probable causes are coal dust, or makeup." My hand shook as I pressed my drink under my lip. "Sure," and I stared at the auburn-haired woman next to me, "I've heard of the disease."

Her green eyes—yes, they were green—seemed to burrow into mine.

"Well, it's all news to me." Pinstripe had ignited her cigarette and she tossed her head back, inhaling, eyelids mercifully closing.

In panic, I glanced into the mirror behind the woman's head, searching the image of the bar for a friend, an acquaintance, a former trick, anyone! to distract me, hopefully to annul the horror that breathed through me. But all I could make out were the vague forms of suited, hulking strangers. No help from the bar crowd. No escape or excuse to exit the very situation I had pursued, groped toward, and apparently wanted to rub my nose in...the memory and even the love. Margo had always seized me with her pretense of a body and her layers of makeup meant to mask her honesty, her courage and intelligence. As though she knew that no one could directly contend with her essential magnificence, she must have contrived her mannequin façade to shield others from her real depth.

The woman yawned, her carmine lips stretched and then pursed. "And so, as Darren, here, tells about his case..."

"I'm brought in on the case because..." Pinstripe hesitated.

She filled in. "The woman's husband, colored, gets accused of what looks like murder. Now who's going to properly defend a black? God, I practically had to sneak Darren, here, into this bar, tuck us around this dark little table in the corner. And him dressed like a tycoon and all. And with him a lawyer, as I said." She turned to me, "You gotta name?" Her eyes flashed. The question was abrupt and, that late into the conversation, unexpected.

I returned her stare in wonder. Wouldn't she know my name? And yet this woman didn't speak as Margo had spoken, with condensed accuracy. And Margo would never have interrupted the man accompanying her, even if her ultimate intent were to dismiss him.

"My name is Robert."

The black man stuck out his hand, and I experienced a distasteful squeeze as our palms pressed.

"And you're a painter?" The woman blew smoke in my face, lips curling, playful.

"How could you know?" I felt that I must have instantly grown pale. My heart beat up in my throat. Ghosts can't reflect. I strained to see, but her face was so near to me and the beveled mirror so close to her head, that I quickly exhausted any attempt to discern whether she could replicate herself or not. I gulped my drink, an ice cube smacking my teeth.

She squashed her cigarette suddenly and forcefully into an ash tray. "You've got blue paint under your fingernails, so all I'm asking is whether you paint walls or canvases. That was an innocent enough observations, wasn't it?" She pouted at me, blinking slowly, then added, "I hope not walls. Blue walls are repellent. I like all walls to be white, white as a Russian winter."

With a shiver, I felt my Adam's apple rise toward my jaw. I shifted my leg away from the chair, preparing to stand, to stride out of there, away from the bar and into the street so that all of this, whatever was really happening, would stop. It was the word 'Russian' that did it, the land whose writers Margo coveted, and the fact that, almost imperceptibly, this woman's language had altered, refined itself, become more succinct.

Beginning to put weight on my left foot, I noisily cleared my throat and dared to toss off, "Your case, Darren, sounds like Crime and Punishment, but in reverse. Yet mirrored, echoed. You know, the novel by that Russian whatshisname."

Aware of my shift in posture, Darren offered, "Don't let us hold you back from joining your buddies at the bar." He gestured behind his shoulder. So, my predilection was obvious to the streetwise lawyer. Is that why he had permitted me to remain at their table for even a brief time? Had he known me to be a former lover of his wife—but apparently he didn't!

Margo, for it must be Margo, out of space and place, laughed deeply, confiding a code word from her past, "Dostoevsky? Oh, that's the book you mean." Bantering, flip.

"Cut this crap!" The lawyer belligerently stuck out his lower lip at Margo. He must hate her reading, her caring about books he wouldn't concern himself with, her distancing herself, which is what reading often is.

I watched her for a reaction to her escort's insult. Except for the slight shudder of one shoulder, her pose remained stoic, the light glancing with an almost imperceptible cast from a vague shift of her green eyes...which connected, for a second, with mine.

Despite my fear, my wonder and confusion, I sensed my lips jerk into a smile that froze instantly into what must be a sordid grin...of acknowledgment regarding where reminiscence can lead. I struggled to rise from the uncomfortable chair, from this disconcerting situation, and hovered for a moment over the woman who I had every reason to believe just might be Margo with her husband-lover-trick-pimp.

"Don't forget your drink there, buddy."

The moment seemed delicate. This inadvertent stumble into the past that I had hoped was buried proved to be stultifying. Obediently, I reached for my drink, hand shaking, listening to what remained of the ice knock again the glass. "See you around," attempting to arrange my lips into a sincere and apologetic, if nonchalant, grin.

"Oh, yes," the woman pressed herself to attention. "Around, of course."

As though memory were what I was going to be made of. No choice whatsoever. Trying to balance on knees turned to water, I backed from the table. I pivoted dizzily and began threading my way toward the bar.

"So, you've read the Russians," I thought I heard her call after me. As though my attempt to obliterate Margo from my memory were a specific crime for which I must now pay. Or was the crime my initial involvement with her?

Pinstripe's gnarly voice snarled over the cocktail chatter, "We've had enough of that guy, enough!"

"Margo, were you sleeping? The phone rang so many times, I was about to hang up."

"I always sleep now. You know that."

"Are you getting worse?"

"Do we have to talk about it?" After a pause, *"Robert, do you love me? Even with me like this, so ill."*

"Of course."

"I've never asked anything of you before. Not really." Margo's voice went soft. I pressed the telephone close to my ear. Only her breathing came over the wires and then her challenge, "You're not saying anything."

"Lighting a cigarette."

"Well, get settled." Silence. Finally, "You want me to...cry my anguish?"

"No, I...."

"Soon the muscles of my face won't move at all. Shall I tell you again how the skin on my legs has darkened and become hard...." The breathing again, steadily, deeply. "I want to live! But I can't. Please, Robert, get me lots of sleeping pills, a gun, anything! I can't endure it. The waiting. But I want to live...."

"That's why I shouldn't do...what you've asked. And besides, why me? I could be held as an accomplice to murder."

"I'm dying. Turning into a rock. Does that make you squirm? I'm sorry, I have to be so careful with everyone I talk to. I have to make them happy...those who come to attend me. But I've got to do something before I get...more repulsive. Just to know I would have that safety at least. That I could control that much."

"Somebody else can get you a gun. You said someone would. Your husband, maybe."

Her voice rose, a restrained shriek, "I can't pull the trigger. My fingers won't bend."

"Then live!" I held the receiver away from my ear, shut my eyes.

She whispered, "To love you again. I love my husband. But, Robert, I've always loved you more."

"We will always love. Can you hear that?"

"I must hang up now." Her words spilled into

mine, obliterated them. "Remember...."

As though it had been a commandment!

I reached the bar, leaned against it, shoulders brushing the other men. Handsome, many of them. Their eyes, even with mine, searching for the warmth, the intensity, the agreeing to desire. I drained my drink, even nibbling at the lime. But no men now, with the weight of reminiscence crushing me. Not tonight.

Placing my empty drink glass on the shiny counter, I observed my fingers around the glass refract in the glowing mahogany surface, murkily visible in reverse and in chiaroscuro. Yet my fingers kept grasping the wetness that streaked the glass as though I couldn't let go of my memory of Margo, nor did I think I would ever want to.

PART II

The Back Country

15

The Stone

It was late, near midnight, as I bicycled out to what I believed to be my secret cove. At least I had never seen anyone there. The inlet was rocky but with rivers of sand—almost white in the half moon—running among the igneous boulders. Having hefted my bike on my shoulders, I meandered down the cliff past black shadows. The tide was out and chunks of broken coral gleamed, pale as pitted bone.

A week before I had bought the bike for ten dollars and was still very aware of its importance to me. Though thievery on the island seemed to be unknown—no one even locked their doors— my Chicago heritage made me cautious. Because my friendship with Ralph had grown tepid, I felt I could no longer rent his transportation, his freedom or whatever it is that vehicles of all types represent. With Margo back in the States and Jessamine publicly cavorting shamelessly with her Peter from Poukeepsie, I felt as alone as I've ever been. Just me on a tiny spot of land, a thousand miles from anywhere.

With a bottle of rum as a friend, my intent was to indulge myself in the bathos of isolation. Leaning my bike against the cliff, I kicked off sandals and wandered through broken shells toward the water, my knapsack with the half-full rum bottle gurgling on my back. I already knew that the goal was to transform loneliness into solitude, but I remained too emotionally jarred to bring that about.

The only child desperately needs friends, lovers, and their own children. They live their childhoods as starvelings. They are the hungry nobility, the wretched aristocracy. They remain forever the pawns of others. Their precarious position in the hierarchy of existence prepares them for unfulfillable expectations. And a sense of being always culpable, because without siblings to share the blame, if you didn't do it, then who the hell did!

When I was tiny, my father took me for a walk over a bridge that spanned a river he said he used to ice-skate on. Though it was summer and I rustled in my short-panted silk sailor suit with the glisteny black kerchief around my neck—we'd just been to the birthday party of one of his old girl friends—he told me all about how the river froze solid, and when the snow wasn't too deep you could skate for miles and miles. Well, I already knew that because he'd told me before. So I tugged impatiently on his sleeve, "Why are we just standing here?" I squeaked.

"Because," my father said while leaning over the railing, "it's right here under this bridge that while skating one day I glided over a frozen baby under the ice. It was staring up at me."

"Were its eyes open?" I demanded to know.

"They were shut," he said. "The babe was in a shoe box," he continued while squinting down at the murky, rolling water. "Face up, though. Mouth open with bitty bubbles caught in the ice."

I knelt down on the wood, sticking my curly head out over the water, my father pulling me back by my shiny tie, "Was it a boy, was it a boy, was it a boy?" I excitedly shrieked.

Soon after that I began searching garbage cans—where I knew shoe boxes were likely to end up—for a brother. A cute, bubbly one. Morning upon morning after my father had gone to work and my mother was in the basement doing laundry, I rummaged. While the rag man shouted his plaintive "Rags, rags, bring out your rags" as he whipped the flanks of his skinny horse, I searched for what I never found. I did occasionally come upon shoe boxes, but all they contained were wispy wraps of tissue paper.

My butt nestled comfortably in the sand as I leaned against a rock and twirled the cap off the rum. "Pride of the Islands" the label boasted as I held the bottle up for the moon to strike the amber. I took a swig, joying in the harsh sting as it seared my throat. Now, having no choice, I would at last come to terms with my fear of loneliness. They put criminals into isolation cells for their benefit, I tried. Benefit my ass, hissed a wave. We all die alone no matter what, I attempted to assure myself about the commonness of my plight. Not surprisingly, that knowledge did not help. Love, if I ever attain it, would be but a momentary illusion, as I had already discovered. Experience didn't mollify me either.

I sucked on the bottle, letting trickles of rum bite my tongue as I wallowed deeper and deeper into sorrow. I scratched my back against the rock and stretched my legs out into the still warm sand. I was beginning to enjoy myself enormously. Not that I managed to annul my terror, but with each burning sip—the stars drilling my eyes with their icy indifference—I gradually eased my way toward accommodating misery. My intention always has been not to dismiss inevitable unhappiness as an enemy, but to embrace it lustfully as I might a sexy companion, because what we try to escape pursues us. It's best to welcome whatever there is that is, hold close to misery and fear and whatever embarrasses you and become one with them all. Or they'll get you.

I wriggled out of my pants and shirt. The moon bathed my skin with the winsome glow of the unworldly. I scrunched deep into the sand. Already half-erect, I admired myself and stroked the swelling sleekness, gently, gently, watching it rise toward the moon. I secrete when I even think about sex. Always have. No spit necessary for this one. I oozed an ambrosia, slick and gleaming.

I stood, the bottle in my left hand, right hand tugging my balls and kicked through the sand to where the Caribbean snaked phosphorescent froth onto the beach. The slight breeze laved my body with the blessing hands of an overwhelming, almighty something-or-other. I tucked the rum bottle in the shadow of a rock and began galloping through the shallows—spray sparkling over my body in a veil of fire, penis slapping my stomach. All god because all animal, I turned and plunged deep into the water. The sea felt warm as blood, and like the only child I am, I tried to impregnate the entire universe. I yawped at the bursts of spewing stars, ambitiously stretching to penetrate the glowing cascades of the Milky Way.

* * *

Better to get with child the heavens, I concluded the next morning while stumbling unsurely out onto the Gable's porch, than to get with child real women. It was Sunday and Mr. Edmonds lingered over his coffee while slumped in his wicker chair. He eyed my disheveled appearance with alarm. He already gathered that I had begun to drink too much, and might have guessed at my now lonely state since it so approximated his own.

"What did you do until so late last night?" he sniveled into his cup like a furiously jealous parent.

"Went swimming," I decided to inform him.

"Heard you struggling up the steps near dawn. With a-thunk, a-thunk, a-thunk." His grin was even more infuriatingly wan than usual. "My friend, I care." His gold eyetooth flickered.

I thought how we weren't friends, we were replicas, and no one dislikes anything more than his replica. "So what did you do last night Mr. Edmonds? Toss and turn in your crib?"

He sputtered, "None of your business." He angrily twirled his foot with the gray or just plain dirty socks that frumped under his ankles.

I was about to inform him that my escapades with my desperate body were likewise none of his business when Daisy—who must have heard or sensed our bickering—had the dignity to intrude herself under the guise of providing Mr. Edmonds with a bowl of unrefined sugar for his coffee.

"Oh, Mr. Sweet, have you ever been to Concord Falls?" she suggested. "They is a lovely tumble of water I hear. They be some ten mile down the coast road. Never been there myself, but all visitors must see them. It's Sunday so no trucks or buses will force you off the road in your new bicycle."

She was impressed by my bike which was painted orange with blue wheel-spokes and pedals. On the island, it was equivalent to owning a Cadillac.

"Yes, go," said Mr. Edmonds. "I've never been there either but have been told the falls are a splendor."

In an action rife with the contempt with which lonely people can treat each other to fortify and exacerbate their loneliness, I moistened my third finger, swathed it through his sugar bowl and carelessly sucked the sugar off onto my tongue. "I'll go all right. To Concord falls where you've never been."

Mr. Edmonds peered into the bowl and then focused on my finger. "That was nasty," he said.

I stiffened the finger at him and trounced down the stairs, thinking that now I had managed to exile myself from the Gables, my home away from home. And by total accident into the horrendous wonders of a world I would never know again. It would all begin under Concord Falls that Sunday when I had nothing better to do than to go where I had never been.

Angry at both Daisy and Mr. Edmonds for, as I saw it, dismissing me from their casual brunch I knew would follow, I sped off on my bike fueled with rage. There's nothing better for empowering tendons than unrighteous anger. That is, until the heat of noon began to take its toll and my hangover bowed my head which dripped with sweat. My breathing had become stertorous, when a native guy pulled alongside me on his bike. He was ugly as a still attractive guy had any right to be: crooked nose, glaring popped eyes and a navel bunched like a pile of orange peels. His pecs, however, bulged, and the nipples on his dusky bare chest stuck out like fretwork on a downy quilt. "Youse go Concord, sir?" he called out.

I mumbled absurdly, "Yes, to peace," while gasping at the humid air. I stopped my bike whose blue-spoked wheels were barely turning anyway and imitated him by clawing off my shirt. We were miles from St. George's and the shirt-on-in-town rule no longer applied. On one side of the road waved a field of sugarcane, on the other rustled deeply shaded rows of bananas. He pulled along side me and blinked his enormous eyes. I instantly bonded with him as to the brother I had never found. "Is that where you're going? To Concord?"

"No place else for a length and some." He scratched under both gnarly armpits. I fantasized his leading me to a burbling brook where we'd lie down on cotton grass, our legs slowly twining about each other's, fingers fumbling with our belts, but he said, "Soon as youse got breaths back, mun, Ise race ya." He nodded at my orange bike and its blue wheels with awed appreciation.

To Grenadians, slow and easy are the passwords to acceptable behavior. I could only suspect that my whiteness mounted on my splendid machine spurred him to so American, and for him, risky a challenge.

We were off, him in the lead, my eyes glued to his high, firm butt and the streaming of his bristly hair. He stood to pedal furiously, the knobs of his spine throbbing above his belt. I heaved myself upright, stabbing at my pedals, swearing that I would never drink so much as a drop of rum again, while wondering how far, God, how far down the road must that babbling brook be—when his front wheel hit a rock and he was down, long legs and arms twitching at the road like a tarantula in death throes.

So much for sensuous slides down smooth embankments. I back-pedaled and braked, narrowly missing his moaning head. The stained whites of his eyes glazed in the sun while a still-spinning wheel whirred over a crumpled foot. I jumped off my bike, letting it tumble into a shallow ditch beside the road, and leaned over him. My ideal self assumes I'll react with skill, compassion and efficiency when confronted by an emergency. Actually, my legs shake and I forget to breathe. I slumped down onto my knees and decided to take his pulse, which turned out to be shallow and fast. Other than having proved he was alive, I didn't know what that kind of heartbeat meant, so I said what everyone says at a moments like this, "You'll be just fine," while thinking how brash and foolish it was for him to race me in the wretched contraption he was riding.

He rolled his head on the cracked macadam. "Ise hurtin. Me leg..." He pointed to the one under the wheel. I saw that it was gashed, blood seeping through the wiry hairs.

"Can you move it?" I decided to perform professionally. I actually had begun my college experience by majoring in biology, thinking that I might want to be a doctor. But while trying to discern a vein from an artery in a split-open cat—arteries had been pumped with red dye, the professor claimed, veins with blue—it became evident that my color-blindness would prevent me from passing Anatomy 101. To my eyes, the blood on my racing buddy's leg glistened sticky black. "Try moving it." I reached to touch the leg. It moved. I felt along the entire bare limb asking does this hurt, does that. When I got to his thigh I observed his lack of underwear and the wrinkled length of his foreskin. Since he hadn't shouted out in pain during my ministrations, I concluded he would soon switch from shock into survival mode, so I decided to while away the time by asking his name.

"Throckmorton," he wheezed through a clogged nose. "Me is Throckmorton." I was glad he repeated the name because black names are typically so startling that whites need to be assured they've heard correctly.

"I'm Bob," I introduced myself.

"Mr. Boob, sir," he clutched my arm wincing from the motion. "Ise needs medicines."

"But from where?" I stared up the empty road.

"That there way." He gestured in the direction we had been racing. "In Concord."

I hadn't realized Concord was a town as well as a falls. I had never come across a map of the island. But then I'd never looked, believing that one's sense of adventure gets stifled if you know where you're going. Besides, as Melville wrote, "True places are not on any map," and I've always pretended to seek out true places.

I wriggled his bike out from under him and helped Throckmorton sit up. His head pressed against my lap, and I began to hope we might spend the rest of the afternoon glued to each other in the heat on the empty road. I couldn't carry him, so I adjusted myself under his rancid armpit like a crutch. He gathered his feet under him and we both struggled upwards, he taller than me by a foot. In this manner we staggered off toward Concord like Civil War survivors oblivious of color, though he continued to refer to me as "sir". And I continued to be intrigued by Throckmorton's blackness.

My introduction to passionate love and how I got imprinted to blacks had been with the only Negro student at my college. America in the fifties was so repressive, so physically and mentally thwarting, that Negroes who were prevented from joining the mainstream were by default freer than anyone. They were forced to be alive, while whites were choking-off their own existence. Whites had to toe the line, obeying what their society demanded. Negroes were only told to stay out. But they wanted in. They wanted their piece of the pie. How badly they wanted in could not be believed by me who only wanted out to where they were. To me, that pie was dolloped with poison.

Throckmorton, his arm across my shoulder, kept collapsing against me while whining, "It hurts, mun." Finally he brightened up enough to ask, "Is youse, Mr. Boob, sir, from Hamerica?" and I had to affirm even his mispronunciation.

"Why you here on the island?" His right leg still bled and I watched blood dribble onto the road. He was so heavy that I tended to keep my head down seeing only my tennis shoes and his bare feet while his sweat mingled with mine.

"To go see Concord Falls?" My question hung there, strangely rhetorical, as we stumbled around a bend in the road where a building of white stucco announced itself to be "CONCOR CLN" in partially peeled blue lettering.

"Medicine, medicine," Throckmorton enthusiastically squeezed my neck in a tight embrace.

As we hustled through the grass, still hooked together like Siamese twins toward what might be a medical clinic, I thought to ask a very American question, "What kind of work do you do?"

"Ise tend to things," he said.

That didn't tell me much, so I wondered, "Where do you live?" Throckmorton's response came quickly, "Anywheres, mun."

Because I feared that after he entered the building—where I knew the care was free as the British had socialized medicine even then—I would never see him again, I mused aloud what I had been curious about since we met, "Are you married?"

Throckmorton snickered as I helped him over the threshold into the waiting room. "No mun with sense marries." He glanced at me sideways as though suspicious as to why I would ask such a silly question of someone so obviously intelligent.

The waiting room was windowless and stuffy. Bare benches straddled the walls. Only a few turbaned women occupied a far corner whose children sucked at their breasts with frail smacking sounds. I propped Throckmorton on a perch near the door and arranged his legs straight out in front of him. I glanced at his wound. "Bad one," I bravely observed now that he was within a doctor's reach.

"Hit stings," he commented crossing his big arms over his chest. "You sits with me, Boob sir?"

"For a minute," I said adjusting myself beside him. "I've got to go back for our bicycles before long."

"Ise forgets theys," he grinned at me.

Since Throckmorton apparently had no work, no particular place to live, and was not married I became curious about his belief system. "Do you have a religion?"

"Huh?" he responded.

"I mean, it's Sunday. Do you go to church? Have a God?"

"God?" He glanced at me quizzically.

"Yes. What is God to you?" I had decided to turn myself into an anthropologist since I seemed not to have done well as a doctor.

His eyes rolled up as though he might be thinking. One of the children began to whimper and the woman in a blue turban hushed it. "God's a stone," Throckmorton tossed out. Then he laughed. A high, strangled sort of laugh. The women stared at us.

I laughed too. Our chuckles filled the waiting room. "I've never heard that one before," I chortled. "You mean like the stone that just almost killed you?"

"That too," he said.

"God is a stone?"

"God is in, not of…nothin'." He slapped his good knee as though he'd struck on a profundity.

Which maybe he had, so I pursued, "So where is this stone God of yours to be found?"

A black man who might have been the doctor—soiled white smock, greasy stethoscope swinging from around his neck, smudged eye-glasses circling beady eyes—appeared from the back to choose Throckmorton for his next patient, ignoring the women and children.

I helped Throckmorton up and headed him toward the doctor by patting his tight buns as he twisted his head around to whisper, "Stone God behind Concord Falls. Not in, but of stone, behind. Which youse knows all along. Thas why youse goes there, Mr. Boob, sir. Aaaamen!" And he sniggered hysterically as the doctor grabbed for his hand to lead him off.

16

The Falls

By the time I had returned to the clinic with both bikes in tow, Throckmorton was waiting for me, his leg swathed in a bulky bandage. He sat on the front step, the knobby knees of his long legs even with his ears. He smiled engagingly. "Thankee, mun." He rose to hobble over to his bike and lean on it.

"You can't ride with your sore leg," I cautioned.

"Ise walks. Bike for crutch now." Dragging the injured leg, he began wheeling his bike through the grass toward the road.

"Want to show me where Concord Falls are?" I called after him.

"No."

"Where are you going?"

"Jus goin', mun." And he waved haphazardly without looking back.

The heat was overwhelming. I blinked constantly in the futile effort to keep sweat out of my eyes. The whiny rise and fall of cicadas whirred from tall palms through whose sporadic shadow I watched Throckmorton enter the road and turn left, back toward St. George's. He seemed to have dismissed me with so casual a gesture that when I reached the road I felt I should avoid him. In order to do so I must go to the right.

I followed his wheel tracks through the weeds, barely escaped being thudded on the head by a careening coconut, adjusted my behind on my orange and blue vehicle and slowly began pumping my way toward Concord. Or I think it might have been the town of Concord I finally reached. There was a boarded-up, sagging post office and a store made of thatch from which I purchased three bananas, a box of cookies and a tepid coke. I ate and drank right there, squatting next to the bike. Between the former post office and the little store ran a rutted road leading into the interior. I asked the plump and sour lady at the store if the falls were up that road. And she said, "You goes there? Why you goes?"

I didn't know why I was going so I didn't try to explain, but assumed that her reply meant I would be traveling in the correct direction. Also, the road into the back country was lined with the thick branches of ferns arching under tall gum trees beyond which I heard the rumbling of a stream. It was cooler riding that road and I eagerly breathed in the smell of dampness and decay as I slowly and gingerly wheeled my way around potholes of stagnant water.

My sense of being deserted intensified. The only charitable excuse I could offer for what I felt to be Throckmorton's rude retreat and the store woman's impertinence was that afternoons on the island were so hot no one even pretended to communicate. Occasionally I passed flimsy shacks of unpainted wood with rusted corrugated tin roofs, but I saw no people. Or dogs either, which permitted me to relax a bit. Sometimes through an open window I would spot the cords of a hammock swaying as though someone rested there. Tropic afternoons are best survived by remaining comatose.

I could not count myself a sensible survivor. The only moving creatures other than myself seemed to be lizards, scuttling around puddles and darting along tree limbs, their long, thin tails streaking after them like comets. Now and then I halted my bike to chat with them. Well, I was lonesome.

Also, I'm not much of an adventurer. That's why it had taken me some seven months to head myself, even inadvertently, away from the sea and toward the island's interior. To tread into the unknown alone heightens the simplest experience to an almost unbearable pitch. At least it does for me. When you're with someone, nothing seems insurmountable. Alone, one sees and smells and potentially fears everything. I assume that's why we put up with each other's foibles as well as we do.

But moving further down the deserted road toward an

unknown, with the intensified screech of cicadas shocking my ears and the shiny folds of leaves bigger than people blocking all sight, I was reduced to animal wariness. I decided to walk my bike in order to permit my natural instincts to respond. The one advantage of being by yourself is that you can always decide when not to proceed.

The road wound upward. Rocks began poking out of increasingly crumbled strips of macadam. Then a fallen gum tree blocked my passage. The tree had collapsed not many days before because the leaves remained unwilted. The backs of them flashed silver in the sun, all thrust forward from the weighty crash of the tree. I decided it was appropriate to turn around. Maybe some other day I would try again to reach the falls. Besides, the vegetation that had crowded both sides of the road had abruptly given way to glistening white boulders, some big as houses, with flat tops and steep sides, and the sun beat down ferociously causing me to blink back torrents of sweat.

I was turning my bike when out of the corner of my eye I noticed a woman seated on a heave of macadam, her back against a rock in a blue slant of shade. She wore a wide-brimmed straw hat. A straw handbag lay cradled in her lap. She did not move or speak. The shadow cast by her hat prevented me from seeing her face. Other than that she sat upright, I could almost assume her to be dead.

"Hello," I shouted over to her. I thought I had pitched my voice in a friendly lilt, but there came no response. I wheeled my bike nearer to her thinking that it would be polite and very Grenadian to at least pass the time of day. "It's a hot one," I offered.

Her bare, cracked feet twisted in toward each other. "What's youse do here mister sir?" I watched her scrape scum off her lips with the back of a dusky hand.

"Just wandering about." I was beginning to sound as evasive and obscure as Throckmorton. While taking in the glittering rocks and smelling the dampness, I tentatively licked my own lips. There are some places steeped in natural beauty that one senses to be unwelcoming. And the tone of the woman's voice did not reassure me. It was raspy and thickly spittled. I couldn't challenge her by asking what she was doing there because she appeared to belong as did the rocks, and even the crushed gum tree, and the lizards—one who had just skipped across her lap, the tiny dragon as undisturbed by her as she was by it.

"Youse takes sun walk, mister sir," she apparently tried to explain my presence to herself. "No good to do. And not here."

"Why not here?" I glanced around. "It's wonderful here. Are the falls near about?"

"Behind theys rocks," she said. "Now you gets you back to big town." She fetched a sugar apple from inside her bag and carefully began to chew on it. She only had one tooth hanging in the front so she had to push the apple over her gums and into her mouth where presumably a few remaining stumps might facilitate mastication. Saliva and apple bits spouted out to dribble down her chin. "You gets back to big town before you troubled," she coughed and thumped on her chest. "We ain't seen one of youse around... Now you be goin', mister sir."

I felt quite affronted. I suspected what she couldn't abide about me was my whiteness and I wanted to explain that like her I hadn't much to do with what color I was and couldn't we just be friends. So I challenged her, "You don't think I have any right to be here?"

"Thas whats Ise says," she said.

I decided to be bold. "Because you were once a slave, or rather your ancestors were...I had nothing to do with all of that."

"White man devil," she said.

My temptation was to lecture her on the fact that the people from whom she was descended also kept slaves and that's how they got sold to the Europeans in the first place, but I decided it best to let that slide. I did however lean my bike against a rock and seated myself cross-legged on the road near her in an effort to indicate that, devil though I may be, our conversation could well continue.

She reacted by heaving herself to her feet and tugging her straw hat down over her ears. "You no go, I go," she announced. "But youse be beware." She slung her straw bag over one shoulder. Without another word she began strolling down the road in the direction from which I had come, her bare feet easily traversing the jutting rocks and the boiling heat rising off what remained of the macadam.

Instantly I relapsed into a dreadful despair. I watched two vultures gliding soundlessly on motionless wings high near a cloud above me. Cicadas chattered like infernal machines through the tiring heat. The back country apparently wanted to have less to do with me than even the town. Or my own country, for that matter. I must be a pariah. I seemed unable to dance to anyone's drumbeat and all were eager to let me know just how clubfooted I was.

To avoid further confrontation with Throckmorton I had continued toward Concord rather than return to St. George's, and now I felt disinclined to follow the woman for the same reason. If you don't want me, I'm not there. I'm not going to apologize for my life-long defensive behavior, just simply to confess my inability to behave otherwise. So now I was trapped up the road I had been more-or-less forced to travel. Despite warnings and personal misgivings I was determined to tough it out since I seemed to have no choice. At least I would tough it out until the lady racist had time to reach whatever destination she intended for herself. To her friends and family she might be going to tell her tale of the white devil encroaching on their territory. I shuddered to contemplate their reaction.

But then Daisy had described the falls as 'a marvelous tumble of water' even though she had never seen it, and Thockmorton had insisted his stone with a god stuffed in it would be there, and the lady with the shadowed face had admitted that the falls fell beyond the high rocks, so I resolved to carry onward, reluctant warrior though I was, approaching a zone of magnified power still hidden from me but somewhere within the aura of danger inherent in places such as this.

Leaving my bike where it was, I clambered my way between and over large, slippery rocks finally hearing the thunder of what must be the falls as I came upon a narrow path leading downwards. The sun slammed against the rocks increasing its intensity. The whooshing sound of water made every cell in my body desire to be bathed in it. Need and desperation, not devotion or ambition, can cause nearly everyone to do nearly anything. In retrospect, reaching the falls seemed a minor task, at the time however, the freshness of the experience and my tendency to approach any unknown with almost pathological caution turned what should be easy into a trial.

It was my feeling isolated—and having been forewarned—that transmogrified me into a hero of sorts. After all, herohood is as relative and personal as anything else. We start from where we are and go to where we can. The more you take in, the more horrendous each confrontation with the world can become. Mountain climbers, sky divers, car racers must be very dull and unimaginative fellows to demand so much exhilaration.

I slid down a final embankment to face a world that seemed not to have been touched. Or was I in New Guinea, Borneo, or my own liana-infested unconscious? Entering between two last boulders, I found myself in an enclosed valley lush with tree ferns, drooping banana leaves feathered by the wind into a semblance of Archaeopteryx wings, and crowding trees so thick with foliage as to appear purple through the mist rising from the falls. I stood near the river, my sneakers sinking into a cool swamp of green water. Near me, water reeds furled in waving clumps, and scatterings of heart-shaped plants with large lily-like flowers mirrored themselves in the quiet slough.

I quickly shed my clothes, weighting the bundle with my sneakers on a rock, and stepped naked into the stream, careful to avoid the sharpest stones, gradually feeling my way along a strip of sand. I have two rules when hiking, even in my own country: the first is that nakedness, weather and insects permitting, is mandatory in natural settings; the second is that directly proportional to the physical and emotional effort you've invested in reaching the point of your disclosure, the more nudity just has to be acceptable. I've suffered considerable embarrassment by following my second rule. Since Grenada, I've traveled back country in much of the world and can attest that after the age of five, nakedness tends to be a cross-cultural taboo. I suppose that's because of all animals we're the most salacious and must try to disguise ourselves from the fact. 'Who told thee thou wast naked?' wondered the Old Testament God, astonished at Adam and Eve's chagrin after the serpent beguiled them.

So I relished my nakedness while remaining suspicious of my rights, therefore I dipped into the cool water to cover myself as soon as I reached the deep pool under the falls. I almost yelped with joy because my body felt delicious enveloped by the whirling stream, each eddy and swirl tugging, caressing and laving my every part. I stretched out my legs and arms, floating and twirling in a vortex like Leonardo's anatomy drawing of the proportioned man, imagining my cock and balls glinting from wetness and the sun.

I was raised to despise my body. I perspired through torrid summers of all my teen years in long-sleeved shirts and baggy, heavy pants. Not until my junior year in college, when I finally gained courage to imitate meticulously other guys taking a shower, did I learn to wash properly. Bodies, I had been taught to believe, were disgusting. Whatever bodies emitted was disgusting. Since this attitude was primarily encouraged by my mother, male bodies were understood to be particularly detestable. Which may explain why I often saw my mother naked but never my father. Mother was a real goddess on the hoof, using me for a mirror while tolerating her husband as would an insect for one nuptial flight and henceforth as a begrudged drone.

I pressed legs and arms tightly together and lunged backwards deep into the pool, touching the smooth rocks when I scraped along the bottom, reaching out to merge myself with them. I sought to become united with the water and indistinguishable from the moist air I bounded up to gasp into my lungs.

The falls gushed through a cleft of black rock a hundred feet or so above my head. The stream tumbled directly down, the white cascade widening until it roared into the pool in sparkling clouds. Embedded in the dripping rock on both sides of the spilling water clung tendriled plants, ferny and thick-lobed, and one yellow-blooming acacia bush dripping and waving from the booming spray. The noise was tremendous, obliterating rather than alarming, lulling my senses, tempting me toward the ego loss requisite for attaining solitude. I was well aware that had I not been by myself, and had I not felt rejected by all I had ever known, I would have experienced my immersion into the waters under Concord Falls as a mere pleasure and not this luxurious baptism in the font of wholeness.

Then I saw him. Standing stock-still, the bare foot of his left leg lodged against the knee of his right, the leggy triangle outlining the path I also had found to approach the river, the whiteness of the two giant boulders outlining his dark shoulders. He looked to be near my age with a bristly head of hair so thick and black it coated his head like a helmet of ink-dyed isinglass. He wore only short dark pants of a very thin material. Around his neck circled a bulbous, black car inner tube, its color and texture so resembling his skin that it looked to be a yoke supplied him by his own body.

How long he'd been there I couldn't be certain. Surely he had witnessed my abandon, my cavortings, my nakedness. I had to assume he resented my presence as had the toothless sibyl. I politely buried all but my head in the water and paddled just enough to keep afloat while warily eyeing him fearful of racial antagonism. Were he a color-bigot, I was mince meat. Well, that's what I get for blundering into what might well be forbidden territory. And me exposed as a pellucid grub adrift in a puddle.

The more alarmed I am, the more strident my voice gets. "Come on in," I splashed water in his direction attempting to appear relaxed and playful. "The water's fine." Platitudes have been known to rescue many a desperate man, I hypothesized on the spot.

I think he was staring at me, but I could not be sure. The sun was almost behind him and the rocks had begun to cast shadows. Either his eyes were closed or an umbra of darkness obscured them. His body looked to be squat rather than tall as was usual on the island, yet solid with more beef than fat. His right leg remained implanted in his left as though he were a swamp bird or an African hunter stalking prey. I clawed my hands up onto a dry rock and kicked demurely, proceeding with my charade of nonchalance. My bare butt must be protruding beyond the water and I felt woefully vulnerable. The constant crash of the water was so terrific that if he had responded to my invitation I probably would not have heard. I peered down the river into the valley.

"Hey, youse," I finally descried him calling out, "youse Hamerican?"

I kicked on while responding with a forceful burst of voice, "And are you Grenadian?"

From a side glance I noticed him shuck off his shorts and wade rapidly into the pool while adjusting the inner tube around his waist. He collided with the water amidst a splash and then floated inside the confines of the inner tube, his head propped near the protrusive nozzle. His wet muscled chest with its spatterings of kinked hair reflected the sun and glimmered like a metal shield.

Believing that gestures rather than words define human interaction, our shared nakedness and his obvious unconcern regarding my presence encouraged me to relax my guard. I dog-paddled over to where he floated and sputtered, "This your swimming hole? What I mean is, do you live near here? My name is Bob but I'd rather you called me Robert."

"Boobert?" he mis-echoed.

I decided it would do no good to correct him and so proceeded to inquire, "What's your name?"

"Name?" he questioned as though thinking. He had a very African face, wide nose, thick lips and a very round chin. "Youse calls me Junior?" he suggested as though his identity were in question. He smiled, his very white and perfect teeth aglitter. His smile, should memory prove me correct, was poignant. Not especially welcoming, nor sarcastic, but poignant. With a wisp of spittle riding one corner of his lip.

Since I had to keep paddling in place while addressing him, I began to exhale frothy spouts of water until he suggested I cling to the tube, which I did. I let my legs drift alongside his. I felt the current push our thighs together. He shut his eyes, his heavy lips settling into a grin, blissful as the Buddha. I could not even guess how he might have come by the name of just Junior. In my mind I named him Celestine even though I did not realize yet how Catholic the island really was, how the Anglican Church centering my favorite cemetery was more for show than worship. As the Catholic Church well knows, he who gets there first masters imaginations. And the French colonized the island long before the British. The further back country one meandered the further into the island's past one journeyed.

"Hang tight," Junior warned as he began to backstroke us toward the falls, the thick hair of his armpits shaggy from moisture. The stream whirled in circles the closer to the roar we got. Speech became impossible. A cold wind off the falls made me shiver. I glared at him in alarm. My lips must have drained to a wormy pink. But because his poignant smile remained fixed, I didn't let go and swim back to shore. Our thighs were still enmeshed and so when he reached for my hand I let him grab hold and fed my fingers through his while squeezing my eyes tight against the stinging whips of water.

The tube plunged and spun—with me screaming—somehow through the roaring spray and beyond. Eventually I dared open my eyes and there the watery veil poured, heady with exuberance, screening us from the valley. Behind the falls where we bobbed the water lapped serenely. I saw that it leaked in rivulets through cracks in the rocky wall. All felt calm, safe, strangely comforting. Junior indicated where I should stand on a submerged boulder where he was to balance next to me while pushing the inner tube onto a jutting, dripping shelf. With his arms he pulled himself up onto the shelf beside it, his dangling sex swinging like an animal's under his crack. After he had turned to yank me upwards with him, I had no trouble walking the shelf behind the falls to the far corner where he led me.

I crouched with him in the twilight of our cave where, yes Throckmorton, some sort of god must abide within the leaking slags, because Junior and I leaned back against the rock so close our shoulders touched and I felt engulfed by the aura of where we were, as though in a temple, sacred and profound. We began to touch each other. Our fingers lingered, stroked and pulled until the sheets of tumbling water grew whiter and shook as with the spasms of a ghost. When I finally returned to inhabit my body, the valley that lay beyond the falls seemed to have slid into the sudden violet dusk of evening.

Was Junior now Boobert's friend? I had not a guess. Such is the closeness that occurs within the confines of a tremulous thundering where speech is useless.

17

The Bridge to Somewhere

Junior maneuvered us out from behind the falls as easily as he had swept us under. With help from the half moon, I located my clothes. I was grateful for the warmth they offered. Being sprayed for hours by watery spumes had set my teeth to clacking. Junior walked me to my bike which still leaned undisturbed against the rock. Neither of us had said anything, but as I lifted my transportation to aim it back toward Concord he cleared his throat. "In four nights Ise meets with youse. In big town. By bridge."

"What bridge? Where?"

"Queen's Park. The water be St. John's water."

I got on my bike and began threading my way around rocks—since I had no lights I was again thankful for the slippered moon—and thought to call back, "When?"

"Nine," I thought he said.

There he stood encased in the inner tube, the dark of his body gathered up in shadows. I shivered. Love is dangerous. At least the kind that grows on need is. It's like a dung beetle whose gorgeousness depends upon offal. I already knew that. I hunkered down on my bike pedaling like mad through the miles of oppressive darkness, passing an occasional hut and its kerosene lantern, and dogs who scurried from the whir of my wheels while yipping.

I had three days and nights to cool my heels. I don't recall talking to anyone except Daisy whom I told how wonderful Concord Falls were, avoiding all prurient details, of course. Mr. Edmonds, though he heard me raving to Daisy about the beauty of the falls, remained understandably frosty, even protectively securing his sugar bowl under the armpit of his wrinkled coat while sipping coffee. Daisy said that since I'd enjoyed the falls so much, just maybe I might want to rent the cottage on the shores of Grande Etang, the volcanic lake in the middle of the rain forest. "Four dollars a day," she enthused, "and a cook comes with." I didn't know whether she was trying to get rid of me or whether her almost motherly concern for me inspired her to act as a guide. I decided that her motive was inconsequential so far as I was concerned and tucked the idea into my memory for future reference. Had she or Mr. Edmonds ever been to Grande Etang, I asked? They both laughed, fluttering fingers in front of their faces in denial.

"No liquor there," said Mr. Edmonds. "Just monkeys, or so I hear."

I wondered if that wasn't a warning to me. I did drink too much. I hadn't fallen down yet or acted in any way more ridiculous than when sober. But mornings especially my breath must reek since I drank mostly late at night in an effort to bring about sleep. But then an alcoholic stupor was affected by the islanders who could afford it. Because rum was cheap, that included much of the population. It was just that Daisy and Mr. Edmonds drank before dinner, not after, and I had begun to be a before and after kind of guy. Like the natives. I have noticed how, the world over, alert consciousness is considered to be an intolerable state, which only goes to prove what a curse most humans consider awareness to be.

While waiting for Thursday night to arrive and my possible meeting with Junior, I did write on my novel which now attempted to characterize a number of the male faculty at the prestigious high school where I taught who were having affairs with their eager female students. All true, of course. I have only ever lied to protect others or to salvage my reputation. Gay people are born to lie. Or be jailed. Our lies are lies of omission, however, not usually commission. We live with the knowledge that others tolerate our existence easier so long as we keep our mouths shut.

I also kept reading. I had discovered Grenada's remarkable if small library where, thanks to British planning, every book was a jewel. While waiting for my assignation with Junior I remember perusing *The Journal of Albion Moonlight* by Kenneth Patchen. I kept imagining Junior as Albion, because when last I had seen him he was outlined by shadows wrapped in moonglow.

Thursday evening after dinner I pedaled off toward the St. John's river, an unopened rum bottle stashed in my knapsack. I had not the slightest expectation Junior would be at the bridge, or if I would even find the bridge he might have meant. Certainly it could not be the bridge that crossed the main road that followed the shore, so I turned inward on a dirt road paralleling the St. John's river in the hopes that the tangled brush and palms lilting across the starlight might be preserved as a park. Other than that there was an abrupt absence of shacks, I thought I could be nowhere in particular, merely riding into some valley unaccountably devoid of people. Finally I came to a small flat bridge spanning the narrow river. The moon had not tugged its way up over the mountains yet, so the stars were all I could see by. The bridge looked rickety. Boards were missing and water reeds thrust up through the gaps. The bark of tree frogs was so piercing I wanted to clap my hands over my ears.

I leaned my bike against a palm and arranged myself on the least splintery board I could find, my feet dangling over the running water. Because I did not expect Junior to appear, I had already decided to manage an evening's drunk out of the escapade. I had no idea where Junior lived and he had no idea where I stayed. He had no more reason to trust me than I had to trust him. Although I always do what I say, I knew that others did not necessarily feel equally obliged. And certainly not those from another culture whose sense of obligation may be nil.

I twisted off the cap on the rum. The first taste was as loud in my throat as the frogs stinging my ears. I heard the church bell clang once to mark the half hour. Must be eight-thirty. I couldn't make out the hand's position on my watch. Besides would Junior—should that be his actual name—want to meet me again? The island was his home, so surely he lived a rich life here. I was the stranger, the interloper, living a borrowed life which had recently turned sour. I wondered if I should return to Chicago. But the idea of home seemed to have gotten lost somehow and survived only as a grim recollection, distant and cold. My present desire included only him, this illiterate, barefoot, kindly savage with whom I had nothing to share except a greedy body and a needy soul.

The longer I waited, the more I hoped he would rescue me from myself. The church clock bonged nine times, I counted each one. The tree frog's barks choked the silence that followed. I lay on my back letting the stars drill my staring eyes. Encounters between males are not usually repeated because most men don't want them to be. Were it not for my crushing sense of need, I should react typically. But I didn't. Of course, it's easy to love what you don't know. Easy to be enamored of an illusion.

I propped myself up by one elbow and slid more rum down my throat. Fortunately I had never confused sex for love with women. I could dally with the most intriguing, dangerous types and emerge relatively unscathed. And be loved by them even more for that. My essential passive-aggressive nature made me the perfect love object for them. How they were trained by the society to be, I really was. I didn't know whether I had become passive-aggressive as protection against the criminality of my fascination for those of my own sex—you usually don't get arrested for not approaching—or whether I was genetically disposed to passive behavior, or whether somehow it had to do with my mother. Whatever, for me at least passive-aggressiveness has remained a highly successful defense against a hostile world. I recommend it.

Lying prone on the bridge, breathing deeply due to encroaching inebriation, arms stretched out in an attitude of crucifixion or ecstasy—I've never thought Christianity managed to distinguish the one from the other, nor can I—I gradually had to accept that love is a matter for loneliness to settle, for emptiness to deal with. At least erotic love is. Like tropical rain forest soil, it's shallow and not very fertile. But for youths fresh from the produce bins, there is no other love than red: sexual, greedy, and possessive. I feared that was what I felt for the unknown Junior *because* by ten o'clock—I counted all ten bongs—he had not arrived. Had he showed up, knees bent in supplication, I would be free to appraise him with the arrogance achieved from security. After all, you can't grovel before what you've got. But the frogs still screamed, the stars continued to bore pinholes through the iris of my eyes, and my need for him made my head thump disconsolately against the boards of the bridge.

I must have slept. Suddenly there he was standing over me, head tipped to the side, smiling and whispering, "Boobert? Boobert?" The moon curved its horn beyond his head and falls of its light splashed iridescent streams over his bare shoulders and chest. He hovered over me like a Colossus, wearing the same short, dark pants as he had before. His thick thighs tapered into muscled legs whose naked feet pointed into my armpits. His knees looked to be scabby and dusted with gray scales of peeling skin.

"You're late," I heard myself accuse him.

Junior tapped a wrist. "No watch."

"But the church tower clangs every half hour."

He swayed slightly while folding his big arms over his chest as though considering the possibility that, yes, he might have heard the bells but added, "Ise walks. From Concord."

"All that way?" It was at least ten miles, I realized.

He waved a foot with its callused, yellowish sole over my face as he adjusted himself to sit next to me on the bridge, legs hanging out over the stream. The curve of his back glowed. "It easy in the night," he said, "to walks far. Sorry Ise late."

"Time is important." I decided to remain on the offense.

Slowly he turned his sweaty head to stare at me over his shoulder. "Why is that?"

"Time is life?" I wondered even as I spoke where that idea had come from and why I framed my statement as a question. I edged my body over and swung my tennis shoes toward the water next to him. I wanted to touch him. I wanted to put my arm around his waist. But I hesitated.

Perhaps what occurred between us behind Concord Falls had been an accident of sorts. The taboos that held sway in the town of St. George's were typically Christian European. And those I understood. But back country I had no idea what the rules were. Nor to what extent Christian European hegemonies might have infiltrated the forest, nor for that matter what the original Nigerian mores might have been and to what extent they still survived.

I glanced at Junior. "Want a sip of rum?"

Wow, did he! After protracted swallows of the stuff he propped the bottle between his legs as though he owned it. Which was just as well, I decided. I had had enough.

"Lookee up there." He jabbed his black fist toward the stars. I watched as his second finger gradually freed itself from the curl of his thumb and pointed. "That there be Mars," he said. He chuckled, apparently happy to share this observation with me.

"I think I see it," I squinted. "That tiny reddish thing hanging over the mountain?" The stars were even brighter inland than they were on the coast and so to talk about them seemed natural. Other than the moon and the dark heave of a mountain and the onyx gleam of his body, the stars seemed to be all there was.

While scratching his groin he raised the rum bottle to his lips with his free hand and then carefully explained, "Only mad scientists lives there." He snugged the bottle back between his legs.

It took a moment for my mind to absorb this sci-fi fantasy emanating from lips that shouldn't know anything about that unfortunate genre. "Really," I finally coughed out. "How have you heard about the mad scientists?"

"Ise knows. Lots Ise knows. Youse just ax me whenevers."

"All right." I unlaced my shoes and took them off thinking that their whiteness looked somehow impertinent and out of place swinging next to his bare feet. "What do the scientists do up there on Mars?"

"Theys makes big bang things called...called..."

"Bombs? Nuclear bombs?"

"To blow all up. Scientists, they is bad."

"You mean as in Hiroshima and Nagasaki?" I tested his knowledge. What he said seemed all correct and wrong in the same breath. I inched my hand under his thigh as though by accident.

"What's youse say? That be gobblygook," he said.

"Those are the names of cities in Japan that were bombed." As our flesh touched, he did not flinch or pull away. I realized I did want more rum and so walked my fingers over his shiny skin to extract the bottle from between his thighs.

Before I managed the rum to my lips, his arm encircled my waist and he pulled me toward him. "Youse drinks too much," he laughed. "Ise drinks too much." He tousled my hair and stuck a finger in my ear.

I liked the finger in my ear. All was progressing nicely. But what did Junior really want from me? Ten miles is a long way to walk for a date. Especially since I hoped he understood he would have to walk back. The thought of his sharing my bed in the Gables was, for both sexual and racial reasons, out of the question. Daisy would have heart failure. Protective though she was of Mr. Edmonds who admitted slaughtering his mother, love between men would be a crime considerably more heinous.

My hand moved up Junior's thigh and under his short pants. James Baldwin, you were right, blacks can be immense. At least Junior was. Experience had already revealed to me that among blacks this was not always so.

"Now keep your eyes fixed on all those stars," I commanded Junior. "I'll explain something to you."

His big eyes rolled dutifully back, their whites luminous and veined as Carrara marble. His flattened nose and full lips made him appear to me to be the most beautiful comely man I had ever held. His finger began to stroke my lips while I explained, "Many of those stars we see aren't there any more. The light from the stars takes so long to reach earth that what we see now may not be there. Some planets may even have burned out or exploded. Stars blow up too." I wondered if I had even approximated a physicist's stab at reality.

Junior's eyes readjusted themselves, his brows dipping down into a deep crease that ridged his nose.

I rushed on, "So what we see is no longer there. Or might no longer be there." My student was rapidly losing his erection, and I imagine even Socrates might take that as a sign to cease his discourse. I speculatively felt along the warm underside of Junior's testicles.

He nuzzled my neck and licked in my ear. I wondered if he didn't have an ear fetish. He said, his voice husky, "Scientists tells you that what youse sees ain't?"

"Well, yes," I admitted.

"Bet theys knows what time it always is too."

"Always," I assured him. He undid my belt and had me out of my pants so quickly I barely had to shift my butt. "And yet to the scientists, time is relative," I mumbled on, feeling a soft breeze waft between my legs and then the fumbling of his hand. I guessed he wanted, but was not certain what he wanted, nor precisely how to attain satisfaction from what he wanted. Which was just as I had perceived his desires to be under the waterfall: curious and determined but faltering in his own curiosity.

We both reached for the rum bottle at once and snorted with guffaws as we shared the liquor, letting it dribble down our chins.

"Knows youse what's really funny?" he smacked his lips. "Sees you that there smiley moon?" His features assembled themselves into a frown evoking deep seriousness.

I wondered if there were a subtle battle being waged for who might master the field of knowledge. Or, to put it more succinctly, whose culture had the most convincing mental weapons. So far I felt certain that to him I had failed miserably. My claiming that time was of the greatest import and yet was relative—which I explained meant that time was comparative, that is to say fast and slow depending on...I had hesitated, confused—but I rallied to summarize my half of the conversation: "So what really is you can't see at all, and what you can isn't any more than an illusion," which only convinced him that the scientists of my skin color were precisely as he described them, quite mad and should be banished to Mars.

I decided to remind him where he'd been in our conversation. "What did you mean to say about the moon?"

"Not for sure that one," he grinned.

"OK," I said inching his shorts down over his reviving cock, "tell me what you mean." I caressed it lightly. He let out a throaty moan.

"That's St. George's moon. The big town moon."

"Yes?"

"Not the Concord moon."

"You live in Concord?" I stuck a finger in his ear. When in the throes of sex, do unto others as they do unto you. Let their actions be your guide. He yowled so loud the tree frogs were humbled into momentary silence. Yes, he had an ear fetish.

"Ise lives in Concord. When Ise don't lives other places. That how I knows St. George's moon be different from Concord moon."

"How is that?" I wriggled my finger in his ears to more predictable sighs of appreciation.

I withdrew my finger so he could compose himself sufficiently to continue. "Different moons over different towns. Always." He massaged my balls. Pulled on the hairs tentatively.

"How do you know that?" I challenged while thinking, good God, must every thought, every gesture, pleasure, pain between disparate cultures be so…disparate? And how dared I be enamored by that difference. And how dared he…if he was.

Junior eyed me directly. I thought I observed his lips tremble with earnestness as he proclaimed, "Because every town youse in… the moon, she in different place in that sky." He pointed upward as though assuring me that all he revealed was incontestably true. "So all towns and mountains has all times different moons."

"Or no moon at all?" I grasped what he meant and winced. Our space, time and causal continuums were perversely opposite. Only our bodies were ours to share. But should an insufferable sense of closeness indicate souls inhabited our skulls, maybe our souls as well.

18

Goat Skull

The sky had already begun to lighten when Junior and I decided it was time to part. The frogs had ceased their yawps, a cool breeze clacked the palm fronds, and the stars blushed out behind a scud of sunrise pink. Dawn terrifies me. It's like being caught in the grip of some monstrous revelation. Whether up all night or being forced to confront its approach by waking, dawn is the only hour in the twenty-four that you don't get to ease into. It may be like being reborn again, yet the moment of birth is a matter of blood and howling, something to be gotten through, more harrowing by and large than enjoyable for all parties.

With face drawn Junior said, "Now Ise goes." His fallen features looked to be registering guilt. Or was it just hang over exhaustion?

"Back to Concord?" I dreaded the thought of his ten-mile return hike. On impulse I said, "Do you want to borrow my bike?"

Silence. A long one. The stream giggled under the bridge as though chiding me for being so trusting. My whiteness meant money, his blackness meant poverty. I wanted to whisper back to the stream that though it wouldn't be easy for me to lose my bike, I didn't believe I would. Whether I was trusting or testing, it seemed worth it to me to find out what motives lurked behind his furrowed brow.

"Concord far." Junior stared at his feet. I stared at my bike. I had only a mile to walk back to the Green Gables. I didn't want material lusts to interfere with our rapport, but I had no intention of paying for love or being paid for it for that matter. In either case I would jeopardize my fantasy of people's caring for each other simply because they cared. There are some illusions I've felt it best never to dispense with. But then I had never met anyone as impoverished as Junior, so I tapped my foot impatiently waiting for his decision. Of course, if he just borrowed my bike as I suggested and didn't steal it, I would think no less of him.

Finally he smiled at me. "Ise likes to walk," he said. "Youse needs bike to go back to town with."

"But then how will we ever meet again?" I flew into a sudden panic. Now that he seemed to be noble, sacrificing, and concerned for my welfare, my need for him doubled on the instant.

"Youse meets me next. Youse come to me," and he held out a big callused hand I eagerly gripped. "On road to falls. Three shacks after tall white rock. On left, further up from falls. Skull on front. Skull of goat, where me mamman is."

I was to meet his mother? I was astonished. What had he in mind, for me to plead for his hand in marriage? I had seldom met a trick's mother before, nor did I cotton to the idea. I dreaded their suspicious glances. Fathers were worse though, and must be avoided at all costs. I hoped that Junior didn't know who his father was, which could be expected on the island.

"But why your mother? Can't we just meet at the falls?"

"Mamman says youse come. She sees you in stone, coming. Says no choice there is for youse."

I was incredulous. "You've told her about me? About us?"

"No," he said.

"I'm to believe she just knows?"

His eyes pierced mine. Though we may come from different worlds, I had already assumed from my experience as a teacher that intelligence can be predicted by the cast of light flickering from eyes. However garbled Junior's speech sounded to me, however unfamiliar and even bizarre his mind set, from the second we met his eyes flashed to warn and intrigue me. Speedy synapses seemed to wryly and whimsically fire and thus undercut his every word and nuance. His thoughts and actions struck me as duplicitous, not in the sense of conniving but rather laden with a multiplicity of implied meanings.

Junior strolled off the bridge permitting my question about his mother's knowing of me to remain unanswered. I addressed his back, "When?" Not only did he seem to have no sense of specific hours of the day, but the days of the week must be equally obscure to him.

He turned. Held his hands behind his back while contorting his body shyly in a gesture of mock compliance. "What's the day we goes under the falls, friend Boobert?"

"Sunday."

"Fine," and he waved me off as he backed through palmettos and ferns apparently to tread a path whose existence I could not detect. The leaves closed with a whoosh over him.

* * *

Cocks crowed and donkeys brayed and parrots whooped as I tiptoed up the Gable's steps to sleep perchance to dream, just as though my waking life weren't now the stuff that dreams are made on.

But I wondered why my daydreams needed to take a nightmarish twist while, next Sunday, I dutifully wheeled my way inland up the road to the falls, pushing against heavy winds and into the splatterings of enormous raindrops exploding across my face like tiny grenades. Grenades on Grenada, I muttered, pumping hard on the pedals. Pretty good. Brigadiers on Barbados. Hysteria makes me rhyme senselessly and alliterate. The tall gum trees clashed limbs over my head, tree ferns sighed and dripped. The more furiously I pedaled the more careless I got, careening through the deepest ruts, spraying water in my wake. Why didn't I turn back? My father taught me only one thing that stuck: finish what you've begun. Not because incompletion meant failure necessarily, but simply because incomplete meant you shouldn't have started in the first place. And if you never started anything, nothing could have meaning. He obsessively finished each golf game with that determination, even after he'd lost one lung to cancer. My persistence in getting to

Junior's shack had much to do with my father's example. Though my mission to join a black male lover in a jungle-thatched hut with a goat skull for a doorknob—or whatever decorative use there might be for a goat skull—would be to him grounds for disinheritance, institutional commitment, or both.

I passed the tall white rock the woman with the hat had warned me about progressing beyond, and was stopped once again by the fallen gum tree whose leaves had dried by now and rustled from the rain. I got off my bike and investigated the impasse. I must be very near my goal, should that high white rock—now gray and glinting with splashing water—prove to be the marker Junior had meant. I felt relieved that no particular time had been mentioned when I should arrive at his house. Because of the rain, I had slipped my watch off my wrist and into my pocket, frankly too tired to bother looking at it. It must be midafternoon, and that was all I needed to know. Surely Junior would not expect a white guy to go all that distance braving wind and rain. But then Junior's mother had apparently pronounced that I had no choice. With which the spirit of my father within me seemed to agree. So there I was, slightly shivering and wiping rain from my eyes, searching for a way around or under the collapsed tree. I didn't worry that Junior would not be home. Since leaving St. George's, I had passed neither people, dogs, or chickens. I was glad to have somewhere I was supposed to be safe at last from the storm, my journey in its own way as sacrificial as Junior's walk of twenty miles for an assignation with me. Tit for tat, to give is to get.

There was by now a cleared passage under the white-barked trunk through which I dragged my bike. I observed with relief that the road then curved downward. On the left squatted three rickety shacks with roofs of woven thatch, the furthest one graced by a skull, a small one. Yes, it must have been goat, whose horns curled up to catch the last drops and sparkled that moment in the first weak rays of sun. Tropic storms are like that. You never know when they'll begin, but can be assured they won't last long. Already the cracked macadam road steamed. A yellow striped woodpecker noisily drilled a tree. I heard what might be a warbler toss music through the air. Enchanting.

Until I neared what I assumed to be my lover's shack, to be accosted by a cloud of flies—a type of sweat fly I assumed, for they attached themselves to my forehead and wriggled over my thighs. I was wearing short pants. I leaned my bike against what must once have been a tiny porch—only broken boards remained—and whisked both hands and arms over my face. I called, "Junior? I'm here." I dodged gaps and protruding nails that marred the few steps. "I finally made it," I shouted. "Hello? Hello?" Since there was no door, I entered.

The room I walked into was devoid of people and furniture. The three windows lacked curtains, as though the occupants had moved out or fled. I noticed the traces of something heavy recently having been skidded across the raw plank floor. And then he came up behind me, both black hands closing over my belt buckle. At first surprised, I then turned and burst out laughing.

Expecting his usual bare chest with its steely pecs and pert nipples, I could not help being amused by the red sweater straining over his muscles. The sweater was much too small for him, its ragged hem frayed two inches above his navel. The sweater's sleeves were short and puffed into wilted flounces of exasperated yarn. Clearly, the sweater was meant for a woman or a trash can.

"Sweater gift, a gift from England. From the Queen. Special. Today cold. Rain falling for all time long. Why, my Boobert, youse laugh? I wears for you. Sweater from Queen big time." He swelled his chest while plucking at the puffs in the sleeves. He seemed to be proud of the sweater, as though it were a sign of knighthood bestowed by Elizabeth herself.

I compressed my lips and managed, "Did you get the sweater after hurricane Janet?" I remembered how during my first meeting with Jessamine she had told of the perils of hurricane Janet and that the British had sent warm clothes to the sweltering colony to signal their commiseration.

"Janet. Yes," he said.

"The sweater is nice," I tried to agree. Especially, I thought, the way it revealed his navel. Unusual for back-country Grenadians, his button was deeply indented as though whoever birthed him had gnawed off the umbilical cleanly. "But the sun is out now. Aren't you hot?"

"Youse takes your shirt off?"

"Sure." I pulled the T-shirt over my head and waved it about as a kind of fan to fend off the flies which I irritably noticed paid more attention to me than they did to him.

Junior yanked furiously on the sweater to extract himself from its tawdry confines while unaccountably muttering, "Now youse hears this. Ise walkin' down the road and Ise sees me brudder Jacob." He tossed the sweater into a corner on the floor and placed both hands on my shoulders while seriously searching my eyes. "And Ise cuts his head off." I thought of the poor goat's skull poised above the door and twinged with alarm. "What's it?" he laughed in my face. A fly walked the crease above his nose. He did not seem to notice.

"Huh?" I said.

He repeated again, slowly, explaining that what I heard was a riddle and that my intelligence, which he guessed must be superior to his on all counts, would be proved to him were I able to answer the riddle. "Hit easy," he assured me. "Listen. Ise walkin' down the road and sees me brudder Jacob..."

"And you cut his head off," I chimed in. "And so what is it? And that tests my intelligence?"

Junior's brow hunched in disappointment. He went over to one of the paneless windows and slumped on the sill. Clearly, I was supposed to have shouted out some obvious solution to the riddle and we would have been buddies forever. Helplessly I swatted at flies, reliving my childhood experiences as a dunce in all spelling bees and word-matching tests. Like a squid on the defense, I squirted out an ink cloud, "E equals m c squared?"

"No sense," came his appropriate response.

"Well, help me then. What in the hell really is Jacob's head you've cut off?"

He looked up at me, his lips compressed into a grin, his eyes brimming with compassion. "A hammer? A nail? A tree? Or a coconut." He tried helping by offering me a multiple choice exam, an educational device that also has left me stymied. I blurted desperately as I do under such circumstances, "A nail," guessing that the correct answer must be hidden near the middle of the word list.

"Ah Boobert, Boobert," he slapped at a fly entering his pant leg, "youse tries again. Ise knows youse can come to it."

Fortunately for me a woman's voice called from the shack's other room, "Juney? Juney? Has that man arrived?"

Junior stood. "Yes, Miz Samuels. He here."

I whispered into his ear, "Who is Mrs. Samuels?"

"Me mamman," he whispered back.

"You call your mother Mrs.?"

"Respect be proper," he said. "Come," he nudged me toward the room. "She be expecting youse." He stuck a finger into my ear and twirled it as though pulling wax out. He breathed into the lobe, "Head of Jacob be coconut. Coconut. Coconut," while chuckling hilariously as though even ignorance and a weak imagination were ultimately forgivable offenses. The tension between us now being defused, I snickered too at the shocking absurdities that continually separated our minds.

I eventually learned that riddles are African tests of wit and are known as Nancy stories. At the time, of course, I could only be grateful that Junior accepted my ignorance with such grace.

As I took in the room into which Junior steered me—its strangeness, mystery, horror and startling wonder—I was relieved that we had entered laughing. The visual onslaught that greeted me could have registered on my face as fear and loathing, reactions

I felt it impolite and possibly dangerous to expose.

Upon a bed long as it was wide lay an enormous woman whose stench must enamor the flies. Flies with golden bellies beaded the ragged sheet that partially covered her. Some of them flitted like winged, scuttling nuggets. The sweat flies courting my armpits were of a different species, I noticed. Junior urged me to draw closer to the bed. Through a buzzing cloud that rose toward the ceiling a woman stretched a light-skinned hand toward me and announced, "I am Mrs. Samuels. And what be your father's name? You are most welcome." Unlike Junior, her English almost resembled the Queen's. The yellowish mulatto cast of her skin in no way matched Junior's slate-black features.

I tentatively bent down to take her offered hand in mine, trying not to breathe, not to shudder. Her fingers closed firmly about my wrist, a pressure I first concluded was meant to pull me in with her—where ever she might be going. In retrospect I have decided her real intent was to be gracious, even ladylike, could a naked, fly-ridden woman whose watermelon breasts tumbled over fold upon fold of flesh be construed as partaking of dignity.

And yet 'dignified' is the most apt word I can find to describe her. She seemed to wear whatever disease that confined her to the bed as a badge of honor. Her face was noble, strong-boned, aquiline-nosed, with dark deep eyes, a fortuitous amalgam of the races that composed her.

I released her hand to swipe at a fly tickling my lower lip and stuttered, "My—my father's name?"

"What a handsome chest you have," she tossed out while adjusting her bright, glowing, moon of a face into a pile of rags serving as a pillow. I had honestly never been introduced to a female before while so scantily attired and I felt my face flush. "Now, what about your name?" she went on. "I have to know who you are. Your lineage. Juney, offer your friend a box to sit on. Sorry about the flies. But you get used to them. Eventually." She sighed.

Junior retrieved a wooden carton mounded with old newspapers he shook off and slid behind my knees. On shaky legs I lowered myself onto it. "Ise be back in some time," with which Junior abruptly left the room. I felt the terrible absence of him. I stared out the window at the twisted, gnarled trunk of a hacked-off tree for courage. "My surname is Sweet," I admitted. "Like sugar."

Very gradually Mrs. Samuel's entire body began to quiver and shake, her mouth finally gaped to expel a wheeze. "And like a cookie," she spasmed, fingers fluttering through her light brown, wavy hair. "Are you sweet as that?"

"When caught off guard," I responded from habit.

"Well relax," she said. "Be one with who I am."

A strange request under the circumstances. My eyes began to focus on the odd paraphernalia clinging to the wall at the foot of her bed near the window. Three wood boxes were stashed against the wall, a fourth balanced on top. Above, three goat skulls hung in a triangle within which dangled cat skulls and bird skulls arranged haphazardly around a human skull. Out of the eye sockets of the human skull jutted feathers of assorted sizes, colors and configurations. Below that was nailed a tattered, fading depiction of St. Patrick, his foot resting on writhing snakes, clothed in a vestment grasping a golden crook. The halo circling his conical, striped hat winked almost as gold as the abdomens of the room's whirring insects. 'I heard a fly buzz when I died,' is all I could think as I tried to absorb the Voodoo collage of an altar before me. Below the picture of St. Patrick lay a leather-bound, cracked and peeling Bible stained with candle drippings. The Bible rested on a slate slab, precisely the color of Junior's skin.

I went over to the Bible, curious to see what page it was opened to, and read 'The Revelation' and noticed underlined: 'I am he that liveth, and was dead; and, behold, I am alive for evermore, Amen; and have the keys of hell and of death. Write the things which thou hast seen, and the things which are, and the things which shall be hereafter.'

"Mrs. Samuels?"

"Yes?"

"Why is your Bible open to this passage? Why is it underlined in pencil? Did you underline it?"

"Who else?"

Despite her smell and the flies I went back to my box, sat down, and hunched over her. "I'm trying to be a writer. A recorder. An expresser."

"Why else would you be here," she stated, rolling onto her side so that only her bare back with its flawless, slightly yellow skin was visible. Where the flesh rolled around her hip, I focused my eyes. She was as beautiful and shapeless, as meaningful and meaningless as all magnificence is to me.

"But it was Junior who forced me here." My love for him, I thought but did not mention.

"Speak not of force," she whispered, "only of the inevitable. About all I know of things is that they're inevitable. Damballah-wedo is in me. The serpent spirit."

I glanced at the picture of St. Patrick trampling the snakes of the Emerald Isle. "And is that a portrait of your Damballah-wedo, over the Bible and under the skulls?"

Since my Voodoo marriage to Jessamine, I had not heard Damballah-wedo mentioned by anyone. And I had hoped never to hear of the chief of the Voodoo pantheon again.

She turned onto her back once more. With every breath her huge stomach heaved cascades of droning ingots. "Because I is of all races, white and Carib and Arawak too, with blood from home howling through me. Yes, hear this you Mr. Sweet, Africa howls through my veins. Know that I know how you came here to the island to stomp on your own snakes that make a feast and nest inside your skull. Damballah-wedo is a cannibal, chewing all others down himself." She arranged the rotting sheet over her breasts and demurely scrunched it under her layered chin. "Release yourself to he who knows. Lose, lose it to the joy in the stone. I am tired. This daughter of house slaves, generations back, exhausts. I am ill, for so many long years. I sleep now. Junior will feed you. Then you come this night to feed me also and I will...I will...when it is dark..."

The eyes closed in her lovely face, her mouth remained open, and a fly droned down to scale the tip of her furled tongue.

19

A Severed Tree

I wandered toward the back of the thatched cabin looking for Junior. Rattled as I was from my confrontation with his mamman—should that be who she was—I felt the need for a familiar presence. I had been plunged into a lethal but splendorous world whose trappings and every word and gesture alarmed as much as it fascinated me. I was desperate for a connection to counterbalance my own trepidations, which increased my desire for Junior, intensified my love or need. I've never been certain which was which, or if indeed both words are not irrevocably linked.

Night struck like a hammer blow. Tree frogs began their screeching and fireflies dazzled the heavy air. If there was a moon, no light from it penetrated the heavy canopy of drooping trees. Finally I came upon him where he hunched over a small fire about which were piled a semicircular ridge of stones centered by a collapsed chimney. Sparks from the fire so mimicked the whirls of fireflies that I almost passed it by.

He was naked. Well, this was his own backyard. Besides, deep in the forest as we were where no breeze could work its way in, the temperature remained tepid. I aped him by shucking off my pants and adjusted myself on a stone beside him. Dark skins merge with everything. White skins shine like beacons, especially in the dark. Though I felt awkward, I determined to enjoy every minute of it. Junior was simmering some sort of stew over a grill of twisted metal. I enjoyed watching him rise to bend over the pot which he stirred with sections of bamboo bound together to form a sort of ladle.

"How you likes me mamman?" he wanted to know.

"Is Mrs. Samuels really your mother?"

"As much mine as anybody's." Junior reached for two once-white enamel bowls chipped and dark around the lips. Awkwardly he slopped the results of his cookery into them. "She fine woman and mamman to me."

"But you don't look like her." I heard myself add with horror, "Or speak like her." Though his 'Ise' and 'youses' made it difficult to understand him, I swore never to correct his grammar or pronunciation, even though I made my living by doing just that in my own country. I didn't want to drown my lover in red ink.

"I speak your language when I wants," he said handing me a bowl. "It's just that it slave-master language, which mamman knows and taught me when she taught me too the reading and writing, but is not a good or proper language to use on this island. Bad memories. Bad...how you say? implications."

There seemed to be no utensils, so I tried dribbling the stew into my mouth. The thick mass was too hot and tasted like boiled barley. But since my pronunciation of English had been declared oppressive by my companion whose need I needed, I resolved to brave up to the food. By my second sip the stew just seemed strange, possibly nourishing. I was hungry and the mixture of sweet potatoes and other vegetables, whose tastes I failed to identify, might last me until I could get my hands on some rum to wash it all down with.

That the subtleties of grammar arose to separate the classes, I already knew. I just wasn't prepared to accept my speech patterns as officious and reminiscent of terror. So I mumbled into my bowl, "I'm sorry."

Junior, who had swallowed his dinner in a gulp, poured himself some more. I couldn't take my eyes off the velvet of his body. Observing the dangles, bulges and ripples of his seemingly inexhaustible grace made me feel, through him, joined with the forest, to its warmth and darkness.

"Have more," he entreated while watching me as I went to ease more stew into the bowl, my skin, I knew, luminous in the firelight, my body's hairs flaring chest and legs. I liked his staring at me, it made me feel alive. We seemed mutually connected. Junior's eyes permitted me to be.

I slurped the stew while posing in front of him, my back to the fire. "You can read and write then?" I had been as surprised by Junior's offhanded mention of his literacy as I was surprised by almost everything about him.

"I does both enough," he said stroking the hairs on my testicles. He was not very hairy compared to me. We were both becoming as wrapped up in our differences as we were in our similarities. But such can it be when races and cultures attempt intimacy of any kind.

"Enough literacy for what?"

"I can help sometimes others." Unbidden, his pronunciation, if not his sentence structure, was imitating mine. He accommodated himself to the language he despised, as did his Mrs. Samuels. For my benefit, obviously. But then, did that mean they both humored while despising me? I didn't know. I didn't want to know. "Like for my friend," Junior chatted on, "that the government charges for breaking his rib."

"What?"

"He breaks his rib, like Adam, and so he knows his girl Arabella will say her child is his. I writes letter for him to government telling he can't pay no matter what."

I sat back down next to him, my eyebrows lifted. "I don't understand."

Junior glanced at me slyly. "When man breaks his rib, he knows then for sure that child will be claimed to be his. Which is troublesome. Because government passes rule making man pay for all children claimed on him."

"But what's that got to do with breaking his rib?"

To my amazement, Junior stood, propped one bare foot on a rock, and began rhythmically slapping his thighs with both hands in a mock imitation of drum beats. He tipped his head back like a baying wolf and burst out in a smooth baritone,

"Adam in the garden, hidin', hidin'.

Adam in the garden, hidin' from the Lord.

Adam in the garden, he knows how Eve made from his rib.
He knows the Lord knows all he does to Eve is his. So..."
A long pause, and then,
"Adam in the garden, hidin' from his rib."
Another but longer cessation of both hands and voice, broken
finally by a running wobble and an extended embellishment of
the vocal line:
"Lordy mun, how Adam from his God he hides."
Appreciatively I clapped and laughed. But Junior glared down
at me. "Not funny," he said.
"But the song is funny."
He scowled. "Not to all them Adams out there hidin'."
I arranged my features into what I hoped might be an acceptable
frown. "I've been an Adam like that. Have you?"
Now Junior did laugh. A deep, uproarious, hiccuping kind of
spasm. "Not me, mun. Ha, ha," and he held his stomach while his
privates flopped.
We had a number of usual behaviors in common, I thought.
"But I still don't understand why you wrote a letter to the governor
because your friend broke his rib."
"You don't get it?" He backed near the fire as though to warm
himself. "Woman comes from Adam's rib, right?"
I couldn't imagine how to respond.
"Your Bible tells how that be true."
"Yes, the Bible does, but..."
"So anything that happens to man's rib shows what his joy has
brought about. I writes letter explaining that about my friend, but
that he poor and can't pay. Except some day when his rib come
back together. That will be a long, long time in happenin'. I signs
the letter 'sincerely your own' and has mamman correct it all for
me to make it just right."
"But do you believe the condition of a man's ribs are proof of
paternity, I mean fatherhood? What about sex?"
He brushed a mosquito away that danced in front of his eyes.

"Sex?" as though I'd dared a disgusting obscenity. "Sex?" he questioned again. "Don't know what you talk about." He managed to clap the mosquito between his hands. He showed its body to me, a dabble of blood and twisted legs, mangled against his palm. Behind him one log sank into the other and smoke and flames spired into the darting fireflies.

"Sex is this," I grabbed his crotch.

"This be just fun." He reached for me. "Don't have to write no government a letter afterwards." And we sparred and parried and funned ourselves over the stones and on the ground struggling to avoid the fire.

I gasped, "Nor have to worry about ribs."

"But it's ribs that do it," he insisted while squeezing me in an illustrative hammerlock. He could be rough, in a playful sort of way.

I was not certain then, but discovered in the following weeks, that Junior saw no particular connection between orgasm inside a woman and childbirth. His neighbors apparently didn't either. As it was eventually revealed to me, on the island spirits assured conception when the moon was full, especially under the yawning branches of a bo tree. A woman could be quite alone while accomplishing this feat. All she had to do was open her mouth and let some light from the Moon Spirit glide over her tongue. When I tried to correct Junior's version of reality by sketching in my notebook a penis and testes and a vagina and ovaries—which I scribbled with charm and a degree of accuracy, or so I told myself—he shook his head in disbelief. He was incredulous at the span of nine months to accomplish the miracle. It was like trying to explain to a butterfly how it was once a worm.

Junior cupped his chin into his curved shoulder blade to protest, "Nine fucking months?"

"You don't have to be fucking all that time," I calmly insisted. "Just once. Possibly."

"Better with you," and he wrapped an arm around my leg.

"Oh, I'm easier on ribs. I'll admit that. And, with me you'll never, like your friend, have to pay off the governor."

"You just fun."

"I hope so," I replied, not quite believing it. Nothing is just fun. All that we do has repercussions.

Junior left me snoozing on the sandy soil. I dimly heard him saying, "Got to keep pot hot for mamman when she calls." I felt the heat intensify when he added more wood to the fire, but I was so groggy from whatever ichors flow after satisfying sex that I failed to aid him, even to lift my hand.

I snapped awake, however, aware of my nakedness, when Mrs. Samuel's voice floated out of her window toward us: "Juney? Any food left?"

I had just lifted my head when Junior arranged my fingers around a full, warm bowl. He efficiently pulled my short pants up as far as my thighs and told me to stand. I carefully balanced the bowl as he zipped me up and buckled my belt. "You take dinner into her. She will like that."

Still groggy I padded around the house, once more managing my way through raised nails and gaps in the steps, to sway unsurely through the empty room. I was again startled by what I saw as I edged through the doorway into her room. Night had transformed it. Transformed Mrs. Samuels as well.

Whatever her illness might be, it had not crippled her into total immobility. Her bed flickered from the wavering lights and subsequent shadows of numerous candles that only she could have arranged about. Over the call of a nightjar outside, the candle's sputtering obsessed the room. Candles were lodged in every cranny available in her Voodoo shrine. They were affixed into holes in the skulls, their flames making the feathers protruding from the eyes appear to move, to flutter along deep shadowed runnels of space. Spires of incense rose, the smell weighting the air as though St. Patrick and the Bible were lodged in their accustomed environs. The place reeked of Catholic mystery, with the added depth of the even more direct Voodoo confrontation with death. It's not that I don't respect the profundity behind religious nonsense, it's the worshippers and believers I fear for and just plain fear, who mistake metaphor for the real and err by misconstruing symbol for fact.

Cautiously delivering Mrs. Samuel's supper into her waiting hands, I noticed that her head was neatly ensconced in a wound orange turban which she aimed at me while approximating a welcoming nod.

"Your back is covered with sand," she observed. "Where have you been lying, Mr. Sweet?"

I tried crawling my hand over my back. I heard sand spatter the floor. "Resting," I excused my condition. "By Junior's fire. I must have fallen asleep."

Sipping the stew, she whimsically responded, "Quite natural. Good food and rest, irresistible companions. You like my offering to your gods, my gods, and all the gods?" She waved stubby fingers at her altar.

"Oh yes," I politely assured her while settling back down on the wooden carton which Junior had earlier supplied me. "I'm sure your Damballah-wedo watches over you."

"But sir," her tone challenged, "I explained this afternoon how Damballah-wedo is a cannibal of the heart and of the mind. Like love." She glanced at me warningly, her lashes closing contemplatively over narrowing eyes. "Would *you* find comfort by being watched over by a cannibal?"

Frustration with her and my own desperation caused me to be blunt. "I too know God is a cannibal. Why else would we be created to be absorbed by him?"

"That's why you prefer to deny what is?"

"But I don't deny it. I—I merely play with it. If God made us from clay in his image, then I'll mold shadows of him as my fancy compels me."

Mrs. Samuels, evidently in league with meanings that are indefinable, subversive and beyond the ken of rational knowledge, proceeded by insisting, "But you can only create as the gods command you to. You have nothing to say but what they insist upon saying through you. They whisper, you transcribe. At best, Mr. Sweet, you are a secretary. Did you ever think you had anything to say?"

I was especially irritated by that remark, because when I had confessed to my mother that I wanted to become a writer she had triangled her plucked eyebrows to archly and rhetorically inquire, 'What makes you think you have anything to say?' I tried defending myself, 'It's showing, Ma, not saying.' She had only laughed, reducing me to devastation. 'Movies show every thought,' she pressed on, 'so what is there left for words? Scribblers are passé. Imaginations are on hold. Only what we see can release us from ourselves. Which is the object, after all, of entertainment. Devote yourself, Bobby, to making money. Money is the only sign of success we have. And I want you to succeed. Money, money....'

This parental recollection bothered my head and caused me abruptly to change the subject. Since I was involuntarily administering to, and I supposed amusing my lover's mambo mother, I shifted gears to ask, pleasantly enough, I thought, how Junior got his name. "Apparently from you," I probed. "How is it Junior came to think of you as his mamman? He doesn't resemble you much."

Mrs. Samuels rolled and heaved her languid bulk in my direction. She was attired in a house dress that served as a nightgown. It was purple, speckled with flowers, hyacinth and roses mainly, ripped under the arms. Her breasts lay enormously wrapped in sheaths of these shimmering flowers. Heady speculations on the nature of life and the gods took second place to her adoration for Junior and his origin. I could tell, because at my question her vast body curled itself under the rotted sheet while she muttered, "You wants to know about my Junior? He appeared from nowhere. Nameless, hungry, forlorn as wandering children tend to be." She passed her now empty soup bowl over to me, sparkling clean as a licked dog plate. "And I took him in because..." I stowed the bowl between my feet on the floor. "Because I had...destroyed, somehow, my own real son. Destroyed him through belief. Not in the belief of Damballah-wedo so much as disbelief in what I knew to be true but couldn't obey."

She arranged herself as comfortably as she could on her back, arms folded over the rise and fall of her tremendous stomach, short thick fingers interlaced. The yellowish cast of her face glowed from the flickering candles. "Have you noticed how outside that window," she squinted her eyes while adjusting her head into the pile of ragged cloths that served her for a pillow, "there is the large stump of a mango tree?"

I had noticed it, before the night fell while I first spoke with her and because Junior had forbidden me to go near it when we were out back. The trunk had been severed awkwardly with a twisted fringe of near-white bark along one side. Despite that, my intent had been to lean against it while he cooked. But Junior waved me off with the suggestion that I might be warmer by the fire, and I naturally obeyed him. So I assured Mrs. Samuels that I was aware of the severed tree whose roots undulated like molting pythons around the house. I had even tripped over them while attempting to reach Mrs. Samuels as I carried her dinner.

"Trees are life," she said. "That tree, the mango, grew and grew, shading us, my little son and me, the two of us content. And the tree fed us. It fed us well throughout the year. Year after year. And butterflies came to suck the rotten fruit and birds took their fill from them also."

I wondered what any of this had to do with Junior. But as Mrs. Samuels spoke, her lips mumbling over the richness of her reminiscence, I understood that I had been meant to hear this. For her enlightenment as well as for mine. It's not just that Mrs. Samuels was a natural storyteller, but that without the mechanical accouterments dependent on electricity—radios, movies, records and the like—people must imagine directly through each other the excitement of things. And for every storyteller whose confession is meant to exonerate their own souls, an audience of at least one has to be there to share it. I wondered if that isn't why she had predicted my visit. She needed my ears to hear what she must report. Junior knew this, of course, and remained outside so as not to interfere with her pleasure. As for me, I felt a tad abused and used, though at the same time privileged and awed. The crooning sound of her voice, the mesmerizing wafts of incense, the candle glow, and the occasional clear, hovering cry of the nightjar lulled my memory back to where it had never been, yet I recognized as home.

"What was your real son's name?" Mrs. Samuels had been so determined to know my surname and insisted I refer to her as Mrs. Samuels that I was curious as to why she had not yet revealed his name.

She hunched and rolled her bulk across the large square bed toward me. She cupped one hand around her lips and whispered, "Junior."

"Does Junior know he is Junior number two?"

"No," she shook her head. "And I'll trust you not to tell him."

I have always felt especially chosen when someone says 'I've never told anyone this before, but...' Even though, of course, it's almost never true. When, days later, Junior told me he knew quite well he was, as he put it, Junior Two, I was not surprised. At Mrs. Samuel's initial admission, though, I experienced a voyeur's thrill. I leaned toward her. "What happened to your son, Mrs. Samuels?"

"He gets sick. Real sick. Month upon month he begins fading away. Feverish and sweaty and then cold to freezing. And then just weak with watery eyes. He is six years old. His lips cracking. And when some blood smears off onto his tongue and teeth I know I'm going to not be able to stand it. So I run to a priest and plead, 'Come bless my child. Pray to your God to tell me what to do.'"

She couched her head with one hand and thoughtfully stared at me. "I am, for this island, educated in white man's ways. I've been careful, always, to take on only so much of black man's ways. For generations now our mothers has reared us to do the reading and the writing of which I am now worse at than any mother before me. But no matter, from slave-masters we in my family all learned. And I now the only one to keep it going however I can." Slowly she blinked her great dark eyes. "Priest say I don't pray in church, so why should he pray for Junior who is not baptized? 'The fault is all yours, Mrs. Samuels,' he said. But then the priest pulls on the cross hanging down his black dress to explain how since his God cares for everyone, he'll do my son Junior one or two prayers. So I leave him relieved. And wait for my Junior to repair himself. After a week, and he not even eating anymore, I think the priest has no power to change anything. My son just lays there on his bed all day and night, this same bed sheet I spend my last days under once covered him." She fluffed the bedclothes. "We here in Grenada don't have much," she seemed to be apologizing to me. "That is why we live so deep in our minds."

"Would a doctor have been any help? To heck with priests," I said.

"I tried the doctor before even the priest. I believe doctors to be of no account. But I wheeled Junior there, to Concord clinic, in a wheelbarrow, him moaning all the way. The doctor just wanted to know if there was water standing around where we lived. And I said how it's almost a swamp our shack sits in. And the doctor pulled on that black tube thing around his neck and said, 'Drain that swamp!' He gave Junior some round, hard, tiny food to chew which the child spat up and since I could not drain a swamp and Junior only sickened more, I never went back. I only guessed that to save my child the white man's way I had to go to church and drain my swamp and neither seemed much help or possible to me."

She swallowed hard before proceeding: "My white blood doing me no good," she sighed, "and Indian blood dead in my veins before I was born. So I rallied my black blood and called upon the African magic man whose powers had to be beyond those of the priest and doctor." Her voice had a catch in it which she struggled to control.

"He came at my bidding, the magic man did, and stooped low over my panting child. 'Very, very sick,' he said touching Junior's forehead. 'I don't know if much can be done. You should have called on me sooner. Why did you wait?' I wanted to explain to him that there were many knowledges in this world and on this island and that I didn't know whose might be strongest. Was his the strongest? I asked him. 'I'll tell you what to do,' the magic man said. He peeked out my window. 'That mango tree smothers your house. Too big. Too much fruit. Too long roots. That mango tree means death. Cut it down,' and he jerks on a chain around his neck that has a picture-circle of the sun hanging from it. He pulls on it hard. He looks into my sick Junior's eyes and waves his hands over the child's face. 'Cut that tree,' he repeats, kissing his sun as did the priest his cross as did the doctor stick the tube into his ear.

"I couldn't know, Mr. Sweet, what power there was to alter things. So I told the magic man, 'We are poor. That great tree feeds us. That great tree shades us. That great tree shields us from the rain. How can all that goodness be the cause of sadness?' The magic man demands upon his leaving, 'That tree takes away the strength from all who live here in this place. Cut it down!'

"At first I was relieved the magic man had gone, but sad. My black blood did me no more good than did my white. Or Indian, for that matter. I am by blood a combination of all the knowing of this earth. There seems no strength to change things for the better. How could it be that cutting the goodness of the tree would save my son? So in my mind I told myself accept, accept...that has to be what power is.

"But my son, now thin and fading more, with dry eyes and fingers pulling through his hair cried, 'Mamman, do as magic man say. Cut down tree.'

"'But, child, there is no purpose to starve us of food, shade and beauty."

"'Mamman,' his voice came thin as his narrow shoulders, 'please, please for me. I sick. I dead sick. Kill your tree.'

"'For some crazy whim of those who think they know what no one can ever know?' I snuggled this blanket close under his pointy chin." Again, she held up a flap of the blanket.

"For two more days I took care of my Junior both all the day and all the night long. I blew food into his mouth through bamboo I hollowed out. And water too. And love. All the love my wanting self could harvest for him. And I thought and thought about where real power to change things could come from. On the third day he died. He choked and sighed and closed his eyes."

I watched Mrs. Samuel's lips shake and waited for her tears which to my wonder never came. Instead she propped her entire mass up with both elbows sunk into the straw mattress and smiled. A broad, beaming, at first endearing smile. While I stared, it stretched itself and quivered into a bitter, trembling stricture of breath, finally exploding into a horselaugh so intense the candle flames wavered from the force of it.

"With a machete I went out to hit the tree. I smacked it hard, then harder. For all day and half the nights I bit my fury into the tree. Finally it fell, on the day of my son's burial. It fell into the swamp with a wail of snapping branches. The rot of it still stinks the air where it sinks each year deeper into muck."

I stood and reached toward her in order to help Mrs. Samuels recline with as much comfort as would be possible back onto her bed. "You thought the mango tree was evil?" I thought aloud.

"No, no," she stifled a moan. "I have never been certain which advice could be strong enough to save what there is to save. Do you know, Mr. Sweet, what power there is that is the most strong?"

I watched as she gestured helplessly toward her burning altar of skulls and feathers. Chills shook my body. I stared at the picture of St. Patrick and the Bible open to Revelations resting upon the stone that was the precise color of Junior Two's skin.

20

Grande Etang

Though Junior's mamman was a wonderful person, the intensity with which she surrounded herself and the aura that blazed from her being took its toll on me. She had fallen asleep by the time I tiptoed backward out of her room. Junior greeted me where he waited, seated cross-legged on the front step, wearing only his dark short pants. "It late," he said as though it was obvious I could not spend the night there. In truth, I didn't want to.

"Do you really live here in this cabin?"

"Yes and no."

"Do you have a job?"

"No work on island. I wants someday to be a carpenter."

I squeezed his upper arm while threading my way past him down the three steps to retrieve my bicycle where I had leaned it against a tangle of greenery. I arranged myself on the seat. Junior tossed my shirt at me which I caught, twisting it around my waist. It was going to be a long, hot ride back to town and I wanted to feel the wind against my skin.

I said, "I have an idea. I've heard about a house for rent at Grande Etang. A guest cottage. Since you have no job and don't seem to live anywhere in particular, do you want to go there with me? For a few weeks? I won't enjoy myself if I'm alone. Why don't you come with? Please."

His smile beamed at me like a half-moon. "Ise goes with youse." Excitement, apparently, slipped his tongue back into pronunciations natural to him. "Boobert is me friend."

"Is there someone to take care of your mother?"

"All peoples in these parts watches over her. She is who they come to when theys wanting advice. The important thing is that she be kept alive, every person agrees. For the betterment of us."

I thought of how the older ones and the ill were isolated in my own country and treated as if they were irritating irrelevancies. Books were the first to be responsible for that, I suspect. Especially the printing press that could churn the books out in ever greater numbers. You don't need wisdom or history or even unanswerable questions prodding your mind into alertness by elders when books will sustain you even better. And more cheaply, and with less effort.

"Next week, then. Saturday at noon. Meet me at the Green Gables. Do you know where that is?"

"You lives there."

Once again, I experienced that transparent feeling which I so often suffered on the island. Did everyone know everything they wanted to know about anyone? Obviously, yes.

I had less than fifty dollars left. I had been on the island for eight months. I wasn't certain I could afford a taxi as far as the crater lake called Grande Etang which was the island's highest point. So I looked at Junior questioningly, "How will we get there?"

"Truck. Many trucks sometimes cross island there. We jumps on a truck."

It was settled then. I had sealed my future with a spontaneous decision to share with my lover not only the island's back country but, as it would turn out, the interior of myself as well.

*   *   *

The following Saturday I sat on the front steps of the Gables between my suitcase and typewriter. My bike lay at my feet.

"Someone will come with dinner food," explained Daisy who had arranged for my reservation at the guest house on the shores of lake Grande Etang. She attempted to calm my worries during our farewell breakfast. "Be very careful while in that jungle." She cheerfully chewed her toast, then swallowed while avoiding my eyes. "It's not a healthy place to be."

"Diseases? Are there diseases there?"

"It's that you're not going alone. And that you may not be alone.

Oh, I don't know what I'm saying really." She chased her toast with coffee.

Mr. Edmonds whispered over at me from his table in the corner, "Better that you just leave this island. Go back to where you came from. You've no business hurling yourself off into mountain forests nobody with sense would care anything about."

Abruptly they both stood and strolled out onto the porch leaving me to brood over my poached egg. My stomach was queasy as it tends to be when in the throes of shifting from a known toward an unknown, so I had asked that my egg be poached. Disconsolate, I smeared the yolk over my toast. Did Daisy know Junior? Acquainted with him through Ralph, possibly?

When you don't know what you're doing or why you're doing it, my motto has always been to stagger onward. Put your trust in whatever nook of your unconscious that came up with the plan in the first place. But Junior was still a stranger. We were as mismatched a couple as anyone anywhere.

And yet by noon, I nevertheless had planted myself on the Gable's front steps surrounded by my few belongings, heart thumping as though anticipating an executioner. When by two o'clock still there was no sign of Junior, I sifted through what might be left of my mind for alternatives. I couldn't return home yet. Not in my present state with the dogs of defeat nipping my heels. I fondled the key Daisy had given me to open the guest house at Grande Etang. Do we engineer our own fates more than they are engineered for us? I seemed to have no choice except to proceed in the direction I was heading. I would splurge and hire a taxi, I decided. The island was only ten miles across at its center. The price to attain the middle of it could not be that exorbitant.

When Junior finally arrived, barefoot as usual but encased in a purple T-shirt with the words 'The only thing we have to fear is fear itself' stenciled between his nipples, I didn't know whether to weep or laugh. An island straw bag was strung around his neck dangling off one shoulder. He shone with sweat like a grease monkey. He poked into the bag and cavalierly withdrew a toothbrush still in its wrapper and four packages of new white Jockey underwear. "To journey with youse," he grinned.

Though I could well have done without the thought of his ever wearing underwear, the toothbrush made me sigh with relief. Whoever this guy was, he strove toward propriety in all things. We couldn't touch in town of course, so I simply stood and said, "Lead on. Where do we catch a truck?"

"At the market," he muttered while picking up my suitcase and typewriter. The market was only two blocks down Green Street, so we set off parallel to the gutter over the cobblestones. I wheeled my bike. We didn't talk, nor could we, because Junior hung back from me some five paces, like a servant. Again, I concluded, proper for the circumstances. No townsfolk could comprehend our friendship much less the love I felt for him. But did he love me in return? I shoved that fear out of my mind just as his T-shirt admonished me to. I did wonder though, how Roosevelt's turn of phrase would have played some ten years later had the Allies lost. Only from winners can aphorisms be taken as meritorious and not absurd.

Wheeling my bike toward the roofless truck Junior indicated, I saw the truck was loaded with tractor supplies and boxes of ale from England, due to head across the island, ten miles as the crow flies, but a tortuous thirty or more across the heights of Grenada from the town of St. George's to Grenville situated on the island's other coast.

Junior had already hopped aboard, having heaved my suitcase and typewriter on top of the ale boxes. Then he reached down to haul up my bike. How I was to hoist myself into the truck I could not imagine. Where had Junior planted his feet? I began to claw at the unhooked back of the truck. The driver had started the engine and everything shook while the truck's six or more occupants sang out to me in chorus, "Jump, mun. Jump!"

And so I did, as I always do whenever encouragement and

desperation converge. Someone banged the back of the truck closed with a shattering clang. We were off, me sitting perched on a tractor wheel, Junior on an ale box beneath me. The truck roared through the crowd that always infested the corrugated tin-covered market. Everywhere buses were parked, all with spectacular names scrawled in paint along their sides, such as: 'Tinker Bell,' 'Wandering,' ' To Nowhere' and 'Hope Springs.' Shoppers and traders crowded amidst the fly-clung fruit and split-open carcasses of suspended cow and goat, beneath which mildewed shirts, pants and undergarments sulked in plucked-over disarray.

"We goes now," Junior shouted at me.

But to where, I wondered. Really, to where? I recalled with nostalgia my basement apartment in Chicago with its shipping crates for furniture and its four chairs and one Formica table, all of which I had given up in order to seek my demise on a tropic isle. Oh, the hell with it. The hell with all of it. When you've got nothing to lose, lose what you haven't got. It's easy.

The truck quivered, shook and roared its way out of town. The steeper the narrow road became, the slower the truck chugged around each blind curve. At first, all relatively flat areas on each side of the road were dotted with breadfruit trees, shacks, children, goats, pigs and slovenly dogs. Then tree ferns appeared, looping over the roadway, heavy with moisture, luminous with clinging drops. The higher we climbed, the thicker the foliage became. Sword-like leaves six feet or so in height waved in the wind above dark piles of pitted, volcanic slag. We passed waterfall after waterfall through whose runoffs over the macadam the truck hissed, tossing sheets of spray. Heavy clouds whirled overhead. Here in the mountains prevailed a different world, a world whose colors were green, gray, and black through which the wind blew restlessly.

I noticed Junior and the other natives shifting their eyes uneasily, folding arms over their chests, clinging with greater tenacity to whatever in the bouncing truck could offer support. Inclement weather was not what they were used to, and I guessed they couldn't wait to get over the mountains and into the warmth of the coast again. Junior looked especially miserable. His eyes and nose began to water. I wondered if he wasn't gritting his teeth.

Over the grinding and roaring of the truck, speech was difficult, so not surprisingly for this part of the world, someone began to sing. Others soon joined in and there was much smiling, clapping of hands and rhythmic jerking of necks. Junior, roused from his shrinking torpor, bellowed with glee. It was a rather long song as I recall, most of the words engulfed by truck noise and for me, rife with incomprehensible pronunciations. But I do remember the refrain: 'Why is I so black and ugly.' The last word in the refrain was drawn out and melodic, each vowel holding to a downward spiral of notes, 'o-og-lee.' Each time the refrain was repeated came hoots and howls of appreciative laughter and the slapping of hands on each other's bare shoulders. They loved the song. They loved the words, especially the refrain. Junior showed all his tonsils and reached up to squeeze one of my ankles in sheer joy.

I listened in wonder to their…acceptance. From where else other than acceptance can enough strength come to proclaim one's ugliness with such enthusiasm? Humans are not the most lovely animals on the planet. Just stand on any city street corner for fifteen minutes and observe. The pigeons have it all over us.

After the song, when no one could come up with another verse, a man shouted over my shoulder that I should sing. Without hesitating, I gaped open my wormy lips and howled: "Why is I so white and o-og-lee, o-og-lee, o-og-lee," to be greeted by the wildest round of applause, whistles and congratulatory hand thumps on my back as I have ever received. Junior stood and hugged me tight.

So that's the road to appreciation, I thought, just imitate your surroundings. Which I've seldom been able to do with any honesty. I could no more accept who I was, nor where I had come from, nor the race I represented than I could accommodate myself to my need for Junior and our relationship, skewered as it was on a rotisserie turning over the glowing coals of lust.

The clouds spun darker in a near perfect circle over the mountains, increasingly more leaden, finally leaking drops that splashed big, cold and discomfiting into our eyes and down our noses. The truck skidded to a stop, though the motor kept being impatiently gunned, while Junior tossed my suitcase over the side. I grabbed my typewriter indicating that Junior could busy himself with my bike which he dangled with one arm over the side and followed its fall by dropping himself over at the same time. I scrambled up onto the vibrating side of the truck but uncertainly paused there unable to dare the requisite leap. "Go, mun, go!" the chorus behind me urged, until I finally tumbled onto the macadam, typewriter clutched to my chest. Though rubbery and limber as youth always is, I sank to my knees and shook my head in an effort to regain equilibrium. As my vision cleared I made out Junior standing over me rocking with mirth. God, these people laugh a lot. I watched the truck disappear around the next curve trailing veils of exhaust.

Then silence. Deep, penetrating, intimidating silence. "Where the hell..." I tried standing and shaded my eyes from the gray glow of a cloud that enveloped us. Tattered, spooky remnants of the cloud crept along the road and through the palms and the shimmering leaves that yawned broodingly over our heads.

"Ise sees the house." Junior pointed up a brief side road that curved in front of a white porch with octagonal wood insets. Two Victorian gables pointed through wisps of cloud. They were glistening and sharp, centered by two windows. White wood filigree outlined the triangles. Where the cottage was not embellished, the wood was painted gray. I just had time to take this pleasant image in when abruptly, from everywhere at once, the rattling shrieks of cicadas thrummed our ears. The insects had been intimidated by the diesel roar of the truck. With their competition removed, they brutally trilled through the rain which now began to pelt us hard.

"The weather..." I whined while running toward the house.

Junior followed me, my suitcase now balanced across the bicycle's seat, wheeling the ensemble up the steps. "Season of big rains," he informed me. "Up here, rain all the time now."

No wonder I had little trouble renting the place. The governor knew what he was doing, as usual, except when it came to native religious practices. He had grasped the island's mind but not its heart. Exiling me at my own request to a rain forest uninhabitable for months at a time must be his version of a lark.

But the coolness and dampness were perfect for roses. The front porch was entwined by them, their pink and yellow heads nodding from tendrils winding through the octagons, festooning the balustrade.

The door unlocked on the fifth try and eventually we hurried into the musky interior. A large round table with chairs and clumped shadows greeted us. "Everywhere it's dark," I groaned.

Junior found a kerosene lamp that hosted a box of island matches which he struck some twenty times before the lamp gushed into flame. The resultant glare and humping shadows put me into a real funk.

"So this is the climax," I muttered.

"Of what?"

"My life." I went over to Junior and squeezed his butt. "There's a bottle of rum in my suitcase if we didn't break it." We both dove to spring open the latches. The bottle proved to be intact. We went out onto the porch, crouched against the wall, and shared the rum, taking a gulp each at a time. We listened to the rain hiss through the leaves and waited for night to fall.

If we looked out and down to our right, a small and round lake glimmered in the last light, its silver, mirrored surface pocked by rain. Lake Grande Etang, which in French means 'big pond,' was perfectly round like a wide open sullen eye. Everything about us seemed round to me: the clouds formed a circle above the mountains, the lake which had resulted from a volcanic explosion now glared cyclopean, wounded, reflecting circuitous surprise. With each swig of rum I felt cuddled yet hustled through a funnel, the experience as frightening as it was meaningful and soothing. I put my arm around Junior and shyly licked at the sweat staining his T-shirt. "I'm glad you're here with me." My tongue affectionately worked its way under the shirt's short arms and lapped the wiry hairs.

"Ise hungry," he muttered, staring off into space.

My tongue furled back where it belonged. Air, food, shelter, then sex. I tried to accommodate myself to the inevitable hierarchy of needs. I looked back down at the big pond: the orb, the mandala, possibly for me of realization. But realization of what, I had not a clue. The mystery of that eye, glinting darkly now in the waning light, was intensified by the black stippling of water reeds around its edge and the abruptly rising mountains which were unrelievedly clothed in crosshatched clumps and spirals of towering vegetation.

"Somebody is supposed to appear with food," I said. "Maybe they live upstairs." I had noticed that a stairway to the upper floor was blocked by a crumpled rug of unusual size. I couldn't imagine how else in this trackless wilderness, within whose chilly dampness even a banana tree could not survive, that food fit for humans might be possible.

I left Junior to go inside to unravel the mystery of how our dinner might miraculously appear, when to my amazement I saw preparations for it already there. The kerosene lantern sputtered, now in the middle of the table where two white welcoming bowls shone in its glow. Around the bowls glittered spoons, knives and forks. A person, possibly a woman, maybe startled by my appearance, darted through the shadows to fade into the dark of the room in back.

"Juney," I called, "come now. We're going to eat. In splendor."

I turned to see him balanced by both outstretched arms as though holding up the doorframe. "Me mamman calls me Juney. Not youse."

"Christ," I fumed. "I'm sorry. But then," I decided to retaliate, "my name isn't Boobert as you refer to me. It's Robert. Rob—ert."

"Lookee, Boobert," he said, "Ise eats, but not there at that table with youse."

"But why not?" My hopes for a romantic kerosene-lit dinner seemed dashed.

"Ise knows where Ise belongs. And so should youse." Junior remained stolidly framed within the doorway, the whites of his eyes glaring at me.

I breathed deeply, then stalked over to the table and sat in a chair facing him, an upraised knife in one hand, an upraised fork in the other. "You, Junior," I tried being commanding but my voice wobbled, "will eat there at this table across from me." With my foot, I wiggled the chair I meant. The room rumbled with the scrape of its legs.

"No," he said retrieving his arms from the doorframe and folding them across his chest. "Not proper. No ways."

"But we've eaten together before. Just last week, as a matter of fact. At your mamman's house."

"No one else there but mamman and she not see anything we does."

Slowly it began to sink into my reluctant consciousness: our intimacy, our racial differences were more taboo on the island than in my own country. I tried to mollify him, "We're alone here. If you want to remain secret buddies, that's OK by me. But on this mountain cloaked in its rain forest, we're as isolated as anyone can get. Aren't we?"

As I spoke I became aware of a shadow bending over me. I looked to the side and saw that the shadow—darkly swathed in black cloth as it was—had actual substance. It might be a woman, short, squat but wiry. Her red turban was caught up in a bundle of material that wafted over her face like a Moslem housewife. All I could make out was a black, wrinkled forehead and yellowish, darting eyes. She placed a covered tureen in the middle of the table while mumbling, "Sir, please you, sir." When she straightened and became aware of Junior standing stock-still in the middle of the room she gasped, threw up her arms, and fled.

"See, no one here cares about anything. She just comes with the house. Must live down the road. Servile and harmless," I tossed off. With feigned indifference I plucked off the tureen's lid. I saw it was raw fish head soup, within which floated lumps of what I took to be bread.

Junior approached the table and carefully ladled out a bowl for himself. He smacked his weighty lips appreciatively. I smiled as though being complimented on my cooking. Everything was going to be all right then. I found a cloth napkin and dramatically draped my knees with it. I watched happily as Junior filled my bowl. Though I had disastrous memories of raw fish head soup on Jessamine's porch, I already knew the dish was popular back country but failed to put two and two together. It was as Junior shuffled off to the porch determined to eat alone and I was left to ruminate on matters at hand that I began to wonder if there weren't something familiar about our servant. Something, to be blunt, scuttling, underhanded, detestable.

As I spooned the soup and then prepared to munch a bit on the speckled fish head, aiming with my teeth for just above the bluish film that sealed the eyes, I thought of Jessamine's maid, Lemba—and quickly dismissed my suspicion. Just because Lemba had served me my first raw fish head soup is no reason for my assuming all fish head soup had to be served by Lemba.

I wished, however, that Junior and I might eventually dine together, that our differences would not remain as insurmountable as they now seemed. That love could just be the miraculous phantasm it was, unburdened by the fingers of reality I imagined tightening around my throat.

I listened to the rain pressing hard against the surrounding jungle. I heard it strike the roof and rush into gutters and plummet through the roses and shivered.

21

The Pool of Longing

We found some rollaway beds in the back room and slid them near the front window. All dishes had been removed, and after hearing the sound of water running in the kitchen and the slam of a backdoor, silence descended. I didn't know what to say to Junior, so for once I kept my mouth shut. The anxiety between us remained as continuous as the rain. The weighty, moist air inside the house caused the walls to sweat. Cold sweat. But the wind finally stopped and the cottage temperature became almost comfortable, though I guessed the meager food helped warm me even more. We were only some 2,000 feet up, and because the island wasn't located far from the equator, what chilly discomfort I experienced might be perceived as more psychological than physical.

The next day Junior and I seemed to feel better about each other and after wolfing some bread and marmalade from the kitchen, despite the still soggy weather, we set out to explore the rim of the lake. Its water was so tepid we decided to swim and bathe. Afterward, we lay side by side in the muck, watching our legs and bobbing organs be nibbled at by guppies. Schools of them. The male guppies sported spectacularly long and brilliantly colored tails. It was like lounging in an aquarium. We could barely feel the nibbling and what we could feel was arousing, affecting us like a piscatorial vibrator.

I like to imagine being one with the creatures, water and clouds. The touch of leaves brushing skin is for me ecstatic pleasure. In the weeks that followed, Junior and I took to wandering naked through the mountain forest. Though Junior's callused and leathery bare feet proved more than adequate for slugging through even the slickest mud, I kept my sneakers on. At that height there were few mosquitoes and even fewer flies. Sporadic showers throughout the day made wet skin that quickly dried more bearable than the damp cling of clothes. Though we occasionally came upon a green boa curled around a tree limb, no poisonous snakes were said to be present. I always kept my eye out, however, suspicious that a fer-de-lance could have stowed aboard a ship from neighboring St. Lucia where they were an established menace.

By unspoken agreement, we had sex only in the forest. Many times a day. Coating ourselves with mud became a usual invitation to foreplay. There was always another small stream or waterfall to clear the mud should we tire of its weight and pull on the skin. As we merged with the earth, the leaves, rocks and streams, so we merged with each other until no sense of separateness was left. We stretched out on the flat tops of boulders, in patches of ground-blooming orchids, in the spreading crotches of the larger trees letting the harsh leaves of bromeliads scratch our backs. And when an occasional streak of sun did slash through leaves, we luxuriated in its golden warmth while wrapping our tongues around each other's, hermaphroditic as slugs.

Yet as we returned to the governor's guest cottage each evening, a sense of estrangement always settled like a broody bird of prey between us. The moment we pulled our clothes on and approached the house, I felt the malevolent bird hunch its weighty wings to push us apart. We had even begun to sleep in different rooms on the first floor, a gesture toward separateness I came to appreciate. Bad breath, farts, jabs, and groans from the dreaming other are best avoided. Not only because Junior's snoring was irritating, but because the only child in me is so accustomed to solo sleeping I've come to believe that the self requires a nightly healing. Not having to contend with each other all night, lovers can be freshly reunited each morning and thus avoid the stickiness of stifling familiarity.

Besides, as I well knew, the oneness Junior and I shared naked all day in the jungle was a lie whose repercussions I chose not to face. Not yet, not yet. But one plus one does not equal one. Any fantasy of unity is short lived as a fish stranded on a beach. How to forestall the stench occupied much of my conscious time.

With head on my stomach, playing with himself as he often did like the monkeys hooting in the tree above us, Junior demanded one day, "Ise wants to go with you. Back where you lives. In that there Chicago."

He knew I would not stay much longer in Grenada, so the suggestion from his point of view seemed reasonable. I ran my fingers through his bristly hair. "What would we do together in Chicago?" I responded cautiously. It was as though he had just said, 'Separating would be painful. We need to continue our togetherness. I love you.' I was moved by what I thought he had said. Often words actually spoken have little to do with the real message. It was the first moment I assumed he yearned toward me as I yearned toward him. I had already gathered that among the back-country folk, romantic love was unknown. When put in cultural perspective, romantic love is a misapprehension of reality not all peoples of the world suffer. Had I somehow transferred the disease from me to him or was he being chillingly opportunistic? His wanting to join me in Chicago cautioned me to wonder.

I scraped a glob of monkey shit off my forehead. We were near a sugar apple tree and the mono monkeys were tossing the tiny ripe fruit into their mouths and at each other, leaping hysterically from quivering branch to branch. Being beneath them was a visual joy but frequently a tactical disaster. Junior hadn't responded to my question, so I asked again, "What will we do together in Chicago?" I wiped my fingers on a leaf.

His eyes rolled up and back toward mine. "We goes to all the waterfalls there. Together. And always under them we swim. Everything in your Hamerica is big, so waterfalls be high, very high there, deep pools under them." And he smiled a smile so long and engaging, his teeth so white, his lips so full and lush that I wanted to cry. Suddenly my eyes filled and I had trouble breathing. I plucked through the humus, found a wide leaf, honked my nose.

"Chicago is a crowded city," I sniffed. "And it's dirty, with one putrid river running through it. With slums where poor people live much worse than anyone on this island. And," I tossed the soiled leaf aside and squinted accusatively at the cavorting monkeys, "there are no waterfalls. All the land is flat, not even a hill."

"You don't tells me a truth." Junior jerked his head off my belly. "No place be as your Chicago is. If so why youse lives there? Ha!" He stood, swaying over me.

I thought about how beautiful much of Chicago was: its boulevards and thrusting skyscrapers, its parks shading the shoreline of Lake Michigan whose waves rolled and crashed like an ocean's. Its nightclubs and posh hotels, museums and symphony and opera halls, none of which would be easily available to him. At the best he'd be pushed off into a housing development on the south side, at the worst he'd be selling pencils at the entrance of a soot-blown subway.

"No orchids, no monkeys, no palms, and in winter it gets very cold when even your fingers and nose can freeze, and the snow as you walk on it pings while your breath falls as ice."

In frustration Junior turned his back on me and waved at the monkeys, shouting for them to be gone. "We goes now to where water deep. And warm. Hit warm there." He reached down to take my hand and pulled me up. Nuzzling my chest hairs, he ended by nibbling a nipple, pulled back and grinned as though saying that no matter how cloudy our futures, today was today and realities are best left for tomorrow.

I followed him over boulders and along animal trails winding through chunks of volcanic slag all bound with the probing roots of broad-leafed trees tendriled by waving vines. He caught a cicada and held it by its whirring wings. We marveled at its size before he let it go. During each cascade of rain, before sun darts flashed the foliage, their raucous cries whined into so piercing a screech that we had to shout in order to be heard. So we fell silent. Forests are too dense with sound, too crowded with sights, too languorous to permit locution. I felt subsumed, absorbed in the sheer act of being. Death seemed as improbable as birth. All was suspended within the limpid drops of clinging rain—a world within a world within a world.

Between the split ribs of sap green palm fans, I noticed smoke, or an errant cloud, drifting through the canopy to spread across the gray sky. Junior whispered, "People fear coming here. Afraid hit all explode. Go up in fire."

I whispered back, "Well, will it?" while watching the white spumes weave beyond the meshed tangle of tree limbs.

"Me mamman say might soon again. Mamman say not to come here." He paced foreword, tossing over his shoulder, "Thas why we here."

I scrambled after him. "Then you've been here before?"

"I don'ts believe in much folks say."

"That's wise," I agreed, always taken back by Junior's brave assertions. So often he showed himself to be unique, spontaneous. He was like me who perpetually struggled to break through the sustaining net that binds, as though no social fabric could trap him— except of course when it did.

The spiraling cloud made me wonder if we approached a camp site or possibly a place where someone lived. A forest fire in such a damp area should be impossible. I am always hesitant to intrude upon unsuspecting strangers, so I hung back. Besides, there might be dogs. I seemed no longer aware that we both strode naked, so that was not an immediate problem. I wanted to call out to Junior, but he just raced on slogging through the mud. Before too long I caught up with him where he wobbled across a spongy, moss-rich fallen tree trunk jutting over a thermal pool. I should have guessed that so near a crater all volcanic activity would not have ceased. The pool was almost round, in imitation of the lake Grande Etang several hundred feet below. Thick and curled as pubic hair, feathery moss clasped the labial folds of slick rocks sloping toward the clear, gray-tinted water. Holding his nose while snorting air Junior plunged deep into the abyss. His streaming hair looked very black against the wall of bleached rock surrounding him. I watched his legs kick until he breached the surface puffing out, "Hit warm as, as…"

"Blood? Warm as that? Warm as life?"

Intolerant of verbal metaphors, concerned only for life lived, Junior splashed water over my sweaty, mud-caked body. "Filthy, mun. You filthy. Come be washed. With me. Be clean in this now."

I lunged into the warmth, sliding down past his body, pointing toes expecting to touch bottom but never did, needing to flail my way up and crawl along his chest to break for breath.

"Youse likes this other part of the island?" He playfully, I hoped, pushed my head back under implying, 'Trust me. Trust me.' Which so long as we nestled in that soothing orb, I knew I could. The innermost world within me stretched free through paradise, wafting my limbs, helpless, reaching through memory down to where, eyes shut and body furled, I floated through heaves of anticipation. Finally desperate for oxygen, I fought against his hand and emerged sputtering. "Don't do that again!" I paddled furiously to keep afloat.

"Ise jus' playin'."

I lurched out of the pool to sprawl on a rock, my butt and head sunk far in the soft moss, eyes open to the wraith-like dance of steam ghosting the heavy leaves. I wondered if I weren't the one who was really just playing in this other part of the island where most persons feared to wander and lava roiled not far underground. I closed my eyes against the brightness of a rush of sun glancing off the shining leaves. It was myself I could not trust.

That night as we trudged back toward the cottage the harpy eagle, dark and strong, thrust wide its wings between us. Junior had yet to agree to eat with me at the table, continuing to have his dinner on the porch. Lemba, if indeed that was who served me, proceeded with her duties without speaking. She moved with a scuttling somnolence. Existence in the Victorian cottage was the opposite of what life seemed for me in the jungle. I had gone wild. Any accouterments of civilization affected me now as would a cage.

One morning it rained so hard I decided to write more on my

novel which now boasted some twelve first person points of view each sounding alike. One of the students at the high school I wrote about had an abortion, the fetus was cremated, and the teacher who had been the father officiated at its mock burial. Once again, all true. The writing of fiction always squeezed what I knew of reality out of me. Mere projections and blatant imaginings, on the other hand, have always been reserved for my essays of supposed insight. The honesty in me is never where you expect to find it.

While I scribbled in my notebook, the rain stopped and the sun poured forth with unusual force and magnificence. The cicadas screamed in exasperating excitement. Not to waste a moment of the sun's warmth, Junior wheeled out my bike. Having borrowed my dictionary he peddled round and round the circular drive in front of the cottage, studying page by page the hefty book balanced unsurely across his pumping knees. Through the window I watched his lips curl about unfamiliar words after which his eyes would close in the obvious effort to remember. The sight of his perusing my Webster's while circling around on my bike with its orange handlebars and blue spokes captured for me what poignant means. Savage as Junior appeared to be, he strove always to be otherwise. Otherwise though I was, I hungered to be savage.

That evening, after our separate dinners and before we collapsed a room apart in distant beds, Junior announced, "We needs, friend Boobert, some entertainments. You and Ise goes to that entertainment. Tomorrow night. Miles from here. We must start walk early afternoon. We reaches there about right times then. Important. By night. In the dark things appear and must be hushed back down under ground. You sees what makes your heart drum."

"Good night," I muttered indifferently while flopping onto my bed.

"Tomorrow," he flung at me.

"Tomorrow then." And I shut my eyes, ignorant of the personal trials the next dark of night would bring upon me. But I dreamed. I dreamed once again the most repeated dream that has pursued my life. So many times a year in fact that I don't need to recall specifically the dream that set me to tossing and groaning that particular night. They are all woven out of the same cloth. All make me moan through the unsettling re-experiencing of loss. And always over a cat. Or at least a cat symbolizes for me rapture and its inevitable disruption.

Though dogs may be my nemesis, from childhood on when my mother's feline love Patsy—whom I seriously believed to be my furry sister and fellow battler against dogs—cats have been my totem creature. I have always rescued and nurtured them, identified with their mousy triumphs, thrilled when they deigned to lick my fingers with their grainy tongues, wept inconsolably at their untimely deaths. If I have a soul tangled somewhere within my cerebral wiring, that soul meows, buries its shit, and obsessively preens each and every hair.

Always in my dreams I am searching. The cat, a former or present pet, has strayed. Usually there is a house, big, fetid, empty, whose many rooms might contain my soul—crouched in a dark corner, under a piece of furniture, shut in a closet, howling plaintively from the coal bin behind the furnace in the basement. Its life depends on my finding it and, by extension, my life as well. The longer I search the louder my soul yowls and the more cavernous and numerous become the rooms of my mansion-mind.

I never find the cat. I never find my self. I am left always to wake trembling, vacuous, yearning. Why I dreamed my dream of longing that night I did not know. I think now it was a premonition.

22

To Feed the Dead

Beginning from the cottage, that afternoon we walked downward heading in the general direction of Grenville. Sometimes we followed the road but most often trod paths so narrow and vague, so encroached by foliage, that were Junior not my guide I would have found the journey impossible to negotiate. We didn't talk much, as we usually didn't when in the forest. I had no real opportunity to question him as to where we were going or why. His rapid pace and occasional show of impatience when I heaved myself too slowly over a fallen tree made me curious about why this 'entertainment' we neared was important to him. We who had fed off ourselves too thoroughly for our own good needed a change and an entertainment might do nicely. Uninterrupted weeks of heaven can stultify as well as fulfill, I began to realize. Pleasure, all pleasure, is limited by time. We're always pursuing our metaphoric tails, snapping at happiness, cringing with pain from the bite.

By evening, we came upon a small field crowded with people. Felled gum trees lay tumbled about. Hurricane Janet had devastated the area. It hadn't rained all day and we were down far enough for the moon now full to breach the clouds and make the white bark of the gum trees glint like splintered bone.

Junior instructed me to wait under one of the larger trunks while he investigated the gathering. Was this the 'entertainment'? Was he wandering through the people to prepare them for, or warn them of my Caucasian presence? I heard a drum begin in rapid beats and someone shout, "Baron Saturday." Or was it 'barren Saturday?' Had the words not been repeated, I could not have registered what I heard. 'Baron Saturday?' It made no sense to me. Defensively, I crouched further under a limb. Another drum began syncopating nicely with the first, both accompanied by more cries of "Baron (or Barren) Saturday," louder and louder.

Despite last year's hurricane and the devastation it had wrought in this small valley, palmettos survived along with high tangles of towering bamboo whose minnow-shaped leaves swam across the pale sky. I was grateful for the bamboo's stalking shadows within which I hoped I was hidden. How had Junior known about this place? He had been there before or he couldn't have found it. But what about this particular night? Unless a festival were constantly enacted here, he had to be aware of this calendar moment. Had he been informed by that cowled woman who brought us our dinner, the one I had never managed to exchange one sentence with, whose very presence drove Junior and me apart and whose yellow eyes seemed to piss on me?

After an hour, I finally heard Junior pushing through the palmettos in my direction. "Boobert? Boobert?"

I stood to indicate my presence. He shoved what might be a goatskin pouch into my hand. "You drinks this."

I pulled open the gut which bound the pouch and cautiously sniffed the contents. Since he had a similar pouch hanging around his neck and swigged from it, I asked him what it was. "Good for entertainment?" he smiled at me.

I dripped some on my tongue. Though throughout my life I've always been a kind of human garbage pit, indiscriminately consuming most of what might be available, I have always feared that someday and somehow I would be poisoned. But Junior and I had exhausted the bottle of rum I brought with me to Grande Etang over a week before, and the liquid from the goat pouch fired my tongue as would a satisfying liquor. And yet another taste penetrated the stuff that I could not identify, something tart, sharp and bitter. I licked my lips speculatively. "You first." I prodded Junior's pouch. Every paranoid needs a taster.

He eagerly complied, gulped lustily, then ran his tongue over his teeth and burped and farted at once which made him laugh and set me at my ease. Drums proceeded thumping in the cleared space where the people mingled. Toasting to the air of excitement around us, I drank deeply in imitation of him. "Let's talk," I said after a brief fit of coughing. Whatever we drank was strong.

"So youse talks."

"What is going on here?" I waved an arm toward the milling bodies some hundred feet away that began to arrange themselves into a circle, arms on shoulders, shuffle-dancing under the moon. Some had what appeared to be shovels tied around their waists. The shovels scraped and dragged the earth as their asses shook. "And who or what is Baron Saturday? This Saturday person?"

"He the cemetery man." Junior wiped his mouth with the back of his hand and shunted his eyes evasively.

"Is this a real Voodoo something-or-other? How come a white man is allowed to be here?"

"Ise prepares for you the way. Boobert me friend, and so they say yes, bring friend forward. And so after we drinks, you comes with me. I don't knows what be Voodoo. This be entertainment."

Religion an entertainment? Junior taught me much just when it seemed most unlikely. I began to see that religions do what all entertainment does: they take you out of yourself, suspend your disbelief on threads of musical offerings and the hopeful insistence that reality is appeasable.

"You don't take this seriously then? This is just fun, like our being together?" I needed to know. I realized sex was just the same as religion. In both the ego is expunged, and faith in the dream of oneness overpowers the fact of separateness.

"Come shango. Youse shangos with us." Junior held out both hands to pull me toward the drumming, the dancing, and the sporadic whoops and singing.

"Shango?" I shouted over the din.

"Lightning," he said. "The dance of lightning down to earth. Shango. Shango." We had both drained our goatskins, and if he felt drunk as I did, it was little wonder we stumbled while nearing the foot-stomping assemblage.

We stumbled for good reasons though, over a short, wooden cross protruding from the ground, and in our effort to right ourselves entangled our feet in other crosses. We clanked into them like croquet balls colliding into wickets.

I was grateful not to have been impaled on a cross. We left the cemetery and entered the throng of dancers. Junior pushed and wedged me into the gyrating line.

I enthusiastically attempted to imitate the sidestepping, heel-heavy slamming of feet and the swinging of butts. However, I was not enthusiastic about the hand into which mine had been delivered. It was Jessamine's.

The initial tug and pull upon my fingers struck me as familiar. I was so busy concerning myself with what my feet were doing—trying to accommodate myself to the heave and swell of the writhing participants each interpreting rhythms in their own fashion—that it took me a while to distinguish the nodding, white-tasseled, nun-like head on my left to be anyone other than just another dancer in search of ecstasy.

Recalling our Voodoo marriage, it struck me that possession is what it was all going to be about. Jessamine, her breasts jiggling in time to the drum beats gasped out at me, "So there you are, Boob."

Her feet thudded, intermixing with mine. I had not seen her for over a month and assumed she still cavorted with her Peter from Poughkeepsie. So I acknowledged with a jerk of my head, "How is your friendly Peter?" I admitted to myself how I was not in the least disturbed to be informed he'd flown back to Poughkeepsie as might any migrant fowl. "Sorry," I commiserated with a smirk. "But what are you doing here in the jungle, so far inland?" From roots we grow, to roots we go. Her beginnings in the back country should have forewarned me of her penchant for entertainments. Our surprise marriage should have been omen enough. I winced as my heels ground into the soil. The drums had flurried into a triple rhythm which staggered my typical Western four or six beat mind.

Out of breath, I cut my response to the rhythm in half and then to a fourth. Just as everyone stopped dancing, the drums sank into a rumbling whine.

Across from me, I noticed another woman garbed in the same headdress as Jessamine, starched white with long tassels dangling astride her ears. At that moment she broke free from her circling brethren and sauntered toward the center of the dancers, a shovel grasped with both hands. "I am here for the Master Saturday to dispense with me as he pleases," she cried out. "Hear me, hear me, all the Laos who I will serve so they will serve me." She began to dig with her shovel directly into the grave mound at her feet. The earth flew every which way as her digging increased in ferocity. Despite the murky leaps of shadows, finally I recognized the digger as Marilee, the desk clerk from the St. James Hotel. What was going on here? Old home week? I recalled that Marilee had buried a child, whose grave I had seen her tend last Halloween when first I had arrived on the island. But other than that she was Jessamine's best friend, I knew nothing else about her.

But there she was digging deep, until a tiny box lay brightly exposed to the moon. She flung aside her shovel, fell to her knees shouting, "Damballa-wedo, pray with me for this death I have caused and suffered. Pray for me now, and with Jesus and his Mary forgive my trespasses. May the ghost of my little one rest, sleep, and haunt me no more." She was surrounded by women who, carrying baskets slung around their waists, knelt beside her so that Marilee could dip into their baskets. With her fingers she dribbled the gruel, seeds and fruit rinds, thudding them upon the uncovered box. "Take this, my darling," she groaned, "so that food may lull you back to that great sleep I have offered you. Sleep, sleep, my lovely girl, and no more come back to me. I have wept you goodbye, and I feed you now to renew your rest forever and ever. Amen."

Jessamine had sunk in reciprocal supplication to her knees. I joined her. "What happened to Marilee's child?" The drumming quickened again. A song of wailing rose from the women, their high strong voices sighing across the moon as would a wisp of cloud.

"Marilee had no milk of love for her child and no man came forth to save her from what she had to do...."

Before Jessamine finished speaking, she was on her feet running toward Marilee, not to console her but to grab Marilee's shovel. With the shovel Jessamine began to turn the earth over a different grave, faster, faster until another even smaller box began to appear. "To mine, to mine," Jessamine called to the stars, "and to the Baron Saturday, guardian of graveyards, and to all who dare believe the dead remain dead. Only the dead are alive."

The basket-bearing women crouched about her. Jessamine too reached into their wicker troughs to bring forth seeds and gruel, the hearts and rinds of fruit. She flung the offering onto the box with spite and cruelty. Her body shook, teetering over the open grave. She clutched her fingers deep into the back of her neck. "My son, my son," her voice shook, "who could not be, whose father denied concern—because I knew you, child, not to be from the slick of moon-shaft on my tongue at midnight. You are the imprint of an unrighteous man who walks this earth. I have fed you, my baby boy, once more so that you can sleep satisfied, so that not one breath of yours may ever walk the world or accuse my heart or spirit more... I plead this in the name of Mary and Saint Patrick and the Baron and the holy Damballah-wedo: visit me no more, stop your crying. Rot, my son, and let your tears dry—as I have mine."

The renewed drumming struck sharp into my heart, jabbed like lightning spikes of the Shango god. I had conceived a son?

It's not that I didn't know I was responsible for standing by and doing nothing while what I had engendered was snuffed out in Jessamine's womb. During the graveyard ceremony, Jessamine's anguish and fear drove the fact home to me. Knowing and feeling are different levels of realization.

As I watched Marilee and Jessamine toss their bodies in spasms on the ground I sweat profusely while cold prickles froze my veins.

And I felt dizzy, possibly from the odd drink with which I had been plied to prepare me for the onslaught. Junior bobbed in knee-wagging circles around me, his ass pert and grinding. "Junior," I bellowed, "for God's sake, stop it."

"What's from me youse wants?"

I put it as plainly as I could, "To hold your hand."

"Not here, not here," he sang out. "We friendly only. Only friendly in this place."

The drums rippled into a smacking frenzy. I watched Junior bend over, hands gripping his knees, feet kicking up sprays of dirt. I understood how he was with his own people now and that the reality of our relationship must be suspended. I couldn't hold his hand on Chicago's Michigan Avenue either, day or night. This I knew because I had held a guy's hand once in a park behind the Art Institute and we were both arrested, mug shot, and fingerprinted, but since we were jailed for only one night considered ourselves lucky.

Junior pointed at the twitching Jessamine. "Youse knows that island woman?"

"I used to play the piano over at her house," I shouted above the drums. "Isn't her name Jessamine Hempstead?"

"Her mamman, Mambo Lemba, tells me you is to go over to her." Leaving me with that revelation, Junior spun off into the crowd, all of whom were twirling and whirling in the same manner as he, one oscillating head could not be distinguished from another. My guide had deserted me.

I started walking through the graves over to Jessamine. The graves were by now so trampled it made me wonder if the graveyard were real or mock. If the place were a real burial ground, the disrespect shown by the dancers who had flattened the mounds and crosses with their lunging feet seemed incomprehensible. But if it were all mock, that is to say symbolic, the entire proceedings made sense. I neared Jessamine whose back contorted into swarming leaps of tendons as she raised off the ground, supported by digging heels and plowing head. I bet to myself that in the box she had dug up one would find nothing. Unless she had transported the fetus home with her from the abortion in Trinidad by smuggling it in her purse. I had long since concluded that on the island nothing was impossible.

But that Lemba, who I had assumed to be Jessamine's maid was actually her mother, gave me pause. Had Lemba been the servant who served us our food in the governor's Victorian cottage? I now hovered uncertainly over the possessed Jessamine. Lemba squatted on the ground near her daughter's gyrating head and I saw that a trail of black material wound around her neck and fell in folds across her black chest. On no other island person had I ever observed a black drape such as that. Not on the Lemba I had known at Jessamine's, only on the Lemba who must have secretively maneuvered herself into the employ of the governor to plague my life and curse my dear Margo. Her yellow eyes spat fire at me.

"Will she come out of it? Will Jessamine be all right?" I inquired of Lemba in as conciliatory a manner as possible under the circumstances.

"Jessamine, she being ridden." Lemba nodded her head to the thumping drums. "Ridden, ridden hard she be."

I walked around my writhing former mistress to bend over Lemba. "If you are her mother, then..." my voice failed because so much was now clear. Lemba's motives for disconcerting me and anyone close to me were now obvious. My presumed desertion of her daughter had somehow to be expiated. I suspected that she too had been done wrong by men, which it is in men's nature to do and women's nature to avenge. Her attaining the prowess of a mambo had been the method through which she gratified her anger. Since her hexes could only work on believers, I nonchalantly assumed myself to be invulnerable.

Lemba could dribble urine and menstrual blood over any door stoop I inhabited for all I cared. She probably already had, come to think of it. The entrance to the cottage had seemed damp and viscous from more than just the rain for a week. Let her pour grave dirt into my coffee. Yet I felt toward my stomach speculatively. "Well, are you Jessamine's mother?"

"My child be no more youse to hurts. She be ridden now by Baron. Humping her. She given unto the spirit, humping, humping. Not youse, not no more a man, but gods take her." Once again, I wondered what language Lemba thought she spoke. I stared at her, my knees weak. If Jessamine had her way, this rocking mambo whose temperament was vicious as a pit bull would have been my mother-in-law. Mom, I want you to meet your... My knees got the best of me and I aimed them toward the rim of my son's grave and sank, kneeling.

"Watches youse now your sweetie humped by the forces, forces no white man knows how," she barked into my ear.

I tried to focus on the distorted semblance of what had been the naive and lovely Jessamine. Under her skirt I could sense her vulva twitch and drip. Behind me, a fire had been lit. I smelled the smoke and heard the crackle. Light from its flames danced over Jessamine's puckered face. Her mouth opened belching forth, "Dam, dam, bo, saltangum, go, go. Wedo, ballah, shango oh." Her lips pushed high over her teeth, lolling like an eel squirming for water.

Though I had a friend in college prone to grand mal seizures and had pried his teeth apart with whatever might be available and cushioned his banging head, I was still not prepared for the intensity, the vibrating and the quavered screaming of Jessamine's willing, cataleptic abandonment. For some unaccountable reason, her white, nun-like cap with its dependent tassels remained fixed on her head, the tassels whipping her forehead and wide open but glazed eyes. "Dam, dam, saltangum go, wedo, ballah, shango oh," over and over, shouted and moaned, sighed and whispered.

Lemba placed a hand on her daughter's butt. Jessamine screeched with orgasmic verve. "She now be with the all," Lemba squinted her eyes. "She be earth, water, sky, the fire."

Actually, Jessamine yelped and twitched very much as she had with me. I felt I could not share this observation with her mother, however. If God is orgasmic fervor, so be it, since I am not convinced there is any other proof available. And whatever instigates the rapture—another person, one's self, service to a purpose— possession has to be the fulfillment.

"Onward!" I tried to abet Jessamine's cause.

"No men. No youse. No more my Jessamine needs." Lemba misconstrued my encouragement as an affront.

"But I agree. I am with you, Mambo." She could not guess how much.

Lemba narrowed her eyes to mere slits and spat to make palpable her distrust of me. "She with the Baron."

"Yes. Jessamine is dead now to herself." Absorbed, I thought, by passion itself.

I felt a hand on my shoulder. It was Junior, eyes bulging, out of breath. His fingers painfully kneaded me down to the bone. I gathered he could dare that much intimacy. "Big blaze, big fire," he yelled over the incessant drumming and the buzz of rattles that now rose above the bawling of the crowd. "Sacrifice starts soon. Good Friday for Baron Saturday," and he squeezed my shoulder even tighter as he squirmed with laughter. I didn't know whether to register relief at his cynicism or shock at his ability to joke at several religions at once. Surreptitiously I kissed his hand in admiration before he pulled it away.

Why must most religions depend upon blood sacrifice? Because gore sells? Drama, drama, drama...the word echoed through my mind as I followed Junior to merge with the crowd who with stomping feet and jerking heads pushed into a tight ring around the fire. Now without censure I could press my body against Junior's, as actually I could against anyone's. A stud behind me lay his meat I could feel through his pants across my backside, a woman eagerly stroked my arm as though it were her own. We were one, staring at the fire, hearing it burst and sizzle above the steady throb of the drums.

"Obeah, Obeah," a man's voice sung out in a deep, full bass. "Obeah," the woman scratching my arm echoed. "Obeah, Obeah." The odd word sprang up like sparks from diverse segments of the gathering. I didn't know what 'Obeah' meant or who or what it might designate, but the word sounded important especially when repeated. It was like attending a Catholic Mass in Latin where all is rife with mystery because what is flatly intoned is incomprehensible to most parishioners.

"Obeah sanctus domine patris," the rich voice chanted. That *was* Latin. Did he know what it meant? To clarify mystery is to dislocate its essence? Gods are for those who don't want to know what they claim to want to know. My mind was a whirl of conjecture when the deep voice disengaged himself from the throng and stepped toward the fire. He was directly across the flames from me and appeared to be muscled and tall, his dark face running with sweat. I wondered if he was the same mambo who had cast snide aspersions at my banana while covertly marrying me to Jessamine. That incident had inaugurated so many of my woes on the island. I clamped my teeth. Yes, that's who it was. The bastard.

Junior explained to me over his shoulder, "That mambo there be the mighty one. Don't no one dares gets on his mean side. Much strong magic he makes. See, he tucks under one arm a black cock and under the other a cat? They is the sacrifice. To make us all whole," he snickered sarcastically while holding his nose and grinning. I assume he meant his gesture to assure me that he thought the idea of sacrifices to make us whole stank. His comments regarding the powers of the mambo, however, I believe I was to take seriously. Which, from experience, I had no trouble doing.

I hadn't seen a cat before on the island; too many dogs, I suppose. The doomed, scrawny creature staring wide-eyed from the mambo's armpit must be the greatest grandchild of some French or English planter's pet.

"Should be all black, the cat," Junior hooted into my ear. "But too many sacrificed. None left. Got to use whats youse got." Again he laughed at the foibles of Voodoo.

I arrowed in on the cat, watching its white whiskers tremble, its white front paws dig into the man's arm. And then I could see that its whole body quivered, like the possessed Jessamine. It looked to be weak from hunger, pitiful as it tried to curl in on itself, terrified.

Junior squeezed against me and fell silent as the mambo tipped his great, shining head, pinched the black cock's beak closed between thumb and forefinger and, precisely timed to the crescendo of the drums, began biting into the twisting neck. Even over the drumming, I heard his teeth gnash, breaking through the bone, unless it was the sound of a snapping limb from the fire which at the same moment sent a spray of sparks over the crowd. One of the cock's wings shot out from the confines of the mambo's arm and spasmed, the long dark feathers streaked with blood. Blood also speckled the mambo's face, the cheeks especially, which gleamed with runnels of it. I watched him lick the corners of his lips before he fell again upon the fowl's throat, gaping it open, shutting his eyes from the blackish spurts as much as from the effort it must take to accomplish so primordial a task. Decapitated, the cock was let fall to the ground where its thrumming legs spun it through the onlookers who kicked the body into the fire, the feathers igniting into crackling bursts.

"Obeah!" intoned the mambo, his teeth still clenched upon the cock's head. "Obeah!" roared almost everyone except me and Junior. Though I could not rightly appraise the extent of Junior's cynicism, this weaponless slaughter of a fertilizer of more hens for our dinner was basic as things get.

I had been aware that across the fire from me and not far from the mambo's now prancing feet cavorted Ralph—Daisy's servant boy, my erstwhile trick and the chief dispatcher of chickens at the Green Gables—but I had not wished to acknowledge his presence. I was no longer surprised at the number of faces I recognized. The crowd was large, the occasion apparently important, the island small, the population bored and desirous of excitement. My light brown, wavy hair and sun-red skin and six feet of gangling inappropriateness made me an object to be shunned, admired, ignored, but not for a moment invisible. So if I noticed Ralph, he certainly had seen me. I grew apprehensive of his presence, because as the mambo jiggled his behind, right after he finally spat out the chicken head, Ralph bounced his way over to the mambo and lay one large hand across the cat's back. The mambo, now in full voice, brayed beautifully from the somber depths of his diaphragm, "Domine sanctus, pacem, pacem, pacem." Obviously he had been an altar boy while growing up. The dry hiss from the rattles whined above the low thuds from the drums. Ralph yanked the cat from the mambo's arm and held it by the scruff of the neck over the fire, the animal's eyes wide and moist. It tried to kick its white-pawed spindly legs away from the heat of the flames.

The closer agony approaches a species linked to ourselves, the more we can identify with the suffering and horror. The sacrifice of human beings is of course preferable. The Aztecs knew exactly what they were doing, though a thousand hearts a day may have been a tad excessive. The New Testament got it just about right though, as perpetual sales of the Bible and fresh Christian adherents everywhere make clear. To crucify God Himself is to aim accurately at where symbols need to go. Pressing over Junior's shoulder, I observed with growing distress the terror of the cat dangling from Ralph's clenched fingers.

Was I dreaming and was my recurrent search for the missing cat I could never find about to culminate in a nightmare? As all primitives know, you don't mess with their totem animal. And my brain is as primitive as any warrior of the bush. My bush soul is mine to rescue, I thought, while circling my arms around Junior's waist for security. "We've got to stop this awfulness!"

The crowd surged expectantly, all eyes fixed on the dismemberment of what I, and I alone in all that shoving mayhem, must emotionally acknowledge to be the annihilation of my symbolic being. For me, the sacrifice was quintessential, the expiation exact.

Junior twisted his head toward me as far as he could. His large Adam's apple rode the satin of his throat as he mouthed, "Don't youse acts so like white man. Not here. With me in jungle fine. But, Boobert, not now! Not here."

Chagrined, I dutifully arranged my arms rigidly at my sides. Still pressed against him by the crowd, I felt estranged from him, abruptly distanced. To know that he merely tolerated my white behavior during our forest nuptials, when I had presumed it was I who was grand enough to tolerate his native wiles, depressed me into silence. After the first startled moment, however, I realized his admonishing me must be well-intentioned. Any further protestation on my part would not only disrupt the communal hysteria but could well endanger my life. I would be the sole antagonist in this volatile, drum-whipped morass of bodies.

Besides, in my own country, had I ever even considered bursting in upon a Catholic mass to vilify the wafer and wine imbibers for persisting in their cannibalism? Sacred is defined by custom. Profane is to dare interrupt that custom. I'm a very profane kind of guy—in my mind. But action and I have never combined forces.

I watched my bush soul struggle and pant when pulled out of the fire, quivering and slobbering fear and pain as it was thrust by Ralph against the mambo's chest. I shivered with anger and dread. Ralph had now grasped the cat's hind legs with one hand, while the other clasped its neck. He turned the creature over, belly up, presenting the offering to the mambo's stained teeth. "Obeah, sanctus, sanctus, sanctus," the mambo roared again. The drumming and rattling and other cries of "Obeah, Obeah," carried over the fire and into the full glow of the enormous moon. And I wanted to puke. Because as the mambo buried his face into the glistening fur of the sacrifice and my soul, the cat howled horribly, not once but three times, as the mambo's teeth ripped through the hair and then the jugular.

I leaned so hard on Junior that he had to brace himself to keep standing. Calls of "Jesus, Lord, Damballah-wedo, Baron Saturday, Holy Mary and Saint Patrick," flooded the crowd. The cat's eyes closed then sprang open again, sightless, as its head tumbled off the body and Ralph tossed the jerking legs and spattered remains as far into the fire as his arms could heave.

I have never felt so empty. To my bush soul I whimpered, "Requiescat in pacem, buddy." I clung to Junior's shoulder. If he fell I too would fall and all would know that with the immolation of my totem beast I was now vulnerable.

23

Possessed

I recall reeling from the burning of the decapitated cat on, inwardly paralyzed but outwardly imitating my fellow revelers. Like Junior, I grasped my knees, spun in heel-thumping circles, my butt high and taut, a puppet whose every motion is controlled by wires of percussive sounds. My jerking, stomping charade of replicating the gyrations of the dancing horde around me gave me moments of relief, a sense of cohesion, the savor of belonging.

Junior whirled near me, "Good, mun. Youse doin' good," and he was gone again, lost in the jostling crowd. After the entire assemblage of drum-struck people began to break away from the fire to begin their solo dancing, I noticed Ralph and Junior clap hands over each other's backs and, smiling, exchange convivialities. Fear of abandonment has always made me a suspicious person. If you don't assume most other people have not your best interests at heart you're soft in the head. Observing Ralph and Junior in their jovial tête-à-tête gave me a jolt. So that's how Junior knew I was staying at the Green Gables. But how much did Junior know about me and Ralph? Or any of my other mishaps on the island? I tried calming myself. Paranoid is as paranoid does, Robert. What I attempted to settle in my mind was to what extent this entire Voodoo festivity had to do directly with me. How much was circumstance, how much had been arranged? Oh, come off it. Junior had indicated he knew many persons present, why shouldn't he? Partly down the mountain on the island's other side, we were only five miles as the crow flies from St. George's. Small places are wonderful because so many people must become friends or are at least acquainted. And know everything about each other too, which is the bane of small places. Just enjoy your vulnerability, your accessibility. And since all religions are a jumble of ritualized symbols, interpret this Voodoo commemoration of whatever it commemorated precisely as you wish. Dig your heels deep into the graveyard dirt, swing your ass, squeeze your eyelids, synchronize your heart to the drum-pulse and merge into mob ecstasy.

Which I had difficulty doing. For seconds at a time I would let myself go only to be thrust back into myself with a clunk. Especially since I kept colliding with dancers who revolved near me. "Sorry, man," I excused myself. "Sorry, sorry, sorry," as though my existence required perpetually reiterated apology. The sacrificial demise of my bush soul had made me particularly uncoordinated, left me panicked. My knees hurt. My calves twisted into painful knots.

A rhythmically flagellated mess, I wrapped my arms about a wooden post in order to steady myself. When I opened my eyes I discovered I had inadvertently stumbled into a large hut. The walls were made of bamboo, the roof thatched with dried palm fronds. A phalanx of blacks milled about within the enclosure. A more organized group marshaled themselves around a table along the back. The table was piled high with bowls of food and candles, skulls and the ubiquitous Bible, its cracked and peeling leather crowning a carton proclaiming "Best English Ale". Though people came and went—laughing and groaning in various stages of catalepsy—no one paid me any particular attention. Most of the men had their shirts off, many women were halterless, so I freed myself from my T-shirt and went to crouch on the dirt floor, back against the bamboo wall, knees propping my chin. The hut seemed airless. Body odors both pleasant and unpleasant pervaded the interior.

A dwarf, wobbling on his fat, bowed legs, strutted about the enclosure, a tin bucket balanced on his frizzly head. People dipped their goat-skin flasks into the bucket and then pressed the flasks to their lips and swallowed. The dwarf seemed to be a peripatetic bar tender. When he scurried near me I held him still a moment by grasping his shoulder and dipped the goat flask I still had strung around my neck into his bucket. I hoped it was the same drink

Junior had offered me earlier. Before the dwarf waddled off, I stared into his wide dark eyes, admired the tangled pelt of hair ranging his chest and the shiny ochre of his mulatto skin. Though not as cute as the dwarf in Manhattan's Everard Baths, who had graced me with clap nine months earlier, he nevertheless struck me as a masculine version of the exquisite. Dwarfs seem helpless while they overwhelm, sacred by happenstance and sensibly selected to be divine throughout history. I did not question the importance of his presence among Voodooists who are so metaphorically eclectic as to be the spiritual vacuum cleaners of most mythical detritus.

I gulped from my goat pouch. The liquid was the same. I swilled its burning between my teeth and over my tongue. 'Take this in remembrance of me.' Holy, holy are the fluids utilized by humans merging their unconscious into their conscious. However this union can occur, so be it and amen. Praise whatever substance, sexual convolution or creative re-creation that is capable of melding the disparate into one.

I sipped away, contentedly nodding my head to the inexhaustible rippling of the drums, monotonous yet soothing. Junior materialized across the room leading by the hand a fantastic creature who looked to have come straight from an anthropological exhibit. I had no guess as to what sex the personage might innately be. But the painted face (white slashes intermixed with orange), the pendulous burlap dugs sewed onto a shirt and swinging from the chest to saucily circumscribe a bulbous navel, made me assume it to be a man. Except then I saw the enormous male organ replete with dangling testicles (all stuffed and wrapped in burlap) which made me wonder.

Junior leaned over me to challenge, "Youse gots no thing like this in your Hamerica."

I stood in order to finger admiringly first both breasts and then the male appendage. "Like in Africa," I remembered from museums, "and Oceana too. An hermaphrodite, the synthesis of knowledge."

Junior said, "Huh?" And then cocking his head, "Me thinks

youse likes this being-person. Hit gots everything."

"That's more or less what I mean," I blathered on as though our conversation were rational. "Gender fuck. Well, more than mere gender fuck, all important gods are both female and male. In most religions in their fashion."

It was the liquor. Not only had it raced to my brain, but now it wagged my tongue. Wagged it totally inappropriately for the circumstance. But I needed to really talk in my own manner. For months I had been in a verbal straight jacket, restrained by simplicity but also by innuendoes I did not understand. I hadn't been able to express myself and felt that I was in danger of losing whatever identity remained to me.

After my outburst Junior stared into my eyes. "What youse says youse says," he said. His head rhythmically swayed to the drumming like a hypnotized cobra. He put his arm around the masquerader who he seemed to know well and they shuffled toward the Bible, the candles, the skulls and the bowls of food.

I was hungry, not having eaten since morning, and it was now late at night. If the bowls of food on the table contained the cock and cat sacrifices, then so what. I didn't know if many people had ever cannibalized a transmogrified version of their own souls but desperation made me quite willing to suspend any sense of delicacy.

Arriving at the table, I stood alongside the costume's tremulous organs and the shirtless Junior. As it turned out, you didn't get to choose what you ate. Women behind the table simply shoved morsels into your mouth as you leaned over stubby candles and the skulls of possibly monkey, goat, dog, cat and two human skulls that I had no trouble identifying. The hermaphrodite seriously endangered its burlap breasts by singeing one in a candle flame. Noticing smoke exuding from the painted aureole, I tossed what remained in my flask on it. The ladies behind the table shrieked with good humor, as did the costume. Its uncontrollable penis had already dislodged the Bible off the British Ale carton and a bare-breasted girl in a dirty white turban busied herself attempting to rearrange the book's disheveled covers.

Junior elbowed me in the ribs. He had come to stand on the other side of me and by leaning forward over the table and opening his mouth and pointing at his tongue indicated that if I wanted food I would follow his example. So I aimed my mouth at the girl with the dirty turban, said "Aaaaah," whereupon she obligingly stuffed me with a burnt wad of meat while drawling, "Take this, sir, and never you forgets."

Savoring the meat, I couldn't identify the greasy tang of the rubbery flesh. Was it cat? It wasn't anything I had eaten before. I think I munched my own soul.

Suddenly, the drumming stopped. The people ceased speaking, singing, talking in tongues. At first the silence seemed piercing. Junior faced the entrance of the hut. Still masticating a sacrificial morsel, he quickly swallowed, then muttered, "Stay where youse is. Important," he warned me. "So no special notice be paid. Respect be when no notice shown. Respect be just what is." Nevertheless he crossed his arms over his chest and bowed his head while male bearers of what appeared to be a litter edged their burden between the hut's supporting posts.

The dwarf dashed into the room's center, bucket now hefted in both hands. He plopped the bucket down and with a coke bottle filled with the bucket's contents began splashing the liquid in a pattern that eventually described a big square. Were imagination to supplant a chalice for the coke bottle, holy water for the liquor, a bishop or possibly the pope might be expected to appear. The French-Catholic planters had sowed more than sugarcane in the island's soil, and the hungry imaginations of the ritually starved slaves gleaned what they could for their own purposes. I have since learned that this scattering of liquid is to honor and join the four corners of the earth. At the time I thought it was a waste of good booze.

The litter, made of tree limbs cushioned with matting, was eased down in the approximate center of the dwarf's square. Upon it lay

Mrs. Samuels, back bolstered by her soiled rags, voluminous breasts naked as I had first met her, torn sheet snuggled about her middle, pudgy fingers curled around a mango. Despite the hour, she still managed to be accompanied by a bevy of flies whose gold abdomens flickered in the candle glow as they groggily rose, only quickly to settle back again among the comforting hairs of her armpits.

I stood smiling. Mrs. Samuels recognized me and jauntily waved her mango in my direction. Everyone else, even Junior, seemed stunned by her presence, but I welcomed her with all my heart. Femme fatales scare the stuffing out of me. But earth mothers such as Mrs. Samuels made me envy her entourage of flies seeking succor within the ample folds of her always sweaty skin.

She must have guessed my feelings, because she beckoned to me with the mango she held raised by her palms as if it were an orb. I believe it was her massive immobility that made her awesome in the eyes of others. Immobility commands even as it evokes pity. "Mr. Sweet," her voice rich with liquefaction, "join me please." Then as I approached her, hands behind my back, head respectfully bowed in imitation of Junior, she continued, "I have duties here this night, but first I ask you how has it been these weeks between you and my Junior?"

Because no person spoke or appeared to move, I felt terribly exposed. The content of her question, though typically matriarchal, did not put me at my ease. I squatted cross-legged on the sheet between her feet so that no one but Mrs. Samuels might hear my answer. "We have shared more than two dare share." I decided it would be up to her to interpret my meaning.

She squinted, creased her forehead, pointed the mango's navel at me. "That word 'dare' is a strange word, isn't it? I will think about it." She tossed the mango in the air and expertly retrieved it while laughing. "How is your writing going?" as though we were at a cocktail party, she being solicitous of my preoccupation without any real concern on her part.

"Every which way."

"And have you discovered yet that you had anything to say?"

This repeat of the same question she'd asked me from her bed at the shack infuriated me. "Would anyone dare think so?"

"That word again," she said. Her lips puckered and she bit into her mango, the fruit that signified her doubting nature. I did not know if she were the most powerful of mambos or simply a run-of-the-mill mambo whose influence emanated more from her bulk than her obviously fertile mind. "To realize," she smiled expressively, "that you hardly dare be the self you maintain nature made you. Come, come Mr. Sweet, who are you really? And dare you be responsible to your answer? More responsible, I hope, than you've been in the life you've tried so far."

I burst out, "I came to this island to kill myself for being who I am."

"I'm sorry to hear that," she simpered not unkindly, but not sympathetically either.

"It's hard being who you are," I heard myself whine and winced from the churlish timbre of my voice. I tried to reclaim my dignity, "Maybe I can dare permit myself to be abandoned, exiled... reviled." I excitedly squeezed what I suspected to be her big toe, a pressure she obviously did not register.

"Reviled?" she questioned. "Revealing never gets reviled. Reviled is what those who don't reveal are doomed to. But you know that. It's just that you didn't know you knew it. Dare that, Mr. Sweet. Dare the shock of knowing what you know and when you forget, as you will, remind yourself again and again... But I have my work to do." She glanced warily about the room, her eyes reflecting the candle light. "This is the night of grandest happenings...for everyone. And I'm already tired." She closed her eyes and whistled out a long sigh. She mumbled, "I'm the spinner of webs for flies. I net, then suck them dry...for food. Troubled flies taste the best."

"Am I a fly?"

Her eyes flashed open, her grin infectious. "Is your belly gold? Is your fate a web?"

"I don't know what you mean."

"I pray not, Mr. Sweet. If you did know what I mean no web could ensnare you and all those like you. I would then dwindle to a strand of straw...I don't want to think of it. So I won't." Mrs. Samuels busily smoothed the sheet, stretched it taut over the mound of her heaving stomach.

With a wallop the drums began again with refreshed frenzy. Rattles and the haunting whoo-whooing of a blown conch shell revived the dancers and the shouters who howled, "Wedo, O Wedo, come Damballlah papa," and "Obeah," and "Legba." Jesus and Mary got fair play among the most exuberant, as did Baron Saturday and the Ezili who I had the misfortune of hearing summoned during my marriage to Jessamine.

Though people fluttered and spun about Mrs. Samuels, she seemed determined to brush them aside. I disentangled myself from my position between her feet and rose into the sound, my ears greeting the mayhem as would a drowning person seek air. Mrs. Samuels gestured with her mango orb at the bearers who lifted her high, circled the litter once about the room and wafted her—flies, rolling breasts and bitten orb—out of the bamboo hut and into the night. She hadn't acknowledged Junior who did not approach her. Though respectful always, Junior undoubtedly knew her as well as I was getting to know her. And flawed motives—Mrs. Samuel's feeding on the miseries of others, for instance—that make us invaluable to society as a whole, can seriously impinge upon any personal relationship.

Junior came over to me. "Too much the noise," he squawked into my ear. "Too much entertainment tonight. Ise goes now."

"But I'm staying."

"Do as youse wants. Always best that way."

"Where will I meet you?"

Staring at his feet, "By tree, under bamboo, where youse was before." He began backing off. "Ise finds youse."

My feet had already begun to jerk and plunge into the dirt as though physically compelled to accompany the pulsating beats. From the corner of my eye I watched Junior push his way out of the hut—in boredom? disgust? with foreknowledge of what would happen to me? Probably a mixture of all three.

His leaving bothered me not at all. I wanted to whirl, to funnel my way in and hopefully out of myself with rhythmic abandon and needed no one to interfere. I was grateful all danced alone. The reality of that permitted me to descend to where I had to go. Out of joy I would descend. Since speaking with Mrs. Samuels, a feeling of release took over me. Not due to anything she said, but what her presence stimulated me to promise. 'Dare ridicule. Dare the reviling.' If all societies, from the rigidity of their customs, go mad, decay, and eventually disintegrate, then to be excoriated by them is to be ultimately honored. Pushed by genetic determinism, I would go my own way. Choiceless, I would accept. There was no option other than to be the me I am. This thrill of recognition drove my feet deeper toward the heart of the earth.

From then on, nothing was verbal. All was sensation. I was a revolving, foot-stomping, ass-waving bundle of reacting muscles and firing nerves. Until finally I succumbed to the lure of the earth itself, convulsing on the ground. It had begun with a numbness of my toes, then my entire foot, which I at first ignored. While in a fit of losing yourself it's not possible to comprehend what's happening to your body. I grew alarmed yet oddly welcoming and wholly receptive as the seizing numbness crept through my belly and finally paralyzed my shoulders. That's when I fell, gasping, trying to cry out, but only meaningless words contorted my tongue, and my entire body heaved in turmoil, taken over by some vital principle, alien and obscure.

Joy is ego loss, pain is ego gain. My joy, though short-lived, was ecstatic as a humped nun stunned with adoration.

24

In the End Is the Beginning

I can't remember exactly how Junior and I got back to town. We must have retraced our journey to Grande Etang because I did retrieve my suitcase containing the novel I had been writing. In the long run this proved to be pointless, the fate of most artistic endeavors. When I arrived in Chicago I stored the manuscript with other belongings in the basement of my parents' house. The basement flooded from a freak storm so the book ceased to exist within a month of its completion.

I do remember that Junior and I vacated the cottage more quickly than I wanted. We were standing on the porch looking down at the glaring eye of Grande Etang that had seen us for who we really are. "We knows now that we knows," Junior said. Our arms wound over each other's shoulders, black and white snakes entwined, gorged with the essence of our inseparableness.

When we reentered the town, however, our accommodation to each other instantly became assailed by the restrictions of civilization. I had just enough money to stay a week in St. George's after which I must return home. Because saying goodbye to Junior would be unbearable, I did not even question that we must find a room together. The Santa Maria Hotel was too expensive. Abiding at the St. James would put us under the ever watchful eye of Marilee. So without much hesitation I presented us, bag and baggage, in front of Daisy's Green Gables, my home away from home.

"You're alive," Daisy said as though surprised to see me after opening the door to my repeated knocking. She did not seem pleased and glanced uncertainly at Junior who stood properly behind me with my typewriter in its case balanced rakishly on his head, my suitcase dangling from one muscled arm. He had scrunched himself into his T-shirt that declared 'All we have to fear is fear itself.' He hadn't confided in me how much he dreaded the town, but his posture—unnaturally stooped and legs bowed at the knees—advertised his discomfort.

"I missed you, Daisy," which if I had thought about it might almost be true. I've always found it easy to despise and adore people simultaneously. Her multicolored skin flickered like an aurora borealis in the evening light. One sandaled foot edged back into the shadow cast by the door. "Thanks for arranging my stay at the cottage by Grande Etang. It was wonderful. Thank you very much." I jauntily cocked my head and grinned. "I'll always appreciate you." Which was true.

Though sometimes I lay it on a bit thick, I've never known a compliment not to please. Daisy's face melted into a welcoming smile. She stuck out her hand. "You want your old room back, Mr. Sweet?"

"What a fine idea," I quickly pushed around her as I squeezed her hand and began trudging up the stairs. "Bring my luggage," I snapped at Junior who obeyed with a drawn out, "yes sir". My plan was to ensconce Junior in my room without mentioning that he would be remaining there with me. Daisy's disapproval of both our relationship and racial mix might be defused were she not directly confronted. My knowing I was about to leave made me push the envelope.

Daisy flatly refused to serve us dinner together and Junior refused to eat there in any case, and so I proposed what I had done habitually throughout my life when blocked, mocked and confounded, I suggested to Junior that we escape to the movies. Junior had never seen a movie, and since he'd showed me so much of his world, it would only be fitting I introduce him to what I could of mine.

It was a Sunday night and the movie house was jammed. The marquee, as usual, was blank, lettering never being available. Those who could afford it simply filled the small interior each Sunday to languish in the fan-whirring darkness over imaginary worlds far away that made them discontented with their own. The theater had a balcony with real seats that lined up to form some five rows. The ground floor had wood benches, splintered and in disarray. The balcony was reserved for natives whose skin color was copper-toned, ochre or sienna, for the Governor and an occasional white visitor. The ground floor benches accommodated those whose skin was ebony, black onyx or dark slate. The ticket taker gawked at me when I asked for two twenty-five cent, ground floor tickets. "Broke," I tried to excuse myself.

"But, sir, no, no," the ticket taker insisted shoving a dollar balcony seat at me. "Not proper," he insisted. "The cheap not right for you, sir."

I had been there many times before and knew quite well that Junior would be tossed off the balcony no matter who he was with or how much we paid, whereas I had never witnessed anyone expelled from the benches except when too drunk or rowdy. "No money," I repeated. "Two tickets for the ground floor."

"But no…," the ticket taker persisted, his mouth with its two remaining teeth gaping, the pores of his midnight skin exuding sweat.

I offered him the British West Indies equivalent of fifty cents and, though shaking his head in disbelief, finally he complied with my wishes. "Very, very hot on benches," he warned.

Which turned out to be no exaggeration. The ceiling fans did their womp, womp only over the balcony. The inferno into which Junior and I tried to adjust ourselves was a fiery furnace. But since Junior had never seen a movie, I anticipated being intrigued by his reactions whatever they may be. The lights were still on and I observed a mere smattering of dark folk scattered among the benches. However, glancing up and behind me I noted that the balcony was full. In the front row sat Jessamine with her friend Marilee staring down at us, their eyes pinched from dismay when they recognized me. Mr. Edmonds, who had not spoken to me when I passed him on the stairs at the Gables, crouched in a back corner, the light shimmering unmercifully off the wrinkles of his tan suit coat. Daisy sat rigidly next to him in a black blouse with ruffles which seemed to tug at her ears.

"Are you excited?" I whispered to Junior. "I wonder what movie we'll see."

Junior didn't respond. He slid his butt inches away from me down the bench and held his jaw with clamped hands, elbows digging into his knees. I didn't appreciate being in the spotlight either. Especially since repressed Ralph, the assistant cat-sacrificer, plopped his gorgeous bod in front of us. He was with one of the whores I recognized from the docks. She lay her head on Ralph's shoulder, fingering the bulges on his upper arm with her yellow fingertips. I was about to urge Junior to sit with me on another bench when the lights snapped off and the screen burst into life with the film's title *Gone with the Wind* blazing in technicolor. I had expected an American horse opera or a British comedy one couldn't laugh at. No wonder anyone who was anyone attended that night. I had even observed the Governor, resplendent in his official white jacket and glittering medals with his quadroon mistress anchoring the balcony.

I had seen the film some five times, so I concentrated on Junior's and the audience's reactions. When Clark Gable spat out his famous, "Frankly, my dear, I don't give a damn," there was an audible gasp of horror. Junior did not swear. No one swore in those days except for me occasionally and Joan Collins when trampled by my foot. Clark Gable's expletive hung in the air, sizzling as a Fourth of July rocket. Junior inched his way back to press against me whispering, "Damn, but Ise loves youse Boobert." Under the protection of darkness I squeezed his knee.

On our walk back to the Green Gables after the movie the dogs were particularly noisome. They crouched and sniveled through gutters and yipped and snarled with low-throated growls. Junior grabbed a stick and smashed them across their muzzles or on their heads. The canines skulked back into the shadows. Was that how the rabble, whose morality I could not tolerate, were best treated: with assertive contempt?

The entire town of St. George's now cast both me and Junior as pariahs. Which was apt in my case so far as the citizens were concerned. Even though they may not have understood why a very white man publicly displayed himself next to a very black man at the movie house, my ignoring color demarcations was cause enough. Daisy made it clear that my servant and I had best leave her property as soon as possible.

I was only going to be on the island a few more days, so I ignored her. I maintained a strained though still gratifying relationship with Junior and, since I was ostracized, expected no further communication from anyone else I had known in St. George's. But the next evening as Junior and I returned to the Green Gables from having ferreted out food from shack people, whose hearts and cookstoves easily became accessible at the sight of money, I found a note from Jessamine poked under our door. The note paper was smudged and crumpled as though Lemba had delivered it with reluctance between clenched fingers.

"My mind is again in a termoil & I feel I must write you & try to express my true emotions. I am still very deeply in love with you my darling else I couldn't have become completely yours & still want to love you & be with you always. When I love you I feel exquisitely happy & nothing else seems to matter. When I leave you I want you with me again & am afraid of that deep feeling which has taken control of me. From all you have told me dear I know I must not expect too much, but if I continue loosing you I'll probably go insane when you do leave to go back to your people & all that you hold most dear & I'll know there is no hope. As I told you dear, I take love very seriously & will never change. Lets be friends. As before I am afraid to accept any happiness as I feel it will be taken away when you leave & my life will become more empty than it was before I met you."

I collapsed on the single bed Junior and I now uncomfortably shared. It was as though Jessamine had no recollection of the events at the Voodoo ceremony. Junior stared out the window at the sea. My toothpaste painting of the graveyard that inadvertently featured Jessamine's husband's tomb still hung over the washbasin. I narrowed my eyes at it. While Junior and I were at Grande Etang, during the torrid afternoons, the crosses and stucco boxes had continued to drip and slide into what was now an indistinguishable morass.

Junior mumbled, "Letter from that Jessamine Hempstead?"

"Yes," I sighed miserably. "But how would you know?"

"On the island we has our ways." He leaned out of the window, and as though addressing the clacking palm fronds said, "She sees us in movie house. She scared but don't know why. She come from my people back country, so don't mind we together but don't know what we do...together. Youse goes to her. I goes to me mamman." He turned to face me. "Mamman needs me. It wrong for me with you in big town. Ise no good for you here. I go..." He hesitated. His wide nose flared. He licked his full lips.

I raised on my elbows, my mouth suddenly dry. I barely managed to croak, "Can't you stay until I leave Wednesday?"

"Youse wants all my blood?" Slinging his straw bag containing his toothbrush and still unworn undershorts over his shoulder, Junior leaned down to kiss me hard on the mouth, pivoted and started toward the door.

I knew his decision to leave was correct. But I pleaded, "I don't care about Jessamine," which was only partly true. I did care for her. Even though I did not love her as she apparently loved me, I was almost as shaken by her letter as I was by Junior's abrupt threat of departure. And yet I was the one who would leave both of them. I was the one who didn't belong anywhere.

I scrambled to my feet and grabbed Junior's hands. "Take my bike. I won't be needing it. It's yours. And here," I reached for my dictionary and thrust it into his bag. "Remember me."

I pray physical death envelope me with as much awe and suddenness and blank darkness as did Junior's severing himself from me that day. After hours of mourning, still numb, I walked the cobblestones to Jessamine's house. The flamboyant tree under whose scarlet canopy we'd first communed had dissipated into long, dry seed pods that scraped in the evening wind across the tiled roof. Her living room was crowded with people, some of whom I recognized, but most were strangers. She came toward me, arms outstretched. "Boob, Boob, welcome," as though a week before I had not witnessed her ritually reburying our son while entranced by the guardian of graveyards. I held her close for a moment wondering if perhaps she actually didn't remember what had happened under her seizure by the Voodoo spirit. I was relieved, in either case, that we did not have to confront each other alone. "We're friends?" she wondered aloud, apparently referring to her note.

"Friends," I assured her. "But who are all these people?"

"Pentecostal Baptists. From Canada." Jessamine disengaged herself from me and waved at two white men wearing glasses who leaned on the piano. "He's here," she called to them.

"Brother," they both shouted rushing over to me.

"What's going on?" I was still so in shock over Junior's departure that I had difficulty concentrating on Jessamine's eyes which flashed enthusiastically.

"Now that you're here, my heart is big enough for all. I'm thinking of joining with the Baptists. They give me meaning so I might better withstand the sorrow of your leaving."

"What?"

The two white men, preachers I assumed, pulled on my arms. "Mrs. Hempstead has assured us God would send you to play hymns for us on the piano." Steering me toward the instrument, they opened a hymn book and whether by the will of God or the always subtly manipulative will of Jessamine, I reluctantly accompanied the crowd whose voices rose in splendid, full-throated response.

And He walks with me and He talks with me. And He tells me I am His own. Both Jessamine and I, so caught in grief for loves we could no more know, forced our twin voices to carry richly and strongly over all the others. I concluded my favorite hymn with a crashing, rolling chord in E minor.

I've always preferred weeping in E minor. Except for Jessamine and me, however, the chord had the opposite effect, because before I had even released the damper pedal the two preachers exuberantly bellowed, "For Jeee-sus-ah! The saving and the healing Lord!" Led by them, the entire assemblage charged out of the house and toward a church on River Road. Jessamine and I stumbled in their wake. I was so disturbed that night by witnessing their inappropriate and dangerous attempt to heal the ill who had access to free medical care that I scribbled down my reactions, which were printed the next day in Grenada's newspaper *THE TORCHLIGHT* under whose banner read: *Savoir c'est Pouvoir*— 'Knowledge is Power.' Sandwiched between "Lost, Stolen or Strayed one full Bred alpine Ram goat. Finder will be rewarded $10" and "It's good to know that the well known Happy Sewing Machines price is reduced considerably," my comments appeared as follows:

Hale and Hardy Health Healing along River Road

"At night River Road is a black and quiet place. Occasionally a whisper of light sneaks through the boards of a shack. Sniveling and lean, a dog barks. Generally, River Road is a black and quiet place. But a little further up past a bend in the road totters that not-so-white church of the Pentecostals. The stars are obscured by the light that washes its dirty front, and the silence is shattered by shrieks over a microphone. The Reverends Hale and Hardy raise their tightened fists into the air, roll their spectacled eyes towards the church's roof and hoarsely scream, "Come to Jee-sus-ah! We KNOW you've done wrong. Come to Jee-sus-ah!" Though the desire on the part of Hale and Hardy to make their congregation hysterical with feelings of guilt is of pathological interest, they cannot be condemned objectively for this infringement upon the dignity of man. However, they can be condemned for being 'faith healers' and thus persuading their followers to avoid medical treatment when gravely ill. 'All those for healing come forward,' trembles the voice of the Rev. Hardy while behind him poses Rev. Hale, eyes closed, forehead shiny and chin up as though he were about to transubstantiate. If we are too proud and indifferent to bring light to River Road, let us at least not condone by our silence the grotesque malpractices of this Canadian witchery.—R.B.S."

If my public appearances with Junior had not exasperated the color-conscious islanders, my editorial comments on their newest religion certainly did. But then I thought, well I'm leaving so what the heck. *Savoir c'est pouvoir.* My departure was now beginning to be welcomed by even me. Especially because I received a letter from Margo who, after puzzling over my continued absence from Chicago wrote: "You are probably happier on the island—but I am selfish because I miss you. I suppose I should try and convince you I am in dire need of help—this is the surest way to get a speedy answer from you. Perhaps you will think I am, after this letter. Oh, God. Pain in all its fury has found its way through most of my body and settled in for what I fear will be the death of me—narcotics to lessen the pain, and doctors for sticking needles and drawing blood and rows of test tubes holding their sides to keep from splitting and giggling with glee. Robert, I am so afraid that when you come home there will be some terrible strangeness between us at first. God. That would be a bore. I could not bear it. Just come over—take a shower and lie on the bed and talk to me. O.K.? Remember the orange shell with the black stripes we found on the beach. You know, the one you liked. I put that one in my suitcase because I wanted to be sure I would have it when I got back to Chicago. You are really lousy when it comes to calculating a few simple figures. How you are ever able to maintain any semblance of a budget, I will never know. What I am trying to say is that I had some time on the way home to figure out your expenses, and I must owe you at least the amount of the enclosed."

Days later, while waiting at the airport with its narrow runway through the mountains, trying to balance unsuccessfully my typewriter in its case on top of my head in imitation of Junior, I noticed the banana grove. The banana grove where, hidden like Adam, I waited out the rain expecting Margo's plane to appear. The banana grove from where I had watched Jessamine accompanied by her mother, Lemba, preparing for her bitter flight to Trinidad. I had hated Lemba, who might or might not be the source and instigator of Margo's illness, even before I had gotten to know Margo well and even before I guessed what power Voodoo might have. Now I was glad I never shared all this with Margo. There is much we need not know, much that should remain untold, because there is so much about our own lives we cannot understand.

For instance, I did not have the prescience to know when I mailed Junior an electric saw from the States to encourage his interest in being a carpenter that he would barter the saw for a cow who had calves which he sold in order to come to the United States only as a migrant worker. Or should I just not have sent the saw? Because the contents of his letters mailed from Florida still wrack me:

"may this few line of mine reached you quite safe the reason of dropping this few words is my position in florida is very bad now I am working two days a week for $12.00 and I have to pay $11.55 for food and place to sleep a week and florida is very cold now so I am asking you kindly to send me some old close for me please."

To what extent must I hold myself responsible? He next wrote: "I love America. I need to talk to you face to face. In order to stay in the states I will have to get married to a girl. Please give me advice what I must do in life. Let me know what I must do."

We can't bear the blame for the actions of others, only for our own. But my not answering that letter constituted an action. I stared up into the bilious gathering of evening clouds, choked—even before I departed the island—with nostalgia, guilt and understanding enough to try again to form a life. As if I already knew that memory, for better and worse, is who we are.

A small, dark man with wiry white hair wanted to know if he could carry my suitcase up the plane's steps when it arrived. I said, sure, and he pertly inquired, "Youse gone back to your Hamerica?" After which he seriously mused, "And does George Washington, be he still reigning there?"

"George Washington, he dead," I informed him.

The man seemed to be politically oriented because he chatted on, "All the islands be federated soon. St. George's be the capitol of federation." He smiled with toothless excitement.

"Why?" I wanted to know.

"Island of Grenada has no piezonous reptiles," he quivered with appreciation for his home. "And is beautiful."

I agreed, longing already lodged in my heart. 'Like being swallowed by Jonah's whale,' I thought as my plane swooped low between the mountains to taxi noisily toward the limp weather sock, reflecting orange in the last gleam of the tropic sun.

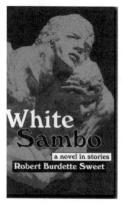